PRINCIPLES OF ANGELS

PRINCIPLES OF ANGELS

JAINE FENN

GOLLANCZ

LONDON

Copyright © Jaine Fenn 2008
All rights reserved

The right of Jaine Fenn to be identified as the author
of this work has been asserted by her in accordance with
the Copyright, Designs and Patents Act 1988.

First published in Great Britain in 2008 by Gollancz
An imprint of the Orion Publishing Group
Orion House, 5 Upper St Martin's Lane, London WC2H 9EA
An Hachette Livre UK Company

With thanks to Barry Andrews and SHRIEKBACK for permission
to reprint a verse from 'This Big Hush', from the album OIL AND GOLD,
© 1985, Island Record Inc. All rights reserved.

A CIP catalogue record for this book is available
from the British Library.

ISBN 978 0 57508 2 915 (Cased)
ISBN 978 0 57508 2 922 (Trade Paperback)

1 3 5 7 9 10 8 6 4 2

Typeset by Deltatype Ltd, Birkenhead, Merseyside

Printed and bound in the UK by CPI Mackays, Chatham ME5 8TD

www.orionbooks.co.uk

The Orion Publishing Group's policy is to use papers that are natural,
renewable and recyclable products and made from wood grown in sustainable
forests. The logging and manufacturing processes are expected to conform to
the environmental regulations of the country of origin.

For D. The only thing that matters more

Is there a flame in the dark?
Is there a bright heart star?
These creatures look the same now
We freeze wherever we are
We wake alone in the blackness
We sleep whenever we fall
One dream all around us
This big hush infects us all

'THIS BIG HUSH', SHRIEKBACK

Desperation is a tender trap
It gets you every time

'SO CRUEL', U2

CHAPTER ONE

Taro lay still, eyes wide, ears straining, an arm's length from death.

There it was again, the sound that had woken him: a shrill whistle off to his left. A moment later, it was answered by two longer ones, away to the right.

The sound of a hunt.

He stood carefully. He'd spent the night on a mazeway, one of the thousands of ledges lashed and pinned to the vanes hanging below the floating disc of the City. The labyrinth of open-sided mazeways and enclosed homespaces formed the twilight world of the Undertow, Taro's home. Below him, the early morning light broke the planet's barren surface into a mosaic of orange rock and black shadow. Taro looked away, blinking to clear the bright after-images of a quick and easy end to his troubles. *Gotta stay sharp.* The hunters were probably after a meatbaby, but since his world had gone to shit three days ago, he was fair game too.

He picked up the pack he'd been using as a pillow, stuffed his blanket in the top and, keeping his back pressed against the vane that supported the mazeway, began to edge sideways. After three steps, he froze. A shadow flitted across the T-junction ahead, where this mazeway ended at another, wider one.

Another whistle, closer, but coming from hubwards, the direction the hunter had gone. Looked like they hadn't spotted him. So he just needed to stop his legs shaking, get his breathing back under control and move off in the other direction – but cautious-like, as this was disputed territory. He'd been so tired last night that he'd just picked a quiet dead-end to stretch out on. He hadn't even tethered himself, even though the gap between the mazeways ran to three metres here, and wasn't properly netted. That kind of carelessness would get him killed now he didn't have an Angel to protect him. *No, don't think about that, don't think about Malia.*

The next whistle came from further off.

At the junction he had a choice: rimwards or hubwards, the direction he thought the hunt was headed. He peered that way: the mazeway went off long and straight, with plenty of support ropes and a fully net-ted gap. The nets at the far end were swinging back and forth. Someone – probably the hunt's prey – had gone that way recently: a meatbaby's twisted limbs allowed them take to the nets where most downsiders wouldn't risk it.

'Hoi, Angel-boy!'

The voice came from rimwards, behind him. Taro's first instinct was to run – but then he'd be heading into the hunt. And the speaker should've seen that Taro wore City colours in his hair, so he would think twice before attacking. Taro flicked a finger to release the catch on one of his wrist-sheaves and turned slowly, feeling the hilt of his fleck slide into his hand.

A lag a couple of years older than him was standing a few paces up the rimwards mazeway. He held a vane-cutter – not a good range weapon, but perfect for butcher-work – and wore strands of orange and green plaited into his lank pale hair. Limnel's colours. Resh, that was his name, Taro recalled, one of Limnel's seconds, with a rep for mindless thuggery and unquestioning obedience to his gang-boss.

Resh nodded at the blade in Taro's hand. 'Don't be stupid,' he lisped through the gap between his two missing front teeth. 'You ain't the dish o' the day. But yer in me way.'

Taro stepped back to leave the path clear. 'Mazeway's all yours.'

Resh sauntered up to him. 'Yeah. Some of us gotta work fer our food, y'know? Oh, wait, so do you now, doncha? Shame it's an invite-only hunt.'

Taro said nothing. Until three days ago he'd been one of the lucky few: Angel lineage, protected and revered. But since his line-mother had joined his birth-mother in the Heart of the City – or whatever paradise or hell really lay beyond death – he was on his own, as Resh couldn't resist reminding him.

He held his breath as the other youth passed him. In a world where water was currency, washing was a luxury, but Resh smelled bad even by Undertow standards, the rancid stink of sweat mixing with the sour reek of burnt mash on his breath.

A sequence of three short whistles came from hubwards. Resh glanced back at Taro and said with a sneer, 'Boss's offer's still open, y'know. Fer now.' Then he headed off purposefully. If the rumours were true, Resh would be in no hurry to finish off the hunt's prey. Meatbabies might have twisted limbs and simple minds, but they were more or less human. Resh would have other pleasures on his mind first.

Once he'd rounded a couple of corners and could no longer hear the hunt's whistles, Taro stopped. He was still shaking, and his throat was parched.

After checking no one was around, he sat down and opened the leather hammock that, now he had no homespace to sling it, doubled as his pack. His remaining possessions made a pitiful tally: the clothes he stood up in plus his flecks, the knives fashioned from slivers of vane material and worn at each wrist; and in the pack: a harness of twisted cord with a plaited rope tether; one thin blanket; a spare shirt, as dirty as the one he wore; a bent metal spoon and a bone-handled eating knife; a plastic bowl and cup; a rusty hand-mirror; and, wrapped in rags to cushion it, the flute carved from his birth-mother's arm-bone, his only memento of the stranger who loved him, but who had died before he had the chance to love her, leaving him in the care of her sister. He found what he was after at the bottom. The water-skin was all but empty. He sucked the last few drops from it, tipping his head back against the vane.

So, Limnel would still let him join his vagabond troupe of muggers, liggers, thieves and tarts. The gang-boss had made the offer the evening after Malia took the fall, striding into the homespace Taro had shared with his line-mother without a by-your-leave. 'So, boy, word is yer all alone now. I could use someone like you. Take up the old hobby full-time, neh?'

Taro, still in shock at losing his protector, his last surviving relative, had murmured, 'No thanks, Limnel. Don't think so.'

The gang-boss had looked around the central common-room, lingering on the dark stain on the nets strung across the gap in the middle of the floor. 'You won't hold onto this place long by yerself, y'know. Think about it.' Then he'd left.

The next morning, soon after dawn, a medium-sized troupe – five adults and three children – came round. They were armed with flecks and one ancient-looking boltgun, but they didn't want trouble. They wanted somewhere to live, and there was no reason why they shouldn't have this place. From the smell of them they were shit-gardeners and a large, isolated homespace that had once belonged to an Angel was perfect for their necessary but anti-social trade. They eased Taro out almost apologetically, waiting while he bundled his things into his hammock. He didn't take anything of Malia's. Her room had been out of bounds when she was alive and he couldn't face going in there now she was dead.

He had asked everyone in his small group of friends for a place to stay, but no one had space in their troupe for an extra mouth. He thought he might at least be able to beg safe crash-space for a day or two, but had no luck, though one ex-girlfriend had given him a refill of water. He couldn't be sure how much his cold reception was due to his association with a now-fallen Angel and how much resulted from Limnel putting the word out that he wanted Taro for himself. At the time he'd seen this rejection by those he'd considered friends as justice; he didn't deserve a break, because his line-mother's fall had been his fault.

For the last two days he'd been living in the mazeways, keeping out of everyone's way, sleeping only when he was too tired to move. The unexpected meeting with Resh had fractured the numb self-pity he'd been wallowing in since Malia's death. Throwing his lot in with Limnel was the only sane option. The gang-boss would be a harsh master, but he would have a safe place to sleep and the protection of belonging to one of the biggest gangs in this quarter of the Undertow.

But first he needed money to buy himself in. And for that he had to go topside.

Taro stuffed the water-skin back and slung his pack over his back, then carried on walking rimwards, accompanied by the ever-present sigh of the wind below the vanes. He checked the daubed tags marking the gang territories and managed to get back into safer mazeways without having to stop and check water-trap colours – which was a relief, as he didn't much fancy hanging over the edge of a mazeway to check out the troupe colours fluttering from the ropes of the nearby 'traps.

He managed to get within a few mazeways of the edge without meeting anyone else; anyone around this early had probably decided to lie low in the wake of the hunt. He passed a few strangers near the edge, downsiders whose daily business was with the rollers and coves in the City above. No one challenged him, and some gave way to him. They weren't to know that he no longer had the right to wear City colours. He should un-plait the red-and-black from his hair, but he wasn't ready to cut that final tie to his line-mother, not with her death still on his conscience, her fall yet unavenged.

The vanes were shorter this close to the edge; Taro felt he could almost reach up and touch the underside of the City. Ahead, the sparkling orange of the forcedome enclosing the City marked the edge of the world.

A close-woven net about six metres wide hung down from the rim, its bottom edge bolted firmly to the outside edge of the wide mazeway where Taro stood. These were the best-maintained nets in the Undertow, as they provided the only route topside. Every respectable troupe – those, that is, that didn't call themselves gangs – considered it their duty to check for damage and repair faults. Everyone's lives depended on it.

Though Taro had done it hundreds of times, that first step into the rim net always sent a surge of fear through him. Dry mouth and churning guts warned him unnecessarily how close he was to taking the fall. He wiped his palms on his breeches and stepped forward, using his long toes to grip the edge of the mazeway. The net was made partly from plaited rags and lengths of cord, though the support ropes that ran up from mazeway to rim were the real thing, bought or stolen from topside. The outermost mazeway was inside the rim of the City, so the net didn't hang vertical. You had to fall off the mazeway into it.

He leaned forward. As gravity pulled him off-balance his eyes fluttered closed and his hands spasmed as they reached for the ropes. The impact was gentle, but it still winded him.

He paused to catch his breath, then started climbing, slow and careful, always making sure he had at least two limbs anchored before moving on. Ignoring the hypnotic glow of the forcewall in front of him and the bleak, rock-scattered ground far below him, he looked only at his hands, thought only of the next move.

To get up the outside rim of the City, he needed to be on the other side of the net, to go from being inside facing out to outside facing in. He worked his way to the edge, then hooked his right hand round the reinforced edge of the net. *Right leg now, get a good solid hold.* A small pause – time for a silent prayer to the City, for all the good that might do – then he swung out and round.

He wasn't used to climbing with anything on his back, and halfway through the slow-motion pivot his pack slipped, pulling him off-balance. He felt his grip begin to loosen. The rope started to slide away under the sole of his right foot. He clawed for purchase, his head full of panic, his body too sluggish—

—until he caught the rope with his toes and curled them round it, ignoring the shooting pains of a sudden cramp. The nets above him creaked, but his grip held. His flailing left hand came round, found rope and grasped it. The creaking subsided.

He hung still until the nets had stopped moving, deafened by his heartbeat, staring blindly back into the darkness of the Undertow.

When he'd calmed down he dragged his pack back up onto his shoulder and started climbing up the sloping rim until his nose was pressed against the grey material of the City. He inhaled its sharp yet comforting smell. Down in the Undertow the scent of the City was masked by the smells of people – sweat and piss, burning tallow and composting shit – but here it filled his head, a reek like mother's milk gone sour.

The rest of the climb was easier: the nets lay against the City itself, hanging from bolts that made safe, easy holds for hands and feet. The only problem was the gravity. With every step his limbs felt heavier, and each move took more effort than the last. Why the people who lived on top of the City's disc wanted gravity that made them twice as heavy as those who lived below, in Vellern's natural gravity, was just one more topside mystery.

When he finally pulled himself up onto the flat ledge at the top he was tempted to lie there for a few moments and catch his breath … but he knew better than to block the way. He rolled away and pulled himself onto all fours, getting used to being heavy, then stood, blinking until his eyes adjusted to the light. He kept his gaze down; looking up at the forcedome arching overhead could set off a vertigo attack worse than looking at the ground when you were downside. Behind him there was no sign of the route he'd used, which was as it should be. Topsiders did not go into the Undertow …

Only, one had, and that was how Taro came to be without home or lineage, with nothing in the world but the bundle on his back.

He started to walk sinwards around the ledge. On his left, a couple of metres away, the fence that ringed the City hummed faintly, a warning to the ignorant. The pylons supporting the fence were thick, holding up the wire and fire, and supporting the circle-car tracks running overhead. The passage of an unseen carriage was announced by a faint swish and the pop of displaced air. Mostly the fence enclosed blank walls, some of the cleanest in the City – no one had any reason, or the opportunity, to tag or deface them. Every few metres Taro passed an alley mouth, giving a view through the links of the fence into the sidestreets. He stopped at the third alley and turned to face the fence. He drew in a deep breath, and reached out to it.

His fingers brushed cold, dead metal and he let his breath out, a subconscious sigh of relief. Long before he'd been born, this part of the fence had been cut to allow downsiders like him into the City proper. Unlike the semi-organic material of the vanes, this would never grow back. He moved the flap away from him and climbed carefully through the gap. Once on the other side he pushed the fence back into place, lining up the edges so the exit was hidden again.

In the sidestreets the light levels dropped to a more comfortable level. The walls were covered with cryptic graffiti and as he made his way down the narrow alleys, he stopped to check over his shoulder every now and again. The wedges between the main Streets were home to some smoky coves, citizens whose business made them as dangerous as any gang-lag in the Undertow.

This route topside brought him out in the wedge between Soft Street and Amnesia Street. Soft Street was where the rollers came for pleasures of the flesh, but every pitch was owned. Amnesia Street was largely free territory but he didn't fancy being a punter's drugged fantasy. Best idea would be to head for Chance, the next Street sunwise from Soft, though it was a long walk.

He turned a corner and spotted a group of topsiders unloading crates from a cart into the back door of a dingy building. Intent on their business, they hadn't seen him.

He doubled back and picked another route, taking him past one of the automated waste-reprocessing plants that lurked in the centre of the wedges, away from tourist eyes. The deep rumble of machinery was less of a give-away than the rotten-sweet smell drifting from inside. He looked down at a rustling by his feet; a rat sped by along the base of the building, intent on its own business.

Thanks to the distraction, he didn't see anyone step out of the door opposite the waste plant until it was too late. As soon as he registered movement he froze, and focused on the lone figure looking straight at him. He knew he should turn round and get out of there, but he couldn't run for long in this gravity. Besides, they might not be alone.

Then he recognised the person blocking the alley.

The man had a fleshy, almost jovial face, and no hair on his head other than girl-thin eyebrows. He wore a narrow-brimmed black hat and an improbably smart but unfashionably cut dark grey suit. He was as short as a topsider, and a little porky, but this was no ordinary cove. There was only one person in the world who looked like that, and though Taro had never met him, he had heard the description enough times. He was looking at the most powerful man in the City: the Minister, the head of the Kheshi League of Concord.

Taro stepped forward, crossed his wrists over his chest and bent his head, the downsider gesture of submission and respect.

The man approached. ' Taro sanMalia?'

'Me life is yours, sirrah,' he croaked. The Minister had called him Taro sanMalia, though he no longer had a right to that name; Malia had been his aunt, not his birth-mother, and though she had adopted him, with her death his lineage name should revert back to his dead mother's. Was it possible that the master of the Angels didn't know that one of his agents was dead?

8

'Your life? Indeed it is,' the Minister replied. 'But all I require is your service. I wish you to witness a removal.'

'Witness a removal? Aye, sirrah – to make sure it's legal?' By the rules of the Concord there needed to be ten witnesses, but they weren't usually downsiders. Removals were topside business, and the witnesses were most often tourists; that was what a lot of the rollers came here for. Taro was not sure why the Minister wanted him.

'There will be plenty of people watching the mark. I want you to watch the Angel. Or rather, to report on her performance and when she returns to the Undertow, to follow up on her movements down there. Do you think you can manage that?'

Taro's head was reeling. He couldn't believe he was here, having this conversation. After three days of hell, he was standing in a topside alley being given his first mission by the Minister, who knew nothing of Malia's fate.

He said the only thing he could. 'Aye, sirrah. I'll do me best to serve you an' me City.'

'Good. The Angel in question is Nual. I expect you'll need to do some research.'

Though any personal fame among the Angels was discouraged by the Minister, who preferred them to be held in awe and viewed from afar, Taro knew the names of all thirty-three Angels currently in the service of the City. He searched his memory for some fact about the Angel Nual, to show the Minister he knew his stuff.

'She lives under the Merchant Quarter, don't she?' he asked after a short pause.

The Minister nodded, waiting for Taro to continue.

'An' ... I don't think she's a pureblood downsider.'

The Minister gave the ghost of a smile. 'You could say that. Nual is scheduled to remove Salik Vidoran, Second Undersecretary for Offworld Trade, in Confederacy Square later this morning. I expect she will take the shot from a vantage point beyond the City's rim, and she won't hang around afterwards, so you are unlikely to see her, but you will be able to watch the crowd and check the reaction of the mark to the threat. I would also like you to note any unusual occurrences in the aftermath.'

9

Should he tell the Minister about the unusual occurrence in his own life, the death of his line-mother? Surely he must know— No, let the Minister bring it up. Stick to the task at hand. 'Nual's one of the best, ain't she?' he asked.

'She never misses,' the Minister agreed. 'She is also one of the most reclusive. I want to know anything you find out about her current activities downside. Quietly, and without attracting undue attention. I will expect full details after the removal, and updates every morning. You can make your reports from any public com booth in the Leisure Quarter. Just go in and ask to be shown *the one who has everything*. You'll need this to get into the State Quarter.' The Minister held out a small strip of pale grey plastic. Taro stepped forward, nervous of getting so close to this legendary figure, and took the credit bracelet. The Minister continued, 'The ID is valid for 24 hours, and there is enough credit for the circle-car fare there and back, plus a little extra. There will be more once you start delivering useful information. Any questions?'

'No, sirrah.' He should tell him now, tell him what had happened to Malia.

'Then go. I am a very busy man.' The Minister nodded in dismissal and stepped back to let Taro pass.

Taro had betrayed his line-mother. He had betrayed his City. He must confess.

But he found himself already walking away from the Minister into an uncertain future.

CHAPTER TWO

Elarn woke to silence. No, not quite silence; there was the near-subliminal hum of the life-support systems, a constant reminder that she was in space, a long way from home. Back on Khathryn she would wake to sea and wind, natural sounds, louder, more chaotic, but real, and comforting.

She has been dreaming again, the ever-present nightmare at the edge of consciousness. In the dream, she is in her house, her lovely safe spacious house. But she is not alone. Her visitors have disabled her security and let themselves in, and now they are coming for her. She is hiding, crouched in a wardrobe like a naughty child, but she can't hide from them forever. For years she thought she could, but they have finally caught up with her.

She had always managed to wake herself before the sinister visitors found her, thank God, but she suspected that might not always be the case. Though she had risked spending the interstellar transits in stasis, rather than dealing with the reality-twisting horrors of shiftspace with drugs, the dreams had been getting worse ever since.

She got up and dressed slowly, paying attention to the details: fair hair piled artistically, clothes smart and formal, cosmetics applied with caution to flatter the stern lines of her face. Must present a good impression. Confident, competent, but not to be approached too closely. Today, for the first time in her life, she would be walking on a new world – or rather, on a massive construct floating above an uninhabitable planet.

As she got herself ready, she had the com-unit play back newscasts from Vellern. She had requested downloads as soon as the starliner emerged into Tri-Confed space three days ago, hoping to learn something more about her destination. Initially she'd had trouble finding anything useful among the welter of adverts, local scandals and unregulated mass entertainment, but digging revealed some in-depth political analyses, sufficiently sophisticated that she had trouble picking up the nuances, ignorant as she was of the background of the situations being discussed. The level of detail should not have been much of a surprise, given the bizarre and brutal process of government in the Confederacy of Three. When a mistake by those in power could lead to them getting their heads blown off, political analysis became strangely popular.

The Tri-Confed system was ancient, one of mankind's oldest territories. The originally settled planet, referred to simply as the homeworld and not even graced with a capital letter any more, was barely habitable, scarred by environmental mismanagement and centuries of warfare between the three main continental nations. The three power-blocs had extended their conflicts, alliances and uneasy truces into the rest of the system thousands of years ago. By this point, their different homeworld environments had already impacted on their genetic make-up. Kheshi tended to be sallow-skinned and dark-haired, Yazilers were pale and Luornai were darker-skinned, with red or dark hair. Or perhaps, Elarn had thought when she had first read this, they had come from original Old Earth stock, back when skin shades were associated with political or cultural groups.

Some time during the dark days of the Sidhe Protectorate, the three sides had reached a compromise. Vellern, a mid-system rock too small for terraforming and long since stripped of any resources worth fighting over, was chosen as the site of a new unifying government. So they had built the Three Cities, expending massive resources to out-do each other in scale and grandeur, and had begun sharing power according to a complex process codified down the centuries and referred to as the Concord.

A soft chime announced that breakfast had now finished, but a light brunch was available in the day lounge. As though it was anyone's business when she ate! That was another thing she hated about space travel: you were always on a schedule. It wasn't as though anyone needed to go anywhere in person these days; beamed virtuals were as good as being there in the flesh. They had certainly been enough to let her have a profitable and fulfilling career without having to leave the world she had been born on. She could transmit a concert via beevee direct from the studio in her house, her producer adding acoustic tweaks and whatever backdrop he felt suitable for the particular market: space scenes for non-planetary nations, natural beauty for the urban fan-base, ecclesiastical architecture for the devout ...

Still, whatever she felt about being told when to do it, as she had no idea what the arrangements would be once she was down on Vellern, she should eat soon. She made her way down the corridor to one of the luxury ship's three lounges, where a selection of light mid-morning snacks were laid out, just in case any passenger experienced hunger pangs in the three hours between breakfast and lunch. There were perishable delicacies including fruit, a sweet-leaf salad and a tray of semi-crystallised flower-petals among the usual cornucopia of dried meats, cheeses, pastries and cakes. Presumably they had picked up fresh supplies when the ship made a brief stopover on the Confederacy home-world yesterday morning; ecological wreck or not, homeworld would want to make sure an élite interstellar liner had everything its occupants might possibly want. Vellern was a popular tourist destination, not just for those from the three Confederacy nations, but from everywhere in human space, with all the attendant wealth that brought in. There were plenty of affluent people who found the idea of a place where everything was available and nothing – allegedly – forbidden very appealing, even if Elarn did not share this view.

She began to browse along the buffet, picking out a couple of pastries and a savoury roll. She still needed to pack, which would give her an excuse not to take lunch with her fellow travellers. The only thing worse than being enclosed in an artificial environment for two weeks was being forced to share it with strangers.

'Will you be visiting Khesh City, Medame Reen?'

Elarn jumped, almost dropping her plate. The speaker lounged on a comfortable couch under a currently blank screen, one of several dozen people she had been introduced to and promptly forgotten. When the ever-changing seating plan had brought them together for dinner, he had flirted with her in a desultory manner; her and every other woman at the table not physically holding on to a partner.

'I mean, obviously I'll be taking trips to Luorna and Yazil too,' he continued, as though she had already replied, 'but with Khesh coming into Grand Assembly, removals will be at the highest level for years. That's where the real action will be.'

'I'm sure,' she said, turning her attention back to the buffet.

'I ask because I wondered if you had any plans for your stay.'

So he hadn't had any luck with the other unattached women. Good.

'Actually I do,' she said, hoping that would be the end of it.

He sniffed, and raised an eyebrow. 'Concerts, you mean.'

At dinner on the second day out of Khathryn, one of the other passengers had asked Elarn outright if she was *that un-augmented singer of ancient religious chants who did all those charming plainsong recordings.* She had resented the woman's patronising tone, and would have liked to have denied her identity, but she was a lousy liar.

As a result she had found herself reluctantly agreeing to give an impromptu concert, which she treated as practice for Khesh City, where she would be performing live in front of paying audiences. The evening had gone fairly well, despite her nerves. This man had not, as far as she could remember, been in the audience.

'That's right,' she said brightly, 'concerts.'

He frowned. 'I must admit, I would have thought singing religious songs to audiences used to unrestricted pleasure and legal murder might be a case of— well, how does that ancient proverb go? Pearls before swine?'

'Possibly,' she conceded, wishing there was some polite way she could end the conversation.

He gave a nasal laugh. 'Oh Medame Reen, please don't take offence. It's just that you're so, well, unusual. Not the kind of person one normally meets in one's travels.'

To hell with polite. She had had enough of these people. 'You mean I'm not a more-money-than-sense thrill-seeker who thinks they're better than the rest of humanity just because they can afford the unnecessary luxury of interstellar travel?'

He sat up straighter. 'My, my, that sounds like a nasty case of parochialism. Not everyone is content to live their lives at the bottom of a gravity well, only ever seeing the universe via beevee, you know.'

'Most people don't have the money to do anything else.' Elarn knew she shouldn't argue, shouldn't risk making enemies, but anachronistic snobs like him annoyed her and before she could stop herself she added, 'Or would you rather we were still under the dominion of the Sidhe? Plenty more shiftships around back then, and no beevee to mesmerise all us planet-bound hicks.'

That got him. He looked shocked. 'Of course not! Goodness, woman, I'm not saying we should go back to living under the rule of those despotic bitches – I'm as grateful as you that they're all long dead!'

Elarn's brief triumph dissolved into dismay. Rather than continue the conversation, she snatched up her plate and walked off, not trusting herself to reply to the wretched man.

Two words echoed round her head as she fled back to her cabin.

If only.

CHAPTER THREE

So this was how the other half lived. So far, Taro wasn't feeling that impressed. Mainly he was feeling sick, 'cause the circle-car changed speed so smooth-and-easy that his guts reckoned he was hardly moving while the rooftops whizzed past scary-fast. It was bad enough being topside where there was no ceiling; up here on the circle-car rails there were no walls either. Though he was sitting down, he kept thinking he was about to fall over.

At least he hadn't had any trouble getting a seat. When he boarded at the end of Amnesia Street, the carriage's other occupants had stared at him with a mixture of fascination, fear and, in the case of the coves, disgust. For the rollers, the romance and danger of the Angels rubbed off on all downsiders, but locals thought everyone who lived in the Undertow must be filthy thieving scum. Several rollers had stood up to give Taro a place to sit. When he took his seat, those near him had edged away, leaving him plenty of space. He probably didn't smell too good to their delicate topside noses, but that wasn't the only reason they were wary of him. He knew what they must be thinking: you need ID to get on the circle-car, but downsiders aren't citizens. They don't get ID unless they are agents of the Concord; if not an Angel, then at least someone with official standing with the Minister.

Taro had always expected that he would work for the Minister one day. He knew he would have to start small, just one of the many downsiders who ran errands and gathered info for the leader of the Kheshi League of Concord. He would have to work hard to get noticed, as his sex was against him, but one day the Minister would see his potential and make him an Angel. Angels never went hungry, or homeless. They never had to worry about waking up to find they were being robbed or raped. People didn't mess with Angels ...

Except that someone had messed with Malia – and not just anyone, an agent from another City. And Taro hadn't had the balls to admit that to the Minister. This wasn't how he'd imagined his career in the Concord starting. The circle-car had already passed the ends of several Streets – Chow, Elsewhere, Slice, Freak – and now it was at Groove Street, the last before the wall that divided the Leisure and State Quarters. He had been tempted to go the long way round, to see the Guest and Merchant Quarters too, but given how the ride was messing with his belly and head, he was glad he'd decided against it. Before boarding the circle-car he'd taken the time to visit a Soft Street fast-food joint, one that would serve downsiders, and used some of the funds on the cred-bracelet to get an over-sweetened drink and a something-like-meat roll but much longer in here and he'd be wasting his money all over the floor. He closed his eyes, turning down the chance to look over the unknown Streets of the State Quarter in favour of not throwing up. When the mellow-voiced announcement said they were approaching Confederacy Square he opened his eyes, eager to get in among the buildings again, but as the carriage pulled up at the end of the Street he found himself gawping down on an open space as wide as eight or ten Streets put next to each other. It was full of people, the most Taro had ever seen in one place: hundreds, maybe thousands of milling rollers, and the coves guiding, guarding or fleecing them. The tourists were taking holo-pix, reading their guidebooks, hanging round the clusters of sales and betting booths and generally making like they happened to find themselves there in that very place this morning almost by accident. Only the sinwards end of the square was empty. That section was dominated by a building twelve storeys high, fronted by a massive balcony supported by a row of huge black pillars.

That had to be the Assembly building; Taro had heard somewhere that those pillars were made of real stone.

The enclosed lift ride down to Street level was a relief after the wide-open spaces surrounding the circle-car, though gravity bit extra hard when it stopped, leaving his knees aching.

He wasn't sure how long he had before the removal was due, or where to watch from, but he decided to get nearer to the Assembly building, as that would be where the mark would most likely be heading when he took his final walk. He wanted a good view. This was what Angels did, what made them special. These people were here for one reason only, even if they were pretending otherwise: to see death at its most skilled, its most just, its most perfect.

Because almost all removals took place in the State Quarter, Taro had never seen Malia do her duty for her City. And now he never would.

But today he would see the Concord go on without her, and know that justice would continue to be done. He aimed for a point to the right of the statue in the centre of the square. The statue was the size of a small building, three figures reaching up so their fingers just touched a floating ball. He supposed the ball must be Vellern, and the old coves in robes were meant to be the three nations of the Confederacy. Maybe that kind of thing made Tri-Confed citizens feel all warm inside, but Taro thought it was just plain ugly. His height gave him a clear view sinwards over everyone's heads, where he could make out the line of floating grey grav-batons sealing the officials and politicians off from the plebs. Every few minutes groups of smart-dressed coves walked out of one of the smaller buildings and crossed to the big one, some of them looking pretty nervous as they emerged into the open. Whenever anyone appeared, the interest level amongst the watchers in the square went up for a while. Occasionally Taro stopped and looked back rimwards, on the tiny chance he might see the Angel getting into position, but the orange static of the forcedome was as featureless as ever – and painful, if you stared at it for too long. The buildings here were higher and cleaner than those in the Leisure Quarter, decorated with columns and carvings, and the ground was free of litter and dirt. The punters were better dressed too, but who was to say that after the excitement was over some of them wouldn't head back sunwise for a different sort of gratification?

He'd just drawn level with the big ugly statue when the crowd noise changed. The hubbub died down, and he started to hear the name 'Vidoran' as attention focused on the rimwards corner of the square, all pretence at casual curiosity forgotten. Hurrying a little now, he cut in sinwards and rimwards. Most people moved aside without him having to say anything; to the less observant, or stubborn, he used his elbows and muttered, 'City business, make way, please.'

By the time he had found himself a good vantage point, everyone had fallen silent and all eyes were on a group of three people walking along the sinwards edge of the square. That must be Consul Vidoran in the middle: perfect suit, perfect hair, perfect smile. He was playing it cool, smiling like that, walking out to his death like he hadn't a care in the world.

Just to this side of him and a couple of steps behind he spotted a woman in the high-necked red tunic and black cap of the City militia: an official guard, here for the sake of form. She looked nervous. Taro didn't blame her. Removals could be messy, with frequent collateral damage. She should be safe enough though; from what he knew of her rep, Nual never took out bystanders. Of course, the militia-woman didn't know who was going to perform the removal. No one here did except Taro, and possibly the Consul, who was about to experience invisible, silent death from an Angel's gun.

The past no longer mattered. He was here, in the centre of things, an official agent of the Concord, one of the Minister's chosen. He was part of history.

The third figure was on the far side of Consul Vidoran, so Taro couldn't see him very well, but he was wearing green and yellow: Yazil City colours. That made sense; Taro had heard something about the Consul doing some smoky trade deal with Yazil City, which was presumably why he was up for removal. The Yazilers probably felt obliged to put one of their men on the line too.

As the three of them turned to head towards the Assembly building, the third figure drew slightly ahead.

Taro saw him clearly for the first time – and knew him.

Nual sat on air.

She floated a few metres out from the edge of the disc of Khesh City, legs crossed, toes pointed to control the gravitic implants that kept her aloft. Her mimetic shimmer-cloak hung around her in loose folds, rendering her invisible against the forcedome.

Her head was bowed, her gaze fixed on the black object in her lap. The laser was as long as her arm, with a heavy triangular stock and a slender barrel. A sensor pad on the trigger was coded to her alone and would discharge a lethal shock into anybody else who tried to fire the laser.

She raised the gun to her shoulder and rested her cheek against the smooth stock, watching the distant throng in the square with un-augmented vision for a few seconds before shifting her head to put her eye to the sight. She would be visible from directly in front now, the foreshortened gun a dark smudge against her pale, narrow face.

Through the sight the distant mass of people in Confederacy Square resolved into individuals. She let her gaze wash over them, getting a feel for the crowd, reading her target's approach in their faces. They were a varied lot, united only in their desire to vicariously experience another's death. One figure, conspicuous by his height, caught her eye: a youth with a thin, dirty face and scraps of red-and-black fabric plaited into his long dark hair. A downsider, Angel lineage judging by his colours. Interesting. The Minister must have sent him as an observer. From the look on his face he thought this was the best thing that had ever hap-pened to him.

She was about to move off him when the youth's expression changed from self-satisfaction into shock and hatred and she gasped as the force of the downsider's emotions washed over her. She turned her head away from the gun-sight to catch her breath. Whatever was wrong with the boy, she couldn't let it break her concentration. She had to stay focused. She swung the sight away from the downsider's contorted face to the place where she expected to get a visual lock on the target; some twenty metres in front of the Confederacy Monument. That's where Vidoran should emerge from the shade cast by the rimwards buildings.

She slid a finger under the trigger-guard. The sensor warmed to her touch.

Taro was stunned.

He knew that man – not his *name*; punters rarely bothered with such niceties – but he would never forget that face, that body, nor would he ever forget what the bastard had done. What the fuck was he doing here? He wasn't just an honour guard, a token gesture from Yazil City: he was a Screamer, an agent from the Yazil League of Concord.

The Screamer was walking in front of Vidoran now, scanning the crowd. He noticed Taro and a corner of his mouth twitched, before the twitch resolved itself into an expression of mild surprise. He looked away and moved on.

The Screamer's indifference jolted Taro out of his paralysis and he started to shove his way through the crowd. He wanted to shout, attract the fucker's attention, but his throat was constricted. In his head all he could hear was his own voice, shouting *I'll kill you!* – the silent vow he'd made the last time they had met. The wall of bodies gave way as he pressed towards the grav-batons separating the crowd from the three figures crossing the square.

Something was wrong.

Was she just fazed by the youth's strange reaction or was it her own unease? The senses she tried not to rely on had told her not to accept this mission, but to refuse would make her rogue, fair game for her own, or any other, League. She just wanted to get the removal over and done with so she could return to the dark sanctuary of the Undertow.

He was close now. No distractions. No thought. Just focus.

Her vision tracked across the back of a man's head: blond ponytail, flash of yellow and green. Yaziler. Not in uniform, might even be a Screamer. Interesting, but not important now. There was someone else on the other side, a woman: Kheshi guard. Ignore her too.

And there, in the middle, his back to her now, was Vidoran himself, moving without haste, thoroughly self-possessed. She watched him for a moment, then took a deep breath, poised on the cusp, that glorious, awful moment between life and death.

Taro thrust the last few people out of his way and slammed into the grav-batons. The invisible force-field winded him, but the pain released his voice. He pressed himself against the barrier and screamed at the top of his voice—

'—I'll kill you, you fucker!'

For a timeless moment, everything froze.

Then the Screamer leapt backwards, pushing Vidoran down. Taro was vaguely aware of the politician falling and of the look of puzzled surprise on the face of the Kheshi guard before she fell.

Nual dimly registered the boy's distant cry, but there was no time to reconsider. She was committed to the shot now.

Her finger tensed on the trigger-pad, began to draw back

There was a flurry of movement and Vidoran dropped out of her sights.

Too late.

She felt the subtle vibration as the gun discharged.

Taro was still shouting as the Kheshi guard hit the ground. The Screamer stared at him for a moment, his face expressionless, then looked around, searching for the real threat, the person who'd fired the shot. Vidoran was already scrambling towards the Assembly building when the Screamer turned and ran over to the politician, putting a protective arm across his shoulders as he hurried him back into the shadows.

Someone was screaming. Taro, hoarse and out of breath, tore his gaze from the Yaziler's departing back and looked at the militia-woman, lying where she had fallen, her upper body curled in on itself and her legs twitching wildly. Her high, thin screech was only the sound in the square.

Nual expelled her breath in a low moan.

Vidoran was already under cover and out of the line of fire. She hugged the gun to her chest, flicked her legs out and dived down below the disc of the City, away from the faint sound of the guard's agony.

The crowd were in shock. They'd wanted violence, but not like this, not an innocent bystander. Within the Concord an individual's death was a matter of ritual and tradition: clean and efficient, an almost antiseptic state-sponsored thrill. The accidental shooting of a guard instead of the mark because of a random distraction wasn't part of the deal.

People had pulled away from Taro; they had heard him cry out. This terrible thing was his fault. No one approached him, no one said anything, but he could feel the weight of their eyes upon him, glaring at him in accusation and confusion.

Taro ran, oblivious to the pain in his limbs. No one got in his way. By the time he reached the edge of the square, the screaming had stopped.

CHAPTER FOUR

From space, Vellern was an orange-brown wasteland. The screens showed magnified views of the Three Cities as the liner passed over each one. The text at the bottom of the screen currently read: *Passengers for Khesh City please wait in the reception lounge for the shuttle.*

Elarn Reen wished there was something else to look at while she queued with the other passengers. The dome of the force-field that enclosed the City reminded her of a boil on desiccated skin.

The queue started to move and Elarn shuffled along with it. The shuttles were tight on space, so no personal luggage was allowed. She had to trust that her possessions were on their way to her hotel in the freight shuttle.

When the queue reached the airlock, an insincerely smiling steward bid the passengers goodbye. Ingrained politeness made Elarn return his smile.

The shuttle was cramped, and the screen at the front played an endless loop of adverts for hotels, bars, massage parlours, specialist shops, dance clubs and restaurants. Elarn stared at the backs of her hands.

'Excuse me, medame?'

She looked up to see another steward bending over her.

'I have a message for you. The message had to be re-routed to the shuttle, as you don't have a com.' The woman made not having a com sound like an offence committed only by the ignorant or stupid.

'Well?'

'It's from a' – the stewardess checked her wrist and Elarn thought how she'd take an attention-span over a piece of tech any day – 'Medame Shamal Binu. Is this person known to you?'

'Yes, sort of.' Shamal Binu was the local agent Elarn's manager had assigned to handle her professional engagements. Elarn had seen a holo-pic of the woman – she looked every inch the kind of impresario Elarn would never normally have allowed near her – but she had yet to speak to her directly.

The steward continued, 'The message reads: "Apologies, I have been unavoidably detained and may be a little late meeting you at the transit hall." Did you wish to send a response?'

'No, no. That's fine.' Actually it was far from fine. After days alone in the opulent confinement of the starliner, she was now being left in the lurch by her only contact on this planet.

'Medame? Are you all right?' The steward was still hovering.

Elarn waved her away. *I'm scared and homesick, and I don't want to be here at all, not that you care.* She looked up at the screen. At least the adverts were gone now, replaced with pictures showing their steep descent towards Vellern's barren surface. As Elarn watched, the disc of the City became visible as a dark smudge beneath the translucent force-field. Before she could make out more detail the screen went blank. The adverts were back briefly, followed by an announcement telling passengers to remain seated until instructed to disembark. The image of the approach to the City must have been a recording, probably typical of the kind of tricks and illusions she expected here.

She waited while the other passengers filed off, running the words of one of her favourite songs through her head to try to relax herself – words with lost meanings, in a lost language, intended to celebrate a religious ecstasy she had never experienced. But the alien, ancient shape of the sounds calmed and relaxed her.

By the time she followed the tail-end of the crowd out there were only a dozen or so people left with her. She entered a great circular hall, decorated with a complex spiral-pattern in black and red on the ceiling and with black doors all around the windowless grey walls. She followed her little knot of tourists through one of the doors which had tell-tales blinking green, and gasped. She and her fellow tourists were standing in a transparent bubble clinging to a thin spine running from the shuttle-pads down to the middle of the massive disc of Khesh City.

As the elevator descended she was treated to a panoramic view. The first thing she noticed was that there was no sky. After a life spent under the dramatic open horizon of Khathryn, she found her mind rebelling at the idea of being stopped by the orange force-field. The sun was visible only as a small bright patch high in the wall of static, but there were no clouds, no horizon. While the 'sky' was featureless, the disc of the City itself was intricate with detail. She knew it was ten kilometres across but she could see nothing to give it any scale. Only as the elevator dropped lower did the thin lines radiating out from the centre of the disc resolve into boulevards dozens of metres wide, and the jumble of shapes between them into low, close-packed buildings. She gripped the handrail and leaned against the elevator wall as she looked down. The greenery directly below – the famous Gardens, presumably – was shrouded in a faint mist and broken up by various structures. She spotted one big building, a sports stadium, maybe, and what looked like an amphitheatre, and a cluster of buildings round a large pool. The view disappeared and the elevator went dark for a brief moment before they emerged into light again. The elevator was inside now, decelerating through a high-ceilinged hall whose floor was alive with figures and holo-projections.

When the door opened she followed her fellow travellers through an ornate free-standing arch. Elarn's suspicion that the structure was not just ornamental was confirmed when two gentlemen in red uniforms decorated with black piping stepped forward to accost the idiot who had pestered her that morning. Elarn, already through the arch, slowed down to overhear what was being said by the men, who she assumed to be the Khesh City militia, the nearest this place had to formal law enforcement.

'We have reason to believe you may be carrying a propellant pistol, sirrah,' one said, his hand firm on the tourist's arm.

'What? How do you—? I mean, what makes you think—?'

'You have been scanned, sirrah.'

Much as she enjoyed seeing the man discomfited, Elarn couldn't help wondering what other, less orthodox checks might have been carried out on Khesh City's visitors. The man protested, 'I was told that personal weapons were legal here. In fact, I was *advised* to carry one.'

'Yes, sirrah. You may buy or carry non-projectile or gas-powered weapons for self-defence purposes. However, if you wish to bring your own weapon into the City, you'll have to pay import duty. That was clearly written in the small print of your travel documents.'

The man spluttered, but held out his credit-bracelet.

Elarn allowed herself a small smile and joined the trickle of tourists sauntering across the open area beyond the arch towards a line of floating grey batons. The area on the far side of the batons swarmed with people, many of them pressed up against the barrier, trying to attract the attention of the new arrivals. Tacky holo-adverts flashed above the crowds: 'Diamond Mall – jewellery from across the universe'; 'Try a bodysculpt for a You you've only dreamed of'; 'Whatever your pleasure, you'll find yourself fulfilled on Soft Street'. The graphics on that last one stopped Elarn in her tracks: apparently there were no laws against public obscenity here. The human hucksters beneath the holo-ads were also trying to sell things – weaponry, narcotics, maps, trinkets, themselves – and as she passed through the gap in the barrier, the sound of the competing sales pitches melded with the soundtracks of the holo-ads into a barrage of noise.

Elarn recoiled from the onslaught. Even if her agent had been here, she doubted she would have found her. But she couldn't stand around in this place all day either. The best thing she could do right now would be to find somewhere quiet to wait, somewhere she could keep an eye out for Medame Binu. She lowered her head and started to push through the crowd, muttering apologies that no one noticed. She found herself constantly jostled by the press of people, but her obvious lack of interest meant no one bothered her directly.

A hand shot out and grabbed for her wrist. Elarn snatched her arm back and looked up. Standing in front of her was a fearfully pale girl well over two metres tall, wearing a mismatched collection of ragged, ill-fitting clothes, and plenty of dirt. Instead of shoes she had strips of fabric wound round her feet. Orange and dark-green rags had been plaited into her otherwise unkempt hair. Her dark eyes were huge, and the left one was made even bigger by a curved pink scar that pulled down the outside corner. Elarn realised that this was someone to whom the concept of personal hygiene was obviously unknown. She drew a quick, frightened breath.

The girl put out a hand in a warning, shushing gesture. The other hand performed a complicated flick and when Elarn's eyes followed the movement, she saw that her attacker was holding a short, jagged-edged grey blade.

She managed to look away from the knife, hoping to find help. Now, finally, people were avoiding her. She was an island of calm in the sea of hustlers as people passed by quickly and avoided looking her way.

She must not panic. The relative safety of the arrival area was only a few metres behind her. She took a step back, then another.

Her heel hit flesh.

The gravity was only a fraction more than she was used to, but it was enough to make a difference. She toppled backwards, falling hard. As soon as she hit the floor an arm snaked out from behind her and clamped across her neck. Something dug into the small of her back and foul, hot breath fanned the side of her face.

Elarn froze. Though she was terrified, some detached, analytical part of her mind recognised her attackers from recordings: they were *downsiders*: exotic, brutal and immoral. Deep inside she felt the scream building, the scream she must not allow to escape.

She needed to stay calm, to try to reason with them, convince them to leave her alone. If she panicked now, they would be more likely to hurt her. And if she let the scream out, she wouldn't stop screaming until everyone here was dead.

She took a couple of rapid breaths and forced herself to speak 'Wh— what do you want?' she panted. Perhaps if she kept the downsiders occupied long enough the militia would see what was happening and come over to help her.

'Bracelet, please, medame,' said the downsider in front of her in a matter-of-fact voice.

'Bracelet?' echoed Elarn stupidly, until she realised the girl wanted her credit bracelet. There wasn't much on it – the guidebooks had advised against carrying too much stealable credit – and though it also held Elarn's City ID, this skinny thief was welcome to it. Chances were

she'd let her go once she had the money. 'Yes, of course, but I need—'
She shifted, and the pressure round her neck tightened. She struggled to
speak. 'You'll have to let me sit up to get it off.'

The girl crouched down and Elarn flinched: for a moment she
thought the downsider was going to use that vicious-looking knife on
her, but instead the girl looked past Elarn and nodded.

The pressure on Elarn's neck relaxed, although she could still feel a
knife pricking into her back. She sat forward and reached over to thumb
the clasp on the front of the bracelet. *She just had to do what they said and
she would be fine.* She could panic later.

Sudden movement made her look up.

The downsider girl was scrabbling backwards, staring up at something behind Elarn. In her terror she suddenly looked very young. She
swore under her breath – *Shit and blood!* – then turned and was gone in
a flurry of scrawny limbs.

From behind, Elarn heard a sharp crack, followed by a soft sighing
sound. Somehow she knew that however bad the attempted mugging
had been, this was worse. She threw herself forward, away from the
sound, her heart in overdrive, and started to crawl away, but she had to
look back, even though she knew she'd regret it.

A downsider boy was sprawled in front of an athletically built young
man with a handsome, cruel face and blond hair swept back over his
shoulders. The man held the boy's head in his hands; the boy's neck was
bent sharply to one side, his eyes were wide with surprise and the tip
of his tongue protruded from his lips. He wasn't moving. Elarn looked
from the boy to the blond man and met the calm, dead eyes of a killer.

For a second, she thought she was going to lose control of her blad-
der, but she couldn't – wouldn't – let herself do that. She couldn't faint,
either, much as she wanted to; a lifetime of being in control wouldn't let
her take the easy way out.

She tried to gather her legs under her to stand, but, no matter how
strong she was in her head, her body refused to co-operate. All she could
manage was to twist herself off her knees to a sitting position. She had
never expected to die this way, killed by a random lunatic on an alien
world.

'Are you all right?'

Something was being held out to her. *A hand?* A man's hand, clean, elegant. Not the hand of an enemy. She grabbed the hand without thinking. It was firm and cool.

'Here, let me help you.'

Elarn let the man pull her to her feet. Even through her fear she could see he was immaculately groomed: his dark hair and small beard were cropped and shaped, and his red-trimmed dark green suit looked made-to-measure. He had a narrow, aristocratic-looking nose, dark brown eyes and lips which, though thin, had a sensuous twist to them. It was the most wonderful face in the world.

'It's all right, medame.' The man's voice sounded close to her ear; Elarn found that she had pressed herself into him. 'Scarrion won't hurt you.'

For a moment Elarn was confused; then she realised the man was referring to the killer. Should she trust someone who kept company with murderers? But the man said, 'He's my bodyguard. I saw what was happening and told him to help you.'

'He … he broke that boy's neck.' A stupid thing to say. She must be in shock.

'And if he hadn't, that boy and his friend would probably have killed you. Besides, it was only a downsider.' The man raised his voice slightly, addressing his bodyguard. 'Fetch the militia and get them to clear up this mess, please, Scarrion.'

The blond man hesitated for a second, looking between Elarn and her saviour, who addressed him with a nod. 'We'll be fine for a while. I think the lady needs some air.' The bodyguard dropped the body as though it were a sack of rubbish and strode off through the crowd without a word. Elarn noticed a small dribble of blood running from the corner of the dead boy's mouth, and a new, unpleasant smell emanating from the body. So this was what death was like.

'Let's get you away from here.' The man put an arm round her shoulder and turned her from the scene.

Elarn let him lead her through the crowd, most of whom had seen enough to move aside and let them pass. Her legs still felt like they wanted to bend the wrong way and she couldn't stop her teeth chattering, but with every step she regained some of her composure.

As they left the transit hall, the noise level fell. Elarn found herself at the side of a small tree-lined square where a queue of peculiar little vehicles waited to take the arriving tourists to their hotels: pedicabs, three-wheeled pedal-powered contraptions with a double seat in front of the driver. A fountain played in the centre of the square and pots of red and white flowers decorated the walkways. The trees that surrounded the square had glossy leaves; they looked healthy. After ten days in a space-going box breathing recycled air Elarn found the smell and sight of so much vegetation a pleasant surprise, but the 'ground' out here was still the same grey material as the floor of the hall they had just left, a reminder that despite the plants disguising it, she was on a man-made construct, floating three kilometres above the planet's surface.

Her saviour guided her to one of the varnished wooden benches just outside the door. 'You're sure you're not hurt?' he asked solicitously.

'No, I'm fine, really. Just a bit shaken. I can't believe that everyone ignored what was happening like that.'

'Ah. I take it this is your first visit to our City? I'm afraid that's fairly typical, especially when downsiders are involved. It's safer to just pretend it isn't happening, to avoid drawing attention to yourself.'

Elarn had assumed from his cultured manner that he must be a visitor, but he'd said 'our City'. 'Do you live here, then?'

'I'm being rude. Allow me to introduce myself: I'm Salik Vidoran. And yes, I am one of the minority who think of this City as home.'

'Elarn Reen. I'm very pleased to meet you.' Salik Vidoran? Elarn had heard that name recently.

'Ah, here's Scarrion.'

The bodyguard stopped outside the doors and scanned his surroundings. Unlike his employer he was dressed ostentatiously, in embarrassingly tight dark green trousers and a loose cream-coloured shirt shot through with golden thread. He was a little barrel-chested. When he spotted them, he nodded, but didn't come over – watching for threats, presumably. Elarn was quite happy for him to keep his distance.

Salik Vidoran stood. 'May I get you some transport, Medame Reen?'

'Er, no, thank you. I'm being met.' She wondered what he would assume from that, whether she should say more – just in case, for example, he took her comment to mean that she had a partner.

'Of course. I can wait with you, if you like. My day's appointments have just been cancelled and I'm at something of a loose end.' His smile was dazzling. She found herself smiling back.

'Well, if you— Oh!' That had to be Shamal Binu, disembarking from a newly arrived pedicab. She was slender, and looked almost like some exotic bird, right down to the feathers in her hair. She spotted Elarn and waved enthusiastically. There were pink and lilac feathers at her wrists too, colour-coordinated with her short-skirted suit.

'Ah.' His tone said that he shared Elarn's first impression of Medame Binu. 'I do believe your ride is here.'

Elarn turned to him, but he was already standing up. 'Thank you,' she murmured.

He smiled down at her. 'Might I be impertinent enough to suggest that we meet up again? Perhaps after one of your performances? Assuming I have leapt to the correct conclusion and you are *the* Elarn Reen?'

So there was one person at least in this uncivilised place who appreciated music. She smiled. 'Yes, I am. And yes, I would like that. Thank you, again.'

He left, and Elarn tried not to peer after him.

Moments later Shamal Binu arrived in a flurry of feathers. She mimed two quick kisses to the air behind Elarn's left and right ears, and then stared with the intensity of a bird of prey spotting a mouse at Salik Vidoran's departing back. Without looking at Elarn she said, in a voice surprisingly deep for one so slight, 'Unbelievable. Here two minutes and you've already snared the man of the moment.' She turned back to Elarn and favoured her with the full force of her make-up. 'Now that, my dear, is style.'

CHAPTER FIVE

At first Taro welcomed the burning in his legs, because pain stopped thought. But gravity soon got the better of him and by the time he was out of the Square into Confederacy Street he had to stop running.

Ahead, an open gateway marked the hubwards end of the Street and the edge of the State Quarter. Taro attracted nothing more than a hostile stare from the baton-boys on the gate. They couldn't have heard the news; if they knew he'd caused the death of one of their own they would've beaten him to a pulp, valid City ID or not.

He found himself in the Ringway, the circular street that ran around the Gardens. From here you could get to the hubwards ends of all thirty-two Streets. Ahead, the dark pillar of the spine towered over the green chaos of the Gardens. Taro plunged into the wall of foliage.

Branches scratched his face and the change underfoot from flat City material to uneven, root-impacted soil nearly tripped him up, but he carried on, deeper into the Gardens, until the sounds of the Streets tailed off to a distant drone and all he could see in any direction was green. Only then did he allow his legs to buckle and he fell to his knees, tears streaming down his face. He made no attempt to stop them. For three days he'd been numb with shock and guilt; now he gave way to grief.

Eventually the tears ran out. He rolled onto his back and looked up at the shifting pattern of leaves against the orange sky. All this growing stuff around him made him feel safe, cut off from the screw-up his life had become.

Something cold dropped onto his face. He flinched. Another drop. As though mirroring his mood, water was falling from the sky. He'd been in the Gardens once before when this happened; the roller he'd been with, a Kheshi homeworlder, had told him the water fell from unseen structures in the trees to feed the Gardens. Maybe that was true. Right now it felt more like City magic. He opened his mouth and closed his eyes, swallowing whenever one of the fat drops landed in his mouth. He lay there until the ground below him began to feel damp, then slowly climbed to his feet.

He knew what he had to do.

He had messed with the sacred process of the Concord by disrupting a removal. *His* reason had been personal vengeance, but the Screamer had broken more rules than he had. The Minister needed to know what had happened. And Taro must be the one to tell him.

It was possible the Minister had decided that Taro's actions – no doubt known to him now through other watchers, or whatever more arcane means he used – deserved punishment. If so, hiding in the Gardens would only postpone it, maybe even make it worse.

Taro pulled his pack up onto his back; the extra weight was a burden, one he could do without, but he had no idea if he would be able to come back for it, or if it would even still be here if he did.

Stepping through the hedge back onto the Street got him a few odd looks from rollers in passing pedicabs. He ignored them and set off sunwise. If the Minister had decided that he was to be punished, it would happen now. He tried not to jump at movements seen out of the corner of his eye; if an Angel came for him, she would strike from above. Chances were the first he would know about it would be when she ripped his throat out. If that was what had to happen, so be it, nothing he could do. Just keep walking.

The Leisure Quarter started less than an eighth-turn sunwise from here; this close to the centre of the City, that was about a few hundred metres. Taro took it slowly, keeping close to the Gardens as he passed the silent gated Streets of the State Quarter. He heard Groove Street long before he reached it. Dancers and acrobats spilled out onto the path and the early crowds surged and flowed. Holos played above the buildings, showing the kind of fun to be had within: animated crushes of bodies moving to pounding rhythms; a lone dancer shaking her stuff in a metal frame. He ignored it all and walked to a row of niches set into the wall on the sinwards side of the Street.

Taro had never used a public com booth before. They were there for the few topsiders who didn't have personal coms, though you still needed City ID to use them.

As he ducked under the clear plastic hood, the sounds of the Street faded out and the screen in front of him jumped into life. A soft voice, the same as the one in the circle car, asked him to state his request and have his credit bracelet ready. Taro wondered if he was hearing the voice of the City. Plenty of downsiders thought of it as their living protector, but Taro had never quite managed that leap of faith. He pulled up his sleeve, ready to put the bracelet in the reader, and said, 'Show me the one who has everything.' His voice came out as a croak and he had to repeat the request before the voice responded, 'Your request is acknowledged. No ID or payment is required for this service.'

The screen went blank; even the adverts on the walls died away, and for a moment Taro wondered if something was wrong.

Then the Minister's voice came from the still-dark screen. 'I think you have some explaining to do,' he said.

Taro took a deep breath and said, 'He killed Malia.'

'Who killed Malia?' The Minister's voice, though clear and perfect, sounded strangely toneless.

'The Screamer, the one with Consul Vidoran.'

'And that explains your behaviour in Confederacy Square.' Still no clue as to how much the Minister already knew. But no indication he was angry either. 'Was there any particular reason why you failed to mention the circumstances of your line-mother's death when we met this morning?'

'I should've, sirrah. I was surprised, meetin' you like that. Scared, too. It's been so hard since ... since she died.' The Minister deserved the whole truth. No more hiding, no more self-pity. 'An' I was ashamed.'

'Ashamed? Surprise and fear I understand, but what had you to be ashamed of?'

'It's my fault. Malia's death. I led him to her. Not on purpose, but, it's still 'cause of me.'

'Explain. From the beginning.'

35

Taro swallowed hard. 'Malia'd been in a mood fer a while, after one of her lovers … anyway she wanted me out the homespace, said I should go earn me keep. She got like that sometimes. She lets – *let* – me share homespace with her 'cause me blood-mother was her sister, but whenever she was having a sh— a bad time, she wanted to know I wasn't just livin' off her rep. I'm a—' Taro paused, not sure how to put it delicately.

'Prostitute,' said the Minister, still without emotion. 'Yes, I know.'

Well, that saved him having to be subtle. 'She said I could take a pitch on Soft Street. She'd had a word with one of the pimps there. That's where he picked me up. I thought he was just another roller. He looked normal enough; wasn't even wearin' colours.' Taro swallowed the bile rising in his throat. 'He—'

'Scarrion.'

'Sirrah?'

'His name is Scarrion.'

'He – *Scarrion* – kept me fer the night.' Taro still had the bruises. He had put up with the harsh treatment, consoling himself with the thought that the idiot roller would regret not spotting that Taro had Angel lineage. Maybe he'd ask Malia to track him down and pay him a visit later that day … Except the Screamer had probably picked Taro just *'cause* of the colours in his hair. Probably made the pleasure he got from giving pain even greater. Taro shuddered, then continued, 'When he threw me out in the morning I headed home. He must've followed me. I thought I heard someone behind me a couple of times, but I was a bit strung-out, thought I was imaginin' it. Even if a roller's gonna hit the sidestreets, no way they'd try and get downside. When I got back I crashed out fer a while, maybe half an hour, not long. I woke up when Malia came in.'

Taro could see her in his mind as he spoke: *his line-mother floating in the common-room in the heart of their homespace, smiling, a little stoned, in a good mood for once.*

'I saw movement, on the other side of the common-room. I called out, askin' who was there.'

Malia glances over her shoulder, casually, not worried. She's an Angel: no one would dare threaten her, especially not here, in her own home.

'Suddenly I got this freaky feelin' in me guts and everythin' went all slow and heavy, like in a dream, when you try to move an' you can't. S'pose the Screamer must've used his implant.'

And now Malia's expression changes: confusion, alarm. She tries to leap for the unseen intruder, but she's clumsy, uncoordinated. She falls, tangling her foot in the nets strung across the gap in the middle of the common-room, but bounces back almost at once.

'The Screamer came out from where he'd been hidin' once we were down. He had a boltgun – dunno where he got that from. Malia went for him, but she was all over the place.'

She tries to jump for his throat, blades extended, but the net still catching her foot pulls her off-balance. She's trying to get her leg free when he raises the boltgun. He's smiling, looking pleased with himself.

'He didn't give no challenge, no formal declaration of feud, nothin'. He just shot her.' He couldn't stop his voice shaking.

The bolt shatters her skull. Taro feels something soft and warm spatter his face. Her body flops onto the nets, then slips slowly, slowly, through. Taro looks on, unable to move. The boltgun doesn't have the range to hit him across the common-room and the Screamer is looking around for the safest way round the floor-gap. His head swings at a noise outside. He opens his mouth again.

Taro's last thought before the assassin's sonics knock him out is to silently make the promise he tried to fulfil in Confederacy Square: I'll kill you! I swear it!

Reliving Malia's death now brought the anger back. 'Sirrah, I know I was a fool,' Taro admitted, 'but I'd never betray me City. He killed an Angel fer no reason, *here*, in our City. By the rules of the Concord you gotta call feud on him fer that, or at least tell the Yazil League so they can!'

'Do not presume to tell *me* the rules of the Concord.' The Minister's cold dismissal cut through Taro's anger.

'I'm sorry, sirrah. I forgot meself.'

'Quite so. And have you forgotten any more details you think I should perhaps know?'

'No, sirrah. That's all. I'll take the rap, whatever punishment you've decided for me.' Taro stood a little straighter as he spoke.

'I think you have already suffered enough for your mistake. Nothing can change what was done. Your shame is understandable. However, this news does not alter your mission, which is to watch Nual and report on her. Malia's death is not yet common knowledge, so you may still be able to trade on your heritage to find information.'

'What about the Screamer, Scarrion?'

'Scarrion is not your problem. If you are lucky, you will never meet him again. You must forget the past; your future is mine, as my spy. I await your next report.'

Taro wasn't sure whether the Minister had gone until the soft voice stated, 'Thank you for using the City-com network,' and the adverts started playing round the walls again.

He ducked back out of the booth and looked at the bracelet on his wrist. It was still valid, and there was a small balance left: enough to buy him a decent meal, or maybe a pedicab ride to save his aching legs. He thought for a moment, and realised he had another use for it.

CHAPTER SIX

As the pedicab pulled away down the tree-lined avenue, Shamal Binu leaned towards Elarn and said conspiratorially, 'Meeting Consul Vidoran like that is quite a start to your visit.'

Elarn remembered where she had heard the name now: among the media dumps from Vellern there had been several adverts, calling for this man's death: 'Consul Vidoran – who's he really working for? Not the people!' Another had been less subtle: 'Remove Vidoran now! His time has come!'

She turned back to the agent, trying not to flinch at the woman's constant invasion of her personal space, and asked, 'So, what has he done? To have people want to ... *remove him*, I mean.'

Medame Binu waved a hand vaguely, feathers swishing. 'I'm afraid I couldn't tell you in detail, my dear – I can't say I follow the Concord that closely. He made some trade concession to Yazil, or something like that – just the usual political wheeler-dealing. I doubt it would have put him on the hot-list if we weren't hosting the Assembly. He must have annoyed some powerful people, though. I can't remember the last time so much advertising space was assigned to one hot-list member.'

'The hot-list being the people eligible to be "removed"?' Elarn tried to keep the disapproval out of her voice.

'Precisely.' Medame Binu smiled, apparently delighted that this primitive offworlder had made the effort to acquaint herself with sophisticated City customs.

They were clear of the trees now, travelling through gentle urban parkland, complete with picnic tables and families playing ball games. The bucolic effect was slightly offset by the mass of buildings beyond the greenery and, beyond that, the orange of the forcedome. Off to the left, something looking like a squat white cylinder on its end was visible over the treetops. That must be the amphitheatre, Elarn thought, distracted for a moment by the view. Seen from above it had looked like a small upturned cup, but down here its scale became apparent.

She turned her thoughts back to her politician saviour. 'And did you vote for him, Medame Binu?' she asked, almost to herself.

Medame Binu apparently had good hearing but very little idea when she was being mocked. 'Shamal, please, no need for formalities with me. And as for Consul Vidoran, well no, I didn't use my vote this month – as I said, I don't take that much interest in politics unless it affects the entertainments industry. Besides, who'd want to see a handsome creature like that get blown away?'

'And will he? Get *blown away*, I mean.' Elarn found herself distressed by the idea that the most likeable person she had met since leaving home could be about to die.

'Oh, you haven't heard!' Shamal Binu leaned closer, her hand brushing Elarn's knee, then withdrawing slightly as Elarn flinched. 'They tried – this morning – but the Angel missed. *Missed!* It caused quite an upset.'

'So should he be out and about like that?' Elarn asked, startled. 'I mean, won't they try again?'

'Oh no.' Medame Binu patted Elarn's knee. 'It's pretty rare for an Angel to miss her mark, so when it does happen – like this morning – we believe it was fated: the will of the City, we say. He'll have been let off his duties in the Assembly for the rest of the day, and his career'll be wrecked, but unless he makes any more foolish decisions, his life's safe enough. And tomorrow he'll be yesterday's news.' Then, as if bored with the subject, Medame Binu gave a small flicking gesture, taking in all they surveyed, and asked, 'Anyway, what do you think of the glories of Khesh City?'

'It's quite a change from home,' said Elarn, diplomatically.

'I'm sure, I'm sure. You'll just love Lily Street: it's very genteel, the quietest Street in the Guest Quarter. And the Manor Park is one of the nicest hotels – not the most ostentatious, but good quality. I thought you'd like that better than one of the bigger establishments.'

One of the more *expensive* establishments, you mean, thought Elarn. But the wretched woman was right: she would prefer quiet and civilised, if there was anything like that available here.

They turned onto a wide boulevard that edged the Gardens as Medame Binu wittered on breathlessly, 'I've arranged a room with a view over the Street, and I've had them install sonic damping. I did try to book rehearsal space, but this has all been such a rush, what with only getting the call from your manager a couple of weeks ago. Basic costs are all covered, but extras you'll need to settle yourself. Have you had a chance to look at the itinerary I sent you?'

'Yes,' Elarn said, 'I noticed several dates were provisional.'

'I'm still in negotiation with the venues – but we're definitely on for tomorrow night: a lovely little salon above a very exclusive boutique in Silk Street. Not that large, but *very* select. Anyway, you'll have a full day to rest and get your bearings before that. Some people take several days just getting used to the City's layout.' She giggled in a way that suggested that even though she lived here, she herself sometimes got lost.

'I'll just have to do my best to adjust,' Elarn said drily. 'Would I be right in assuming that as we turned right onto this street, and we were facing outwards – rimwards, rather – that we are now travelling sunwise?'

'You have done your homework.' She sounded impressed.

Elarn, ignoring the agent's patronising tone, continued, 'And would I be right that of the four Quarters, I need only worry about the Guest Quarter, where I am staying, and the Merchant Quarter, where I'll be performing?'

'Right again – unless you want to visit the Leisure Quarter, of course. I wouldn't advise it, really, I wouldn't have thought it your kind of place. If you must, let me know, and I'll recommend a reputable agency to provide a guard. You might want to see a bit of the State Quarter too – I am still hoping we'll be able to get you in for a performance at the Salvatine Cathedral on Grace Street in the State Quarter. That would be something, wouldn't it? That place has a good capacity, and lots of prestige. Which reminds me: I've left the day after your first concert free, as that's the one that corresponds to your holy day.'

'I'm not a Salvatine.'

'What?' Shamal Binu stopped in mid-flow as the pedicab swung left under a huge floral arch.

'Were you not aware of that?' Elarn tried not to sound smug at finally having fazed her agent.

'No, but— You *are* from Khathryn, aren't you? And Khathryn is a Salvatine theocracy run on religious law—'

'It is,' Elarn agreed, 'and I'm a registered agnostic.'

'But you sing religious music—'

'I sing it, yes. That doesn't mean I believe it.'

'Oh well, we don't need to mention that, do we?'

Not if it decreases my curiosity value, thought Elarn. The agent's reaction confirmed her suspicions that her appeal lay not so much in her vocal talents as in her novelty: *Come and see the religious recluse making a once-in-a-lifetime trip out into the big scary universe.*

The agent continued, 'But you don't have any implants? No tone monitor? You'll understand that I need to be clear on this, given the sort of audience we're hoping to attract.'

'No implants. Even agnostics are subject to Khathryn's laws forbidding personal enhancements; being agnostic merely means I am not expected to take part in religious activities.' She resisted the temptation to add: *but yes, I do live all alone in a big sprawling mansion at the top of storm-lashed cliffs.* She could hardly blame Shamal Binu for trying to make the most of this opportunity to tout an exotically straitlaced performer, but neither did she intend spending more time than was absolutely *professionally* necessary in the woman's company.

The agent's com chirped and, with an apologetic smile at her client, she raised her wrist to take the call. Elarn took the chance to study the early evening crowd in Lily Street, which was positively sedate compared with the crush in the transit hall. She was amazed at the variation in body-shape and personal style, though there were no downsiders here, thank God. Many people wore arm-bands, or coloured tokens pinned to their clothes, presumably denoting their loyalty to the world or City within the Confederacy they came from – or maybe had just decided to support.

In contrast to the people, the buildings had an underlying uniformity:

their heights varied by no more than a couple of storeys and most of the frontages were aligned. Though each was decorated differently, with a profusion of balconies, statues and porches, Elarn was acutely aware that this place was a construct, a habitat that had been made, not a natural settlement that had evolved over time. The thought brought back the barely constrained unease that had afflicted her for the last two weeks. This was as much an artificial prison as the ship had been ... and a far more dangerous one.

Medame Binu finished her call and turned to Elarn. 'I was hoping I might meet you for lunch tomorrow, but I've had to reschedule a meeting,' she said. 'Things are just *insane* at the moment, what with the Grand Assembly bringing in all the extra tourists. Perhaps you should com Consul Vidoran, see if he's free.' She laughed girlishly. 'Only joking! But a girl can dream, eh?'

'Actually, I was thinking I might look up an old friend.' For the second time Elarn had the satisfaction of seeing her agent taken aback.

'I had no idea you knew anyone in Khesh City.'

'We met on Khathryn, a while ago.'

'Really? Was this perhaps a ... *special* friend?' Medame Binu sounded almost breathless with anticipation.

Elarn was tempted to tell the woman to just *grow up*, but of course her agent had no real interest in Elarn other than as a source of income. And she was the only contact Elarn had here, unless she did manage to meet up with Salik Vidoran again, so she might as well use her. 'A special friend? Yes – but we didn't part on the best of terms.'

'Ah,' said Medame Binu. 'I see.'

Elarn was quite sure she did; no doubt having a long-lost ex-lover in the City increased her romantic appeal. But more publicity meant more chance of alerting her quarry. She'd had to put up with a certain amount of fuss, as a professional engagement was the only way she could afford to travel to Vellern – and as out of character as this mini-tour was, it was also the excuse she needed to come here.

Shamal Binu continued, 'You know, the City has an excellent directory service.'

'So I've heard – but I suspect my ... *friend* ... may have taken the chance to buy a new identity. I believe such things are available here?'

The agent nodded sagely. 'Well, yes, people do take advantage of the lack of restrictions in all sorts of ways. In that case you need an infobroker. My hairdresser used one to track down the directors of a cosmetics supply company on one of the Yazil moonlets after the company went bust. They were trying to avoid paying their creditors. From what she said, he did a pretty thorough job. Now what was the man's name? Marain— Meraint? That was it. I believe his office is in Talisman Street.'

'And is he discreet?'

'Oh yes, decent infobrokers always take the confidentiality of their clients into account. It's part of what you pay for.'

Elarn sighed. 'I would rather no one else knew about this.'

'Of course not.' The agent couldn't quite keep the disappointment from her voice. Another selling point missed. 'Ah, here we are: the Manor Park Hotel. I think this will be just right for you.'

The pedicab drew up in front of a pale green building decorated with attenuated black columns. It was lower and narrower than the hotels on either side.

Madame Binu flapped around Elarn as she climbed down. 'You've got my com number? Don't hesitate to call if you need anything – anything at all. And don't work too hard. Take the time to explore a bit. I'll pick you up at six tomorrow. Bye for now, my dear.'

CHAPTER SEVEN

'Where'd ya say ya got it?' Limnel nodded at the lag's departing back. The gang-boss lounged on a battered but comfy-looking couch that must've been a bitch to winch down into the Undertow – as must the etched metal cabinet next to it.

Taro eyed the cushions scattered round the edge of the room. After the long walk through the Leisure Quarter, the climb back down and the wait while the guard on the homespace's main entrance went back inside to find his boss, those cushions looked well prime. But Limnel hadn't invited him to sit.

Taro kept his tone respectful. 'The Minister gave it to me.'

Limnel leaned back in his seat. 'The Minister gave yer a valid cred-bracelet? What fer? Some sorta pay-off fer losin' yer ma?'

After years of having to give Taro respect because of his lineage, Limnel was making the most of having the upper hand ... and Taro was just going to have to live with it. 'I just started workin' fer him,' he said.

Limnel brushed an imaginary fleck of dust off his sleeve. Despite having a face that reminded Taro of a rat with a broken nose, Limnel fancied himself quite the dandy, and he wore topside suits, made specially to fit his lanky downsider build. 'So,' he said slowly, 'yer've just started workin' fer the Minister, but ya wanna buy yerself into me troupe. Am I missin' somethin' here?'

'It's like this, Limnel. I don't have a home, an' I'm gonna need to work to get one. I'll work fer you, in return fer a place to stay—'

'Don't put yerself out, boy,' muttered Limnel.

Too arrogant. He needed to butter the gang-boss up. 'I'll pull me weight, do me part, an' work hard. I don't expect no favours 'cause of what I once was. The deal with the Minister is only casual. I just gotta report to him regularly.'

'Report? On what?' Limnel's interest in the Concord didn't extend much beyond the occasional betting scam, but Taro couldn't afford to piss him off by holding anything back. The Minister hadn't said not to tell anyone about his mission.

'Anything I find out about the Angel Nual.'

Limnel waved vaguely. 'Never 'eard of 'er.'

The lag who'd taken the cred-bracelet away slipped back through the bead curtain and handed the bracelet to Limnel. 'Only got a coupla creds on it, but the ID's valid till midday tomorrow.'

Limnel slipped the thin strip of grey plastic into the inside pocket of his jacket. 'Reckon I could find a use fer this. Awright Taro, yer in, fer now at least. Ya do what yer told, when yer told, and any shit ya hafta do fer the Minister ya do in yer own time. Clear?'

'Aye.'

'That's aye, boss.'

Taro tried not to grind his teeth, 'Aye, boss.'

Limnel glanced at the com he wore on his wrist above his own cred-bracelet. More of his style-over-substance, Taro thought, as the City's bulk blocked com signals from above, but the gang boss was just checking the time. 'Yer've missed the first shift; the sluts 'ave already gone topside, but I'm sure we'll find ya somethin' to do.' He turned to the lag still hovering by his elbow. 'Show our boy 'ere where to stash 'is stuff, then send 'im along to the 'trap room to give Osin a hand.'

The lag, who didn't bother to introduce himself, led Taro back through the troupe's meeting hall and down a side-passage, down another passage, and round a corner. He nodded at a faded brocade curtain at the end of the passage. 'Whores sleep in there,' he said. He turned to the row of cubby-holes set into the wall. 'You can leave yer pack here – there's a gap top right.' When Taro hesitated, pack half off his shoulder, the lag continued, 'It'll be safe. Ya jack another troupe member, yer take the fall.'

Taro heard the murmur of conversation and smelled burning tallow from the other side of the curtain, but the lag led him back the way they'd come, then down another side-passage to a long room with half a floor. The open section of the room wasn't netted so the three water-traps hanging from pulleys set into the ceiling could be lowered and raised through the gap. Two of the 'traps were down, their ropes twisting and creaking. The third one was on the floor beside the gap. The man sitting cross-legged next to it looked up as Taro entered.

'New recruit,' said Taro's escort. 'Boss's sent 'im to 'elp ya fer a while.'

The man, who must have been forty years old, more than twice Taro's age, continued to stare at Taro long after the lag had left. Finally he said, 'Yer Taro, ain't you?'

'That's right. You must be Osin.'

Osin gave him a slow, shy grin. 'That's right. An' the boss wants you to help me?' He sounded unsure.

Taro smiled back. 'Aye. I'm joinin' the troupe.'

'Oh.' Osin looked round, as though wondering if he should have tidied the place up in case of visitors. 'You ever cleaned a water-trap?'

'No, but I'll learn.'

'Bolted. Have a drink first if y'like.' He'd seen the way Taro was looking at the jars and waterskins along the wall.

Taro thanked him before dipping a cup into an open jar: it tasted top prime.

Scraping off the green grunge that accumulated in the corners of the metal trays was nasty work, but Taro did his best and didn't complain. After they'd got the tray clean, Osin had Taro re-plait the troupe colours into the rope where he'd been repairing it. Taro was just easing a scrap of dark-green rag through the strands when Osin said, 'Sorry to hear about yer line-mother.'

Taro looked up at Osin's friendly smile. Here was someone who got no joy from seeing an Angel's line-child brought low. 'I— Thanks,' he murmured, then, thinking he might be willing to pass on gossip, 'Osin, whadda people say happened?'

'Happened?'

'To Malia.'

Osin looked uncomfortable. 'They say it musta been another Angel. Only I hadn't heard feud had been called on her. Didn't look like the type to go rogue, from what I'd heard.'

'But that's what people think? She was killed on the Minister's orders?'

'Most people, aye.'

'And who don't think that?'

'You know Federin? Lives with Fenya, the water-trader just hubwards of here.'

'The remembrancer?' Taro recalled sitting on the floor of Malia's homespace while the old man – he'd been old even then – recited Malia's lineage, mother to daughter, back more generations than Taro could count on both hands. That had been Malia's formal adoption of him, soon after his birth-mother died. 'Aye, I know 'im. Did 'e see somethin'?'

'Well, y'know how he is, a bit gappy these days.'

'So they say – but what does 'e *think* happened?'

'Says he saw a roller in the Undertow, about the time Malia died. Crazy, I know. 'Course, you'd know the truth.'

'Aye, I would.' Taro suddenly didn't want to continue this conversation as his head filled with the sight of Malia's headless body, the Screamer laughing behind her. 'Osin, d'you know anythin' about the Angel Nual?

Osin looked confused, 'Was she the one who ...' He saw Taro's expression and stopped, shrugged, and said, 'Wish I could help, but she ain't local, is she? Don't know much about any Angels other than them as watch over us 'ere. Sorry.'

Osin was happy to talk now the worst of the work was done, so Taro asked him about the gang set-up: seven extended families, plus several odd members with no blood ties, making more than sixty members. Taro needed to know who did what, who to avoid and who to be nice to, and Osin was glad to pass on the info. The boy in charge of the whores was called Keron; he was best friends with Resh, and liked to let Resh have 'freebies' with the new or juicy ones. 'You'll be safe though,' he told Taro. 'Resh prefers girls.'

Finally Osin looked at the dark landscape below. 'Dinner soon,' he said, and stood. 'We'll put this'un down and check the others after we've ate.'

Dinner was served in the gang's common-room, which was bigger than most troupes' entire homespaces with no floor-gaps. The vanes inside the space had been cut off just below ceiling-height and the cut pieces laid flat to give a fully enclosed – if uneven – floor, supported by ropes attached to the stubs the vanes had been cut from. Light came from clusters of lamps hanging from the ceiling. Limnel and his seconds sat at a trestle table at one end; everyone else sat on the floor, grouped on *this* cut vane, or inside *that* framework of ropes, territories Taro needed to learn and respect.

He'd arrived late, after a detour to fetch his bowl and spoon from his pack. He spotted Osin with a group of older men on a sunken vane; the 'trap mender waved for Taro to join him. But he was attracting attention from all over the room, especially from a group of a dozen or so brightly dressed youths in the far corner: his new troupe-mates. The girls had cut their shirts so they fell off the shoulder, and both sexes had dark eyeliner around their eyes, and red-stained lips. They weren't hostile so much as curious, but they weren't inviting him to join them either. He nodded to Osin, waved at the tarts and chose a space by himself against the wall.

Cooks entered, carrying a couple of steaming cauldrons slung on yokes. A murmur of appreciation went up as someone spotted meat in the stew. Taro, remembering this morning's hunt, was less wild about it – right up to the point the smell hit his stomach.

The troupe ate quietly, conversations muted. When the bowls were empty and the slops washed out in cauldrons of steaming water brought by the cooks, silence fell.

Limnel stood up. 'Three announcements this evenin'. Firstly, Shera's 'ad a boy. It was an 'ard birth and she's still at the healers. Yers can go visit her, but go in yer free time, an' take a sunwise diversion so's yers don't go through Rinya's territory. No point flauntin' our colours and causin' trouble with 'er gang until I says. Second, fer those of you who know Daim an' Arel, Daim took the fall. We ain't got no one else to partner Arel, so she's joinin' the sluts. And we got another new whore' – he nodded at Taro – 'who some of yers might know. Taro's on probation, earnin' his new colours.'

49

That got Taro more curious, not-quite-hostile looks. When Limnel sat down again, people started to get up. Taro stood and moved towards Osin, but a lag with narrow-set eyes and enough topsider blood in him to make him shorter than anyone else Taro had seen there so far came down from the table to intercept him. 'I'm Keron,' said the boy. 'Yer one of me sluts now.'

Taro nodded and made to follow the giggling mass of pretty boys and girls as they headed out the main door, but Keron grabbed his arm. 'Oh no, yer ofta see a special client.'

He led Taro out the back of the hall towards the room where Limnel held court, talking all the time. 'She likes to try all the new boys. After her, anythin' ya pick up topside'll be top prime.' He gave a nasal laugh. 'Tell yer what, why don't I give yer a little 'elp? How about it, eh? Somethin' to make sure things is well bolted?'

He grabbed Taro's arm again and pulled him into Limnel's room, which was currently empty. He picked his way through the cushions to Limnel's couch, lifted out a carved wooden box from the cabinet and placed it on top, then started fiddling with the tumbler lock on the front of the box.

Taro stayed by the door. 'You sure Limnel ain't gonna mind?' he asked a little nervously. 'I mean, ain't this his private stuff?' This was just the type of smoky business he wanted to avoid: the new boy getting the blame for whatever shit anyone wanted to lay on him.

Keron shook his head. 'No, no, the boss is prime with this.' The box clicked open and Keron gestured for Taro to come over. 'This gear's new, but he's got shitloads of it – this box is fer general use, all 'is top people know the combination. Fortunate fer us 'e's so generous. Here.' Keron held out a snorting spoon loaded with golden powder.

Taro hesitated. He'd drunk booze and shared smokes and powders with clients before now, but the look in Keron's eyes suggested that this was more than a mild mood enhancer. Serious drugs were either a final resort for the lost, or a luxury for those who could handle the risks, like Angels. Malia had gone on binges more than once, using burnt mash or topside designer chemicals, and Taro understood why; earning your glory killing strangers had its price. He didn't have any reason to go chasing oblivion like that. But he wasn't being given a choice. Keron was his new boss.

'C'mon, Taro. Ya'll thank me fer this later.'

Taro wasn't so sure, but he obviously had no choice. He guided the spoon under one nostril, pressed the other one shut and sniffed.

It hit fast, hard and beautiful, singing through his head and setting the tips of his fingers tingling. Taro drew a long slow breath, feeling the universe settle into place.

Keron was saying something, but Taro only managed to catch up partway through. '—pure blade, eh?'

He smiled at Keron, his friend Keron, though smiling made his face feel funny. Keron smiled back, eyes bright. For what may have been a minute or an hour, they stood together, swaying gently, Keron still holding the spoon. Then Keron exhaled hard, put the spoon back in the box, and said, 'Let's get ya to the bitch 'fore the rush fades.'

Taro followed Keron, trying not to trip over anything, past a couple of curtained doorways, then round a corner; the next opening had a solid door instead of a curtain. A stocky woman with a face like she was sucking on a bone was bending down locking the door. 'Hey, watch it!' she barked when they nearly ran into her. Taro had an idea he'd seen her earlier, sitting at a table somewhere. He smiled at her. She should chill out, join the party.

She smiled back, but Keron shook his head at her. 'He ain't fer yer.'

The woman grabbed Taro's crotch. 'I dunno, Keron, I'd say there's plenty fer everyone here.' Taro wriggled obligingly. Sex: now that *was* a top prime idea. If he felt this good now, imagine how good he'd feel when—

Keron pulled him away, though not before his breeches had got a lot tighter.

'Can't I just—?'

'No. Not yet.'

Keron led him past the door to the next opening, which was covered by a red mesh curtain. He pulled the curtain aside. 'In ya go, Taro,' he said. 'Jus' do whatever the lady wants.'

The room was small, no floor-gap, and empty save for a grubby mattress. A woman lay in the middle of the mattress, half under a thin blanket. She was arse-ugly, and one arm and one leg were withered, twisted as a meatbaby's. Sweet incense burned on a shelf next to the lamp, though underneath it Taro smelled something like rotten meat. She glanced at his face before her gaze dropped to his groin. Her face fell into a sucked-in grin. Taro grinned back, even though she wasn't looking at his face any more. She held out her arms and he fell onto the mattress next to her and started to struggle out of his breeches; he preferred the first one they'd met, but right now he wasn't feeling all that fussy.

She batted him away and muttered, 'With yer mouth first, boy. Take yer time.'

He wriggled down the bed and obeyed. She tasted dry and sour and his cock protested at being ignored, but this was what she wanted and he was going to give it to her. He was good at this, he knew he was. Sex was his salvation. There'd been other stuff, some time in the past, bad, painful stuff, but in the end the path of the grind was the way and the truth. Give pleasure, obey and be happy.

After a while she had him move up and mount her, warning him to be careful of her dodgy leg. There were some scary sights on the way, but then he was in her and she was laughing and pushing back against him and he had the rhythm she wanted almost at once and he moved the way he knew she'd love and she did, she did, she did. She gave a short yelp, squeezing him between her thighs and he thought he'd come too, only he didn't, he stayed right up there near the peak.

'Aye there, boy, that's prime, top prime,' she breathed into his ear. 'Now, again.' He obliged, but this time he couldn't hold it in any longer and he came like the City was falling round his ears.

It was the best ever. Nothing else mattered. This was what life was for.

After he was spent she had him withdraw and work her again with his fingers and mouth. He was getting a little tired now, but finally she pushed him away and sat up, saying, 'Enough, boy.'

She wiped herself off with a rag and started getting dressed. Taro lounged on the mattress, at peace with the world. He was a little worried that he might have to move at some point, as his legs appeared to have stopped working, but really, if he died right now that wouldn't be so bad.

At the curtain the woman turned and said, 'That was good, boy. I'll ask fer you again. What's yer name?'

'Taro,' he said dreamily.

After she'd gone he curled up on his side. He was just slipping away to an even happier place when he felt someone shake his shoulder.

'Can't sleep 'ere, Taro.'

Keron helped him up. He still felt good, but somewhere at the back of his head the beginnings of a killer headache had begun to sidle in. Limnel passed them as Keron led him back to the whores' sleeping room.

'How'd he do?' the gang-boss asked.

'Quality, boss. She loved him.'

'Prime.'

Limnel turned to Taro. He raised a hand and took one of Taro's braids. Taro let him. Why not? Limnel wasn't such a smoky boss to work for.

He teased out a strand of red cord from the braid, twisting it between his fingers. 'Ya know what, Taro? I think we're gonna get along just fine.'

CHAPTER EIGHT

It had been a busy morning and Ando Meraint was looking forward to getting out of the office for lunch, but when the door chime went he decided to check the cameras anyway. If he was going to make enough money to keep up with his darling wife's gambling habit and still send his daughters to a decent school on one of the better Kheshi habitats, he needed to stay open to every opportunity.

His cameras showed a mature, striking-looking woman at the foot of the stairs. She wasn't wearing City colours and she was dressed with a level of taste rare outside the State Quarter. Meraint pressed the buzzer to let her in.

The woman was paler and taller than most Kheshi. Her clothes were expensive and she wore her light-brown hair plaited and piled elaborately round her head. His scanners hadn't picked up any weapons on her, not even a knife. She wore an expression of calm determination.

Ando Meraint found it paid to work out what people wanted and give it to them, and he extended this to treating people the way he thought they wanted to be treated. So he met her at the door, showed her in and offered her refreshments.

She accepted the courtesy of being shown to her seat graciously, but refused the drink. 'I'd like to get straight down to business, Sirrah Meraint, if that's all right with you.' Her accent confirmed she wasn't local.

He settled down behind his desk. 'Of course, medame. How may I help you?'

'I understand that you find, filter and collate information.'

'That's one way of describing infobroking, yes.' A very succinct way, in fact. He called up the basic price-list. 'You'll see the services and associated charges displayed on the flatscreen set into the desk in front of you.'

She scanned the screen, pressed her lips together, then said, 'I hope you won't think me rude, but I have to ask: in a City without rules, where information is freely available, what precisely would I be paying for?

'A reasonable question. Firstly, it is a common misconception that the Three Cities have no rules. For example, the statutes of the Concord are both explicitly stated and rigidly enforced.'

'I know, I've read them. I found them surprisingly dry reading, considering the process they regulate.'

Her tone conveyed a mixture of distaste and unease. Meraint concluded that she was either doing a good job of affecting disapproval, or else she was one of those rare visitors who was not attracted by the idea of a democracy by assassination – which was one thing he had in common with her. 'I must agree, medame. However, I was about to add that whilst the Concord has little direct effect on most people's lives, other regulations do exist. Visitors can sometimes find themselves subject to fines or private lawsuits without even realising they have transgressed.'

'I can imagine. But you haven't answered my original question. If the information is there for the taking, just what is your role?'

'My service pulls together all publicly available data. I also have access to various private systems. Searches on some of these are included in the price, though certain specialist ones may cost a little more.'

'What about surveillance?' she asked. 'I have seen no evidence of it, yet I assume we are all being watched and recorded. Would you be able to access surveillance data?'

Meraint was revising his opinion of her as the conversation progressed. Beneath her calm exterior, this woman was cautious, thorough and more than a little nervous.

'There is some centrally regulated surveillance, but most recording devices are installed by the owners of the premises they are intended to protect. Accessing private surveillance footage would be an example of an extra expense.'

'I see. And can I be assured of your confidentiality?'

'Entirely. The fact that some of my customers would be operating outside the law on other worlds makes the system self-regulating with regards to the sanctity of data. For certain clients, a breach of trust could have consequences far more unpleasant than merely being taken to court.'

She looked a little alarmed at that and Meraint cursed himself for frightening her when he was actually trying to impress her.

She thought for a few moments, then nodded. 'All right. I think I understand what I'll be paying for.' She traced down the list with a manicured forefinger. 'So would a "full search" give me all the information known on a person, including that not publicly available?'

'That is correct. Everything on record about them, sorted and arranged according to the criteria chosen by the client: personal, financial, business, whatever you choose.'

'The person I need to find is not listed on the public com system.'

'Ah. You are sure they are in the City?'

'I believe so. But they may have bought a new ID.'

'That does happen. However, if the information is available, a full search will root it out – hence the higher price.'

She looked mildly taken aback at his reference to money. 'I will spend whatever is necessary, Sirrah Meraint,' she said firmly.

That was what he liked to hear. 'Of course – and you will find my charges very competitive. As is standard in our business, fifty per cent is payable up front, the remainder on successful completion. Now, if you would just like to place your cred-bracelet over the reader?'

The bracelet held only a moderate balance, but that just showed she wasn't stupid enough to carry excess credit. As she withdrew her wrist her glance fell on the holo-pic on the stand beside his screen: his twin daughters, Shiana and Jialle, walking through the Zoo last year. Shiana, always the practical one, had a finger lifted to point to something out of shot, while Jialle's mouth was open in a silent *oohh!* of delight. The picture held her gaze and she stopped, her hand still half-extended.

Meraint cleared his throat. 'Thank you, Medame Reen.'

Her mask of calm dropped and Meraint glimpsed a flash of panic in her eyes. Then she sat back, her expression returning to one of polite interest. 'Of course. Your credit reader displayed my name. I'm still getting used to these things.'

'That is correct.' She must come from a pretty unsophisticated world. Though he avoided dwelling on the motives of his clients, he suspected this one was not after information for personal gain, which made a pleasant change. 'The City does take a little getting used to,' he admitted.

She allowed herself a smile. 'You could say that.' She paused for moment, then continued, 'I— This is going to sound a bit odd, but I did wonder, when you addressed me by name, whether you had recognised me.'

'No, I can't say I did. Should I have?' Yes, that was an odd question.

'Actually I'm here to perform, but my area is very much a niche interest, so I would have been quite surprised if you *had* heard of me.'

That explained it. He was going to have to disappoint her. 'No, I'm afraid I was just taking your ID details from my reader, nothing more.'

Far from looking disappointed, she looked positively relieved. 'I suppose you'll need some more details from me. For the search.'

He smiled. 'Firstly, a name.'

'Lia Reen. Her name is Lia Reen.'

His client flushed slightly as she said the name. Same surname, too. It looked like this *was* a personal matter – a long-lost child, perhaps, which might explain her reaction to the picture of his children. 'Is that L-I-A?'

She nodded. 'And Reen like me.'

'I'll need some basic search parameters to get us started. Is she a visitor, or a City resident?'

'A visitor – she came to the City six or seven years ago. I'm not even sure if she's still here.' She looked down at her hands; her earlier bravado appeared to be deserting her.

Meraint kept his tone light, trying to put her at ease. 'That'll give us somewhere to start, at least. Is there anything else you could give me? Age, nationality, stuff like that.'

'I have a picture. Here.' From her bag she produced a flatscreen head-and-shoulders of a young woman, standing outside, presumably somewhere on Medame Reen's homeworld. She wore a green cape, and strands of dark hair poked out from under a broad-brimmed hat. Both hat and cape were covered in tiny beads of moisture – rain, presumably. An open sky full of purple-grey clouds was visible over her shoulder. The girl had pale skin and delicate features, with sharp cheekbones, a slightly pointed chin and a small, sensual mouth. Her eyes were dark and mesmerising. Meraint thought it a memorable, beautiful face, but somehow disconcerting, as though she were far older than her appearance suggested. She looked nothing like the woman sitting in front of him.

He cleared his throat. 'Do you mind if I scan this in?'

'No, of course not, if it will help find her.'

He placed the picture under his image reader. It beeped and he handed the picture back. 'Facial matches can be difficult, but I'll put requests into the public image libraries if we don't get anywhere immediately. She looks to be in her late teens in this picture.'

'That's right.' She made no move to narrow down his guess; talking about the girl was making his client uncomfortable.

'So she would be in her mid-twenties now. And her nationality?'

'She would almost certainly have had a Khathryn passport.'

'Khathryn? Right. Let's see what we can find.' He started a couple of basic searches using his desk keypad; he always preferred the confidentiality of using a keypad over the ease of voice commands. After all, if his clients knew where to look and how to perform the searches, he'd soon put himself out of a job.

Medame Reen sat quietly while the initial searches returned several 'not found' results. Unlike some clients, she did not believe he would get results more quickly with someone leaning over him asking if he had anything yet. After a couple of minutes the possible matches started coming in.

'Aha, here we are. Or perhaps not. There was a Lia Reen here during the time window you've given me but she was in her eighties and was visiting from Luorna City. And another ... no again; this was a forty-year-old woman, recently sex-altered, homeworld listed as Pasture, one of the Yazil orbitals.'

A red warning light flashed in the corner of the screen.

Elarn Reen, looking at him again, must have seen his expression change. 'What is it?'

58

'Probably nothing. Just a glitch. Corrupt data perhaps.' He hoped.

'Please, Sirrah Meraint, what exactly is the problem?' She clasped the arms of the chair and leaned across the desk, trying to see the screen, not that the information would mean much to her; he always used on-screen encryption to discourage client curiosity.

He tried to keep his tone light. 'Looks like I've just activated an archival flag. Nothing to worry about.'

'Meaning that the data is there but has been archived, presumably?'

'Yes. Probably.' Or that there was a trace on it and his software was trying to deflect the trace into archived records. But the client didn't need to know that.

'You don't sound sure, Sirrah Meraint.'

'This kind of data generally stays live for at least a decade before archival. It must have been transferred accidentally.'

'Is that common?'

He considered lying, but he preferred to stick to the truth where possible. It made things simpler. 'Not really.'

'But presumably even if it has been archived you can get it back?'

He'd been distracted by trying to reassure her but now he turned back to the screen. The warning light blinked out, replaced by a message that indicated there were no further matches for the search criteria. It looked like it had been a trace; fortunately his software had been up to re-routing it. 'Not in this case, I'm afraid.'

'Oh. Is it possible the records were deleted?'

'In theory, yes, but unlikely. The City systems run regular archival sweeps, but as far as I know, nothing is ever physically deleted. We record ID details and credit balances for every visitor, and that's not the kind of data we just discard. I'm sorry. Given that I haven't found anything, there won't be any further charge for the service.' He just hoped there wouldn't be any unforeseen consequences. The fact that his software had come up with a 'not found' message implied the information had either never existed or it had been deleted. So why the trace?

She held out her wrist. 'No, take the full fee. Consider it payment for your time.'

She probably thought she was buying his loyalty. Perhaps she was. If she really was looking for a lost child, then he would do his best for her.

And the extra credit wouldn't go amiss. 'Of course, if you insist. Shall I run the image-scan anyway?'

'I … yes, you'd better. I need to be certain.' She sounded almost relieved that he'd failed.

'It might take a while. I'll let you know if I come up with anything. My com number is on the transaction receipt on your bracelet; do contact me if there's anything else I can do for you. It has been a pleasure doing business with you, Medame Reen. Please allow me to show you out.'

She stood abruptly, but forced a smile as she left.

Meraint decided that, late or not, it was time for lunch.

When he got back to the office an hour later he had no reason to suspect anything was wrong. The outside door was closed and no alarms had been tripped. It was only as he sat down behind his desk that he noticed that the twins' picture was missing.

The hairs on the back of his neck started to rise and he froze, listening. Someone was in the kitchen alcove, behind the curtain on the far wall. He could buzz for building security, but they charged a small fortune just to stick their heads round the door, and the only other time he'd had to call them – to deal with a drug-addled dissatisfied customer – they'd taken a frighteningly long time to arrive. His best defence was right in front of him. Meraint pulled his chair forward, resting one arm by his keypad and slipping the other hand under the desk to stroke the trigger for the set of three dart-guns concealed there. Even if only one hit, the drug in the hollow needle should sedate the intruder within a couple of seconds. Two, and most people would be unconscious. Three would take down *anyone* – assuming there was only one person of course. And assuming he could convince the intruder to come into range.

The curtain of the alcove was drawn back and a man he'd never seen before emerged, glass in hand. The intruder looked round in faint curiosity, as though he was checking out the office suite with a view to making an offer to buy. From his blond hair, heavy build and ostentatious suit of gold-trimmed dark green, Meraint concluded that he was from Yazil City. When the intruder finally deigned to look directly at him, his expression was disconcertingly neutral, almost blank. Without

60

a word he raised the glass in a silent toast, drained it, and set it back on the work-surface.

Meraint decided to go for the casual approach and, hopefully, lull him into range. 'Can I help you, sirrah?' he asked pleasantly.

The man regarded Meraint and said, 'You might be able to, yes.' His voice was low and sonorous but husky, as though talking were not something he did often. His blue eyes looked hard. Meraint thought he had seen him somewhere before.

'Would I be right in assuming that you require information?'

The Yaziler walked out of the alcove, but did not approach the desk. 'Information, yes.' He sounded disinterested, as though he did not much care what Meraint did, up to and including shooting him.

'Good. Right. If you'd like to take a seat and tell me what I can do for you, I'll see if I can help.'

The Yaziler favoured him with a *Do you think I'm stupid?* look and started to pace along the far side of the room. There was something in the way he moved that reminded Meraint of the predators in the Zoo. The Yaziler reached the end of his short walk and turned on his heel. 'What did she want, Sirrah Meraint?'

'Who would this "she" be, exactly?' Meraint reckoned that he'd cross the arc of fire for a couple of seconds when he walked back in front of the door, though the range would be extreme. He hoped the sweat on his palms wouldn't dull his accuracy.

'Please don't be difficult,' said the Yaziler. For the first time some emotion came into his voice, as though he was hoping Meraint *would* be difficult, to give him the excuse to be difficult in return.

'I'm trying not to be, believe me. I'm just not sure what you're talking about.' And he had thought Elarn Reen was just looking for a lost child – there was obviously more going on here than that. But he had no intention of selling her out to this Yazil bastard if he could avoid it.

'Medame Elarn Reen. Offworlder. Scared, lonely, probably never been kissed.' He made the word 'kissed' sound obscene and insulting. 'She came here. What did you tell her?'

He'd been so distracted by trying to talk to this madman that he'd missed the shot. He'd have to wait until the Yaziler turned and came back across the room. 'I'm sorry, sirrah, but my service is confidential.'

'Really?' The Yaziler turned and started to retrace his steps. He sounded bored again.

Meraint tensed, ready to press the trigger the moment the man crossed in front of the desk. 'Of course. My clients rely on my confidentiality.'

'Really?' repeated the Yaziler. He reached into his jacket and pulled out the picture of Meraint's children. He looked down at the image and said, 'It must be nice to be relied on.'

Meraint pressed the trigger.

Nothing happened.

The Yaziler stopped pacing and smiled. It wasn't a nice smile. 'Your guns appear to be broken.'

Meraint recognised him now. He'd seen this man walking behind Consul Vidoran in the news footage from Confederacy Square. He was a Screamer. No wonder he was so calm. Meraint felt a pressing need to visit the toilet.

'All right, I'll tell you. She was trying to find someone.'

'Who would that be?' The Yaziler walked over to the desk and perched on one corner.

Meraint barely resisted the urge to push his chair backwards, away from the threat of the Yazil assassin. 'She wanted to know about a woman called Lia Reen.'

The Screamer looked impassive. 'Lia Reen?' he repeated. Meraint couldn't see how Medame Reen's estranged child – if that was who she was – had any relevance to Consul Vidoran. Neither, apparently, could the Consul's bodyguard; it sounded like he had never heard the name before.

'Yes. I think she might be an adopted daughter. I didn't ask.'

The Yaziler pursed his lips. 'And what did you tell her about this Lia Reen?'

'Nothing. The search failed. No matches.' The Screamer didn't need to know about the trace on the file. Whoever had put that on was someone with more clout than a mid-level politician.

The Screamer raised an eyebrow, as though questioning whether such a thing were possible. 'That's a little odd, isn't it?'

'Not really. Medame Reen lost touch with her years ago. She wasn't even sure the girl had come here.' Not entirely what she had said, but he would tell the Yaziler whatever got him out of his office the fastest.

The Screamer looked down at the picture in his hands. Meraint flinched at the thought of the killer's fingers on the image of his children. 'So Medame Reen did not get what she wanted?'

'No. I did my best, but—' Meraint forced a shrug, feeling his shoulders jump up round his ears. 'I can only pass on what information is available.'

'Obviously if you think of anything else, or if Medame Reen comes back, you'll let me know at once.'

Meraint looked at him in panic. The unpleasant thought that he might have to deal with this psycho again had not crossed his mind.

'I said, you'll let me know.'

'I ... yes.'

'Good. I've sent the number of a confidential voicemail service to your com.' He smiled down at the image, kissed his fingers, then touched them to the picture. 'What charming little girls you have.' He put the holo-pic back, face down.

Meraint continued to stare as the Screamer slid off the desk and left. Only when the door clicked shut did he put his head in his hands and let out a low moan.

CHAPTER NINE

Some bastard had held a party in Taro's head without inviting him. He swallowed. His throat tasted like hot leather. He rolled over onto one side, coughed, and managed to open his eyes on the third attempt.

He was lying in the whores' sleeping room. Morning light oozed up through the nets of the floor-gap, illuminating a dozen or so boys and girls asleep, curled up in pairs or trios. Others sat around talking. Soot and damp streaked the walls above the lamp brackets; lower down, some people had drawn on the wall, or tacked pictures to it to mark their space. The place reeked of stale sweat and cheap perfume.

He levered himself upright. Giddy heat flashed through him and his head wanted to roll off his neck, but he wasn't going to give in. No, he was going to get up now, 'cause it was either that or piss where he lay, and that wasn't a good way to make friends with his new troupe-mates.

He staggered up to the brocade curtain, drawing curious glances from the other whores, and made his way to an alcove he remembered passing yesterday. No one had pointed it out, but the smell told him all he needed to know.

The piss-pot was nearly full. He guessed that, as the new boy, he'd be the one taking the poo-pot to the shit-gardeners and the piss-pot to the water-traders. Something to look forward to. Then, as memories of the last day seeped back, it occurred to him that this wasn't such a bad idea. He wasn't sure which water-trader Limnel's troupe usually used, but if he took the pee to Fenya's, maybe he could talk to her partner and

64

find out whether Federin really had seen Scarrion on the day Malia was killed.

He reeled back to the sleeping room and asked of no one in particular, 'You want I should take the pots out? I don't mind.'

A youth about his own age with pert lips and cautious eyes said, 'No, that's Arel's job.' He nodded to a girl curled tight against the far wall. 'If she ever wakes up. Poor bitch keeps us awake with her moanin', then crashes out when it's time to get up. Good job she's on the late shift. Yer on early, with us.'

A waterskin and a bowl of cold mash were being passed round. He gratefully accepted the drink, but his stomach shrank away at the idea of food. The youth who'd spoken wetted a rag and threw it to Taro. 'Wash yer face. You got a change of clothin'?'

Taro wiped the rag round his face and neck, then tottered off to get his pack. He rummaged in it and found his other shirt. It wasn't much cleaner than the one he had on, but at least he hadn't slept in it for the last three nights. The girl in the corner still hadn't moved.

By the time he'd changed his head had stopped pounding in favour of just throbbing, and his body had settled into an overall tired ache. The tarts were putting on their make-up, and a girl far too young to be in the trade approached Taro and offered to help him. Rather than use his mirror and risk envious looks, he let her put lines round his eyes and dabbed the scent she offered behind his ears and on his wrists. He thought she wanted to chat with him as she worked, but he wasn't sure how the others would react. He was just painting her lips when Keron strode in. 'Let's move those sweet arses topside, boys an' girls.' As Taro walked past him he asked, 'Hoi Taro, how're ya doin' this mornin'?'

'Bad as I deserve, given how prime I felt last night.'

'Oh aye, that shit's quality. Bring in plenty of the foldin' stuff today an' I'll see if I can't getcha a little more of the happy dust tonight.'

That made Taro feel a bit better, until he spotted the looks this comment got him: looked like not everyone had such easy access to Limnel's stash. Maybe it was only those Limnel wanted to keep a hold on – which wasn't good news for him.

Taro followed the whores as they filed through the Undertow behind Keron. The more talkative gossiped while they waited at the base of the nets. Taro didn't try to butt in, but he replied to anything said to him. He let the others go topside before him.

The exit Keron used was sunwise of Taro's normal one, only a short walk through the sidestreets to Soft Street. Their pitch was a good one and it looked like most of them had set places to work from. Keron directed Taro to a spot already occupied by the girl who'd done his make-up, next to a shop selling mechanical sex-aids. Then the pimp sauntered away hubwards towards a bar that, according to the holos playing outside, featured low-g mud wrestling every evening.

Once Keron had gone inside, Taro turned to the girl next to him and said, 'I gotta make a com call. Be back soon.'

She looked at him as though he'd suggested going into a restaurant and ordering a steak. After a moment she said, 'Sure, I s'pose. Better be quick – Keron'll be back soon as he's got his drink.'

Taro ignored the other hustlers as he walked back rimwards to the public com booths he'd spotted.

He didn't have much to report, but he should check in, at least. 'I've made some enquiries but I've nothin' to report yet, sirrah,' he told the emotionless voice.

The Minister's response was just as terse. 'Let us hope there will be soon.' The connection was cut as soon as he'd finished speaking.

Taro returned to his space. It wasn't long before the lag who'd spoken to him earlier came over and asked, more curious than hostile, why he'd gone off like that. Taro decided it wouldn't do any harm to let people know the Minister's eye was on him, but when he said he was working for the Minister, the tart laughed and told him, 'Hope yer not gonna start thinkin' that makes you special – you ain't the only one got Angel lineage, you know.'

The girl beside him chimed in, 'Our older sister shacked up with an Angel fer a while. Never got to wear the colours or take her name ourselves; still, word gets around, y'know.'

'But now—' He shrugged to show their fall from grace.

'Aye, I know,' Taro said. 'Same fer me. I'll deal with it.'

The boy nodded, happy he'd made his point, and walked off. His sister said, 'We was lucky though. Her girlfriend dumped her fer somethin' pretty she found at the Exquisite Corpse, rather than ... you know.'

'The Exquisite Corpse? That place real?' Malia had mentioned the name, he thought – and something about an alien who ran a bar in the Undertow? It'd sounded gappy to him: Malia had been wrecked at the time, so he'd assumed she'd been winding him up. Apparently not.

The girl laughed 'Aye, it's real enough. It's under the Merchant Quarter. Never been there, but they say Angels come from all over the Undertow. Only Angel brood get served, though. Anyone else prob'ly gets used fer target practice.'

'No shit,' murmured Taro. An Angel bar in Nual's part of the Undertow – where better to overhear gossip about her? He still had his colours; that'd get him in. He just needed to work out how to get there.

He was just about to ask the girl's name when Keron came out the bar and shouted, 'Hoi, you two! Less talk, more action!'

She gave him an apologetic grin, pulled her top down and focused on the Street.

Taro knew the drill. When he'd turned fourteen, Malia had given him a choice: find a trade, or find another place to live. Being good-looking and easy to get on with didn't put mash in the pot or water in the skin in a normal troupe, and she wouldn't be around for ever.

Gappy idiot that he'd been, he'd thought she was wrong on both counts, and he'd set out to prove it. An older woman, a troupe leader, mother of a boy who'd dumped him, had come on to him just the week before – but of course he'd turned her down; she was old and he had his pick of the local action. He went back to her and offered himself to her; in return, he wanted the necklace he'd seen her boy palm from a topside boutique. It was as easy as that. He'd offered the necklace to Malia, and told her, proudly, how he got it. *So that's your choice.* That's what she'd said; not, *Well done*, or *I knew you had something special.* She'd looked at him oddly – he'd wondered if she'd been upset at his choice of occupation, but then she'd said, *In the end, we're all whores. You give pleasure, I take lives.*

Over the last three years she'd directly pimped for him half a dozen times, and told him to go find himself some trade two dozen more. Many of his own clients had become regulars – but other than the necklace, she'd never taken anything from him.

Though he did it mainly for the cash, he didn't mind the hustle. He liked sex, and he was good at it; doing it as business made everything simpler: there were no misunderstandings, no broken promises, no hurt feelings. All he had to do was put up an invisible shield, and keep the client on the far side of it. And the hustle was just a way of filling in time until the Minister took him on; he'd always known that was what he was destined for. So what if all his other relationships broke up within a month; he'd never cared for anyone enough to want to prolong things once they started to go stale.

Except the last client had broken through the barriers, and had used Taro in ways that went way beyond physical pain. After Scarrion, he never wanted to sell himself again – but now he no longer had the choice. *Forget the Screamer. Make the score.* He bent one leg up, leaning into the wall, casual-like, making eye contact with anyone who looked like a potential trick, dropping his gaze as soon as they noticed him. Playing it shy always worked best. *Don't scare off the punters.*

The girl next to him pulled her first trick, a fat Yaziler, after an hour or so. She was walking off with him when he noticed a Luornai couple, only a bit older than him, watching him from across the Street. They made their way towards him slowly, then stopped a ways off and started murmuring to each other behind their hands. They had a guard in tow. Taro recognised the Luornai habit: they covered their mouths to show they were having a private conversation, while showing off their wealth – and from the looks of those jewelled hands, these two were loaded. He gave an exaggerated stretch, letting them get a good look at what was on offer. Then, finally, he looked in their direction. The girl, seeing him notice them, came over. With a nervous grin she said, 'Do you do both? Boys and girls, I mean.'

Taro smiled back and suggested a starting price; they could discuss options. Her smile broadened.

As it turned out, they weren't buying him just for sex: they wanted a real downsider, theirs for as long as they were willing to pay. They paraded past shops and bars, asking him all about life in the Undertow: *Are Angels the only law down there? Is it true there are a million downsiders below our feet at this moment? Do you downsiders really eat your own shit?* He gave them the answers they wanted to hear: *Aye, an Angel's word is law; no, we only live in the outer edges of the Undertow, where the vanes are thickest, and actually there're fewer people downside than citizens topside; and no, we just eat mash, the fungus that grows on composted shit.* They pulled faces at this last, and he resisted the temptation to ask what they thought topsider food was made from; it might look prettier, but it was still stuff someone else had already eaten. He showed them his flecks, the weapons created from the very substance of the Undertow, worn secreted at both wrists, both in homage to and in imitation of the Angels' blades. They were offworlders; they had no idea that the colours in his hair meant he had Angel lineage, but they lapped up everything he told them.

When the time came to get their money's worth they went down a sidestreet, setting their guard to keep watch at the entrance. The boy snorted a hit of his drug of choice and had Taro blow him while he leaned nonchalantly against the wall, the girl recording the details and giggling and groaning at the prime squalor of it all. When it was her turn she borrowed the guard's cape to kneel on, so she didn't get too much of that prime squalor on her lovely clean knees.

They paid well over the going rate, and he spent some of the scrip on a tepid pasty from a street-side dispenser. It didn't help much; whatever Keron had given him had left him trashed, and the punters had taken the last of his energy. He spent more of his hard-earned cash on a pedi-cab ride back to the rimwards end of Soft Street. The pedicab rider was happy to take his money, but he still spat at his feet when he dismounted – an ever-popular insult: *Topside, we get our water for free; you shit-eaters have to distil your own piss.*

Taro found Keron at his table outside the bar, eating a bowl of spicy fries. He handed over the remaining notes, having stashed a third of his earnings.

'Not bad, Taro. Not bad at all,' Keron said.

'Good enough to get the rest of the day off?' It was still early afternoon but he'd made as much as most of the others would in a day.

Keron's gaze flicked to the pocket in Taro's faded black jacket. 'Almost,' he said.

Taro hesitated, then pulled out more bills. He had less than a quarter of the Luornais' money left, but if he got the rest of the day free, it would be worth it.

Keron nodded slowly, and Taro was off.

Downside again, and free of topside gravity, he felt a little better, just a bit shaky and dull in the head now. He thought about swinging back via the gang's homespace to pick up the piss-pot, in case that girl, Arel, hadn't done her duty – then he realised his main reason for going back was to try and wrangle another fix, so he made himself carry on hubwards.

The narrow mazeway that led up to the water-trader's door was almost as familiar as the entrance to his old homespace. He'd been bringing his piss-pot to Fenya for as long as he could remember. He'd played with her children when he was younger, and, at Malia's nudging, had introduced Fenya's shy youngest daughter to the mysteries of sex a couple of years back.

He rattled the piece of twine strung with bits of scrap metal and plastic that hung next to the door. A few seconds later a voice shouted out, 'Who's there?'

'It's Taro,' he called. It felt odd, giving his name without the lineage title. He wasn't sure he'd ever get used to that.

The rough slab of faded yellow plastic was pulled aside and the combined stink of piss and the heavy incense Fenya used to offset the smell billowed out.

Fenya herself stood in the doorway. Her face was pockmarked by childhood illness and lined by years of hard work, but she smiled, genuinely glad to see him. 'Come in, dearie, come in. How're you doing? I hear you're with Limnel now.'

'Aye – for now, anyway.' Taro stepped into the water-trader's large common-room. The un-netted floor-gap was big enough to support two large water-traps, both down at the moment, and the room had a dozen exits, some barred, some curtained off. Around the sides were piles of trade goods, stuff people brought to barter for water when they didn't have piss to distil. Taro nodded to a scrawny old man wearing a loose-fitting, multi-coloured robe bent over an unlit firebox. 'Actually, Fenya, I wanted to ask Federin something.'

Fenya snorted gently. 'Good luck. He's no use to anyone today. He's meant to be fixing that firebox, but so far he's hardly got further than taking the top-plate off. Federin! We have a visitor.'

The remembrancer looked up, blinked at Taro and went back to his work. He generally said little unless asked to call up facts from his great store of rememberings. Once that started there was no stopping him.

After a nod from Fenya, Taro went over to stand next to the old man. 'Hoi there, Federin.'

Federin put down the broken firebox and sat back. 'Good day to you, Taro,' he said, looking grave. ''Tis a terrible thing, to pass with no deathfeast. Worse still for an Angel, beloved of the City.'

Taro didn't need reminding about that. 'Aye. It is. And that's what I'm here to talk to you about.'

'You want to know what I saw.'

'I heard you met someone who shouldn't've been there, the day Malia died.'

'I saw her killer. No Angel, no downsider, even. A tourist. Yaziler, I'd say. I saw him go into your homespace. Fool that I was, I didn't dare enter, not till I heard the shot. Then I pulled back the curtain. He saw me and changed his mind. He laughed as he pushed past me. He'd killed an Angel, and he laughed.'

'Did you follow him? See where he went? Did you see anyone with him?' Taro's voice was shaking.

'Follow him? No, I was too shocked to see an outsider down here, and in an Angel's homespace, no less – I came into your homespace to find you lying there, no sign of your line-mother, just the blood on the nets. Did I see where he went? Rimwards, I'd say. Was he alone? I'm not sure, I think I heard him call to someone, quietly, asking something. But I may've imagined that.'

'Thanks fer comin' in when you did. You prob'ly saved me life.' And Federin could confirm that the Screamer had been in Malia's homespace, not that that would help Taro find him again. He drew a deep breath. 'There's somethin' else you can help me with, if that's all right.'

'I'll do what I can.'

'I need to get to the Exquisite Corpse. I'm on a mission fer the Minister.'

The remembrancer nodded to himself, as though pleased to hear that the death of Taro's line-mother hadn't stopped him being part of the Concord.

'D'you know how to get there, Federin? Can you show me?'

The remembrancer closed his eyes and dropped his hands onto his lap, palms up, the way he sat when he was calling up something complicated from his memory. He stayed like that for so long Taro wondered if he'd dropped off to sleep. Finally he opened his eyes, leaned forward and picked up a twist of wire he'd been using to poke the innards of the firebox. He used the point to draw a circle on the sooty base of the firebox. 'Aye, I know how to find the Exquisite Corpse. Our City,' he started, by way of explanation. He drew two lines, cutting the circle into quarters, then scratched a small cross in the quarter nearest him. 'Here we are.' He made another mark, on the other side of the circle to the first, on the border between two quarters. 'And there's the Exquisite Corpse, on the border between the State and Merchant Quarters. And as we—' He traced the way, keeping the wire just above the rough map. '—are back below the Leisure Quarter, that's quite a journey.'

Taro opened his hand to span the distance. The Corpse was about a third of the way in from the rim, putting it right on the edge of inhabited territory. The journey there would be about half the diameter of the City, through unknown mazeways. Quite a journey, indeed, even when he was on top form. But this was the only lead he had to Nual. 'Can't be that bad,' he said. 'It ain't much longer than walkin' a single Street and I've—'

'Aye, it is, much longer.' The remembrancer knocked Taro's hand away, pointing the wire back at the starting point, then flicking it to the right to take in the quarter sinwards of their location, the shortest route. 'Can't go that way. No mazeways under the State Quarter: no one living there to cut them. So,' he brought the wire back and traced a route sunwise, 'we cross the rest of the Leisure, into the Guest – fewer people there, so fewer mazeways and water-traps to navigate by – and into the Merchant that way.'

'That's a long way round. How 'bout I head fer the spine, just turn left when I run out of mazeways and keep circlin' with it to me right?'

'No! Do not think to trespass near the Heart of the City!' Federin sounded agitated. The thin spine that impaled the disc of the City to Vellern's surface was the Heart of the City, the place where the souls of the fortunate dead went after their flesh had been consumed.

'All right I'll try to avoid gettin' too close to the Heart of the City,' Taro promised.

'I don't ask you to believe, Taro, though I might've hoped, being an Angel's child, you'd have more faith. But whatever your beliefs, you must know it's not safe to approach the spine. All energy, all life, passes through that place, and to pass too close is to risk unbalancing all. Even to approach it is to risk your own death.'

Taro *had* heard tales of people burned by unseen light, like an Angel's gun, for straying too near the spine – just tales perhaps … But maybe Federin's worldview wasn't so crazy: one of Taro's clients had been an engineer who worked on reconstruction projects on the homeworld; she came to Vellern for her holidays. She had a plain face, a dumpy body and piss-all social skills, and Taro suspected he was the nearest she had to a regular boyfriend, but she seemed to know a lot about how stuff was put together. She was the one who'd told him about the water in the Gardens. She'd also explained how she thought the City worked: the forcedome kept the bad stuff on Vellern's surface out and the air and water in. The spine somehow controlled the forcedome and kept the disc of the City stable. It also had something to do with power and recycling: Taro sort-of understood the concept of a closed system, though he was still a little hazy on what, other than an infinite supply of rich visitors, lay beyond the forcedome. And when she'd started using terms like 'micro-fusion', 'gravitic compensation' and 'bio-electrical field generation', he'd given up. After that she'd admitted all of this was just best guess – no one really knew how the City worked.

So maybe Federin's explanation was as good as hers. He looked back at the remembrancer. 'You tell me the route to take, an' I'll stick to it.'

'Oh no, you're on City business, for the Minister. Can't trust an important mission to a boy barely able to recite his own lineage.' Federin said firmly, 'I'll take you to the Exquisite Corpse.'

CHAPTER TEN

Elarn needed a drink. She had spent the morning rehearsing some of her more difficult pieces; covering wide vocal ranges to convey sacred ecstasy in a dead language required considerable discipline. Such discipline instilled calm.

She had managed to retain some of that calm during her visit to the infobroker, but finding nothing at all on Lia had come as a shock. Much as she would have liked to take the absence of any records to mean that the girl had never been in the City, it was more likely Lia had somehow managed to get the information erased. Those Elarn was forced to serve were certain their renegade had been here; they had even specified which of the Three Cities to check. If Lia had enough influence to get official records altered, then she might well still be here. Until and unless Elarn could prove the girl was no longer on Vellern, she must assume she was, and act accordingly. And for the next part of her plan, Elarn would need more than plainsong to keep herself centred.

During the pedicab ride back from the Merchant Quarter Elarn had seen an Angel striding through the crowds. From behind, the assassin was an imposing figure, tall and slender, her waist-length white hair and dark red cloak billowing out behind her. People in her path made way without hesitation, but she ignored them. As the pedicab passed the Angel, Elarn had glanced back, hesitantly, not wanting to risk eye contact. But the Angel wasn't looking at her. She wasn't looking at anyone; she moved like a purposeful ghost, gliding through the citizens and tourists without noticing them, her expression distant, cold – and somehow sad. That was the point at which Elarn had decided to give in to the urge for mild intoxication. She had passed several establishments that would have served her, on Talisman Street – a mix of antique and curio shops, offices and licensed cafés – and back on Lily Street, where several hotels advertised bars or restaurants open to non-residents. But she felt uncomfortable being out alone, even though the hotel staff had assured her she should be safe enough, so she decided to get a glass or three of something over-priced and alcoholic in the small bar-restaurant at the Manor Park, where she had eaten alone last night.

She was making her way across the plant-filled foyer of her hotel when the receptionist – mercifully human, a touch Elarn appreciated – called out, 'Medame Reen, I have an— um, a package for you.'

Elarn stopped, puzzled, then walked over. The receptionist bent down and picked up a huge bowl of red and yellow flowers which he deposited on the desk in front of him. Elarn recognised some of the blooms as classic roses; others were more exotic. The smell made her nostrils flare with pleasure.

The receptionist peered round the arrangement. 'It arrived a few minutes ago. Shall I have it sent up to your room?'

'Yes, thank you— Wait!' Elarn had spotted an envelope addressed to her at the base of the arrangement. She bent over to extract it. 'I'll just take this.'

She sat down in one of the comfortable chairs in the bar area and ordered a glass of Eiswein, the only alcoholic beverage she recognised on the list. There were no other guests in at this time of the afternoon and the waiter brought her drink at once. She took a sip: a good vintage, if served a little colder than usual. Finally she turned to the mysterious envelope. Her name was handwritten. She opened the envelope carefully and withdrew a piece of thick, cream-coloured notepaper. She read:

Medame Reen,

Please accept these flowers as a small gesture of welcome after a less than auspicious start to your stay in our City.

I have managed to get a ticket for your performance at the Ares Rooms tonight, and I wondered if I might have the great pleasure of taking you to supper after the concert. No need to reply now, though if

*you need to contact me, my com tag is available on your room's com
unit – another presumption of mine, I fear.*
   With kind regards,
   Salik Vidoran

Elarn read the note through twice, then took a large gulp of wine so
she had something on which to blame the light-headedness. She had
been deeply affected by their encounter yesterday morning, and had
been wondering whether he had meant what he said, about seeing her
again – or even whether she should try to contact him. When the usual
nightmare had awakened her in the night, the normal visceral terror
amplified by recollections of the attempted mugging, she had clung to
the memory of Salik Vidoran; when she awoke this morning she recalled more pleasant dreams featuring her chance encounter with the
handsome Consul.

It looked like she had made an impression on him too.

The wisest course would be to keep a safe, polite distance ... but
Elarn was alone here, and out of her depth, and so far she'd been holding herself together using fear and willpower. If she found someone she
could trust, an ally who knew the City's ways, that might make the task
ahead of her less daunting. She dared not let herself hope for too much,
but the note had lifted her spirits.

It still took another glass of wine before she could bring herself to
implement the next part of her plan.

She walked back to reception and asked, as casually as she could
manage, if the receptionist could recommend somewhere to buy a gun.

She had mixed feelings of relief and disapproval when the receptionist answered completely normally, 'The Manor Park Hotel recom-
mends the Personal Protection Emporium in the atrium of the Hotel
Splendide, which is a short walk rimwards from here. If medame is
considering a visit to the Leisure Quarter, might we also recommend a
guard service?'

She thanked him for the advice, but turned down the offer of a
guard.

*

The Hotel Splendide, fabulously tasteless in purple and gold, contained a miniature shopping mall on its ground floor. The shop to which the receptionist had referred her had a window display of guns that looked more like fashion accessories than lethal weapons.

Inside, the bored shop assistant sat her at a projector table and showed her how to navigate the menus to display the forms of personal armament available. 'We have everything you see in stock, medame, though if you choose the mimetic or colour coordination options it will take a little longer.' As she bent over her, Elarn caught a whiff of the assistant's perfume: rather pleasant, but of course it probably masked pheromones, another enhancement that was perfectly legal here.

Despite her initial impression, Elarn soon saw that the selection was not particularly good; there were various dart and pellet guns using compressed air technology, and tasers and other electrical and chemical stun weapons, but there were no plasma or laser guns, and nothing firing explosive projectiles.

The assistant, sighing at the foreigner's naïveté, told her that Khesh City might trade on its lawless reputation, but there were strict prohibitions on weaponry, an obvious precaution when you were in an enclosed City floating three kilometres above the ground. Those who lived in space habitats would barely notice the restrictions, being subject to such rules themselves, but life on an unspoiled planet meant Elarn had no idea about such things. She wondered what other assumptions about Khesh City she would find were completely wrong. She was used to living under obvious rules that bound, restricted and supported society like an exoskeleton; here it appeared the structure was more like an endoskeleton; it was hidden deep beneath the surface, but it was just as hard, just as unyielding.

After much deliberation, she selected a dart-gun rejoicing in the name of *Silversliver 75*: it was compact enough to fit in her bag but it had – so the assistant claimed – an impressive range and accuracy. It looked as good as any of them to Elarn.

'Excellent choice, medame,' said the assistant, without much sincerity. 'Will medame be taking the standard package with it?'

'What exactly is the standard package?' Elarn asked, looking around for a display.

'Tranq, delivered by needle. The target loses consciousness in one to three seconds, depending on bodyweight and metabolism. There are seventy-five rounds in a magazine, hence the name. We also do a forty-round option, with the same strength of tranq but a larger needle size – in case medame expects to encounter armoured opponents.'

Elarn resisted the temptation to make a sarcastic comment: this was a gun she was talking about, for God's sake. Stress and alcohol were making her flippant. Instead she asked, 'What are the other options?'

'With the Silversliver range you can use everything from euphoric sedative to lethal rounds. Tranq is by far the most popular.'

'I'll take that, then, but I'd like one box – *magazine* – of lethal too, if you would be so kind.'

The girl raised an eyebrow and stated flatly, 'I am required by my employer to make you aware that Vellern has extradition treaties with most major governments in this sector, which may result in your being placed under arrest by authorities representing those governments, should you kill any of their citizens. And although manslaughter of Confederacy citizens in proven self-defence is not illegal within the Three Cities, you may also be liable to lawsuits from the relatives of any citizen you kill.'

'Including downsiders?'

The girl laughed snidely. 'Downsiders aren't citizens, medame. Except Angels, and I assume medame will not be picking a fight with an Angel.'

'Of course not.' Elarn tried not to sound shocked. 'I won't be "picking a fight" with anyone. Nonetheless, I wish to purchase lethal ammunition as well.'

'As medame wishes. If medame would care to wait here.' The girl keyed a stock number into the console and sauntered into the back room of the shop.

Away from the girl's bored regard, Elarn swallowed hard, the sweet aftertaste of the Eiswein bitter as bile in the throat. She had been calmly discussing committing murder with a surly stranger.

The girl returned with a box containing a palm-sized silver weapon. Without being asked she explained the firing mechanism, showed Elarn the release for the ammunition clip, then dropped it back into the box. 'Full instructions and warranty are coded into the box lid, so kindly remember to download them to your com before disposing of the packaging.' Elarn half-expected her to ask whether she wanted the thing gift wrapped, but the girl just deducted the payment from Elarn's bracelet and insincerely wished her a pleasant afternoon.

Back in her room, Elarn took the gun out of the box to practise changing the ammo clip. It was a light, elegant thing, more like a toy than a real gun. She could hardly imagine this little device taking a life … except it wouldn't be the gun, it would be *her*, squeezing that trigger. She slid the weapon into her bag, suddenly repulsed by the touch of the thing.

She went straight into rehearsing that night's repertoire, but found herself unable to engage with the music. Whatever calm her art might have given her this morning was long gone.

CHAPTER ELEVEN

Federin had Fenya pack him a bag, then he hitched up his robe – made from scraps of quality fabric given as payment for his services – and led Taro into the mazeways. Once they were out of familiar territory, the remembrancer navigated by the tags on walls, or by a kind of dead reckoning, stopping at junctions, closing his eyes and relying on memory. Feeling out the City, he called it. Remembrancers had a rep second only to Angels, so they had no worries about getting caught up in the feuds that often blew up between gangs and troupes. With Taro's colours and the remembrancer's robes, everyone they met gave way to them, some with respectful bows.

When they came into the mazeways under the Guest Quarter, Federin told Taro to check the view below. 'My old body's not up to hanging off ledges these days,' he said.

Taro wasn't sure his young one was just now, but he let the remembrancer slip a harness over his head and clip a tether to it. Federin attached the other end of the line to one of the support ropes that held up the mazeway. Taro went down onto all fours, then dropped onto his elbows, hands curled round the edge of the mazeway. He took a deep breath before leaning forward, pivoting himself around his hands to let his head hang off the mazeway. He knew better than to keep his eyes open – looking at the ground below could unbalance you sure as a kick up the arse – but as soon as he closed his eyes all his blood rushed to his head, with his stomach trying to follow it.

He started to tip forward.

A bony hand grabbed his belt. 'Steady there,' said Federin.

Taro remembered how to breathe, and coughed painfully. Federin loosened his grip, but kept his hand on Taro's back. 'Are you sure you're up to this journey, Taro?'

Probably not – but he didn't have a choice. He practised breathing awhile, then said, 'I'll be fine.' A few more breaths and he could face opening his eyes to the upside-down view across the bottom of the Undertow. 'Got it netted now, Federin, thanks,' he murmured.

'Good. The Heart of the City is ahead of you, aye?'

Taro focused on the distant dark line of the spine that ran down the centre of his vision. 'Spot on, Federin.'

'Good. Now give me the colours on the nearest water-traps and tell me where they are in relation to the Heart.'

Taro recited them. After half a dozen Federin told him he had what he needed and hauled him back onto the mazeway – which was good, 'cause much longer and he'd have thrown up for certain.

After that, they stopped and checked the 'traps every few hundred metres, but Federin's perfect memory and dead-straight sense of direction meant Taro didn't have to spend too much time upside down.

Dusk fell as they reached the edge of the Merchant Quarter; the ground below faded from orange to brown before disappearing into darkness, and the twilight of the mazeways deepened into night. Taro started to shiver and pulled his jacket tighter. But at last Federin said they were close enough to their goal that they needn't check any more 'traps. The remembrancer produced a small lantern and tinderbox from his bag. While he was lighting the lantern Taro asked what he knew about the Angel Nual.

'That who you're looking for?' asked Federin.

Taro nodded.

Federin sighed and started speaking in the sing-song voice he used when reciting histories. 'Lives on the sunwise edge of the Merchant Quarter, nearly under the State Quarter. Nineteen chartered Removals. Eighteen successes. No acknowledged lineage.'

'Don't s'pose you know what she looks like?'

'Looks like?' Federin sounded puzzled. How an Angel looked was nothing like as important as her record. 'Let's see. She is not pure-blood.

From what I've heard she's short, built like a topsider. Her hair's dark, I think – even darker than yours – though she wears it properly.' Long and straight: Angels didn't wear troupe colours in their hair. They didn't need to.

Federin handed Taro the lantern and nodded for him to carry on. The candle fizzed and smoked in the damp evening air and he had to pull his sleeve over his hand to hold the hot metal handle.

After a couple more turns they arrived outside the Exquisite Corpse. The bar was off an open area where four mazeways met, beyond a curtained doorway so wide three people could walk in side by side. But the ledge of the mazeway outside was barely wide enough for one person and the gap between the mazeways wasn't netted.

Federin took the lantern and pushed Taro forward.

'Wait. Ain't you comin' in?' Taro asked.

'I've no place here. Neither would you, if you weren't on the Minister's business.' He turned and moved off into the shadows.

Taro edged along the narrow mazeway. He should be grateful there was a ledge at all; it wasn't like Angels needed one. Just beyond his toes, darkness gaped like a pit. He kept his eyes on the curtain of tanned skin that covered the doorway. Music, the buzz of conversation and the occasional laugh seeped out from beyond the curtain. The music sounded like a beat-box, the sort used by topside street-performers, with a low hypnotic voice weaving a melody through the back-beats.

He smoothed down his hair and checked his ribbons and plaits were moderately neat. He should probably have removed his make-up, but it was too late now. He took a steadying breath and pulled the curtain aside.

The place wasn't much wider than the sleeping room at Limnel's, but it was way longer, with a step up to a higher level at the far end. The floor was made of something darker than vane material, and it ran solid from wall to wall with no gaps or joins. The light came from tubes propped up against the walls and hung from the ceiling; the soft purple glow gave the place a feel of seductive danger. The air was warm and stuffy, and smelled of burnt mash, incense and cooked meat. There was more furniture here than Taro had ever seen in the Undertow – tables and chairs clustered along both sides of the room – but no two pieces of furniture were the same. There were plastic tables like the ones in cheap topside bars, comfortable low seats like those Taro had seen in hotels, even a curved metal bench that looked like it belonged in the Gardens.

Most of the chairs were occupied, and everyone was looking at Taro. So much for slipping in quietly and seeing what he could overhear.

He kept his eyes down and took a step into the room. His feet slid away from him and he grabbed the edge of the curtain to catch himself. The floor was slippery – not wet, but smooth and, he saw with a jolt, clear. Thank the City it was night, otherwise he would've been able to see all the way to the ground.

A ripple of laughter went round the room at his not-so-prime entrance. He let go of the curtain and slid one foot carefully along the floor.

A woman and a small girl sat at the table nearest him. The woman wore a dark, long-sleeved dress, and her long white hair was loosely pinned up with a pair of bone chopsticks. The girl, dressed in a patch-work dress of red-and-black, was still giggling at Taro, ignoring the roast meat the woman had been trying to feed her. The woman pressed her lips together and gave Taro a look that said he'd caused quite enough trouble, thank you. When Taro, unable to look away from the little girl's huge plate of food, continued to stare at them, the woman waved a hand to dismiss him. Taro glimpsed the flash of metal at the Angel's wrist and moved on quickly, sliding his feet along the floor, arms out for balance.

Of the six tables on the lower level, five were occupied. Any patrons who weren't Angels wore City colours in their hair. The largest group, opposite the mother and child, were playing jacks with bone pieces, betting paper scrip; the Angel with them was a man, one of only three male Angels in the service of the City. People said that the Minister recruited mainly women because they were smarter and more loyal than men, and that not being natural killers, they wouldn't take too much pleasure in their duty – a lesson other Cities could do with learning, Taro thought bitterly. Then again, Limnel thought most Angels were female because the Minister was a dirty old cove.

The next table up was empty, a glass lying on its side in a pool of clear spirit. Taro slid round to sit with his back against the wall. He recognised the sickly, slightly acidic smell: burnt mash, Malia's favoured drug.

He looked around and checked out the upper level, which was smaller and not so well lit. There were people at two of the tables, and a couple dancing in the space in the middle. The boy looked and moved like someone in Taro's own line of work. His Angel partner had long dark hair and for a moment Taro wondered if his luck had changed, but Federin had said that Nual was short, and this Angel was as tall as Taro. She danced with eyes closed, feet dragging, arms draped over the boy's shoulders. She held a shot glass loosely in one hand.

Beyond her Taro could just make out a hunched figure sitting against the back wall: a meatbaby. She was moving her stunted arms in time to the music, and Taro realised she was singing: the sounds she made were nonsense, but the song had a strange beauty, as fascinating as the dark drop to the ground below.

Taro's eyes were drawn to someone backing into the room through the open doorway next to the singer. Someone – or some*thing*; Taro couldn't make sense of what he was seeing until the figure turned round and he saw it did have the normal number of arms and legs – even if they were freakily thin and angular – and a head in the usual place – even if it was too small and pointy. What had thrown him were the folded wings that stood up from the thing's shoulders. The creature held a tray balanced on one bony hand and now it bustled across to the empty table near the back door and, reaching over with a motion at once both ordinary and impossible, started gathering up used glasses. Taro watched, entranced. This must be the owner: Malia had really meant it when she said the place was run by an alien.

'Hoi! Yer in my seat!'

Taro jumped. The Angel who'd been dancing with the joyboy stood at the end of the table. She swayed forward to stand in front of Taro, leaning into her companion. She wore a long black dress, green eye make-up and a thin red choker.

'I'm sorry, lady. My mistake,' gulped Taro. 'I'll move.'

'Aye. Get out.' She rubbed her head absentmindedly against the whore's cheek and half-closed her eyes. The boy was smiling, but Taro could see fear in his eyes. He knew full-well that he was here to give this Angel whatever she wanted, including his life, if that was her wish. Taro started to ease his way out from behind the table. The Angel held

up one clean, long-nailed hand. 'No, wait. I c'n manage two, I think.'
She giggled, then narrowed her eyes and lunged at Taro. She was too
drunk to complete the movement; the boy barely caught her in time
to stop her sprawling across the table. She laughed as though that was
what she'd meant to do all along, and pointed at Taro's hair.

'Who— Whose boy're you, then?'

He had hoped no one would ask that. 'I claim me lineage from the
Angel Malia,' Taro said, his voice hoarse with fear.

'Malia? Heard she took the fall,' slurred the Angel.

Shit and blood. So the rumours about his line-mother's death had
spread this far. This wasn't going to plan. But you don't lie to Angels.
'She did, lady,' he croaked, ' just under a week ago.'

'Din't hear feud'd been called on her. An' I wouldn't have thought
she'd jump. Still, it's alw'ys the quiet ones, eh?' She elbowed her companion in the ribs and laughed.

Just for a second, he considered blurting out the full truth. If Malia's
fellow Angels knew what Scarrion had done, they'd hunt the Screamer
down and tear him to pieces. But they'd never believe Taro's story. An
agent of another League, taking out an Angel, in her own territory?
Unthinkable. And even if they did believe him, they'd want to know
how the Screamer had found his way down into the Undertow, and
Taro would be have to admit being gappy enough to lead him there. He
could imagine how they'd react to that.

'So, boy, yer a no s-status loser with no right to those colours in yer
lovely locks,' the Angel continued gleefully, 'But you decided to jus' drop
in here fer a drink anyway. Just what the fuck d'ya think yer doing?'

Good question. He needed to come up with a story, fast. There was
one possibility, something that hadn't occurred to him until this moment.
'No, lady, I'm here to—'

'Shuddup.' She wasn't smiling any more.

Taro shut up.

The Angel continued, 'Y'know what? I'm sick of ungrateful, useless
li'l shits who think that bein' lucky enough to have Angel blood makes
'em special. They do nothing to earn their pr-privileges, and they abuse
'em, leaving us to deal with their shit. My sister, she's gone and— Never
mind. You wear the colours, you swagger an' boast, but you got no idea

what we are.' She shook her head. The room had fallen silent; even the singer had stopped, though the beat-box still banged on mindlessly. Taro stared at the Angel as cold sweat prickled his back. She dropped her voice. 'Without death we're nothing. And I haven't taken a life fer my City for over a year. I should've been chosen next. I'm a loyal and ef-ef-effishun' servant of the Minister. But not good enough, 'parently. Hah.' She flicked her hands out at her sides. The joyboy backed off with a squeal. Taro glimpsed movement behind the Angel, but he found himself staring at the long, thin metal blades protruding from the front of her wrists. 'All 'n all I've had a really shitty couple of weeks. An' y'know what? I think I'm gonna take it out on you.'

Taro stared at the Angel, his mind blank, his body frozen. Of all the ways he'd expected to die ... not like this. This was just too stupid, too pointless. Too soon.

She floated a handbreadth off the floor, turning her hands to look at the blades as though greeting old friends, 'Nothin' personal, you understan'. Just need to get some o' that tension outa my system.'

Taro closed his eyes.

'Outside, then.' The voice was soft and feminine, yet oddly toneless.

Taro opened his eyes to see the alien standing next to the Angel, its wingtips towering over them both. Under the canopy of the furled wings it was hardly taller than a topsider. Its spindly limbs had joints in all the wrong places.

For a moment Taro expected the Angel to turn on it, but she just looked over at the alien, pursed her lips and looked back to Taro. 'Solo hates mess, y'know.'

'That is right,' said the alien, 'let us have no blood and guts to make smells and stains.' The voice came from a box attached to the creature's throat, nestling in the short purple-grey fur that covered its body. Other than the box it wore only a narrow pleated kilt. It still held the tray of empty glasses in one hand.

'Fine. We'll take it outside.' But the anger had gone out of the Angel's voice. Taro saw his chance.

'Wait. I've a right to be here. I'm carryin' out Malia's last request.' Not the truth, but not a lie anyone could prove, and it was the best he could come up with under pressure.

'Really?' The Angel sounded dubious.

'Aye, lady. She wanted Nual to 'ave her gun.'

For a moment the Angel and the alien stared at him. Taro wasn't sure whose gaze freaked him most: the blurred violence of the killer or the cold curiosity of the creature from another world.

Then the Angel snorted. 'Nual. Fuck's sake.' She punched the air, her blades flashing. 'That bitch. Takes my hit an' fucks it up. Shit and blood.' She retracted both blades and sat down unsteadily on the stool opposite Taro. She dropped her head into her hands and flicked a hand at Taro without looking at him. 'Jus' go away, boy. Get the fuck outa my sight.'

Taro didn't need to be told twice. He edged out, careful not make any move that she might take as hostile or insolent.

The alien watched him. Its gold-edged eyes were too large and too round, giving it an innocent, almost idiotic look. The Angel had called it Solo.

As he emerged from behind the table, it stepped back to let him out. He nodded his thanks and turned to go, but Solo put out a hand with too few fingers and too many joints. Taro flinched as the clawed fingertips snagged his sleeve.

'You have no gun.' Although Solo's words came from the box, he heard a faint breathy trill below the mechanical voice and saw movement in the long fur on the lower half of its face. He wondered briefly what it ate, before deciding he'd rather not know.

'Sorry?' He stopped. 'I didn't wanna risk bringing Malia's gun so far across unknown territory.' Now he'd started on the lie, he had to hope the shit-gardeners who'd taken over Malia's old homespace would hand the gun over to him when he asked. They'd seemed like reasonable people; they were probably just waiting for him to come back for it, soon as he got himself sorted.

For some time Solo stared at him, not moving any part of its body. Taro had the crazy idea that it had fallen asleep, or shut down, or whatever these things did. Finally it blinked. 'Follow me.'

Taro was confused. 'I—? You want me to follow you?'

'Yes, follow me to somewhere private.'

It pointed to the back of the room with one clawed hand, a freakily human gesture. Taro hesitated. It wasn't far to the door and his path was clear. But there were a lot of fast, dangerous people in here and they were all watching him.

He took a deep breath and followed the alien up the low step onto the upper level and out through the doorway at the back. He found himself in a small room with walls covered in shelves packed with glasses, bottles and boxes. Solo put the tray down on a low shelf and carried on through a curtained door at the back. Taro tried not to stare at the way the pointed elbows of the alien's wings brushed the thin curtain as it held it aside. It led Taro into a larger area with more shelves and a firebox on a metal cooking stand. Like all the other rooms he'd seen so far in the Exquisite Corpse there were no gaps in the floor. The heat of the firebox made the room far too hot. There was a smell in here beyond that of food, a kind of dry, musty odour. It wasn't unpleasant – it reminded him of the time a punter had taken him to a hotel room and shown him a wardrobe of clean new clothes from which he was invited to choose a suitable outfit for the night's fun – but it wasn't a smell he associated with living things. He wondered if it was the alien. He tried to breath through his mouth.

Solo perched on the stool beside the firebox, the naked skin of its wings rustling as it settled itself in its seat. 'Explain,' it said without preamble.

'Er, explain what?' Now he was up close, Taro could see the small details of the alien's appearance all too well: the way its face came forward to a point where the nose should be – only there was no nose, just a pair of tiny holes in the bald patch in the centre; that the skin beneath the thin fuzz of fur on its limbs was grey; the lack of visible ears ...

'Explain why you came.'

The heat was making his head swim. 'It's like I said, Malia wanted Nual to 'ave her gun when she died.'

'Why?'

Talking to the creature was making Taro think how much he normally relied on stuff like the expression on people's faces, or the way they shifted and fidgeted. Solo did not move at all, as though gestures and movement had nothing to do with how its people communicated – which they probably didn't.

'When an Angel knows she's gonna die she often passes her gun on to someone she admires,' he said.

Solo made a musical rasping noise and the box on its throat said, 'I run a haven for Angels. I know this.' Despite the flat voice and lack of body language, Taro could have sworn he was having the piss taken. 'So, I ask again. Why Nual?'

'It's 'cause …' Taro hesitated. All he had to build on was one shaky lie. He was unlikely to get any breaks from the alien. He tried to put as much sincerity as he could into his voice and continued, ''cause Malia admired Nual. She has – *had* – a perfect record. You probably know that. It's just … it's what Malia wanted.'

Solo watched him silently, still as death, not even blinking.

It was way too hot in here. Taro found himself taking deep breaths, despite the smell, just to get enough air. He wondered if the alien would mind if he took his jacket off. 'Listen, you're obviously a very busy … person. Just tell me how to get to Nual's homespace an' I'll leave you in peace.'

'No.' It blinked, once. With the lack of any other visual cue, Taro found himself fascinated by the thing's eyes. Did it blink when it was annoyed? Or was it just random, like with humans?

'What? I mean, is that "no" you won't tell me, or "no" … somethin' else? '

'I know where she lives. I will not tell you. She does not wish to be disturbed.'

'All right, that's prime,' Taro said quickly. 'Is there anywhere else she hangs out? I'd heard she comes in here quite a lot. That's why I came.'

'She does come here, sometimes. I will give her your message. She will choose whether to act.'

Not ideal, but probably the best he was going to get. At least it looked like the alien had fallen for Taro's story, which was good. Then again, he wasn't sure how he'd tell if it was just stringing him along. 'That's great,' he said enthusiastically. 'Thanks, er, friend. I'll come back later, when you've had a chance to talk to her, shall I? Tomorrow maybe?'

The alien levered itself off the stool. 'No. Do not come here to look for her again. She will find you if she wishes to speak to you. Go now. I am busy, as you say.'

Taro backed out of the room and headed for the bar.

He'd just have to hope the joyboy would keep the Angel occupied enough that she wouldn't notice him on the way out.

CHAPTER TWELVE

Shamal Binu was late again.

Elarn waited on one of the damask-covered chairs in the lobby of the Manor Park Hotel. Her stomach fluttered and she had to resist the urge to get up and pace.

Her thoughts kept returning to the gun hidden in her room. She wouldn't need it tonight. She hoped she wouldn't need it at all. But simply having a lethal weapon in her possession appeared to be affecting her ability to concentrate on anything else – and right now she needed to focus on her upcoming performance. The concerts were just an excuse to be here, but she had made music her life, and performing in front of strangers still filled her with anxiety. She always wanted to give her best.

When Medame Binu finally arrived, twenty minutes late, Elarn was relieved to see that she was wearing a high-necked gown in a relatively sedate shade of green. Elarn herself wore a robe of sapphire sea-gauze over a cream chemise, with a black velvet cloak against the evening chill.

Throughout the journey to the Merchant Quarter Medame Binu kept up a constant twitter regarding the other concerts (five confirmed, one still being negotiated); the guests expected tonight (several persons of consequence and at least two critics of note); and the skill of the accompanist she had hired for this evening (allegedly one of the best un-enhanced musicians in the City). Elarn tried to listen, but found it hard to do more than make occasional noises of assent. Luckily, Medame Binu didn't expect any more.

They were halfway up Silk Street when Medame Binu said something and put her hand on Elarn's arm. Elarn jumped and the agent repeated herself. 'I said, you look pale. Have you eaten?'

'No,' Elarn said, trying to focus properly on her agent. 'I'm having dinner after the concert.'

Medame Binu pounced. 'Really? I did have a call first thing this morning, from a certain Consul, asking whether tickets were still available for tonight and what the arrangements were after the concert. I was going to offer to take you somewhere but if you've already got plans—' She giggled like a girl waiting for shared confidences.

'I have,' said Elarn, and went back to looking at the expensive shopfronts lining the Street.

Medame Binu finally took the hint and shut up. For a moment Elarn felt guilty for snapping, but before she could restart the conversation the pedicab stopped in front of a shop displaying gentlemen's formal wear on disturbingly lifelike semi-animated mannequins. The agent paid the fare, then led Elarn to a plain black door next to the shop, waving her bracelet over the reader beside it. The door opened onto a plush, spacious elevator, complete with human attendant, which delivered them to a large white-walled room where yet more attendants were laying out rows of chairs. Paintings hung around the walls, executed in a chunky, rather crude style that Elarn found both repellent and emotive. Plinths displaying vases and bowls decorated in similarly primitive patterns were arranged in groups under the windows and in alcoves and corners.

At the far end a woman a couple of decades older than Elarn sat at a keyboard. Medame Binu bustled forward, introducing the accompanist as Medame Mier. As the woman greeted her with a warm smile, Elarn noticed the crucifix at her throat.

Medame Mier was every bit as skilled as the agent had claimed, and familiar with Elarn's work, even recognising pieces she had recorded both solo and accompanied. For the first time almost since she had arrived, Elarn relaxed, burying some of her apprehension in the mechanics of her craft.

After the run-through, Medame Binu led her through a curtain to a back room furnished with comfortable seats and a table of refreshments, then left her with Medame Mier while she went to greet the evening's guests. Elarn ignored the alcoholic drinks; while they might have helped with her nerves, tonight she needed to keep a clear head. Instead she poured herself some water, trying not to wince at the recycled tang. Elarn was half expecting Medame Mier to suggest they prayed together, at which point Elarn would have been obliged to confess her hypocrisy, but the woman was more interested in gossip. As the scrape of chairs and murmur of conversation beyond the curtain grew louder, Elarn was grateful for the stream of faintly disapproving comments on fashion, morality and current affairs. It saved her from having to think about how many people were waiting out there for her. She was about to ask how Medame Mier felt about the Concord when the noise level outside dropped away.

From beyond the curtain Elarn heard Medame Binu give a short introductory speech, referring to Elarn as 'an elusive and sacred talent', which was about what she had expected. Many in the audience would see her as an eccentric naïf, a refreshingly primitive voice amongst the decadence of Khesh City. But she should not let their parochial attitudes stop her giving a good performance.

Medame Mier held the curtain up for her to walk out and she mounted the dais. Most of the audience were her age or older; she thought they were probably genuinely interested in her music. Some of her nervousness abated. They had paid good money to see her; they wanted her to succeed. She just had to ignore the younger Kheshi who were here only because she was today's fad. In the centre, near the back, she spotted yesterday's fad; Consul Vidoran smiled encouragingly at her and her innards gave a girlish leap.

Her first song, a relatively modern hymn in a still-used dialect, was barely technically competent, but with the first polite ripple of applause her nerves disappeared and she began to actually enjoy performing in public.

The climax, the most technically difficult piece, consisted of fragments of a Requiem whose full score had been lost long before the Sidhe Protectorate; it was widely believed to be from Old Earth itself. She sang it with full accompaniment, her voice leading an invisible choir and as she sang she felt not as if she were making the music, but as though the music were making *her*, giving her substance. By the end she found her gaze locked with Salik Vidoran's, as though this music were a sacrament they alone shared.

The final applause was far more enthusiastic and some of the audience – the Consul included – rose to their feet. She sang two encores in a strange daze, detached, yet joyously alive.

It was only when she took her final bow and retreated backstage that all the emotion of the past few days caught up with her and she swayed, her legs threatening to collapse under her. She accepted a drink from Medame Mier and composed herself before the various important persons started filing in to give their compliments. Finally she was alone except for Medame Binu and her last visitor; Consul Vidoran had hung back, but now he came forward and took both her hands in his. 'Magnificent,' he breathed.

'Thank you, Consul,' she said, her voice low.

'Salik, please.'

'Of course. Salik.' She liked the way his name tasted in her mouth. 'And you must call me Elarn.'

He led her back out to the main room, where the chairs were being put away. His bodyguard, standing attentive beside a plinth, fell into step behind them. Seeing Elarn's nervous glance at their shadow, Salik whispered, 'Don't mind Scarrion. He takes his duties rather seriously – for which I have cause to be grateful.'

The bodyguard rode in a pedicab behind theirs and, when they reached their destination, a small restaurant at the rimwards end of the Street, stationed himself at the bar while the Consul led Elarn into the main dining area.

Like many of the more up-market establishments, this one was themed, but whatever part of Confed history or culture it represented was largely incomprehensible to outsiders. The small tables were made of woven reeds, and stands of ornamental grasses in ceramic pots gave an illusion of privacy. A band of musicians dressed in real animal skins played low-toned pipes and soft percussion.

'I know, I know,' whispered Salik as a waiter dressed in a homespun robe showed them to their table, 'no one comes here for the décor – unless they like tacky ersatz nomad as a style – but the food is excellent. It's entirely fresh, and cooked on that great hotplate over by the wall.'

'Fresh' meant imported, and that would mean expensive, but there were no prices displayed, and no menus; instead the waiter brought round a tray of artfully arranged raw vegetables and meats to choose from.

Elarn was still on a high from the concert, and the first glass of fizzy pale wine went straight to her head; she decided not to worry about the price, or who was paying, or anything else, at least for a while.

Salik chatted comfortably about music and history and the City, giving her the opportunity to join in or to listen, as she chose. Mainly she listened, lulled by the wine and his presence. She had been concerned, amongst everything else, that this meeting, her first 'date' in many years, would be tense and difficult. She was out of practice at this sort of social interaction. But she needn't have worried; Salik was polite, witty and attentive.

The food was as good as he had promised but, despite not having had anything since lunch, she found herself more interested in her companion than her meal.

She probably should have eaten more; when they stood up to go her legs wobbled before locking into place and the room jumped in and out of focus.

Salik put a hand out to steady her. 'You look exhausted. Are you all right?'

She nodded. Exhausted, in a comedown from an adrenalin high, and yes, quite drunk. *Oh dear.*

'I think we need to get you back to your hotel,' he said with a smile, and took her arm. Outside the restaurant he guided her rimwards. 'We're not going to take a pedicab,' he explained. 'I'll pay for a quicker ride.'

'But you've paid for everything tonight,' she said, feeling a little guilty. 'I feel I should contribute.'

'Not at all, I invited you, if you recall,' the Consul said firmly. 'But if you do insist, you can buy me lunch tomorrow, assuming that fits in with your plans – I happen to have a few hours free in the afternoon.'

'I'd be delighted to buy you lunch,' she said, thankful her obvious lack of social graces had not put him off. He wanted to see her again.

At the end of the Street, they started up the steps to the circle-car.

Elarn was momentarily concerned: the circle-car was a very public form of transport, open to anyone with a City ID, and not as safe as a pedicab. Still, she should be fine with the Consul and the ever-present bodyguard trailing silently behind them. But he turned off before they reached the main platform and, after another sweep of his cred-bracelet, led her to a small, four-seater aircar on its own platform. Without a word being said Scarrion climbed in the front with the driver and Salik helped Elarn into the back. The driver wished them both a good evening and as Salik gave their destination, Elarn settled back into the padded seat and sniffed the faint smell of artificial flowers. Her hip and knee just touched Salik's; she could feel his warmth next to her.

They took off so smoothly that Elarn had to blink to get her sluggish vision to follow. Suddenly the entire City was laid out below her like a dish of jewels, the lines of the Streets like great neon spokes.

As the air-taxi passed the spine, Elarn had a sudden sense of just how immense, and how impressive, Khesh City truly was. It was a spectacular example of hubris, humanity showing off its cleverness and ingenuity. She couldn't help wondering if humans had ever really been clever enough to create this alone.

'This City,' she asked, 'is there any Sidhe influence here?'

Salik laughed, and she realised how thoughtlessly she had spoken. 'Well no,' he said, 'given that the Sidhe have been dead for a thousand years.'

So everyone thinks, she didn't say. Instead she said, 'No, what I meant was, it was built during the Sidhe Protectorate, wasn't it, or just after? Did they ... help?'

'I couldn't say. There's a legend that says a renegade Sidhe faction who sided with humanity lived here, even at the height of the Protectorate, so it's quite possible there is Sidhe technology in the City.'

And that would support her theory that they had sent her, rather than deal with their renegade personally, because they did not want to risk running into ancient traps created by the rebel Sidhe who had wanted humanity to be free. The thought made her feel a lot more sober and a lot less comfortable. 'And it's still here, this technology, whatever it is?'

Salik shrugged. 'Who knows? To be honest, the detailed workings of the Three Cities are something of a mystery, even to their inhabitants.

They have worked perfectly for more than a thousand years, and we assume – hopefully correctly! – that they'll continue to do so for the next thousand years.'

His tone was indulgent, but he probably thought this an odd topic of conversation for this time of the evening. And he was right.

'I'm sorry,' she said, 'this place just keeps taking me by surprise.'

'Don't worry,' he said, 'I've lived here all my life and it still surprises me sometimes. I can hardly blame you for suffering from cultural vertigo.'

He put a hand on her knee, just a reassuring touch, quickly withdrawn. She wanted to return the touch, now, while the wine still gave her the courage, but they were already descending, coming in to land at the end of Lily Street.

Walking down to Street level, Elarn wondered where the evening would go now. Part of her wanted to invite him to come back with her; another part was appalled that she would even consider it, so soon in their acquaintance.

At the bottom of the steps he hailed a pedicab and helped her in, but made no move to follow. 'I have a few things to do in the morning,' he told her. 'Would it be all right if I called you some time after midday tomorrow?'

'Of course.' She smiled down at him.

He reached up to kiss her cheek, a light, gentle kiss, neither forward nor presumptive. She leaned into it and closed her eyes.

CHAPTER THIRTEEN

'Where the fuck d'ya go, anyway?'

Taro jerked his head up to find Keron staring down at him, a couple of the other tarts watching from behind the pimp's back.

When Taro had got back from the Exquisite Corpse, the sleeping room had been half-empty, with the night shift still out. Though he was tired, he'd played his flute softly for a short while. People seemed to like it, especially the girl who'd been standing next to him on Soft Street. When the lamps began to burn low and the day shift whores had curled up to rest, he'd put the flute away and dropped off to sleep almost at once.

'I went—' he started but Keron, eyes big and shining, didn't have time for him to wake up. He pulled Taro's arm and Taro let the pimp haul him to his feet.

Keron was speaking again. 'Boss wants to see ya. 'Spect he wants to check how yer getting on.'

Taro coughed to clear his throat. 'Sure, Keron.'

'Came to find ya earlier, when the first shift came in. Ya weren't back. But yer 'ere now. C'mon.' Keron turned to go, then turned back to him and hissed, 'No need to tell him ya got off early, eh?'

'Wouldn't dream of it,' murmured Taro, letting Keron drag him out the door. He could really use another six hours' sleep, or at least a wash and a change of clothes. He wasn't going to get either, of course. They headed straight for Limnel's lair and when Keron pushed him through the bead curtain Taro found the party in full swing, the gang-boss lounging on his couch with a dozen cronies sprawled on the cushions around him, smoking, drinking and laughing. Taro wondered if he was the floorshow. He didn't feel particularly entertaining.

'Ah,' Limnel gestured at him, 'there ya are. Come in, come in. No, I din't say sit, jus' come in. Come in an' tell us all jus' where the fuck ya went off to. We'd love t'know. I mean, I know I said ya could report to the Minister on wossname, that Angel—' He snapped his fingers. 'What was 'er name, Taro?'

'Nual.'

'Right, Nual. Report on her, aye. Piss off fer a day lookin' fer 'er, no. That's not part o' the deal. Not at all. I assume ya *was* lookin' fer her?'

'That's right. I'm sorry, I—'

'Shut up.' Limnel's obvious pleasure at having Taro at his mercy went up a notch in company. 'So where ya been?'

'The Exquisite Corpse.' Seeing Limnel's blank look, Taro added, 'It's a bar, fer Angels, under the Merchant Quarter.'

'That's a ways from 'ere. D'ya find yer Angel?

Taro tried to keep a level head, but he was still half-asleep, the smoke was making his eyes sting and he kept finding himself staring at the carved box on the cabinet beside Limnel. If they were all wrecked and he'd been called in here to be the fool, he'd best play along. Maybe Limnel might give him a little something from that box, if he reckoned that'd make things more fun. 'Nope, jus' some weird-shit alien with wings who wouldn't tell me where she lives.'

This earned him some scattered laughter from Limnel's gang, but the boss looked unimpressed at his feeble attempt at humour. He leaned forward. 'Then I'd say ya wasted yer day, an' a wasted day means no wasted night, neh?' He looked meaningfully at the box by his elbow, which got more laughs.

Limnel eased himself back into his seat and looked round the room. 'Whaddya reckon, boys an' girls? Should we let our newest troupe member join the party, or just leave 'im danglin'?'

That got a variety of responses, from stoned and clueless smiles to friendly gestures for Taro sit down. Resh, sitting by the door with a bottle of burnt mash by his side, muttered *it weren't worth wasting quality gear on that fucker.*

Limnel picked up the box and looked hard at Taro. 'So what'd ya do today to earn yer reward, boy?'

Though he hated himself for it, Taro suddenly realised he'd do almost anything for another hit of that golden dust. He took a long, slow breath and said, 'Nothin', p'rhaps. But I meant what I said. I'll do me best fer you, fer the troupe. If that means workin' harder than the gang members who've been 'ere a while, that's prime. Sorry I went off today, but I earned m'share fer the day and I 'anded it over. I'm payin' me way, like I said. An' I'll be up on the streets again tomorrow.'

'Pretty speech,' said Limnel, opening the box on his lap. 'Time'll tell if it's more than words.' He dipped the spoon into the box. 'C'mere, then.'

Taro's mouth was actually watering. The pile of powder on the spoon was small, far less than Keron'd given him last night, but he couldn't look away from it.

'I'm not gonna stand up, y'know. Not at this time of night. Ya gotta kneel down.'

Taro hesitated, then fell to his knees in front of the gang-boss. Limnel slipped the spoon under his nose. Taro sniffed.

The rush wasn't as rich or long this time, but the pain and exhaustion were instantly gone, and the world was a better place again. He stayed kneeling, one hand out for balance, lost in the high, while Limnel put the box away. The distant laughter of the gang members rose and someone pushed him gently. He slid over to sprawl onto his side in the cushions. He lay there for a while, numb and happy.

After some time had passed, he looked up to see Limnel bending over him. Limnel leaned closer and drawled, 'One thing yer ain't got netted yet: ya can't serve two masters.'

Taro was still trying to make sense of the boss's comment when the bead curtain rattled behind him. He pulled himself round to see Keron standing in the doorway, holding the arm of a girl whose hair hung down over her face. 'Crash'll hit soon: anyone else wanna go while she's still conscious?' he asked loudly. The girl just stood there.

Limnel addressed the room. 'Anyone? Resh? Thought ya might. Can't keep off the grind, can ya, Resh m'boy? Leave 'er down the corridor when yer done, neh? Don't want 'er disturbin' the other whores again.'

Keron dragged the girl away and Resh stood shakily, ready to follow.

Taro wasn't so stoned that he couldn't pity the poor bitch, whoever she was. He sat up, keeping his head bowed, trying not to attract attention.

'Well, yer ain't exactly the life an' soul, are ya?' Limnel was watching him again.

He nodded at the boss. 'Reckon that last batch was a bit smoky. I'd complain to me supplier, if I was you.'

Limnel snorted. 'Very funny. Plenty more where that came from, if yer a good boy. But if yer straightenin' out, why don't ya make yerself useful? Get yer arse down to the room where yer fucked our regular last night, wait outside until Resh has finished – doubt that'll be long – then go in an' keep an eye on Arel. Make sure she don't do nothin' gappy when the gear wears off, neh?'

'Aye, Boss.' Taro struggled up, his limbs more or less under his control again.

Outside the meeting hall he turned left, hoping he'd remember the way, and sighed with relief when he spotted the familiar mesh-curtained doorway, beyond the locked door and just before a narrow gap in the floor. The noises from behind the curtain made it clear he was in the right place. He sat against the wall, feeling tired and dizzy and not so high at all any more, until Resh emerged, tying his breeches.

He looked down at Taro and laughed. 'Not much left fer you, Angel-boy.' He sauntered off, back towards Limnel's room.

Taro drew a deep breath, lifted the curtain and went in.

The room reeked of bad sex. The girl lay curled on one corner of the mattress, half under the blanket, her clothes in a pile by the door.

As the mesh curtain dropped back into place with a faint swish, she whimpered and pulled herself into a tighter ball.

'Not gonna hurt you,' said Taro quietly.

No response. He'd bet others'd told her that today, and lied.

'Yer name's Arel, ain't it?'

She didn't move. Well, he wasn't going to spend the night standing in the doorway. His legs and head were starting to ache again. 'I'm guessin' they gave you a shitload of dope, and fer a while you din't care no more. That right?'

That could've been a nod. He took it as a good sign and sat down on the edge of the mattress. She shivered and edged away. 'Don't worry. I'm not gonna touch you. Just wanna talk. The thing you gotta understand 'bout grind like that is that what you did when you was blasted – what *they* did to you – it don't count. Not really.'

She muttered something and he moved a little closer. 'What's that?'

'Yer used to it,' she repeated, almost whispering. 'Prob'ly think a bit of grind with an ugly-fuck punter is pure blade.'

That was nice. But at least he'd got a response. 'No, I don't. But I know how to deal with it. They ain't fuckin' *you*, they're fuckin' their mothers or their ex or their best friend or' – he laughed shallowly – 'if they ain't got no imagination – like that piece o' shit Resh – they're just fuckin' a warm, moist hole. It ain't nothin' personal. You gotta remember that. You let yer body do its stuff, but whatever the punters do, it's just flesh fer cash. They can't touch you, the *real* you, not if you don't let 'em.'

Until Scarrion. No, he wasn't going to think about that bastard right now. This girl needed him to be strong, so he had to forget the shit in his own life and help her.

She rolled onto her back, arms still clasped tight round her knees. Her face showed a nasty collection of scratches and bruises. He thought her right eye had been hurt bad, 'cause it looked too big, until he realised this was an old scar, perhaps even something she'd been born with. Her eyes were open, staring blankly at the ceiling. 'No, you don't understan'.' She laughed hollowly. 'I ain't meant to do this, y'see. Daim and me worked the rollers together. Nothin' violent or heavy. He'd distract 'em while I palmed them, or sometimes we'd buzz stupid loners with no guard. We were *good* at it. Pure blade. But Daim's gone now.' Tears started to leak out of the corners of her eyes. On the right side they gathered in the gap of her scar before tumbling across her cheek. 'He's dead and I'm alone now and I'm nothin', *nothin'*. I'm only useful fer fuckin' strangers now.' Her sing-song voice died away. Taro knew that look. He was losing her.

'Arel,' he said urgently, 'Listen to me. You ain't nothin'. You said it yerself: yer brave and clever and—'

She was back, riding on anger. 'Don't shit me, just fuckin' don't! Right?'

'Right.' This would be easier if she wasn't smart and he wasn't stoned.

'But what about that shit they gave me? Jus' like you said: enough of the dust and nothin' matters. Anythin' anyone wanted was top prime. But I ... I need more of it if I'm gonna survive. Look.' She held out her hand; it twitched and jittered. 'Look at that.'

'Tell me 'bout it.'

She looked at him properly for the first time, eyes widening as she focused on the Angel colours in his hair. 'Hey, could ya get me more of that gear?'

'I wish.'

'Ah. You ain't one of Limnel's special boys then. Yer new, ain't ya?'

'Aye, that's right.'

'Been told to watch me, huh? Make sure all that powder Keron sorted fer me don't go to waste?'

Taro nodded.

'Right. So could ya mebbe get me a drink? This stuff leaves yer with a killer thirst.'

'I know. I'll get yer some water.' He thought he'd seen a waterskin on a peg near the locked door. He levered himself up and set off. Half a dozen steps down the corridor he stopped, turned and waited.

Arel came out of the curtain on all fours, bare arse in the air. Under other circumstances it might've been funny, but now, as she threw herself down the corridor towards the nearest gap in the floor, it was just pathetic.

Taro raced after her and half-grabbed her, half-fell onto her. She shrieked and flailed, catching him in the balls with her elbow, and a jagged spike of pain went off in his groin. He almost let go of her, but even if he wasn't under orders from Limnel, there was no way he'd let her kill herself, not on his watch.

He clung fast, ducking her blows, until the fight started to go out of her, then he dragged her back into the room, praying he'd get her calmed down before anyone came to check on what the noise was – assuming anyone even cared.

He got them back to the mattress and sat himself up against the wall, the girl in his lap, holding her fast in his arms until her struggles finally stopped and she lay still. Her skin was cold and clammy and now she'd given up fighting the shakes were starting. He could feel himself twitch in response.

She whispered, 'Way I see it, there's two choices. Either Keron keeps me in the dust forever so I'll be anyone's meatbaby fer a hit, or I take the fall. I'm thinkin' number two's most likely. Even wasted, I don't wanna think about some o' the pigs I've hadda fuck. Whaddya think? You bin nice to me, so I promise not to run again while yer watching me, but I think that's how it'll be, in the end.'

Like she'd said herself, there was no point shitting her. 'I think there's a coupla other options,' Taro said quietly. 'First is: you learn to deal with being a whore. I meant what I said, it ain't as bad as people think. You just gotta get used to it.'

'Aye, right and fine when yer've got an Angel to pimp fer ya.'

'Me line-mother's dead, Arel – or hadn't you heard?'

She relaxed into him for the first time. 'Aye, I 'ad. Sorry.'

He continued, 'The other choice is you learn to act, just enough so's Keron an' Limnel let down their guard. When they're not watchin' so close, you run. Got anyone you can go to?'

She shook her head, wincing at the pain as she did so. 'Nah. I was born into the troupe. Daim had people though, sunwise of here, under Chance Street. Mebbe they'd take me in.'

For the first time he heard hope in her voice. Then she laughed. ''Course, both those plans rely on me not jumpin' on the spoon next time they offer me a fix.'

'You and me both,' murmured Taro into her hair.

She turned and buried her head in Taro's chest, crying, sniffles soon growing to great body-shaking sobs. Taro felt tears leaking from his own eyes, crying for her, crying for himself.

After a while she raised her head. 'You can let go now. Promise I won't run.' She slumped down onto the filthy mattress. 'Couldn't, even if I wanted to.'

Taro lay down next to her. She turned, and he put his arms round her loosely. She sighed, relaxing, and he listened to her breathing grow slow and even until he fell asleep as well.

CHAPTER FOURTEEN

Elarn was not sure if it was the wine or the sheer relief of having given a good performance, but last night's dreams had been a lot more enjoyable than her recent nightmares. She could not remember the last time she'd woken up feeling like this – actually she barely remembered the last time she had felt this way about anyone ... she'd not experienced this sort of quivery anticipation for seven years, in fact. Salik Vidoran was something special ... and, potentially, a very useful contact. Of course she had no intention of involving him directly in her real reason for coming to Vellern, not if she could avoid it, but just getting close to someone who knew how the City worked could make things much easier when the time came to complete her mission.

But dreams like last night's also left her a little uncomfortable – the residual guilt of a Salvatine upbringing was hard to shake. The feelings of shame and unease from her sensual dreams clung to her. She got up and took a long shower, dialled to a cooler setting than was quite comfortable, but even after the shower she was still too restless to practise, so she went out for a walk.

Her hotel was about a kilometre from the rimwards end of Lily Street and she set off briskly. Few people were about this early; she saw maintenance men working on one of the streetlights, and cleaner bots scooping up rubbish. She thought she should be safe enough in the Guest Quarter, but she kept her eyes open and gave the sidestreet entrances a wide berth.

The end of the Street was a disappointment. From the elevator Elarn had noticed that the Streets were open at the end, and she had hoped, illogically in retrospect, that she might be able to see down to the actual surface of the planet from there. Instead, a fence spanned the gap between the rimwards buildings, and an uncharacteristically polite notice on the pylons supporting the fence warned of a current that could cause serious injury or even death.

Looking through the man-made fence at the man-made forcedome reminded Elarn that she was in an artificial environment, enclosed and fragile. She turned on her heel and headed back to the hotel.

By the time she reached the Manor Park, breakfast was almost over. She forced herself to eat something, then returned to her room, determined to rehearse properly, but the com was chirping to say she had a message. For a giddy moment she thought it might be Salik, but instead Shamal Binu's overly made-up features sprang into life on the holo-plate.

'Elarn, darling, have you seen the reviews?' she gushed. 'Tremendous! I've attached links. Anyway, the reason I've commed you at such an outrageously early hour – and on what is a day of rest for you – oh yes, I forgot, well, regardless of your religious persuasion, I don't want you working too hard – anyway, darling Elarn, the most *fantastic* news: we've got the cathedral! Isn't that *utterly fabulous*? Day after tomorrow, evening gig – sorry, concert. This is the big one, so there's a rehearsal tomorrow. With a choir – real, live choristers! They'll do the *Requiem* – lovely piece, that – and a couple of others, largely up to you what. Anyway, you need to be there at eleven tomorrow morning for rehearsal, although I'm afraid you'll have to make your own way, my dear– I'm so rushed, you wouldn't believe it. Anyway, good luck, and we'll speak soon.'

Elarn sat down in the comfortable chair beside the bed, put the com onto wide display and checked the links. There were only two reviews, but both were positive.

Her manager on Khathryn had been nagging Elarn for years to do the occasional live concert, and he'd been understandably taken aback when his client had suddenly taken it into her head to go on tour, and not even locally, but in a different part of human space altogether, and starting in a system renowned less for its cultural history than for its uniquc and brutal system of government. Add to that Elarn's insistence that the tour be arranged at very short notice ... well, he was probably still questioning his client's sanity.

Elarn could hardly blame him. She'd had no choice but to use her professional life to get her to where she needed to be; she couldn't have afforded to travel to Vellern as a tourist and even if she had been willing to wait for a trading ship, it would have been slower as well as less comfortable, and the urgency of her mission had not allowed her that option. The tour might be a pretext, but it was still pleasing to be praised – though she was relieved that there were only two reviews, both in what looked to be obscure publications. Anyone casually perusing the entertainments listings would be unlikely to notice her name. That was good. Whatever Lia was doing now, Elarn doubted she had any active interest in the arts.

Lia ...

She wondered how Lia would react if she *did* find out Elarn was here. Someone, presumably Jarek, had done a good job of hiding the girl when she left Khathryn – it had taken her people years to track Lia down. Jarek, Elarn's impetuous brother, was at the bottom of it – he was the one who'd brought Lia to Khathryn in the first place, so really, this was all his fault. Presumably he had provided the information that led the Sidhe to her, though Elarn had no idea why he would decide to do that ... well, all that was immaterial now. The Sidhe would doubtless be watching all interstellar departures from the Tri-Confed system in case Lia – or Elarn herself – tried to escape.

And if Lia did find out that Elarn was here, what then? Seven years was a long time, and the child abomination would be an adult now, with a human face and alien motivations.

You cannot help but love us ... Elarn shivered. Before leaving Khathryn, Lia had come to say goodbye, perhaps even to ask forgiveness for the disruption she had caused, but she had seen Elarn flinch when she came into the room. Lia had looked at her sadly and said, 'I wish you could understand how it is: you cannot help but love us; we cannot help but use you.'

Elarn thought how much easier it would be if she could hate Lia, but while she could be appalled that she had formed an attachment to such a creature – albeit without knowing its true nature – she could not blame anyone but herself … or perhaps her foolish brother, wherever he was now. But if she actually found Lia and then could not kill her, she would be in a far worse position. She must act without hesitation or remorse. She had no choice. That was what she had to remember.

The com was chirping again. She hit the accept button, composing her face into a smile in case it was Salik.

It was Ando Meraint, looking mildly apologetic. 'Medame Reen, I'm sorry to disturb you, but I wanted to let you know that I have exhausted the usual research sources and have failed to find a match on the picture you gave me. There is one last thing I can try, and that's to check the private pay-to-access holo-libraries in case there's an image of her in any of them.'

How tempting to tell him not to bother, to give up now … Elarn sighed to herself; she had to explore all possibilities, for *they* would find out if she hadn't. 'Yes, please. I do have to be sure. Presumably that puts the cost up?'

'I'm afraid so, medame. I can't say exactly how much, but I'd estimate another twenty to thirty per cent. No need to pay now, you can settle up when I have the results of this last search.'

'And there aren't any other implications?'

He looked quizzical. 'There are no legal restrictions, of course – or is that not what you mean?'

'No. I'm concerned whether – hypothetically – the person being searched for might be alerted to the fact that someone is looking for them, once you start looking in more obscure places.'

He smiled. 'That's highly unlikely. These are libraries kept by individuals and private concerns; the chances are the people in the images were not even aware they were being recorded.'

'Then please do go ahead.'

'Thank you. I'll contact you if I find anything.'

Her personal funds were shrinking at an alarming rate, but then, money was no good to a dead person. She shut off that line of thought before fear could stir the scream into life. Instead, she stood up and started breathing deeply, then turned on the music and made herself start on a few basic scales to warm up her voice and to take her mind off the past. But it wasn't working; the scream was still there, ready to warp her music into something alien and terrifying. She turned the accompaniment off and sat down again. She knew she could give a good performance, she had proved that last night. Right now, she needed to do something completely different.

She had been here nearly two days and as yet had seen very little of Khesh City. Today might be a good day to investigate whatever passed for Kheshi culture. There must be some, somewhere, although what she had heard of Kheshi music spanned the spectrum from saccharine crooning to tuneless screeching without ever approaching good taste. Still, they had a strong tradition in the dramatic arts. Perhaps she should see a play.

And maybe she should also invest in a personal com. The pace of life here was so much faster than she was used to. It would mean Medame Binu could bother her, but the agent was obviously busy enough that she wasn't intruding on Elarn any more than was necessary to keep her functioning as a source of income. If she had a personal com, the info-broker could tell her at once if he had any news, though, God willing, the next call she got from him would be to say there was no trace of Lia anywhere in any records he had access to. And there was Salik. She would give the number to him, of course.

She had been half-watching the time out of the corner of her eye, subconsciously counting down the minutes till noon. Not that many now. It wasn't worth going out and risking missing his call.

However, there was something useful she could do while she waited, given her desire to get close to Consul Vidoran. She could try to find out more about him.

It didn't take long. Even using only the free com services, there was plenty on all the serving politicians in the Assembly. Shamal Binu had mentioned a trade deal, so Elarn followed the links to reports on a piece of legislation Salik had been involved in. During Yazil's last term hosting the Assembly, certain Yazil politicians had apparently passed some import/export laws that had meant financial benefits to certain Yazil territories. Salik had not repealed the legislation, but had extended it to cover Khesh City, though not the Kheshi territories dotted throughout the system. Luorna had been left out, and had suffered financially as a consequence.

Further digging into the Consul's background revealed that he had business interests in Khesh City – in such unromantic areas as waste collection, reclamation and building maintenance – which would benefit by this legislation. Just a few days after the Assembly took up residence in Khesh City, a Consul from Luorna had spotted the loophole, and had attempted to challenge Consul Vidoran over it. As he had been absent from the Assembly at that time, the Luornai objection was sustained, and moves were now being made to change the law – but not before Consul Vidoran had made a hefty profit for himself.

So, he had used his position for personal gain. But a random scan of other Consuls' files turned up numerous similar attempts to use the system for profit. He was apparently no better and no worse, just possibly a bit more successful. And, Elarn told herself, if she was seeing this here, then, by definition, all these— these *misdemeanours* had been found out and dealt with. If you played the system on Vellern, you did so in the knowledge that the system could turn round and bite you back. In fact, such accountability made a pleasant change from a culture where greed and errors of judgment were denied or blamed on scapegoats – the Khathryn way of things.

The thing she had a problem with was that the punishment for getting it wrong was *death*. Especially such a relatively trivial misdemeanour – compared with some his colleagues had got away with, by the looks of things. It had to be the timing, so close to the change of Assembly, and the fact that he had not been present to defend himself, that had put Consul Vidoran on the hot-list.

She was closing down the open files – it was gone midday – when something caught her eye. A couple of weeks ago, just after his return to Vellern, Yazil City had sent an operative of their League of Concord as 'liaison and honour guard' for Consul Vidoran. She remembered Salik's bodyguard, his cold gaze, the casual way he had broken that downsider's neck. Now she knew why: Scarrion was an agent of Yazil City, a Screamer. Elarn shuddered. Surely now, though, with the legislation that had earned Consul Vidoran a favour from Yazil City being repealed, their agent would be recalled? She opened searches on Scarrion, but in marked contrast to the information available on politicians – presumably to allow the people to choose who was to succeed and who was to die – there was surprisingly little on the agents who enforced the Concord. Her initial search turned up only unverified rumours. The best she could find was that the Screamer was in disgrace in his own City, and had applied for an extended sabbatical here, which had been granted by his League of Concord who – reading between the lines – were glad to be shot of him for a while.

The com chirped, and Elarn hit the pick-up key. The cold, disturbing data was replaced by the friendly face of Consul Vidoran.

Elarn insisted she would pay, but she let Salik Vidoran choose the venue. He directed the pedicab to a café on the edge of the Gardens where the diners sat at wooden tables under a canopy of trees. The ever-present bodyguard moved off to sit at a nearby table. Elarn found herself tuning out the section of the view that included him.

The menu was not extensive, but neither was it expensive. Elarn ordered a stir-fry while Salik opted for a chili pasty that was, he assured her, very bad for him. She offered to buy something special to drink, but he declined; he had to return to the Assembly in the afternoon. 'I'm being kept busy organising my own demotion,' he observed wryly.

They talked of more personal matters than they had at dinner last night. Elarn felt as though they had known each other for weeks, even months, certainly more than two days. Salik told her he had been born in Khesh City and his father had been a politician, who'd suffered the same fate he himself had so recently avoided. When he decided to follow in his father's footsteps, his mother had refused to speak to him again. She'd moved off Vellern to one of the Kheshi habitats. He was an only child – there being population restrictions on raising children in the Three Cities, another hidden rule, thought Elarn. He had been married briefly, but it had not worked out and he had lost touch with his ex-wife.

Elarn, recognising the parallels in her own life, found herself recounting details of her personal history she rarely even thought about. She explained never having married in terms of Khathryn's culture; under Salvatine law marriage was a lifelong commitment. Though there had been lovers, she had never met anyone she felt strongly enough about to want to make that commitment with. When he asked about family she said, 'My parents had their own prospecting company. Khathryn has a lot of natural resources, plenty for everyone, if you're willing to take the risks to get it. My mother had a talent for spotting market openings and my father was a geologist and natural risk-taker. They made a good team. I spent the first ten years of my life in temporary apartments, on rigs, on board ships, all over the place, but they always promised we'd get somewhere stable when we could afford it, and we did. I still live in the house my mother had built for us, and the money they made allowed me to launch my career as a singer.'

'Presumably they've retired now?'

She sighed. 'They died when I was twenty, victims of Khathryn's weather – or at least that's what the inquest concluded, that the rig accident that killed them was due to the weather. Lack of maintenance by the previous owners or possible sabotage by business rivals were never even considered.' Though it was nearly two decades ago, Elarn was still angry about how her parents' deaths had been swept under the carpet of religious hypocrisy. She took a sip of her drink to cover her outburst, half wishing she had ordered alcohol of some kind.

Salik said with quiet sympathy, 'You're not a Salvatine, are you?'

'No. I'm not. Does it show? My agent would be annoyed.' She looked away, across the Gardens, skimming her gaze past Scarrion eating with one eye on his master, to a small open arena where a pair of jugglers were entertaining the strolling crowds. 'I do respect – even envy – those who have genuine faith, but my belief was already wavering when I lost my parents. That was the final blow.'

'Doesn't being agnostic put you in a minority? I had heard that that non-believers can face discrimination on theocracies like Khathryn.'

Elarn, embarrassed at showing her feelings, was glad of the chance to steer the conversation back onto more abstract topics. 'A little, but I've managed. I suppose it must seem odd to you, a whole world professing one belief system. I think a culture like Khathryn's only works in a hostile environment. People need a constant feeling of their own insignificance to submit willingly to a divine authority.'

'Not so strange, really. Your world has the Salvatine creed. Mine has the Concord.'

She looked back at him and said, 'Yes, I suppose so.' Then she added, without thinking, 'Though the Salvatine church gave up burning its heretics before the Protectorate.' Seeing the shadow that passed across his face she put her hand to her mouth. 'Oh God, that was a terribly insensitive thing to say, after what almost happened to you! Please, I'm so sorry.'

He shook his head, and when she dropped her hand to the table he covered it with his own. 'It's all right. I knew the risks, as they say. I don't mind talking about it. In fact I find it quite therapeutic. I could do with an unbiased and sympathetic listener – though you must stop me if I rant.'

'Please, rant away.'

The warmth of his touch stayed with her when he withdrew his hand. She wanted to touch him back, though she lacked the courage that the combination of wine and adrenalin had given her last night. But something had changed; this sharing of personal admissions had moved their friendship onto another level. Elarn wished she were better, or at least more practised, at interpreting relationships.

As he talked about his career and its recent dramatic disintegration Elarn reminded herself to try to glean what useful facts she could from the information he was offering, but she kept finding herself gazing at his long-fingered hands, wondering how it would feel to hold them, and his sensuous lips, wondering how they would feel on her skin.

As they stood to go he said, 'I hope I wasn't hogging the conversation too much. I took the fact that you didn't fall asleep or get up and walk off as a signal I could carry on, but I expect you were just being polite.'

She laughed. 'No, I really was interested. This place is amazing.' *As are you*, she thought.

He smiled at her. 'I hope you don't mind me saying this, but you're a breath of air in a closed room, Elarn.' He offered his arm to lead to her to the pedicab stand, and she took it, feeling as weak and foolish as a girl.

As they rode down Lily Street she turned her head, knowing the time was right, and felt his lips on hers. His kiss was as gentle as rain, but it awoke something long hidden inside her. She was happy in the moment and nothing else mattered. When she climbed down, he said apologetically, 'I really wish I didn't have to go back to the cursed Assembly this afternoon.'

'So do I,' she said softly.

'Can I call you this evening when I get out?'

'Yes. Please do.'

Back in her room she resisted the temptation to stare out the window to see if she could spot his departing pedicab. Instead she made herself sit in the chair by the bed and turn the com on.

Something was nagging at the back of her mind, something Salik had said at lunch, but when she tried to chase the thought, all she saw was his face. It didn't help that the com was still set to scan for data on him. She reset it to search for events she could attend this afternoon. She should get out, do something unrelated to her mission, her music or to him. She needed a distraction, something to give herself distance, objectivity—

Because she was falling in love.

She had come to Vellern to cause another's death, and now she was falling in love. This should not be happening.

But it felt so good.

CHAPTER FIFTEEN

Thirst woke him. Taro untangled himself from Arel, who murmured something but didn't wake. He slithered off the lumpy mattress, managed to stand upright on the second attempt, and lurched down the hall to get a drink and find the nearest piss-pot. There was no one else around and, from the look of the light coming up through the netted gap, it was still early. Good. He had an errand to run before he went topside. Not that he wanted to do anything except curl up and fall asleep again. He felt like his head was coming loose, his guts had been knotted and he'd been beaten up. Actually he *had* been beaten up, not that he blamed the poor bitch.

He left the waterskin by the mattress; she'd need it when she woke up.

Though he reckoned everyone in this part of the Undertow should be able to hear the thudding in his head, he took it slow and careful, and managed to creep out of Limnel's homespace without being seen. Once in the mazeways he sped up a little; not too much: in this state he could easily trip and end up taking the fall. Out in the relatively fresh air the headache began to ease off a bit, but the shakes were coming on now. Fuck, the comedown on this stuff was fierce. The withdrawal would be a killer but he'd have to face it sooner or later. Even if Limnel did have an ever-lasting supply of dust he was happy to lavish on his troupe-mates – which he doubted – Taro had no intention of living out his days as a slave to chemicals.

He slowed as he approached his old homespace. It felt odd to be in the familiar mazeways again. He should've done this days ago. As the last of her lineage it really was his duty to pass his line-mother's gun on to another Angel, or return it to the Minister. Until last night, when it'd provided a useful lie to save his skin, he'd been too busy just trying to survive to give this obligation much thought. Now he needed to make the lie true before it got him in more trouble.

The shit-gardeners who'd taken over his homespace had already replaced the green curtain over the doorway with a door of wood and plastic, but it didn't stop the smell of composting shit drifting down the mazeway. Taro rapped on the door, then waited until a child's voice asked who he was. When he said he was Malia's line-child a boy of about ten pulled the door open, looking puzzled, then alarmed. Taro suspected he didn't look his best right now.

Taro, breathing through his mouth, said, 'Hoi there. I'm just 'ere to collect somethin' Malia left.'

The boy called back inside. A woman, his mother, maybe, came forward. She didn't invite Taro in. 'I'm sorry but when we claimed this space we gave you the chance to take whatever you could carry. We've traded most of what was left for a new cutter,' she said. She shuffled and looked away, apologetic-like.

'Not her gun?'

'Of course not!' She sounded shocked. 'We respect the Angels. We know the gun's the property of the City.'

'So could I maybe 'ave it now?'

'You'd be welcome to it, if we had it.' Seeing Taro blanch, she said quickly, 'It wasn't here when we moved in. We thought you'd already passed it on.' She looked worried. 'We'd help if we could, but we don't know anything.'

After a moment Taro collected himself. 'All right,' he told the woman, 'thanks.'

Only one person could've stolen his line-mother's gun: Scarrion. For a Screamer to have an Angel's weapon was sacrilege. The Minister needed to know about this.

Taro started back along the mazeways heading rimwards, but from the look of the light below it'd soon be time to join Keron's merry band of sluts. If he went topside now and made the call, he could be on Soft

Street when they came up, which meant Limnel would still get a full day's work out of him. But it'd also show Keron up if he just turned up like that, plus if he looked even half as bad as he felt, he doubted he'd pull many punters today. Better to head back to Limnel's, get cleaned up a bit, have a drink, perhaps even some food, if his belly would accept it. He'd just have to hope Keron would let him call the Minister before he started work. He changed course.

Halfway along a wide mazeway with patched nets he felt a prickling between his shoulders. He spun round, almost falling before managing to grab a support rope. He blinked, firstly to clear his vision, then to confirm what he was seeing.

A woman wearing a red-and-black panelled coat stood no more than three paces from him. She had dark hair, and the most beautiful face he'd ever seen. Taro stared at her, his mouth open, his mind blank.

When she spoke her voice was calm, soft. 'I have been told that Malia's son wanted to see me. Would that be you?'

Taro nodded, then finding his voice, said, 'Aye, lady. That's me ...' He hesitated, then asked, 'Do I have the honour of addressin' the Angel Nual?'

'So you are not entirely without manners.' Her eyes were dark and hypnotic, the proportions of her face almost dangerously perfect. 'I was told you had something for me.'

'I ... thought I did,' Taro's voice slipped. 'Me line-mother's gun. But—' He could hardly tell her it was most likely in the hands of an agent from another City. He gulped and spread his hands. '— but I don't 'ave it.'

'So I see.' She sounded more intrigued than angry. 'You lied. You know that it is a sin to lie to an Angel. A sin punishable by death.'

Oh, he knew. His hasty words last night had made his life forfeit at least twice over. He said nothing.

Nual raised one hand. The blade slid out slowly and she watched it emerge as though it wasn't part of her but some strange and beautiful thing she'd unexpectedly come across. She let the blade slide back and raised her head. 'But I have had enough of killing. I would rather talk.'

She took three quick steps to close the distance between them, until Taro stood toe to toe with her, feeling as though he was impaled on her gaze. After giving a tiny wrinkle of her nose – presumably at the state he was in – she smiled, making Taro revise his estimate of her age down by five years, and said, 'And I think I'm going to buy you something to eat first. You look like you need it.' She put an arm round Taro's waist and pulled him towards her. Taro froze, confused and, against all sense or reason, aroused. She gave no sign of noticing that, just said, 'Put your arms round my neck.'

It dawned on him what she was about to do just before she stepped off the mazeway. He grabbed for her.

Suddenly he was falling, plunging towards his death.

No, not plunging. Floating, held in place by the Angel. Except for his stomach. That was still plunging.

'If you throw up on me, I *will* drop you.' Her voice was soft in his ear, as though she was whispering endearments rather than threats.

He swallowed hard and pressed his face into her shoulder until the nausea subsided. She smelled like the Gardens at dawn. Her body was warm and firm against his, relaxed save for the occasional flutter of tension along her thighs as she controlled their flight. Most downsiders believed the Angels' flight was City magic, but Malia'd once told Taro that they had tiny machines buried deep in their muscles that allowed them to ignore gravity.

When he looked up again he found they were flying below uncut vanes. For one confused and horrifying moment he thought she was taking him to Heart of the City to be punished for his recent mistakes, but then he got his bearings; the spine was off to the left. They were flying under the State Quarter.

After a while he spotted water-traps ahead. Nets started appearing below some of the open vanes, then full mazeways. He was just trying to work out whether he really did recognise the colours on the 'traps from last night when they shot upwards and came out in the open area in front of the Exquisite Corpse. Nual manoeuvred them over the ledge and murmured, 'You can let go now.'

Taro obeyed, though his legs didn't want to take his weight. He was still trying to get his knees under control when Nual pulled the curtain aside and swept into the bar. He followed her in.

At this time of day the Exquisite Corpse was deserted. Nual gestured at a table and went into the back, presumably to find the alien. Taro hoped she wouldn't mind if they sat on the upper level; the view through the floor on the lower level made his balls retract and his stomach turn somersaults. He shuffled across the transparent floor, holding onto chair backs for support, careful not to look down.

She returned a few minutes later, accompanied by the barkeep. Solo put a loaded tray down in front of Taro. Nual sat opposite him. 'Eat,' she said. 'I don't want you passing out on me.'

Taro ate. At first he wasn't sure his stomach could handle food, but after the first few mouthfuls, he gave it his full attention. It was good; really good: cold meat pie, pickles, dried fruit and fresh bread, with a beaker of something sharp and refreshing that made his tongue tingle. He could feel Nual watching him, but she didn't say anything. Finally he sat back and, before he could stop it, gave a loud belch.

She looked amused. 'You live with that gang near your line-mother's old home now – Limnel, isn't it, the leader's name?'

'That's right, lady.' He wished she hadn't reminded him about Limnel: the boss would be well pissed at him for missing the start of his shift. Ah, screw Limnel. He was on City business, back with the Angels. Limnel was nothing more than a jumped-up hustler.

Nual's smile became a frown. 'So, why would a boy I've never met, who lives in a part of the Undertow I've hardly visited and works for a small-time criminal I know almost nothing about tell me that his line-mother wanted to pass her gun on to me? A gun that he doesn't actually have.' She sounded puzzled.

As well she might be. At least she was giving him a chance to explain. 'I panicked,' he told her honestly. 'I needed a reason to be here last night.'

'And why *were* you here last night? You're a long way from home and you bluffed your way in here with colours you no longer have the right to wear: a risky move, particularly here.'

He wasn't going to lie to her. 'It was 'cause of the Minister. I'm workin' for the Minister.'

She leaned forward and asked mildly, 'Doing what?'

'He …' He hesitated, then decided lying at this stage would just get him killed. 'He asked me to find out what you was up to.' There. He'd screwed up again. The Minister had said to watch her, not have break-fast with her.

Her voice became chill as steel. 'Ah. So you're his latest spy.'

Taro said quietly, 'Aye, lady.'

She sighed, then continued more casually, 'He gets concerned for my well-being now and again. Or perhaps he thinks I'm about to go rogue. What do you think, Taro? Should he call feud on me?'

'I don't know, lady.'

She dropped her voice. 'Ordering my fellow Angels to kill me would make his life simpler. Assuming I let them.'

Taro said nothing. Malia had never killed another Angel. She believed having to turn on her own was one of the nastiest aspects of her calling.

She continued, her tone casual-like, but still with a cold edge just beneath the surface, 'After all, he's got an excuse now. I've failed. After eighteen perfect removals, I finally miss my target – so I must be losing it. Why else would I suddenly fail?'

The food turned acid in Taro's stomach. She knew it had been him in Confederacy Square. ''Cause of me,' he whispered, ''cause I fucked up yer shot.'

'Aye. You did. I saw you, through the sights of my gun; I knew you must be the Minister's agent. That made sense. But why did you disrupt my removal of Consul Vidoran?'

That was why she hadn't killed him yet. She knew he'd smoked her rep and she wanted to know why. Then she'd kill him. Or maybe not. He doubted she often bought meals for her victims.

'I din't mean to get in the way,' he said quickly, 'I was tryin' to get to 'is bodyguard.'

She frowned. 'The militia-woman I killed by accident?'

Taro looked down at the empty plate in front of him. 'No. The Screamer.'

'And what did you have against the Screamer? Something more than loyalty to your City, presumably.'

Taro forced himself to meet the Angel's eyes. 'He killed me line-mother.'

She nodded slowly. 'I see. And so you want to kill him.'

'Aye. I swore it.' Taro felt the prickle of imminent tears and dug the heel of his hand into his eyes to stop them, instead sending spikes of pain lancing through his head. *Crying now, of all times. Get a grip!*

'What happened?' Nual's voice was soft, almost tender.

Taro swallowed sharply. 'The Screamer, Scarrion, he tricked me, followed me into the Undertow, back to me homespace. He shot Malia. I can't let him get away with that. I gotta kill him.'

She nodded, then asked, 'Have you ever killed anyone, Taro?'

'I … No. I never 'ad to.'

'Trust me, murder is overrated. It usually causes more problems than it solves. Avoid it where possible. Did you tell the Minister how your line-mother died?'

'Aye. He said it weren't up to me to decide who he called feud on.' His dismay flashed into anger. 'He said I should forget Scarrion and get on with the job he gave me. Like I can just forget what that fucker did!' Taro clamped his mouth shut. This was no time to lose his temper, especially when Nual appeared so calm – a little crazy, maybe, but calm.

'Work for me,' she said, ignoring his outburst.

'What?' This was the last thing he'd expected.

'You have fire and honesty – despite your lies – and a desire to see right done. The arrogant old goat has got you chasing me anyway. Allow me to give you messages for him and report back to me on what he is up to. What do you say, Taro sanMalia?'

You don't say no to an Angel, even one who calls the Minister an arrogant old goat. And when he looked into her eyes he couldn't imagine himself ever refusing her anything.

'I'd be honoured, lady,' he found himself saying.

'Thank you, Taro. Can I find you at Limnel's if I need you?'

'Aye. Or on Soft Street.'

'I have no intention of spending more time topside than is necessary right now,' she said firmly. 'That is why I have recruited you.'

'As you wish, lady. Limnel can send someone to fetch me.' The boss would hate that – but he wouldn't be able to refuse. 'How do I find you again?'

'When you need to contact me you can come here and leave a message with Solo. If it's urgent she will come to get me.'

Taro looked from the Angel to the gangly alien busy wiping down tables on the lower level. 'It's a she? I didn't know—'

Nual laughed. She had a beautiful laugh. 'Aye, Solo is female, at the moment. And she likes you. You bring out her maternal instinct, which is particularly strong right now.' She raised her voice. 'Isn't it, my friend?'

Solo looked up. 'I listen to my body as ever, Nual.' She turned her flat golden gaze on Taro. 'Even though you lie, I think you are a good person, Taro, and a survivor. We orphans must stick together, no?'

'Aye, I s'pose.' He needed all the friends he could get, even ones who looked like they were made up of bits that weren't meant to fit together. And it wasn't Solo's fault she looked so freaky. Humans probably looked pretty freaky to her. 'Sorry I lied to you,' he said, feeling contrite.

'You are forgiven.' The barkeep started to turn, then stopped and put her head on one side. 'Perhaps when you come back, you can pass the time waiting for Nual by cleaning my fryer. It is not a job for a person with fur.'

Between the alien's lack of body-language and the flat tone of the voice-box, Taro had no idea whether she meant that as a threat or a joke. He smiled back anyway. It couldn't be worse than scraping out a water-trap. 'Right, I c'n do that, when I come back.'

Solo nodded – it looked like another learnt gesture, like when she had beckoned to him last night – and turned back to her work.

Nual asked, 'How do you make your reports to the Minister, Taro?'

'I com him every mornin' from a public booth.' Though Nual probably had a personal com it wouldn't work down here. Besides, even assuming Nual let him use it, he wasn't sure how impressed the Minister would be if Taro called from the com of the person he was meant to be spying on. 'I should get topside an' do that soon. He'll be wonderin' what's 'appened to me.'

'Do you know the ways topside to the Merchant Quarter?'

'No. No, I don't.' Shit and blood, the drugs had addled his brain. For a moment he'd forgotten where he was. He would have to cross the Undertow before he came to any topside exits that he knew.

She stood, pushing back her chair. 'In that case, I had better take you.'

CHAPTER SIXTEEN

The demons are coming.

She can hear them, in the next room. She huddles in the corner of the wardrobe, muttering a child's rhyme to cloud her mind. It won't be enough. They will still find her. They have travelled light-years to find her and they will never give up.

They do not look like demons. They wear human faces, but their hearts are black as space and cold as ice. When they pull her from her hiding place, she will have to answer every question they ask with perfect and honest truth. There is no point in lying when your questioner can see into your soul.

Something shrieks. An alarm.

Elarn woke with a start, almost falling from the chair.

The com, screen tuned to dark blue on power-save, was chirping. She thumbed the control on the arm of the chair, hitting accept on her second attempt. Ando Meraint's face appeared, bright as day and large as life. He focused on her, and looked dismayed. 'I'm sorry, Medame Reen, I've obviously chosen a bad time. Shall I—?'

'Yes, sorry,' she managed, still caught up in her dream, 'I— Can I call you back?'

'Of course, medame. I'll look forward to it.' The com went back to comforting blue.

Elarn, heart pounding, pulled herself upright in the seat. She hadn't meant to fall asleep – perhaps, she thought bitterly, it was her subconscious, insisting she got her daily reminder of why she was here. What had she been doing? Looking up distractions ... except that was over an hour ago. There was hardly any point in going anywhere now. She might as well call the infobroker back – hopefully he would be about to tell her that he couldn't find Lia – and wait for Salik's call.

There was something about Salik ... she remembered it now, the thing that had been bothering her just before she dropped off to sleep. Meraint might be able to help her there too. She called him back.

'Medame Reen,' he greeted her. 'Sorry to have disturbed you earlier. I've got some good news.' Elarn wouldn't have thought so from the look on his face.

'You've found Lia?' She tried not to let her expression change.

'Not by name. But I've found what my software states is a ninety-eight point nine per cent match to the image you provided. It was in a private gallery, one of the last I looked at. There are several sad individuals out there who devote their time to collecting images of the— well, it's not exactly illegal to record these people, of course, but it is discouraged.' He was actually squirming.

'What people?' she asked, curious despite herself. 'What are you on about?'

'It might be simpler if I send you the file and you can decide for yourself whether it's her. Do you authorise payment of the amount on the bottom of the screen and a data transfer to your com?'

'Yes, yes, of course.' She thumbed the control pad to confirm her ID. His discomfort might be a good sign: it probably wasn't Lia at all. And while she had him on the line, she should utilise his service for her other concern. 'Sirrah Meraint, there's something else you might be able to help me with.'

'Of course, medame.' He did not look particularly happy at the prospect of more paid work.

'How complete are the public records on politicians' financial and business activities?'

He looked surprised. 'Very, medame. The Concord relies on it.'

'I would like you to check something for me, concerning Consul Salik Vidoran.'

An odd look passed over his face. 'Consul Vidoran? I should think there's more than enough on him on the public com.'

'There is,' Elarn agreed, 'but I believe he was out of the City when things came to a head regarding his recent political mistake. I would like to know where he was.'

'Where he was?' The infobroker echoed.

'Yes. When he left Vellern.' Salik had mentioned over lunch that he had been attending to business matters on one of the Kheshi habitats, but according to the records she had checked that morning, he had no business interests outside Vellern. 'I need to know where he went and what he did. Is that something you could find out for me?'

He paused, then said, 'I should think so. I may have to access files outside the Three Cities; can I get back to you on the cost?'

'Of course.'

He looked unenthusiastic at taking this job, but, thought Elarn a little bitterly, he could always charge her extra if it inconvenienced him. It could simply be an omission, or perhaps she had misheard what Salik had said; whatever, she wanted to be certain she could trust him before she let herself fall any further. After all, he was a politician.

She started to get up, then sat again. A *file received* message flashed at the bottom of the com: the file that might prove Lia was here. She found herself tempted, for a moment, to pray, but made do with hoping fervently the image was not her missing ward.

She hit play.

The file was untitled, save for a date, just under ten weeks ago. So if it was Lia, she was probably still here. The clip was a flatscreen recording no more than ten seconds long. From the quality and angle, it looked to have been shot from a cheap stealth-recorder, probably eye-ware. There was no soundtrack but a line of text scrolled across the bottom of the image as it played out.

It showed an outdoor café in early evening, the white plastic chairs and tables filled with tired, happy shoppers with bags piled round their feet. The image lost focus slightly as it zoomed in on a figure sitting by herself. At first her face was visible only as a pale crescent. She wore a black coat or cloak and her dark hair was worn in a long plait. The woman shifted slightly in her chair, then reached out and lifted something to her lips – a glass in a silver holder. She turned, perhaps looking for a waiter, so that she was in three-quarters profile. Elarn's throat closed as she recognised those fine, delicate features, those luminous eyes. Then the woman shifted all the way round, her brows drawing together in a frown. She stared directly at the camera and started to open her mouth.

The recording ended.

Elarn ordered the com to play the sequence again. This time she watched the text. Statistics, names, lots of question marks. But one name hooked her and, as she watched the turn of the pale cheek and saw the depth of the dark eyes, Elarn's alarm blossomed into fear. For the first time since she had come to this awful City she realised how hopeless her mission was.

That was Lia. And Lia was an Angel.

CHAPTER SEVENTEEN

Taro closed his eyes, let his head loll back and listened to the wind. He dreamed he was a child again, cradled in his line-mother's arms as she flew across the Undertow for medicine to cure his fever.

Except this wasn't Malia. Malia was dead.

He opened his eyes. They were nearing the edge of the City.

Nual murmured, 'Hold tight. Topside gravity will kick in as soon as we fly over the disc.' He adjusted his grip and pressed himself closer to her. He didn't want this flight to end, but she was already spiralling upwards in a long lazy arc. When the maze of sidestreets swung into view below, she dropped sharply. The wind whipped Taro's braids back from his face. Gravity clutched at him, trying to pull him from her arms. As they became heavier she had to work harder to keep their flight steady. He felt her breathing speed up. Then she swung to one side and they were over Chance Street, the ground coming up way too fast. At the last moment she slowed their descent and they touched down gently, though the impact still curdled Taro's belly and bruised his knees.

When he kept his arms round her neck she whispered, firmly but not unkindly, 'You need to let me go now.'

He unclasped his hands and stumbled back.

'I only came topside to make sure you got here safely. I have to return below,' she said, and kicked off, flying back up into the glaring orange sky. Taro forced himself not to stare after her.

Chance Street was still quiet, though holos of dice, gaming wheels and statistics played over some of the bars and casinos. At the sight of a downsider being dropped from the sky by an Angel, the few rollers who were on the Street had scurried into the safety of the nearest buildings.

Fine. They wouldn't be bothering him then. He staggered forward.

The bright light of the open Street hurt his already delicate head and his muscles felt weak as water. Looked like he would get the chance to kick his new habit soon enough: Limnel was likely to be well pissed that he hadn't turned up for work this morning, so not much chance of a treat for him tonight. No point stressing about that now. He'd deal with it when it happened.

He shuffled to the com booths at the side of the Street, hugging himself and avoiding eye contact with the few people who risked looking in his direction.

In the booth he went through the usual routine, but he was barely connected when the Minister's voice cut in and ordered, 'Stay right where you are.'

Taro was happy to. He leaned against the cool plastic of the booth and waited. He'd just rest here for a while, then go out and find somewhere to wait for the Minister—

A loud rap sounded near his head. Taro jumped and looked down. The Minister lowered his hand. Taro ducked out and followed the Minister to a nearby bench. The leader of the Kheshi League produced a handkerchief and brushed the seat clean before sitting down. Taro stayed standing, crossing his arms and focusing on the Minister's highly polished shoes, while trying not to sway too badly.

'Oh, just sit down before you fall down,' said the Minster.

Taro sat, though it felt freaky to be sitting side-by-side with his master.

'Well?' asked the Minister after a moment.

'Sirrah, I found Nual.'

'You *found* her? My instructions were to find out *about* her. But that is good news, under the circumstances.'

'She said—' Taro gulped. Agreeing to work for Nual was one thing, but conveying her words to the Minister was another thing. 'Sirrah, she said if there's anythin' you want to tell her, you can tell me an' I'll make sure she hears it.'

'Using my messenger against me? Typical!' the Minister muttered.

'That wretched girl is a law unto herself. I suppose I should be glad that she has decided to trust you even that far. Must be your innocent charm.'

'I wouldn't know, sirrah. But there's somethin' else.'

'What else? You have, technically, completed the mission I gave you.'

'I think Scarrion's got Malia's gun.'

The Minister turned to stare at Taro, and Taro edged back on the bench.

'I think he stole Malia's gun,' he repeated.

'And why am I only now hearing this?'

Taro recoiled from the Minister's uncharacteristic anger. 'I'm sorry, sirrah! When I asked you to call feud on the Screamer I wasn't thinkin' straight. I was too busy being upset that he'd killed me line-mother. I din't wonder *why* he did it.'

'You think he killed her for her weapon?'

'I don't know, but it's possible, ain't it?'

'Oh yes, possible and logical. It would explain why he took the risk of entering the Undertow. I suspect that he might not even have planned to kill Malia; he just decided to take the chance when it was offered. That would be in character.'

'He can't use the gun, though, can he? I mean, the trigger-pad'll zap 'im when he tries to fire it.'

'In theory, yes, but no security is unbreakable. And if he has gone to all the effort of acquiring it, it is likely that he has the means to overcome its security, which could be very bad news for all of us. We can only hope that we are being unduly pessimistic.' The Minister stared thoughtfully down the Street for a few seconds, then looked back at Taro and said, 'However, dismaying as this news is, my original reason for coming to see you in person remains unchanged.' He reached inside his immaculately tailored jacket and produced a rectangle of clear plastic about the size of Taro's little finger. A thin sliver of black ran through the centre of the plastic. Taro felt a chill run down his spine. 'I see from your expression that you know what this is.'

'Aye, sirrah.' He'd seen a few dataspikes, though he'd never used one. Usually the central core, where the data was stored, was dark grey. He'd only seen a black one once. Malia had left it on the floor of the common-room in their homespace. When she'd returned after carrying out the orders it contained, she'd flung it through the nets to the ground below. The 'spike contained formal orders, encrypted and readable only by the Angel they were intended for, to perform a removal.

'Take this straight to Nual. Do not give it to anyone else, do not show it to anyone else, do not tell anyone else you have it. Understand?'

'Aye, sirrah.' Taro took the dataspike and, without looking at it, stashed it in the pocket inside his jacket. It felt heavier than he expected.

'I think it should get her attention. But just in case she is still being uncooperative, you can tell her, from me, that my patience is all used up. No more excuses. This is her last chance. She will obey these orders, or she will come to tell me in person why not.

'If she does neither, I will call feud on her.'

CHAPTER EIGHTEEN

Ando Meraint marked off the flashing reminder to phone Elarn Reen and added a new entry – *Research recent whereabouts of Consul Vidoran* – then stared at the screen.

He wished he had never taken the job. There was stuff going on in that woman's life that he would prefer not to find out about. Perhaps he should have just lied to her, told her he hadn't found her lost daughter, refused any further work and passed on what he had to the wretched Screamer. But that would have gone against his personal code: he traded in information, not lies. Besides, he liked her. And if he refused this new job, she might go elsewhere. Leaving aside the loss of credit, if the Screamer was keeping tabs on her movements he would know Meraint had not co-operated. Of course, he should have already commed the Yaziler to tell him what he had found out, but that could wait. Meraint trusted the encryption routines on his com line, and the single bug the Screamer had left under a shelf in the alcove had been easy enough to find and disable by 'accidentally' banging the shelf. A more efficient operative might have left more, or hidden them better, but Meraint's daily sweep had not turned up anything else. Like his encryption software, his bug sweepers were top of the range.

So the Screamer had no way of knowing what information had passed between Meraint and Medame Reen other than by Meraint telling him. And he planned to tell him only what he absolutely had to, just enough to keep the Screamer off his back.

He'd spend an hour or so on one of his tasks, then call it a day. A news agency paid him to correlate removal statistics and extrapolate future trends. If they knew who the most likely targets were, they could prepare their reports in advance and be the first to dish the dirt when a new name popped up on the hot-list. He had a pretty good hit-rate, which is why they kept him on retainer. He hadn't predicted Consul Vidoran, though.

It wasn't the most interesting or challenging work, and when the door chime went only a few minutes later he was glad of the distraction. Then he checked the cameras. Though the figure outside had his head bowed, Meraint recognised him by his ostentatious clothes and long fair hair. For a moment he considered not answering, or maybe even heading for the back door, but running away would only make things worse in the long run. If he kept the Screamer happy, he'd have no reason to hurt him, or, more importantly, his family.

He pressed the buzzer, allowing his visitor in.

The Yaziler took his time, sauntering up the steps and entering with the same indifferent grace he'd displayed on his first visit. This time, however, he came straight over to sit in one of the comfortable chairs on the far side of the desk. Surely he realised that Meraint had fixed the office's defences? Of course he did. He was making a point of not caring. It was his way of reminding Meraint that he wasn't acting alone. Meraint had called up everything he could on the Screamer's activities after his first visit and from the look of it he was still very much in the pay of Consul Vidoran.

Scarrion – though he had not deigned to introduce himself when they met, it had been easy to extract his name from the records – crossed his legs and leaned back in the chair. He raised one eyebrow quizzically.

Meraint cleared his throat. 'What do you want?'

The Screamer sat silently for a couple of seconds before answering, 'You haven't called. I was in the area. I decided to check you hadn't lost the number I sent you.' He delivered each statement crisply, like a lawyer stating the facts that would damn the defendant.

'I still have it. I was waiting until I had something of substance to report. A new development, so to speak.'

'And? Are there any "new developments"?'

He could lie … no, he couldn't. Not while those cold, dead eyes regarded him like a piece of inferior meat. 'Actually, yes, and as soon as I finished this job I was going to call you—'

'Ah.' Scarrion smiled unpleasantly. 'Perhaps I didn't manage to impress on you the importance and urgency of my request.' He frowned to himself. 'I think I used the phrase "at once". I didn't use physical violence, or explicit threats to your loved ones. That's probably where I went wrong. Are your daughters really identical in *every* physical attribute, Sirrah Meraint? And how is your wife? Debts make one so vulnerable ...'

'All right, all right, I understand. I've managed to find a probable match on the search I was doing for Elarn Reen.'

'Show me.'

'It's not very long and it's only a probable.' He called up the original of the clip he'd sent to Medame Reen, set it running and turned the screen to face the Screamer. The Screamer watched the short sequence impassively, eyes flicking between the recording and the stats added by the sad little freak whose library Meraint had raided to get the clip. The data showed possible names and estimated kill-rates for the Angel in the recording; three possibilities, based on the physical characteristics recorded by the voyeur. Meraint had an idea that one of the names was the same Angel who had failed to kill Consul Vidoran the day before yesterday. If this was news to the Screamer, he gave no sign.

At the end of the clip he said blandly, 'I'll need a copy of that.'

Meraint swung the screen back and requested a copy of the file. From the corner of his eye he noticed the Screamer was sitting back comfortably again. Bastard was probably feeling pleased with himself, confident that his renewed threats were enough to ensure Meraint's full co-operation from now on. But he hadn't asked whether Medame Reen had seen the file yet, and he was not about to volunteer that information, nor was he intending to mention her question about the Screamer's own master. That Yazil bastard wasn't as smart as he thought he was. Meraint felt a fearful excitement at his secret defiance. He wiped the sweat from his palms and ejected the dataspike into a waiting holder, then handed it over and waited for the Screamer to leave.

His visitor pocketed the 'spike and leaned forward to look Meraint in the eye. He flinched but held the assassin's gaze. 'And if Medame Reen calls you again, you'll be certain to tell me?'

'Of course.' *Not unless I think you've found a way of checking up on me, I won't.*

Scarrion swivelled out of the chair and headed for the door. Meraint half expected another chilling threat as he left, but the assassin just waved a hand casually and slammed the door behind him. Meraint called up his surveillance. He wanted to make sure the murderous little shit was really leaving. Not for the first time he had cause to be grateful for the extra credit he'd shelled out for the panoramic option on his external cameras.

As soon as he thought he was out of surveillance range, the Screamer stopped, looked round and got his com out.

No doubt he was calling his master.

CHAPTER NINETEEN

Taro's plan was simple enough: go back to the Exquisite Corpse and ask Solo to find Nual. Being given orders for a removal from the Minister's own hand qualified as urgent, so the alien should be happy to find her friend.

The plan relied on him being able to find his way back to the Corpse. Chance Street was sunwise of his normal haunts, so if he got into the Undertow from the sidestreets round here he was already part of the way there. He'd only used this way down a couple of times and it took him a while to find it again. Once downside, he headed hubwards, looking out for the point where he could pick up the route Federin had used last night. It might've been the detour to avoid a pair of squabbling meatbabies who weren't going to give way no matter what colours he wore, or the way the midday light put the Undertow in the shadow of the City, or the fact that he wasn't at his best at the moment, but he got all the way to the hubwards end of the mazeways without finding the turning he was looking for. There was nothing ahead of him now but the uncut vanes of the no-man's land leading to the Heart of the City.

He didn't have a tether on him, and he wasn't going to risk putting his head below the mazeways to get his bearings without one, so he retraced his steps. Time to do what he should've done in the first place, if he'd been thinking straight: head back sinwards, find Federin and ask him to guide him again.

It was mid-afternoon by the time he reached the water-trader's neighbourhood. He was just about to turn the corner into the mazeway leading up to Fenya's homespace when someone stepped out in front of him. He looked up to see Resh's familiar leer. 'Boss thought yer might come back this way, so 'e sent us to check. And 'ere ya are, Angel-boy.'

Taro glanced back over his shoulder. A young lag was coming up the mazeway behind him. The boy had a boltgun and a shit-eating grin, obviously pleased at being asked to help bring in the bad-boy slut.

Resh didn't have his flecks out; perhaps he could barge past him and run for Fenya's. He quickly dismissed that option: even if he managed to knock Resh off the mazeway, the other lag might shoot him in the back before he got to the corner.

He spread his hands to show he wasn't going for his flecks and said, 'Hoi, Resh, how's it hangin'?' He resisted the urge to add, 'Raped any more junkies recently?'

'Lot better now we got yer. Reckoned we'd be 'ere till nightfall on the chance ya came this way, but we'd only just got 'ere. Ain't that prime?'

'That's right. I only just got here. And I gotta go somewhere else soon. So, what can I do fer you, Resh?'

'Yer can come with us. Boss wants to see ya.'

Shit and blood. He didn't have time for this.

Resh nodded to his companion and said, 'Cover 'im while I get 'is flecks.' He let them come up and unbind the narrow sheaves from both his wrists. It wasn't a good sign that they wanted to take his weapons but he didn't have much choice. Maybe if he co-operated with Limnel, the boss wouldn't keep him too long. But if Limnel had sent people out to look for him, chances were he was after more than just an explanation why Taro had missed his shift.

Resh led the way to the troupe's homespace with the other lag bringing up the rear. The boy couldn't resist digging the boltgun into Taro's back whenever he slowed down or stumbled, which happened more and more as they got towards the gang's homespace. Taro felt sick and twitchy, fear piling on top of the stress of the comedown.

He wished he had some idea why Limnel wanted to see him all of a sudden. Was it because he'd found out that Malia's gun was missing? Did Limnel have it? No, he might not have much respect for the Concord, but stealing an Angel's gun was just gappy. It wasn't like he could use it and if he tried to sell it on he'd risk another Angel finding out and coming to pay him a visit. Maybe it was something to do with Nual. He might've been seen with her. When Limnel had asked about Taro's mission Taro had assumed that was just his boss being nosy. Now he wasn't so sure. But why would Limnel give a fuck about an Angel who lived on the other side of the Undertow?

Resh left him in the meeting hall with the other lag while he went off to find Limnel. Taro asked what this was all about, but the boy just waved the boltgun at him and told him to shut up.

Resh came back, grinning nastily. 'Think yer better 'n us, eh?' he muttered as he took Taro's arm and led him towards Limnel's room. 'Think ya can leave the boss danglin', jus' come and go as yer please? Yer deep in the nets now, Angel-boy, deep in the nets.' With that he thrust Taro through the bead curtain.

Limnel sat at the far end of the room, smoking a long-stemmed plastic pipe. Despite what Resh had said, he looked chilled and happy. There was no one else in the room, though Resh and his mate waited outside.

Seeing Taro's eyes flick back towards the door, Limnel said casually, 'They're gonna hang round, in case ya decide to do anythin' rash. Yer ain't gonna do anythin' rash, are ya, Taro?'

Taro started to shake his head, winced, then said, 'Wouldn't dream of it, boss.'

Limnel put down the pipe and waved a hand at the cushions beside him. 'Come up 'ere, then. Take a seat.'

Finally being offered a seat told Taro that he was in trouble, but he picked his way through the cushions and sat next to the boss as ordered.

'Ya look tense, Taro. Ya need to relax.' Limnel lifted the box from the cabinet. 'This stuff still don't 'ave a name, it's that new. I'm thinkin' somethin' like "Serendipity". Not as catchy as "Edge" or "Heaven", but accurate in its way, neh?' He opened the box.

'Thanks, but I'm fine,' Taro said, waving it away. He was far from fine and he had to fight the urge to lick his lips at the sight of the box, but he couldn't afford to get wasted now, not when he still needed to get across the Undertow to the Exquisite Corpse.

Limnel looked up, spoon poised over the box and said, 'Am I 'earin' ya correctly? Are ya turnin' down me generous offer? You've been 'appy enough to accept what I give ya up till now.'

'It's jus' that—' He needed a lie. As usual, he found one and went with it before he could think it through. 'I gotta meet a special punter. Solid prime, lotsa credit. A roller with lotsa credit.' Limnel didn't look impressed. 'You'll still get yer share, of course,' he added, hoping that Limnel would think the nerves in his voice were 'cause he hadn't been intending to cut his boss in and had just thought better of it.

'This roller,' said Limnel, 'where ya gonna meet them? At the piss-dealers?'

'No,' Taro saw the fall coming, but his mouth was already damning him. 'At the Exquisite Corpse. I needed Federin to show me the way.'

'So, yer meetin' a tourist at an Angel bar in the Undertow.' Limnel sucked at his lip. 'Right.'

'Aye, yer right. It's not a punter.'

'How 'bout ya stop shittin' me, Taro?'

'All right. I gotta run an errand fer the Minister. City's truth. I hafta go the Corpse. But I'll come right back.'

Limnel sighed in fake disappointment. 'Not good enough. Like I tol' ya, yer can't serve two masters.'

Limnel was right. Taro had to chose, and there was only one choice to make. 'Then … then cut me free from the troupe. Yer right. I shouldn't've come to ya when I still had unfinished City business.' Gappy idea, leaving him with nowhere to sleep and no way of making a living, but right now he had to get to the Exquisite Corpse and find Nual. Sorting his life out would have to wait.

Limnel thought for a moment, then said, 'Think not. I've invested too much in ya to jus' let ya walk away. So why doncha take advantage of me generosity one more time, neh?'

For a moment Taro thought about making a run for it, but even if he managed to get up without Limnel stopping him, Resh and his friend were waiting just outside the door.

He leaned forward and let Limnel slide the spoon under his nose.

'Don't skimp now, Taro. That's right, snort the whole fuckin' lot.'

The rush was as strong as the first time, no less full-on for being familiar. He felt like his brain was trying to escape through the top of his head. His pulse thundered in his ears and his entire body started to sing. For a minute, or perhaps a day, he had no idea where, or who, he was. And it didn't matter.

Movement in front of his face. Something waving. Limnel's hand.

'Now ain't that jus' pure blade?'

'Shit … aye. Pure. Blade.' He'd been about to do something, or there was something he needed to do or … it was gone. Never mind. If it mattered it'd come back to him. Or not.

'While we wait, why doncha tell me what yer've been up to, neh?'

Taro wasn't sure what they were waiting for, but Limnel must know. 'Awright.' If he could remember, that was.

'What exactly is the deal with yer an' Nual?'

Ah Nual. Beautiful, mysterious, crazy Nual. The important thing had something to do with Nual. He wished she was here now. Or, even better, he wished he was with her, somewhere safe.

'Don't ya go off on me now, boy!'

Taro looked back at Limnel. Why couldn't he leave him alone? Limnel was his friend and his boss now. Except the Minister was his boss too. And the Minister had given him something, something important. 'I think I gotta go somewhere.'

'Go where? To see Nual?'

'Aye. Sorta. I gotta go to the Exquisite Corpse an' see Solo – it's a she, d'you know that? – and then wait fer Nual.'

'And when Nual gets there?'

'When Nual gets there I—' He was definitely on dangerous ground here. He had something for Nual, something he had to keep special and secret and give only to her. Shit and blood, what if he'd lost it? His hand snaked inside his jacket to check.

Limnel grabbed his wrist and reached into Taro's pocket with his other hand. He pulled out the black-hearted dataspike. 'Oh fuck. Holy shittin' fuck.'

Bile rose in Taro's throat and he gulped back a sudden urge to puke. This wasn't how it was meant to go down, not at all.

Limnel stared at the chip and then at Taro. He reached a decision. 'Manak! Resh! Get yer arses in 'ere, now!' His voice was too loud. Taro cringed.

Limnel tossed the 'spike to the boy who pulled back the curtain. 'Get a copy of this. It'll 'ave shitloads of smoky encryption on it so jus' take a straight copy, don't try an' read it, in fact don't fuck with it in any way. And bring the original back, pronto.' The boy nodded and ran out again. 'Resh, you keep watch.' Resh looked confused and Limnel spoke more slowly. 'Give me plenty of warnin' if we get any visitors.' Resh's stolid features cracked into a grin and he too ducked back out the room.

Taro wasn't sure what that had been about but he knew things had gone to shit, and it was his fault. 'I'm sorry,' he whimpered, not sure what he was sorry for.

Limnel looked back at him, his eyes feverish. 'That's all right, Taro. Everythin's gonna be prime. Shit. Solid prime, right?'

'I wasn't meant to give that to yer. It was fer Nual.'

'I know. And ya can 'ave it back in a minute. Now jus' shut the fuck up a moment. I need t'think.'

Taro shut up. He should be working out what to do now too, but he wasn't sure what had already happened, or even what he was doing here. All he wanted to do was just lie in the soft cushions, letting his mind drift ...

He looked up as a boy who had been there earlier came up and handed something to Limnel. 'It copied all right, boss, but you weren't kidding 'bout the encryption.'

Limnel took the dataspike, then leaned forward and slipped it back into Taro's jacket, patting the pocket. 'See, Taro, I only borrowed it. Couldn't let a chance like that go by, could I? But if anyone asks, ain't no need to tell 'em I—'

Resh called from the doorway. 'He's at the front door. Shall I get someone to show 'im in?'

'Shit.' Limnel murmured to himself, 'that was quick. No, Resh, just tell him to fuck off back topside again! *Of course show 'im in!*'

Limnel frowned, noticing Taro again. Taro smiled back uncertainly. Limnel had given him the dataspike back. Maybe he'd let him go now. 'Can I— Can I get back to' – Taro strained to remember what he'd been about to do – 'tryin' to find Nual? I gotta find her, see. I've already wasted too much time.'

The boss shook his head. 'Oh, yer ain't goin' nowhere. Understand, this ain't nothin' personal, in fact, I'm grateful to ya, boy. Just by being a prideful little slut who don't know when t'die, yer've opened up some prime new opportunities fer me.' Limnel eased himself off his seat and stood up. Taro heard him say, 'He's all yers.' He looked up to see who he was talking to.

Limnel headed for the door while Resh held the curtain back for Limnel's visitor. For a second Taro thought he was hallucinating, because no way could this be happening.

But it was.

'Hullo again,' said Scarrion.

CHAPTER TWENTY

She had wanted to see a play and here she was, though these were hardly the circumstances she would have chosen. On the semi-circular stage below, masked actors declaimed their lines to an almost empty amphitheatre. This was a dress rehearsal; the play was due to open in a couple of days. In what Salik freely admitted was an attempt to curry favour with the intellectuals of Khesh City, he had made a large donation to the production shortly after he was put on the hot-list and in return he had been invited to attend the final rehearsal, an invitation which was apparently still open, despite his fall from grace.

Elarn scanned the tiers above as she made her way up the steps. In other circumstances, this would have been a pleasant place to visit. The Streets were hidden behind the rampant greenery of the Gardens, their bustle muted to a faint hum. Off to the left the blue dome of the transit hall shone like a jewel in the late afternoon light; she had briefly considered going there instead and getting herself on the first available ship out of the Tri-Confed system. But the Sidhe would be watching for her. She could not leave without trying to complete the task they had given her, even if it now looked as though that task would be impossible.

She spotted Salik and made her way towards him. The few members of the audience she had to momentarily displace frowned at the intrusion, despite her murmured apologies. There was no sign of the bodyguard; this was a private rehearsal so presumably Salik felt safe enough here. He was watching the actors, leaning forward, chin in hand, with rapt attention and didn't spot her until she came up next to him.

He started slightly, then started to smile until he saw her expression. 'Elarn, what are you doing here? Is something wrong?' He sounded worried.

'I'm sorry to barge in like this,' Elarn said, her voice wobbling a little. 'I had to talk to someone – I did try to call you, but the first time your com was engaged, and then it kept going to voicemail.' Fortunately the seats immediately around them were empty and there was no one to shush them. 'I remembered you said this was your last engagement today, so I came here—'

'And I would have invited you to join me here if I could. But sit down, please.'

She sank into the seat next to him. 'Oh, I don't mean— I know this is a closed performance, you told me at lunch. In fact' – she tried to laugh, though it came out as more of a sob – 'I had to prove to the people on the door that I was an offworld visitor with no media connections before they would let me in – and I still had to bribe them! I've never had to bribe anyone before.' Or kill anyone, she thought. Her control was slipping, her carefully constructed façade cracking. She looked down at the masked actors.

'Elarn, has something happened?'

'You could say that.' She swallowed, trying to dislodge the cold lump of fear in her throat. 'Salik, I haven't been entirely honest with you.'

'In what way?' The play forgotten, he turned to face her, his eyes full of concern.

'While I am on Vellern I have to do something terrible. Not because I want to, you understand, but I'm being blackmailed. I have to kill someone, a person I knew a long time ago.' There, she'd said it out loud. But the fear remained.

'Elarn ...' He searched her face, looking, she supposed, for signs of madness. Finally he said, 'Even though we've only met a few times, I did have the impression that there was something you were holding back. At first I assumed it was something to do with your religion, but then I worked out that you aren't a Salvatine. Now I guess I know what it was.'

She gave a brittle laugh. 'You're taking this very well.'

He took her hands, which lay like dead things in her lap. 'I live on a world governed by consensus murder. I was nearly a victim of that very system two days ago. Death does not shock me in the same way it obviously shocks you.'

'So will you help me?' She could not believe she was asking him this. He was a stranger. But there was no one else.

'Help you kill someone?' He frowned. 'You know, there's a whole Street in the Merchant Quarter devoted to lawyers, and most of their cases deal with actions initiated under offworld laws, or private actions by Confed citizens, all filling in the gap where formal laws would rule in any other system. Despite the impression the media gives, killing someone in the Three Cities is not always without consequences.'

'So you won't help.' Elarn sighed. 'I do understand. I should never have asked. It was ridiculous to even think—'

'Shh, Elarn, it's all right. I didn't say I wouldn't help. I just want you to understand that it might be … complicated.'

Elarn forced the words past the lump in her throat. 'You have no idea how complicated.'

'Then tell me,' he said gently.

Below, the performance finished to a light smattering of applause. Elarn felt the lump lift and the words started to pour out of her almost without volition. 'Her name is Lia Reen, or it was. I was her legal guardian for a time. Then she left Khathryn and I had no idea where she went. Her people eventually tracked her here, and now they want her dead. Don't ask me to explain who they are – you wouldn't believe me – or why they can't do this themselves – I honestly don't know, though I think it's something to do with the way the City is set up – but either I kill her, or they kill me. So I organised this tour as a pretext for visiting Vellern. And yesterday I even bought myself a gun. All the time I was hoping she wasn't here, because then I would have tried but failed, and maybe that would have been enough for them. I had almost convinced myself that if she *was* here then I could do this alone, but then I found out what's happened to her. She's not an ordinary citizen. She's become an agent of your League of Concord.'

She paused, before finishing, 'She's an Angel.'

'The person you have to kill is an Angel?' the Consul said, looking intrigued. 'You're right. That *is* complicated.'

144

Elarn heard herself rattle on, 'She's changed her name, of course. She's using her middle name – well, it's more a designation than a name really, a legal label saying you're not a believer; it's part of my name too, though I don't use it. I think she's trying to make some sort of point. Nual means "faithless"—'

'"Nual"?' She nearly missed his quiet interruption, but something in his tone of voice stopped her dead.

'Yes, Nual. What is it?'

'When a removal is to be performed, the Minister – he's the man in charge of everything – he contacts you to notify you. He won't tell you *how* your removal will proceed, of course, though it's safe to assume that the next time you enter any sort of public space an Angel's going to be taking a shot at you. But if you ask, he will tell you the name of the assassin assigned to kill you.'

'Oh God!' Elarn felt like she was about to faint. 'It was her, wasn't it?'

'Yes ... though I don't feel any *personal* animosity towards her. She was, after all, acting purely as an agent of the Concord.' But there was something in the even way he spoke that said this was Consul Vidoran the politician speaking, not Salik the man.

The lump of cold fear was gone now, replaced by a light-headed sensation. 'I suppose that's one way of looking at it. But' – she wanted to raise her head, but if she looked him in the eyes she might never look away again – 'I still need to know. Will you help me?'

He was silent for what felt like hours. Finally he said, simply, 'Yes.'

The last of her strength left her and she collapsed against him. His arms were around her at once, supporting, protecting. For a while they stayed like that, but Elarn sensed, in the wake of the fear, something else, something as old and primal and powerful as terror, and right now, her only refuge from it.

She eased her head back, feeling his breath warm her cheek, and turned towards him, seeking his mouth.

CHAPTER TWENTY-ONE

Taro clenched his fists, let his head sink onto his chest and closed his eyes. *C'mon chemicals, take me away from this.* Colours swirled on the inside of his eyelids, but he could still hear the approach of the Screamer over the banging of his heart.

There was a touch – surprisingly light – on his chin, and breath – strangely sweet – on his face. He remembered how fussy Scarrion was, how clean he kept himself, how he'd made Taro clean himself inside and out before he'd touched him.

The Screamer made a faint 'hmmm' of disapproval and pulled back. Taro thought he heard him say, 'How much did you give him?'

Taro released the breath he hadn't known he was holding and drew in another with a shudder.

From the doorway, Limnel said, 'Just enough t'keep 'im sweet fer ya, sirrah.'

Limnel was wrong there. If he was doomed – and it looked like he was – he wasn't going out like a meatbaby under the knife. Without opening his eyes, without thinking, Taro mouthed the words he was too weak to voice – 'I'll kill you' – and lashed out at Scarrion.

His nails raked flesh and someone yelped. He opened his eyes to see a blur of green and gold resolve itself into the Screamer, scurrying backwards. The other man got his balance back almost at once, leaving Taro to fall, slowly, inevitably, onto the cushions. *Surprised you though, didn't I?* he thought as his face hit the floor. *You didn't think I'd try to fight back.*

The effort had taken the last of his energy. He lay where he fell, tears leaking from his eyes, while Scarrion carried on talking to Limnel, somewhere in another world.

Someone grabbed his braids and pulled him up. He screamed at the sudden wrenching agony and tried to stand to relieve the pressure on his head. By the time he got his legs under him, sheer terror had driven any positive effects from the drug out of his system. He allowed himself to be dragged, bent double and with streaming eyes, to the room where he and Arel had slept last night.

The grip on his head was released. The mattress had been rolled out of the way and he fell forward onto the bare floor. He lay still for a moment, tensed for the next blow. Someone grabbed his arms and pulled him around until he was sitting against the wall. By the time he'd managed to focus, Resh had grabbed his hands and bound his wrists in front of him using plastic restraints. A cable ran from the restraints to an eye-bolt on the wall next to him. He gave Taro a gap-toothed smile and said, 'He don't want ya tryin' that again.'

Taro started to look away, then realised he still had one small advantage. 'He's a Screamer,' he croaked.

Resh stopped working and stared at Taro, his face falling into his usual dumb-but-ready-for-violence expression.

Taro spoke louder, though each word was an effort, 'Yaziler ... is ... a ... Screamer.'

For a moment Taro thought Resh hadn't heard him. Then the lag looked confused. 'What? A Yazil assassin? 'Im?'

'Swear on the City,' Taro managed. He tried to stop his head lolling forward.

Resh looked over his shoulder and Taro wondered if Scarrion was in the room with them. 'What if 'e is?'

'Ha— Hafta tell Limnel.'

'Don't hafta do nothin' ya say, ya shite-rot little whore. And y'know what?' Resh's expression turned cunning. 'Reckon the boss already knows. An' I reckon 'e don't care.' With that, Resh stood up and left. A few seconds later the curtain was swept aside and Scarrion strode in. Taro felt a brief stab of satisfaction at the sight of the fresh scratch on the Screamer's cheek.

Scarrion crouched down against the far wall, his hands resting on his lap. He gave Taro a look of cold appraisal. 'It would appear that hate is stronger than chemistry. Interesting. That's serious stuff, you know, not at all easy to fight. Extremely addictive too, although I expect you already know that.'

Taro stared at him. How come the Screamer knew about the dust? That didn't make any sense.

Scarrion watched Taro's eyes and barked a laugh. 'How do you think a two-bit whoremonger like Limnel got hold of such quality merchandise? From me, of course, for services rendered.' His tone said that in this case *services rendered* included delivering Taro to him.

If Scarrion was mixed up with the drug that meant ... that meant a whole lot of even worse shit he was too mashed up to work out at the moment. One thing he did know was that as long as Scarrion was crowing over him he wouldn't be hurting him. 'Don' understan',' he slurred, as much to postpone the inevitable as because he wanted to know.

'Such naïveté. Quite charming, really. Limnel wasn't part of the plan, but he has turned out to be a very useful ally. Shall I tell you how we met?'

Taro nodded, but didn't speak. Scarrion carried on regardless, 'It was when I followed you downside. You were easy to trail through the sidestreets, but once we got into the – what do you call them? Mazeways? – I lost you, but ran into Limnel instead, and he responded with the standard downsider welcome for trespassers from above. After I took out the boy he set on me I suggested he would find me a useful ally but a dangerous enemy. Limnel is a venal entrepreneur who likes to back winners. He understood at once. He agreed to tell me where to find your homespace in return for which I offered to make him sole supplier of a fine new drug, delicious and compulsive. And as I'd managed to drop my gun during the fight with his late associate, he even gave me a weapon in good faith. I understand that you use boltguns to fire support pins into the vanes of the Undertow? Up close, against flesh, they can be quite devastating.'

Despite himself, Taro whimpered.

'Ah, Taro. Your pretty face is a picture, you know? Yes, yes, Limnel gave me the gun that killed your "line-mother". Actually, I was rather disappointed. I've never killed an agent of another City before and I was hoping for a bit more of a challenge. And it was irritating to be interrupted before I could finish you – though as it turns out, you've been very useful. If you hadn't made that little scene in Confederacy Square I'd be out of a job now. And Limnel tells me you still work for the Minister.' Scarrion raised his hands and pressed his palms together. 'But much as I enjoy messing with your head, we really should get down to business.' He moved swiftly and smoothly across the floor.

Taro pressed his back into the wall, terror closing his throat. It looked like the Screamer'd had enough of taunting his prey. Now the pain would begin.

Scarrion leaned forward and said, 'You're going to tell me what you've been doing for the Minister. Specifically, you're going to tell me everything you know about the Angel Nual.'

Taro was confused. Then he realised that the Screamer wasn't just here for his own sick pleasure. The fucker needed something from him. The thought was enough to knock him out of his despair for a moment. To his amazement, he found himself laughing in the Screamer's face. 'No,' he said, ''m not.'

The Screamer looked surprised. 'Really?' He sounded intrigued. 'You think?'

Taro gathered what was left of his strength and whispered, 'I hate you more 'n I've ever hated anyone. I'd kill you if I could. I sure-as-shit got nothin' to say to you.'

Scarrion gave a theatrical sigh and backhanded Taro across the face. The impact of his head on the wall jarred his entire body. He coughed and tasted blood.

Scarrion continued, 'You are alone, without friends, and without hope. You are only alive because you are useful to me. Continue to demonstrate your usefulness, or, failing that, your *entertainment value*, and you will continue to live. It really is that simple.'

Taro struggled to speak through the pain. 'Won't play.'

Scarrion picked up Taro's bound wrists. 'Don't you want to live, Taro?' he hissed. 'Wouldn't you do anything to survive? If you die, your hate dies with you. Your line-mother will never be avenged. Not that long ago you were willing to let me do whatever I wanted with that scrawny body of yours. Won't you even talk to me now?'

'Talk, aye,' said Taro, the knowledge that he stood at the brink of his own destruction making him lightheaded, 'I'll talk to you ... Fuck you, Screamer!'

'Have it your own way,' said Scarrion, his voice low and husky. Holding his hands to stop Taro pulling them back, he traced one well-manicured nail along the soft skin on the inside of Taro's wrist. Taro flushed, the heat of panic driving off the mad momentary high of his defiance.

'Now, where shall we start?'

Taro flinched, his skin crawling under Scarrion's caress. When the Screamer raised a hand to Taro's cheek he jerked away, banging his head again, sending stars shooting through his vision.

Scarrion grinned at Taro's discomfort. Taro closed his eyes, unable to bear the cold gaze that said Taro'd had his chance to do this the easy way and now he'd turned it down things would get nasty. Just the way the Screamer liked it.

Scarrion stroked the back of one of Taro's hands, then suddenly dug a thumbnail between the tendons. Taro yelped, as much from shock as from pain, and opened his eyes.

The Screamer shifted his weight to straddle Taro's outstretched legs. Taro started to quiver, his breath coming in short gasps, as useless urges – *Fight! Flee!* – raced through him.

The Screamer began experimenting in earnest now: twisting the restraints that held Taro's hands until they bit into his wrists, pressing his knuckles into points on Taro's neck or arms to send numb shocks shooting through his body, drawing a nail along Taro's forearm hard enough to leave a long red track. Taro clenched his teeth, but he didn't resist; he knew from their first encounter how Scarrion wanted him to fight back, how resistance excited him. He forced himself to accept the pain, though sometimes a moan or gasp escaped round the edges of his willpower.

Then Scarrion bent the little finger of his left hand back until the tendons tore. Taro screamed.

Scarrion started to speak in a low, bored voice, asking Taro how often he had spoken to the Minister, what his orders were, whether he had ever met Nual.

Taro shook his head slowly in answer to the Screamer's questions, holding on to the small satisfaction that Limnel was not the ally Scarrion hoped he was. He should've given the Screamer the dataspike, not copied it and returned it to Taro. Taro tensed at the thought. No matter what happened, no matter what else he ended up saying, he must keep the Minister's dataspike from Scarrion.

Perhaps taking Taro's reaction to mean he was ready to co-operate, Scarrion repeated the last question. 'Do you know where Nual is now, Taro?' He paused, waiting for an answer.

When Taro still said nothing, Scarrion sat back on his heels, a look of mock disappointment on his face. He reached into his jacket and drew out a thin, curved metal blade, the kind fleshers used to flay the bodies of the dead.

Taro shrunk back. The Screamer's smile widened. He leaned forward.

A thin line, beaded with blood—

The tip of the knife worked under a nail—

The upper layer of skin flayed slowly from the layers beneath—

And always questions …

… questions that Taro answered now, the only way to stop the pain, at least for a while. He was past resistance, past lying. But he wasn't yet past hope. He said only what he had to say to satisfy Scarrion's desire for answers. But Taro was becoming aware of another desire, one he could do nothing to stop; over the sound of his own cries and mumbled responses he heard the Screamer's breathing growing heavier.

This was just foreplay to him.

Scarrion reached forward to place the knife just above Taro's groin, the point pricking through shirt and breeches. Taro's breath caught in his chest and his vision went black at the edges. Scarrion let the blade rest there just long enough to savour Taro's expression, then withdrew the knife a little, snagged Taro's shirt and slashed upwards. The thin fabric of the shirt ripped and Scarrion pulled the remnants down over his shoulders, pulling his jacket off and pinning his arms to his sides.

In his haze of fear and pain Taro heard himself begging, *Jus' make it quick*, and *Please, let it be over*.

Scarrion, smiling at Taro's cries for mercy, spent a few seconds regarding his prey's pale, heaving chest with gleeful anticipation. He reached out with his empty hand to grab the cord belt holding up Taro's breeches—

—and froze, arm still outstretched. He was staring at something on the floor by Taro's legs.

Taro stopped moaning, blinked and followed his tormentor's gaze. The Minister's dataspike had fallen from his pocket and lay on the floor by his right knee.

For a moment they both stared. Then Scarrion slid his knife back into his jacket and picked up the chip, turning it over in his hands a couple of times. 'Shit,' he said under his breath. Taro, watching him through a dull mist of agony and receding hope, thought that this was the first time he'd heard the Screamer swear.

Scarrion stood up and turned back to Taro. He pulled back his fist and punched him hard enough to send him into darkness.

There were moments, as she travelled from the amphitheatre to Salik's State Quarter apartments, when Elarn found herself coldly considering possible ways to solve her problem: Salik still had some influence, maybe enough to flush out Lia – *Nual*, as she was now – and put her in a position where Elarn had the advantage. More feasibly, his bodyguard was an assassin, already on the edge, and he might be persuaded to kill an operative of a rival City. She could use that. *They* could use that.

But mainly she just clung to Salik and whispered in her mind, *Hold me, save me! Make the fear go away!*

They hardly spoke on the short journey to his blandly luxurious penthouse. As soon as he closed the door she turned to him, ready to surrender to the wondrous, messy union, the loss of self in another. He was there for her, here and now. That was all.

Despite the heat of her desire, it took a while to re-awaken the passions that Elarn had denied for so long, but Salik had the time and the skill to coax complete abandonment from her. As the afternoon faded into night, the world closed in on them until they were the only two creatures in the universe.

Even as she rode the wild tide of back-brain pleasure, some part of her was amazed and frightened at the depth of need he had awakened. She was making love without barriers, with the man who was going to help her commit murder. If the church was right, she was damned, gloriously damned, for evermore.

CHAPTER TWENTY-TWO

Warm breath on his face. 'Wake up, Taro.' Female voice, whispering, nervous.

Where was he? Why did everything hurt so much?

Someone pulled at his arms, not hard, but enough to make the pain worse. He hoped they'd stop soon.

'C'mon, Taro, wake up. I'm tryin' to help yer!'

Help him? He forced his eyes open, the lashes pulling painfully. The left eye wouldn't open properly and kept watering. He couldn't focus on the person who was tugging at him, but opening his eyes was enough to make him remember where he was. He groaned.

'Shit! Stay with me now, Taro. *Wake up!*'

Why was this girl bothering him? He wished she'd go away and let him sink back into the numb, safe darkness. 'Go 'way,' he mouthed. 'Lemme die.'

'What? Fuck's sake, Taro, yer the one said tha's not the way. Remember? Remember me? Arel?'

'Arel?' A lifetime ago, saving a stranger from herself. He'd told her things weren't as bad as they seemed. What a lie that turned out to be. Taro blinked and opened his eyes again. He could see her now, squatting in front of him, sawing at the strap around his wrist with a fleck. 'Why?' he gasped.

'Why what? Oh, why'm I doin' this?' He felt another tug on his hands. 'Firstly, 'cause I owe ya, and I pay m'debts. There, got it.' She pulled the restraints off.

Taro's hands dropped into his lap.

'Yer gonna have to stand up. I ain't carryin' ya. C'mon.'

'Can't.'

'I ain't givin' yer a choice,' she whispered angrily. 'Right. I'm gonna pull ya up. It's gonna hurt, but we gotta get out of 'ere 'fore anyone finds us.' She grabbed his hand and Taro bit his lip as she pulled him up. He'd just about managed to get his legs under him when the dizziness hit. He gave a raw cough then retched, spewing up thin grey-yellow puke, all over his naked chest and across Arel's shoulder.

'Shit and blood!' muttered Arel, stepping back. He fell to his knees, then toppled forwards. She caught him, hands on his shoulders.

'Don' hafta help me. Not yer problem,' he whispered hoarsely.

'Aye, well, if I'd any sense I'd jus' leave ya. Yer not the only one who's in comedown, y'know? Fuckin' Keron decided to keep me hangin' on, so I din't get anythin' last night. I feel like shit. But this' – he saw her eyes flick over him, and wondered how bad he looked – 'it's not just that I owe ya. There's more to it than that. Tell yer the rest when we get outside, mebbe. Give ya somethin' to stay awake fer.' She put an arm round his waist and pulled him up. Taro collapsed onto her. She staggered under his weight, slight though it was, but managed to keep them both upright.

They had trouble getting through the curtain; Arel heaved a sigh of relief that the corridor outside was still deserted.

Taro gave up trying to make sense of the world and concentrated on staying on his feet. He could feel the individual drops of sweat breaking out over his body, and he had to keep gulping to stop himself throwing up again. Arel, one arm round his waist, steered him through corridors he didn't recognise to a narrow door, barred on their side. She hooked the bar off and pulled it open with her free hand.

She helped him through into the darkness of the mazeways. She propped him against a vane and stood back. 'Right. Yer outa there now. All right?'

Taro started to slide down the vane, eyes closing.

'*Shit!* I can't leave ya out here, they'll just find yer again. Know anywhere safe?'

'Fenya,' he managed after a moment.

'The water-trader? All right. But then I'm off to Daim's brother.'

'Who——?'

'Oh, I din't tell ya, did I? Or mebbe I did, when I was pasted. Daim was me partner. Only he's dead now.'

'What?' He remembered something about that, about other people's shit. Maybe she'd managed to get free of hers. Good luck to her if so.

'Tell ya while we get away from 'ere.' She hoisted him up again, walking on the outside so he could lean into the vane. After a while she started to talk. 'Me and Daim'd been close since we was kids, shared a blood father, though our mothers came from different troupes. Soon as we was old enough we started workin' together, jackin' the rollers. We worked for Limnel, but casual-like. We'd give 'im a cut in return for protection an' a place to stay, but we din't hafta do what 'e said, long as we paid 'im off. Worked fine.'

She paused and tensed. Taro sagged against her. No one was shouting at him or hurting him so he decided not to worry about whatever had made her stop. Now he didn't have to concentrate on moving he found himself drifting off, heading to a place with no pain, no regret. Then she pulled him up again and muttered, 'Fuckin' meatbabies. Give me the creeps.' Taro grunted vague assent and they were off again.

When she started talking again her voice was a harsh, bitter whisper. 'Three days ago Limnel suggests we buzz this offworld bitch in the transit hall, fresh off the shuttle. Said she'd be rich 'n' easy, no guard, lotsa credit. Gave a real specific description, and 'e didn't negotiate 'is cut up front. Smelled a bit smoky, but we took the tip anyway, 'cause his info's usually prime. Only some fucker in Yazil colours turns up just when we're about to get our hands on her cred-bracelet. He broke Daim's fuckin' neck. Jus' like snappin' a stick.' She stopped for a moment, and drew a long breath. 'An' that's when me life went to shit. Fuck. There's nets 'ere, Taro. Can ya manage 'em?'

Taro raised his head and focused with difficulty on the gap in the mazeway in front of them. About two metres, hardly worth breaking his stride for on a good day. Today it was the end of the world. 'Dunno,' he murmured.

'I could just leave yer 'ere——'

Taro grasped at her shirt.

'—but I ain't gonna, am I? No, 'cause yer the one talked me outta givin' up. I got rope. I'm just gonna prop ya up 'ere. That's it, 'old onto that support rope by yer 'ead.'

She reached into the pack on her back and pulled out a length of plaited rope with a clip on the end. She put the tether round Taro's middle, talking while she worked. Taro watched her dully, slumped back against the vane.

'Ya said yer survived by not lettin' them touch yer mind. I took yer advice. When the drugs ran out, I just sent me mind back t'the place the drugs took it, an' told meself it weren't me body no more. It weren't easy but I got through the day. When I come back from me shift that pig Resh wanted me but 'e was too drunk to get it up. Left him snorin' down the hall. Thought about breakin' into Limnel's stash, but I'm gonna hafta learn to live without it some time, ain't I?'

'Scarrion ... give ... him—'

'Who's Scarrion?'

'The Yaziler.'

'Oh, shit! What is it ya sayin', the fucker who killed Daim gave Limnel the drug?'

'Think so.' Taro closed his eyes again.

'Shit. Makes sense, I s'ppose. *Hoi!* Taro! Doncha slip away now. I got ya this far and I'm gonna finish the job.'

Taro nodded slowly, head rolling back against the vane, then forced himself to open his eyes.

Arel looked at him and said, 'We're goin' across now. I'll jump first, tether the rope, then yer come over.'

Taro tried to laugh, but ended up coughing. 'Can't jump.'

'Ya don't 'ave to. Ya crawl over the nets. They're pretty tight here, should be easy. And I'll keep talkin'. Jus' move towards me voice.'

Then she was gone.

Taro let himself slide down the vane onto the mazeway, then pulled himself painfully round onto all fours. He stared at his hands, bloody, bruised and filthy, and too close to the edge.

He felt a faint tug round his midriff. He raised his head to see Arel on the other side of the gap, tying off her end of the rope. She kept talking in a low tone, beckoning him to come to her. 'Y'know, when I was with Resh last night, 'e was goin' on about some important roller who'd done this deal with Limnel, and 'ow 'e'd left ya holed up with 'im – he thought that was really funny, the sick little fuck. Said 'e thought this sleaze was from Yazil – mebbe even a Screamer, for City's sake – but I din't get it at first. C'mon, Taro, start comin' across.'

Taro lowered himself onto his elbows, forearms flat on the mazeway, arse in the air. He started to edge off the mazeway and onto the nets, curling his fingers round the ropes, pulling himself forward, slow and careful-like. His stomach fluttered and his heart-rate soared as his world was reduced to the simple need to get across the nets. Arel's voice sounded further away now, as though he'd already slipped off the City into the darkness below. Perhaps he was already falling, very, very slowly.

'Anyways, I'm on m'way back from Resh's to the whores' sleepin' room an' I walk past the fucker in the corridor. 'E's in a real hurry, don't give me so much as a second glance, but I know 'im. I'll never forget 'is face. That's it, Taro. Slowly, now.'

Taro had managed to get most of the way into the nets, fingers en-twined in the ropes, body stretched over a pair of ropes set close and linked by an uneven network of thin cord. He worked by feel now, his eyes pressed shut. Reality was just the ropes under him, and Arel's bitter words.

'When I saw 'im it all fell into place. Limnel set us up with this – what d'ya say 'is name was? Scarrion? So 'e was in with 'im all along. Dunno why, and I don't care. Do know there's no way I'm gonna be Limnel's whore when 'e's the one shafted me in the first place. I was outa there. Yer almost bolted now, Taro, nearly there.'

He was less than an arm's-length from safety. He stretched one hand forward. He just had to reach out and Arel would grab him.

His fingers brushed hers.

One of the cords stretched, twanged ...

Snapped.

Taro flipped sideways. His legs tumbled away. One hand pulled off the rope. The other held, but he wasn't strong enough, his grasp was slipping—

Something jerked him up, winding him. The rope round his waist. For a moment he swung, connected to the Undertow only by the flimsy rope and one numb hand still desperately clinging on. Then he managed to get his other hand back up and groped for the net. A moment later he felt Arel's hand on his wrist, pulling him up, half-dragging, half-lifting him over the lip of the mazeway where he lay panting, the rush of adrenalin making everything clear and sharp for a few moments.

Arel grasped his arm and pulled him up. 'There, that weren't so bad. I 'ad to take ya with me, Taro, if ya wasn't dead. Piss 'im off by taking away 'is toy, and pay m'debt to ya. C'mon, not far now.'

Taro hoped not. To get across the nets he'd cashed in some of the pain for a loan of energy, delivered on a tide of fear. Payback wouldn't be long coming. While he could still speak he murmured, 'Thanks, Arel.'

'Aye. We're even now, right? I ran out on Limnel, so I ain't never comin' back to this part of the Undertow. Don't know if Daim's people'll 'ave me, but anythin' beats fuckin' punters for a spoon of happy dust.' She hoisted him up and carried on. He let himself fall into a daze, just moving his legs, not thinking about anything other than the need to keep walking till he couldn't walk any further, then he could let it all go and fall into darkness, comforting darkness . . .

'Right, we're 'ere.'

Taro raised his head to find they were at the end of the corridor leading to Fenya's place. The short stretch of mazeway swam and dipped in his vision.

'I'll get ya t'the door, then I'm gone,' Arel told him.

Though he could feel his feet moving, the corridor wasn't getting any shorter. Instead it stretched away, pulling him with it. He was vaguely aware of being handed from one pair of arms to another. He gave up trying to stay conscious and followed the corridor off the end of reality.

They have found her. She hid as best she could but it was not good enough. She knew it never would be.

The demons are beautiful, but that beauty is a mask. Elarn can see beyond the mask to where infinity and hellfire lurk in their eyes.

She cowers at the bottom of the wardrobe like a child. They open the door and reach in for her. She cannot resist; she lets them pull her out. One of them leads her by the hand through the familiar rooms of her own home and tells her to sit down. She obeys, like the naughty little girl she is. They ask her to explain what she has done. She does, leaving nothing out, telling no lies, though her voice is a whisper of fear and all she can think about is the coming punishment.

She tells them how her brother Jarek brought home the adolescent girl he called Nual, though the identity he bought for her gave her another name, Lia, and Elarn suspects that when he found her she had no name at all. She reveals how she started to feel something beyond maternal love for the girl; and when she could resist the attraction no longer and tried to take the girl to her bed, she found out what the child really was. In her fear, she drove the girl away, and in doing so she drove away her brother too. Since then she has lived alone and in fear of this day, the day when the Sidhe would follow the trail of their renegade here.

When she falls silent they tell her that despite her fears they will let her live and never visit her again. Her fear, they say, is strong enough to ensure her silence. But she must kill the renegade.

The one who first took her hand stands up, walks over and kneels before her. She is caught in the woman-creature's regard, paralysed and compliant. Elegant hands reach up to her, as though to take something from her, or to caress her cheek like a lover. She finds she still has her voice, or perhaps they are just listening to her thoughts.

'What are you doing?'

The woman replies without moving her lips, *We are giving you the last song you will ever sing. And a safe place to hide it from our enemies.*

Her fingers reach Elarn's face.

And carry on.

Elarn wakes with a rush of indrawn breath.

She clutches the sheets to her and stares up at the ceiling where rain shadows dance on the familiar sculpted surface.

'Lights on,' she rasps. The furniture of her bedroom springs into life around her. Outside, a storm is throwing itself at the house, waves banging and crashing at the base of the cliff below. But she's safe here. It was just a dream, fading now. A nightmare about *them*. She has these dreams sometimes. But as long as they remain dreams, she can live with it.

She sits up. As she shifts in the bed she finds that she is naked. Where is her nightgown? And her body feels odd, heavy, but in a good way. Self-conscious, although there is no one for tens of kilometres in any direction, she reaches down and feels between her legs.

She is moist, sore, and sated. That is not possible.

She shouldn't wake from her recurring nightmare with the feeling that she has recently had good, prolonged and energetic sex. It's not like she has had even bad sex for several years – since she almost took Lia to her bed she has not let herself get near another person. So she must have imagined the sex ... except there is strong physical evidence to the contrary.

She puts her hand out and smoothes the covers. They feel insubstantial, compared with the pleasant ache in her centre. What colour are they? She cannot be sure. It has not occurred to her until now, but under the veil of familiarity, she has lost the ability to name her surroundings. To name is to question and she is not permitted to do that. She cannot grasp the feel of reality.

Which means that this is not reality.

Hands, reaching for her face—

For a moment after waking Elarn lay frozen, unsure whether she really was awake this time. She was still naked, and the pleasant ache she recalled from her dream was still there. The details of the dream ran away like water, but this time she knew the sex had been real.

And now she was – where? In a dark room, in a strange bed: Salik's bed. She was in Salik's bed, where they had made love for what felt like days before she finally fell into an exhausted sleep. She hoped her nightmares hadn't woken him. She listened for his breathing, but heard nothing ... then she heard the sound of a door closing. She rolled over slowly, her body still reluctant to be dragged from the paralysis of the dream.

The bed beside her was empty, but still warm. She raised her head.

A strip of light showed under the door to the living room. Someone was talking in there. Who would visit Salik at this hour? But there were silences in the conversation and his com was no longer on the table beside the bed. He was comming someone, or they had commed him. At this time of night?

She strained to hear, curious, but not concerned … but when she thought she heard the name 'Nual' she got out of bed and silently crept over to the door. Through the gap she could see Salik, still naked, pacing across the far side of the room. He looked agitated and he was saying, '—need to find out what's on that dataspike as soon as we can. Get your man onto it first thing. But that's good news about the gun, very good news.' He listened for a while. 'No, I'll have to leave it turned off while I'm with the delectable Medame Reen. Leave a message if it's urgent. You may as well get some rest. Goodnight, Scarrion.'

Elarn dived for the bed and when he opened the door she was still only half under the covers, so she shifted around, making a show of having almost woken up, then turned away from him. She heard him put the com down on the table, then felt him get back into bed. For a moment she thought he would reach for her and, suddenly repulsed by the idea of his touch, she tensed. But he lay down on his back with a small sigh, not quite touching her. Within a couple of minutes his breathing had settled into the slow rhythms of sleep.

She counted to a hundred, hardly breathing herself, to be sure he was asleep. Then she got up, dressed hurriedly and quietly, and left. He didn't stir.

CHAPTER TWENTY-THREE

She should kill him, that would be the wisest move. But looking at the youth in her bed, Nual was not sure. Even Solo only came to her home-space when she had important business; no one else even knew how to find it. Yet she had crossed the Undertow to fetch this foolish, pretty boy, and then brought him here, to her sanctum.

So much for the human belief that the Sidhe were masters of self-knowledge who always understood the full implications of their actions.

The water-traders had cleaned up the worst of his injuries, setting his dislocated finger and dressing the deeper cuts. He had remained unconscious throughout the flight here and only now, as dawn seeped up through the floor, did he start to stir. He twitched and moaned, no doubt reliving recent events in nightmare.

She needed to know what that nightmare was, what had happened to him. The safest, most logical option would be to ream the knowledge from his unconscious mind and when she had what she needed, to simply stop his heart. After all, what was he to her? Just an unlucky youth, one without lineage or influence, a liability – possibly even a link that her enemies could use to trace her.

He was also the only innocent in this whole mess. And he might be the only human in the City she could trust.

She placed a gentle hand on his arm; he flinched and groaned, but did not wake up.

Nual sighed. She could reach into the upper levels of his mind, not deep, just enough to rouse him, but years of self-control made her hesitate. Even without the promise she had made, she shied away from using her abilities, because of what they could do. *Because of what she had done.*

She shook him gently.

Taro's eyes darted behind their lids and his head thrashed from side to side on the pillow. He didn't want to wake up. He wanted oblivion, death, an end to suffering.

If she couldn't wake him, Nual told herself, she'd have no choice but to read his unconscious mind. Part of her wanted that, wanted to take him, use him, subsume him. It was what she had been born for. She had been in denial of her true nature for too long.

One last try the human way, and if he didn't wake then, she would have no choice.

She said gently, 'Taro. You're safe, but you have to wake up.'

His eyes opened, slowly, painfully. The left one, badly bruised and watering, was barely more than a slit.

Despite herself, Nual felt a rush of emotions well up with his return to consciousness: *confusion-fear-shame-relief.*

The boy's blurry glance swept round the room. She knew he would never have been in a homespace like this. The only gap was the trapdoor of toughened glass, and the grey walls were covered in a bright collage of hangings and posters. Candles – not those foul lamps filled with human fat – burned on every flat surface. The room was furnished with topside furniture: a table, chairs, and the bed he was lying in. Then his gaze settled on her and his good eye widened. He opened his mouth to say something, but all that came out was an incoherent croak.

Nual picked up the water bottle from the table, leaned over and raised his head with one hand. His hair was matted with dried blood, the skin beneath it hot. She squeezed a few drops of water into his mouth. He licked his lips and swallowed, his eyes fixed on her face. His emotions still battered her: *fear, confusion, shame. Love.* She didn't return his gaze.

Don't adore me, you stupid boy. Don't you know I will destroy you?

She looked away and said brusquely, 'You're in my homespace. Do you know how you got here?'

He let his head fall back onto the pillow. 'No, lady,' he croaked.

'Solo came here late last night. A remembrancer friend of yours came to the Exquisite Corpse, asking for me. When I went to the Corpse this remembrancer told me that you had managed to get yourself to his homespace, half-dead. He said you were ranting about having been too weak to resist, that you had betrayed me. So he came to find me. I think he expected me to pass judgment on you.' She smiled to show that this was not her intention. 'I flew him back to his homespace. There you were, damaged, unconscious. I brought you here, though you have your friend Fenya to thank for tending to your injuries.'

The boy regarded her like a frightened animal.

For a moment she reconsidered her decision, and almost dived into his mind to find the nature and extent of his betrayal— But no, she was tired of not trusting.

She spoke more quietly. 'I'm not going to hurt you, Taro, but you must tell me what happened.'

He looked away, staring up at the ceiling, to where Nual had disguised the grey underside of the City in draperies. 'Aye lady,' he murmured, his voice hoarse. 'Then you must decide whether or not to let me live.'

He had been a mess when they first met, confused and under the influence of some drug. His life had obviously not improved since. 'What did you do after I left you at the end of Chance Street?' she asked.

'When?' Taro asked, blinking. 'Oh. Was it yesterday? Aye, only yesterday. I talked to the Minister. He wasn't happy. And he—' Taro closed his eyes. 'I've done a terrible thing, lady.'

'Tell me, what is this terrible thing you have done?' Only the slightest effort and she could read it, this betrayal that was tearing him apart – but he was willing to tell her freely, and she would grant him that kindness.

He turned his head away. 'He gave me orders fer a removal. To give to you.'

'Oh.' He was wearing only tattered, ripped breeches, and they didn't look like they had any pockets. 'Where are those orders now, Taro?'

He put his hands over his face and rolled onto his side, away from her. 'I'm sorry,' he rasped, trying to stop the tears leaking from his eyes. 'I tried ... I really tried. But I weren't strong enough. He— He knows 'ow to hurt me, and not just me body. He took them.'

'Who, Taro?' she asked gently, 'who took the orders?'

'Scarrion,' he said, shaking with fear. 'The Screamer, he found them when 'e— Lady, I swear I tried to keep it from him, only tell 'im what I had to to make the pain stop, but ... But it was no good. *I* was no good. He should've killed me.' Taro pulled his knees to his chest and curled up against the wall.

Nual watched his quivering back and thought through what he had said. It would be just like the Minister to use the ultimate sanction of orders for a removal to get her attention. But who could the orders be for? The rules of the Concord wouldn't allow another hit on Vidoran without further voting – assuming the Minister had really wanted Vidoran dead in the first place – and rumours from the Exquisite Corpse didn't suggest any other hot-list contenders coming up for removal yet. But the Minister didn't always play by his own rules, not with her, anyway.

And now Vidoran's Screamer had the orders, and that was not good at all.

Almost absently, reacting to his need for comfort, she reached out to stroke Taro's hair. His despair washed over her, momentarily eclipsing her own concerns. She leaned over and wrapped her arms round him, letting him cry, absorbing the horror and self-loathing, draining the poison. It felt good to touch someone, even someone this damaged.

He cried for a while, then uncurled slightly and muttered something she didn't catch.

'Taro?'

He sniffed. 'There's a copy,' he whispered. 'I'd almost forgot ... Limnel, the boss, 'e took a copy of the 'spike. Before Scarrion came. Lady, we could get it.'

'Where would he keep it, do you know?'

'There's a lock-up store, near the room where 'e took me. I'll bet it's in there. I can show you.' He rolled over and tried to sit up, then groaned and fell back.

'You aren't going anywhere,' she said, sternly.

'*No!* I mean— Sorry, lady, but ... I have to. Must undo what I've done.'

His despair had turned to hope, almost equally pitiable. She could still take the simpler option and read his mind for the location of the copy, or she could dominate him, make him her willing slave – but she rather thought she needed a friend as much as he did.

'Taro, you're in no state to go anywhere at the moment, and I'm afraid we do not have the time to wait for you to heal.'

'Please! I can't jus' do nothin' – it's all my fault!'

'From the look of you, you did everything you could to resist the Screamer. You cannot be blamed for his actions, Taro. Stay here, rest. You'll be safe. No one will find you here. I will go for the orders.'

'Lemme come with you. I have to.' He needed to redeem himself. And he did not want to be parted from her. Despite her attempts to keep her distance, the link between them was already growing.

There was one way that he could go with her, though it would mean breaking the promise she had made not to use her powers. So be it: she had pretended to be human for too long, and she had spent so long hiding that she had forgotten what it was like to get close to someone. Because of that reticence, she lacked experience using her powers in this way: she could not be sure what effect such a drastic intervention might have on him, or on her. But it was what he needed, and what she wanted. The time was right.

She asked softly, 'Do you trust me, Taro?'

'I trust you.'

Of course he did. 'There is a way you can come with me, but first I have to explain something, and it's going to be hard to understand. It's something very few people know.'

He stared up at her, eagerly, adoringly, waiting on her words. *Damn him.*

'Not all aliens have wings, Taro,' she started. 'I am not human.'

'Not human? But you're—'

She tried not to pick up the end of the sentence he was too embarrassed to speak—

You're so beautiful.

'There are old, nasty secrets being exposed to the light here, Taro,' she went on. 'Do you know who the Sidhe were?'

'I've 'eard topsiders mention them. Din't they run things a long time ago?'

'The time of the Sidhe Protectorate was a long period of stability – or, as some prefer to call it, repression – when the Sidhe ruled humanity. The Sidhe looked human, but where humans are limited to five senses, the Sidhe operated in a wider spectrum. Trying to explain what that means would be like trying to explain colour to a person who had been born blind. And while humans influence the world around them purely by their actions, the Sidhe had the power to influence reality, or rather, how sentient beings perceive reality, by thought. Legend has it their glance could bare your soul, or stop your breath, or induce total obedience. Most of them, the powerful ones, the ones anyone saw, were women. Humans used to say that to love a Sidhe woman was to doom yourself to the death of ecstasy. The men ... well, that's a story for another time.' She sighed. 'Fear of the Sidhe was one of the few things that has ever united humanity. But, like you said, all that was long ago. They're gone now, dead these last thousand years, all that power reduced to nothing more than fairy-tales to scare children. Everyone knows that.'

'Except they ain't,' said Taro carefully.

This boy was not the idiot he liked others to think he was.

She nodded slowly. 'The Sidhe always were a minority. They ruled partly by controlling humanity's access to technology and partly by using awe, adoration and illusion, making themselves into goddesses who were willingly worshipped. When they were – apparently – destroyed, the survivors went into hiding. They encouraged the belief that they had been defeated utterly and were gone forever, which wasn't so hard to do, given how humans always like to believe tales of their own superiority. The only way such a small group could exert any control is by remaining hidden, and by making the possibility that they might still exist ridiculous. And by being united. Just one renegade, one rogue with Sidhe powers and no loyalty to the Sidhe agenda, could threaten their secret hold on humanity.'

'Oh,' whispered Taro. 'And that'd be you, then?'

Nual smiled at his expression. He looked understandably shocked, but not afraid. *Not appalled.* There was none of the hatred she picked up from other humans at the mere mention of the Sidhe. Then again, most humans didn't spend their lives struggling to survive in squalid surroundings beneath a floating city.

'I am telling you this because there is a way you could come with me to get the chip back. I could help you. But it would mean using my— my talents on you. I want you to understand what that means. For the past seven years I have been in hiding, making myself blind, not using my abilities, all so I could survive amongst humans, so I could fit in. But I am still Sidhe. If I try to heal you I will be invading your mind, reaching into you. It may change you. It will certainly change … us.'

'It's all right. I ain't frightened,' he said, straightening his narrow shoulders with a grimace of pain.

No, thought Nual, *you aren't. Brave, foolish boy.* 'All right. Try to relax. I'll do everything else.'

Taro obeyed. Nual knelt beside him and placed her hand on his forehead.

She went in slowly, letting the images and sensations uppermost in his mind wash over her on the way through his consciousness: the blond man smiles as he draws the knife – the boy with the crooked nose and the sharp suit holds out a spoon of golden powder – the Minister hands over the dataspike, his face grave – herself, sitting across the table in the Exquisite Corpse – in a dark room smelling of sex, the battered, naked girl lies curled up on a filthy mattress – the Angel, dark-haired and wide-eyed, jerks backwards as the bolt blows half her head away—

Names and associations adhered to the images. Nual absorbed Taro's recent experiences, allowing them to seep into her memory. She braced herself to accept all the emotions that accompanied them: fear; shame; terror; confusion. Powerlessness. Hopelessness. She felt a growing admiration for the boy's determination to survive, and to do what he felt was right. She would do what she could to help him.

She had no direct control over the physical, but fortunately, the addiction was mostly psychological and she could excise the need, the insistent demand for more. The physical symptoms of withdrawal she could only reduce, not remove, but she could and did encourage his body's natural healing processes, and she infused him with energy drawn from the lives that – now her shields were down – she could feel seething all around her. And she dulled the physical pain, just enough to let him function. She could have easily dulled his mental anguish too – he might take it as a mercy, to lose the memories that haunted him—

No! His mind must remain his own.

169

But she let her consciousness drift like a ghost through the core of his being for a little longer, taking the time to enjoy being in another's mind.

Finally she opened her eyes.

His eyes were closed and his breathing was slow and even. For the first time since she had met him, his face was serene. Beneath the bruises, it was beautiful.

Apparently the effect was not entirely one way. She stood, her legs shaky, her pulse racing.

It was full daylight by now, and as Taro rested and healed she moved carefully around the room, blowing out candles. She fetched her gun, took it from its case, assembled it swiftly and slung it over her shoulder. She was lifting her cloak from its peg, her back to Taro, when she felt him wake.

She turned, smiling, and when despite herself she met his eyes, she felt their thoughts begin to mesh together. He gasped and she looked away. Resisting the temptation to dispense with words altogether, she forced herself to speak out loud. 'Can you stand?'

He nodded and swung his legs gingerly onto the floor.

She walked over to him, aware of the delicious tension of their new bond. 'I'm going to put this on you; when I wear it with my gun it tends to catch, and carrying you as well ...' She let her voice trail away as she reached up and fastened her cloak round his neck.

He closed his eyes.

She knew how her touch was singing through him; she felt it too, the joy of his presence. After years of solitude her mind yearned for this closeness. She had given in to her desire, telling herself she had to, to help an innocent. It felt so good ... *too* good. The line between love and annihilation was so very thin.

She stepped back and he opened his eyes. He looked at the gun on her shoulder. 'You think we'll need that?' he murmured, his voice heavy and sensual, as though he were asking another, altogether more intimate question.

She avoided his eyes. 'The dataspike will have the Minister's preferred time and place for the removal. We may not have the chance to come back here for the gun.'

'What's it feel like?'

She didn't need to ask him what he meant; he had never killed, though he had lived a step away from death all his life. 'The act of taking a life is a wonderful, terrible privilege. For me, it is far more than you could imagine, for when someone is about to die, I no longer have to hide from them. I am open to them, and they to me, if only for an instant. The shields are gone, the glamour is blown away, and in that moment I am complete. Killing is … addictive.' She laughed wryly at the reactions she was picking up from him. 'Aye, that is appalling, is it not? I told you I was a monster.' She kicked the door open.

He turned to stand beside her. Though they were barely touching, she could feel his heat. 'You said *humans* thought the Sidhe are monsters. That ain't the same thing.'

'Contempt for humanity is bred into the Sidhe; for their part, almost every human I have ever met would wish me dead if they knew the truth,' said Nual, somewhat bitterly. 'So why shouldn't I take their lives when they would happily take mine?' But she was not like her sisters. She had been born different, and she had made choices that would alienate her from them forever.

'Don't try to make me hate you. You know I can't,' he murmured.

She nodded. 'Just try not to love me, either. We can't afford to get lost in each other. Not now, perhaps not ever.'

She put an arm round his waist. Though she held him outside the cloak, not wanting to risk flesh on flesh, she still felt that spark of unity when they touched. Before they could give in to the mutual desire that sizzled between them, she stepped forward and they fell together into morning.

CHAPTER TWENTY-FOUR

'Hello? Who is this? Your com appears to be faulty, there's no image.'

'Sirrah Meraint.'

'Ah. You. How did you get this number?'

'I believe I told you, I do my research. I did call your office first, but you weren't there.'

'It's my day off.'

'How nice. Spending time with your lovely daughters, no doubt. Were you planning to take them anywhere, or are you just having a quiet day at home?'

'I— That's none of your business. What do you want?'

'I have a job for you.'

'I've told you, if and when Medame Reen contacts me again—'

'Not that. This is something different. I believe you have access to sophisticated decryption routines and the expertise to use them.'

'Yes, I do.'

'I have some encrypted data that I wish you to apply your skills to. As an added incentive I will even offer payment for this service.'

'Just knowing you would leave me alone would be payment enough, Screamer.'

'Oh, I think our association might be at an end soon enough. This job is extremely urgent, otherwise I would never be so rude as to interrupt your day off. I am hoping for results by this afternoon.'

'This afternoon? I can try – but I don't even have the data. Can you transmit a file?'

'I don't think that would be wise. I'll bring the chip to your office in half an hour. Unless you'd prefer I deliver it to your home?'

'I'll be there.'

Taro rested his head on Nual's shoulder and thought of nothing.

Everything was so simple; as long as he was close to her, the other stuff, the bad stuff, none of it mattered. Right now he was content, cradled in her arms while she flew beneath the world.

'Taro.'

He liked the way her whisper disturbed his hair, the sense of his name forming in her mind before the sound escaped her lips.

'Taro!' she whispered more urgently, 'you must not let yourself get too close. You must resist the temptation.'

He sighed. If only she'd let him complete their union, let it become physical as well as mental, then everything would be perfect, but instead she was forcing him away, keeping her distance – and he didn't know why, when she obviously wanted him as much as he wanted her.

'I warned you this could happen.' He felt her shiver. 'Physical proximity will make it worse.'

'Wouldn't call this worse,' he grinned.

'Taro, we cannot let ourselves get distracted. Remember *vengeance*, Taro. Remember Malia and your oath.'

'I remember.' And he did. Those things still mattered, and he'd have to deal with them soon enough, but not now, not yet.

'Focus on the future. I know it hurts, but you have to. *We* have to.'

He laughed lightly, feeling his ribs (which didn't hurt any more) move against her slender body. 'I will. But things've never made sense before. All that crap in the songs an' stories. *Love.* I always thought ... it's just what yer body does to yer head when you've had a solid prime bit of grind, ain't it?'

Despite her attempt to keep barriers between them, he could sense her amusement.

He went on, 'But it's real. I know that now. It's like ... the world re-organises itself, has re-organised itself, around you—'

'—Taro—'

'No, it makes sense. You and I, we're alike, don't you see? You do,

I know it. Neither of us could ever show our true selves before! It's just like Malia said: you kill strangers; I fuck them, but either way they ain't really people to us. They can't be. So we've both developed barriers – like, those topside delicacies, the ones they grow in tanks in the top restaurants, *shells*, that's it. When you have to use and be used just to live, you end up livin' inside a shell, but if you find someone else who's the same as you, who understands the *real* you, then the shell breaks. It's the best thing that can 'appen. It's the reason we're alive.'

'No, Taro,' Nual said slowly, 'it's an illusion, a side-effect of the way I healed you.'

He nuzzled into her shoulder and whispered, 'I can't accept that. It feels so right. This can't jus' be some random weirdness in me head. This is how things is meant to be: us in unity, no walls, perfect trust. You know it, don't you?'

She didn't say anything for a while, and he could feel her withdrawing further from him, reluctantly but firmly excluding him from her thoughts. Finally she said softly, 'I know it. I was born into unity. But I rejected it. I can never go back.'

Taro said nothing. He didn't have any idea what was really behind her shell, but if she *had* made him love her with her Sidhe magic, he was hardly going to be able to tell. There was no point trying. And if he didn't survive the trouble they were heading into, he'd rather die for her than for the Minister or for some high-and-noble idea of duty or loyalty, or even for revenge – though he would hate Scarrion for as long as he had breath in his body. Nual had never lied to him, and she had done everything she could to help him. He knew she loved him too, at least a little.

He felt her tense just before she whispered, 'Hellfire! This we don't need.'

Taro raised his head to see a figure, another Angel, flying towards them from the edge of the City. She was moving fast, brown hair and red cloak streaming out behind her.

He felt Nual kick out and they changed direction, moving more slowly. 'Keep a look-out for a way up into the mazeways, Taro,' she said urgently. 'We can't face her down here in the open.'

Taro obeyed, scanning the underside of the Undertow for a gap.

'There's a hole in the nets comin' up on your left, just after that water-trap with the yellow-and-brown banners.' He had no idea where they were; he hoped they weren't about to come up inside someone's home-space.

Nual followed his directions. By the time they reached the gap the pursuing Angel was close enough that Taro could make out her face. He thought she looked familiar, but before he could puzzle out where he might've seen her before Nual rose into an un-netted stretch of maz-eway, cutting off his view. There was a gap of some two metres of open space before the next vane. From the stench of blood and boiling fat, Taro guessed they were close to a flesher's.

Nual swivelled in the air and Taro stepped out of her embrace onto the ledge without being told. He wanted to stay with her, except ... *no, he needed to get under cover before the other Angel arrived* – he didn't know if the thought came from her head or his, but either way it made sense. He looked around, but the nearest opening on the ledge was ten metres off, and barred with what looked, even from this distance, like a pretty solid door. He pressed his back against the vane and watched Nual, still floating just off the edge of the mazeway, facing the direction the Angel was approaching from. Despite Taro's feelings for her, Nual's expression disconcerted him: she looked completely calm, a little curi-ous, not at all like someone about to face a crisis.

When the other Angel rose through the gap Taro realised where he'd seen her before: in the Exquisite Corpse, just a couple of days ago, when she'd decided to slice him up to relieve the tension of a bad day. Her gaze flicked across him, confused, and he suddenly remembered he was wearing Nual's cloak; though it felt light as water to the touch, if he'd thought to pull it round himself he could've disappeared completely. He must look well freaky now, with his head and one arm sticking out of nowhere.

'That yours?' she said, addressing Nual but nodding in Taro's direction. Though she was sober now, Taro heard the same anger in her voice.

Nual said nothing.

The other Angel shrugged back her own cloak, which shimmered and started to pick up the colours of the background. 'Don't answer, then. He'll be mine soon enough.'

'Do you have business with me?' asked Nual softly.

'Business?' The Angel frowned. 'You don't know?'

'Perhaps you would like to tell me?'

The Angel laughed and a flash of silver showed at her palms. 'After all those years of perfect service, you've finally blown it, baby.' Taro thought she sounded pleased at the thought of Nual having fucked up.

'You are entitled to your opinion. But I have City business and I must ask you not to interfere.' Nual didn't move, kept her hands loose by her sides.

'City business, eh? That makes two of us. I'm just doing the Minister's bidding. Which is more than you've done, apparently.' She flicked her wrists, extending both blades to their full length.

'Ah. I see.'

'Do you? About time.' She drew herself erect and said gleefully, 'For disobeying the Minister's direct order to perform a removal, I call feud on you, Nual. Defend yourself.'

And with that she launched herself at Nual, who spun away, deflecting the Angel, who flew past her, blades outstretched.

Nual hung motionless, her expression dark. Her blades were not extended.

The Angel leapt again, and again Nual reacted almost before her opponent had moved.

The other Angel swore and came to rest by the vane just across the mazeway from Taro. 'C'mon, bitch,' she invited, 'fight me.'

'No.' Nual's blades were still sheaved.

'Hah.' The Angel tossed her head. She looked over at Taro and her lip curled into a smile. 'If you won't fight for yerself—' she murmured. She turned and leapt at Taro.

The image of the Angel, blades extended, filled Taro's world, then his legs gave way. He felt the mazeway vibrate as she slammed into it, heard her blades scrape the vane above him where his head had been a moment before.

He drew himself into a tight ball, pulling the cloak over his head.

Blades swished through air. He tensed himself for the killing blow.

There was a noisy scuffle, a thud, then silence.

After a tense moment he uncurled himself. The other Angel was lying face-down on the mazeway. Nual, still floating, bent over her, then turned her onto her back. She looked unharmed, peaceful, as though she'd just fallen asleep. Nual laid a hand on the side of her face and stayed like that for some time.

Taro, his racing heart calming a little, untangled himself from the cloak and sat up.

When Nual finally looked over to him, her eyes were distant, her expression serene, inhuman. He felt a shiver run along his spine. 'Is she dead?' he whispered.

'No. When she wakes up she will not remember meeting us, nor will she have any idea how she got here.' Nual straightened and floated over to him, offering him a hand to help him stand.

As their eyes met he felt an unspoken acknowledgement pass between them: he'd seen her true self, and she knew it.

He hesitated for no more than a heartbeat. Then he took her hand and let her pull him into her arms. Her palms, hardened to act as foils to her blades, were cold to the touch.

She was an alien and a murderer. By her own admission she'd fucked with his mind.

But he loved her.

CHAPTER TWENTY-FIVE

Elarn had not let herself think of anything while she lay next to Salik, but on the pedicab journey back to her hotel her head was spinning. Salik had been talking to his bodyguard about a gun, and a dataspike – and had he really mentioned Nual? Perhaps this was not about her; he had a life outside of their relationship, of course he did, and she had no right to intrude on it. She would have dismissed the com call as nothing to worry about … except for the way he had referred to her. 'The delectable Medame Reen' was not a phrase a lover would use, was it? Especially not when talking to someone like Scarrion.

The thoughts chased each other in Elarn's head. What if she was wrong? What if she had misheard him or, in her dream-haunted state, misinterpreted what she had heard? By running away from him, she would hurt him, and hurt herself, all for nothing – and she would be alienating her only ally.

She should never have involved Salik Vidoran in her problems; it was just that she had panicked when she found out what Lia had become. If he really loved her, then it wasn't fair to draw him into that unholy mess. And – she didn't want to think this, but she couldn't let it go – if he wasn't being straight with her, the last thing she should do was put herself in a position of being indebted to him. Love didn't matter as much as saving her own skin and sanity.

But even if he was not the ally she had hoped for – still hoped for, with heart-stopping fervour – she could still get someone else to kill Lia. She had been thinking Salik might let her use his bodyguard for the unpleasant task, but in a lawless place like this there must be plenty of people who would kill for money. It was an obvious solution to her problem, and she might have considered it earlier had she not been too busy being scared and falling in love. Such people would hardly be listed on the com, but the infobroker might know how to get in touch.

By the time Elarn walked into the lobby of the Manor Park Hotel, dawn was washing out the neon brilliance of the Streets. Back in her room, lying fully clothed on her bed, she turned on the com and set it on a low volume, random scan. But the drone of the holo, far from shutting out thoughts of Salik, reminded her of him in the most trivial, banal ways: recordings of Assembly proceedings (*see, you do have a life of your own, Salik, my love*); lifestyle programs showing some of the most prestigious State Quarter apartments (*your rooms were impersonal, but when I was there with you they felt like our haven*); adverts for 'The best guards, all ex-militia: Want a Guide, a Guard and a Night-time Companion? – We can provide all three in one package, men women and hermaphrodites, for your pleasure and protection.' (You *are my pleasure and my protection.*)

She turned the visuals off and turned on some music, one of her own recordings.

She must have dozed off, though for once there were no dreams. The chirp of the com woke her. She struggled to sit up, then stopped, hand poised over the accept button. It would be him. It *must* be him. She should take the call, challenge him about what she had overheard – but that would mean admitting she did not trust him. And how would she know if he did lie? She forced herself not to move, to listen while the call rang out. A few seconds later the 'message received' light blinked on. She stayed where she was and stared at the light.

He would have woken alone, annoyed, then cursed her and commed her to try to get her back under his control.

He would have woken alone, worried, then missed her and commed her to see if she felt the same way he did.

She hit the play button.

He looked dishevelled and tired. 'Elarn? Are you all right? You were gone and I just wondered— Call me. Please?'

She found her eyes filling with tears. Just at the sight of him, damn it, the mere sight ... But she had no intention of calling him back. She had to know for certain she could trust him before she could go back to him.

Brooding would not help. She needed answers, and one at least was already waiting for her. She had asked Sirrah Meraint to find out if the apparent discrepancies between Salik's account and the records of his movements were real. If they were, it meant he had lied to her, and one lie was all she needed to confirm her fears.

And coming back to her main problem, the infobroker could tell her where to hire someone to kill Lia.

Elarn braced herself and called the infobroker's office, but all she got was a recorded message stating that he was unable to take her call. Not even voicemail.

As she shut down the com her eyes caught the time display: half past ten. Was there something happening at eleven? *Oh God!* She was meant to be in the cathedral in half an hour. Elarn laughed, hearing the hysteria in her voice. She couldn't sing at a time like this— Yes, yes she could. That was exactly what she should do: remember the things that mattered before, and that would matter again, if she survived this.

Or she could wait here for Salik to call and explain – without admitting that she had eavesdropped on him – why he had been talking about her as though she were merchandise, what he had meant about a gun and a dataspike, and what he was going to do to save her from having to kill Lia herself. And she could just assume that everything he told her would be the truth, because she wanted it to be.

She pulled on her cloak and set off for the cathedral.

As they dropped back below the mazeways, Taro glimpsed a dark shape and murmured a warning to Nual. A closer look told him it was no Angel, the shape was all wrong, and as it disappeared behind the thin dark line of the spine, he realised it was not just misshapen, but it was larger than a human too.

'Don't worry,' said Nual softly, 'if I'm not mistaken, that is Solo, on her way from the Corpse to my homespace, to warn me.'

'Warn you—? Oh.' About being marked, she meant.

The shape stopped, probably hovering under Nual's empty home. Taro looked away, scanning the underside of the City, not sure what he was looking for. 'Does she know?' he said at last, 'What you are, I mean.'

'Oh, aye. She is as much an exile from her people as I am from mine.'

Taro couldn't even begin to imagine how strange it must be to be the only one of your race in the world. 'That's why you two're such good friends.'

Nual laughed lightly, 'That and the fact that she is immune to Sidhe charms, being an empath herself.'

Taro opened his mouth to ask what an empath was but Nual was already answering his unspoken question, 'She can't be as precise or – or as forceful – as me, but she can read and influence the feelings of those around her.' He remembered how the Angel who'd threatened him in the Corpse – the same one they'd left lying asleep on the mazeway behind them – had suddenly decided not to bother with him. At the time he'd just put it down to the way Angels were, fiery and changeable; now he wondered if it was something to do with Solo.

'Aye,' Nual continued, her voice quiet, 'being able to influence your customers' moods is a useful talent in a barkeep.'

She fell silent and Taro got the impression she didn't much like talking about alien mind stuff. He didn't mind, it didn't freak him like she said it did most humans, but if she wanted to steer clear of the subject, well, he'd respect that. After all, he now realised, without respect there can be no real love.

They flew on in silence. After a while he felt her look upwards. 'We're nearly there, Taro. Can you check the banners on the water-traps?'

Taro had already recognised Fenya's row of yellow-and-silver 'traps in the distance, and several smaller ones were flying the colours of troupes he knew; he spotted Limnel's orange-and-green fluttering from a 'trap to the left. 'There, rimwards,' he said, pointing.

'I think we should avoid the front door,' Nual said. 'Do you know any other ways in?'

Taro vaguely remembered Arel taking him out of a back exit last night but there was no way he'd be able to find that again. He pushed the other details of that night out of his mind. 'I was only there a few days,' he mused. 'Maybe we could come up through the room where Limnel has his water-traps? There're no nets there, and it looks like there's only one 'trap down.'

Nual nodded and adjusted their course. As they got closer Taro found himself peering upwards; though the chances of being spotted were low, he had a sick feeling in the pit of his stomach, a mixture of nerves and shame. He almost wished he'd never insisted on coming back with Nual – but no, he had to face what he'd done, make amends. And he had to help Nual.

She headed for the end of the gap furthest from the creaking water-trap rope. Taro stayed still and quiet while she got into position.

As they rose up into Limnel's homespace Taro's heart jumped. Someone stood with their back to them, leaning over something on the floor. Taro heard the splash of water being poured at the same time as he realised who this was. He felt Nual tense.

'Osin,' said Taro, as much to stop Nual doing anything scary as to get the water-trap man's attention. Osin started, put down the tray he'd been emptying and turned around. Taro might once have found his look of wide-eyed amazement amusing, but right now he needed to keep things bolted down. 'You din't see nothin', right?' he whispered.

Osin, eyes fixed on the Angel who'd just appeared in his workspace, shook his head. As Nual floated to the floor and released Taro, the old man crossed his arms and bent his head. 'Lady,' he croaked, 'you was never 'ere. I understand.' He kept his head bowed while they walked past him.

Outside, the corridor was deserted. Taro heard distant voices, the usual hum of a busy homespace, but there was no alarm, no sign they'd been spotted coming in. Before they carried on he whispered to Nual, 'He's a good man. He was friendly to me.'

'I know,' she said.

Rather than think too much about *how* she knew, he moved in front to lead the way. As they approached the corridor leading to the whores' sleeping room the chatter of voices grew louder.

Suddenly Nual froze and pulled him after her into a side corridor. They pressed themselves against the vane.

A moment later a gaggle of painted tarts wandered out from the whores' room: the early shift, off topside for another day hustling the rollers. None of them even glanced their way. It felt weird to Taro that life was still going on as normal here when his world had been turned upside down.

He took half a step forward, but Nual's voice in his mind stilled him: *Wait. More coming.*

A moment later a couple of young lags passed the end of the corridor, one laughing at something the other one had just said.

Taro opened his mouth to speak, then changed his mind and thought clearly, *<That's Manak, the one Limnel told to copy the dataspike.>*

For a fraction of a second he thought she hadn't picked up the thought, then she responded, *<The one on the right?>*

Taro formed the thought *<Aye>*, and Nual stepped out into the corridor. As Taro followed her, the pair turned round to look at her, and the one on the left crumpled to the ground. Manak, his mouth open in shock, started to walk jerkily back towards the Angel.

Taro crouched, ready to defend them even though he didn't have a weapon, but Nual slipped a wordless reassurance into his mind. Manak stopped in front of Nual. She reached out to touch the lag's cheek with one finger. His face went slack, his eyes rolled back and he swayed on his feet. Nual traced her fingertip slowly down his cheek and neck, then drew a long slow breath.

'The copies of the dataspike are in the secure store, as you thought. He took several copies to give them a better chance of breaking the encryption.' Taro, faced with another demonstration of Nual's powers, was guiltily glad she'd chosen to speak out loud ... which was probably why she did it.

Taro tensed as Manak moved, but a feather-light touch in his mind told him not to worry. The lag reached into his jacket pocket and drew out a metal key, which he silently handed over to Nual. He bent down and started to drag his unconscious companion back down the corridor.

'What's he doin' now?' asked Taro.

Nual, her attention still fixed on the departing boy, said, 'Taking him to the nearest empty room and then having a little sleep himself, hopefully without remembering any of this. Most of the gang, including Limnel, are currently topside, which is good. But we should still hurry.' Her voice was tense and she didn't move until Manak had disappeared through a curtain into a side room.

Taro had started to move ahead to lead the way when it occurred to him that she must've read the directions from Manak's mind. Instead, he followed Nual. In the meeting room, one of the cooks was scrubbing down the table. He looked up as Nual and Taro passed, frowned and went back to his work. Taro was puzzled for a moment, until Nual silently assured him, <*When you are not expected, it is easy not to be seen.*>

There was no one in Limnel's private room but Taro still found himself going cold as they passed it, trying not to remember what had happened here just the previous night.

The key Manak had given Nual unlocked the padlocked door to the safe-room. The small room was lined with shelves crammed with prime loot, in bundles and boxes and bags. At the end stood a huge plastic water-box which had to contain over a hundred litres.

'I'll take the left wall, you take the right.' Nual sounded tense. Taro wondered if she knew how freaky it had looked when she'd controlled the gang members. 'Course she did. He began to see her point: she was a monster – or she could be, if she let herself be. It didn't change his feelings for her, not one bit.

On the top shelf Taro found a bolt of cloth that shimmered like oil in lamplight. Behind it was a wallet containing dozens of plastic packets of golden powder. He knew what that was. He tensed, waiting for his body's inevitable reaction. Nothing happened.

On the shelf below he spotted a familiar cloth-wrapped bundle: his flecks. He shoved them into his belt and checked the rest of the shelf, but it was mostly preserved food, including topsider delicacies, like dried fruit and chocolate. The next shelf held a pair of full-size holo-com units. The one below that had a boltgun, a couple of cutters and several boxes of bolts.

On the bottom shelf he found a bag of dataspikes, the common grey ones. He grabbed the whole bag, no time to check which ones had stuff on. 'Nual, I've got 'em!' he called.

<Someone's coming.>

Taro stuck his head out just far enough to see down the corridor. Four lags were coming their way. One was Resh, carrying a topsider popgun, another the woman he'd seen here on his first day. She had a boltgun. The other two were armed with flecks.

Nual unslung her own gun and slipped a finger under the trigger-guard in one smooth motion, then stepped out into the corridor. Taro stepped out behind her, and was pleased to note Resh's expression.

'We were just leaving,' Nual said tersely.

The lags exchanged glances, but no one moved. Nual sighed and twitched the end of her gun. A deep smoking gash appeared in the floor half a metre in front of Resh. The troupe members scattered.

As they disappeared round the corner he wondered why she hadn't just put them all to sleep.

She must have still been reading him as she said quietly, 'I manage well enough the human way, most of the time. And I have my limits. Time to leave.'

When he looked at her he saw she was pale as a pureblood downsider, her lips pressed into a thin line. Before he could say anything she grabbed his hand and broke into a run. No effort to be stealthy now; they just legged it for the water-trap room. Nual still had her gun out and she waved it threateningly at anyone who stepped out in front of them. No one argued. When they reached the 'trap-room Taro found that Osin had wisely made himself scarce. Without stopping, Nual slung the gun over her shoulder, grabbed Taro and stepped into the gap.

Close to her again, Taro felt how drained she was. He reached out, willing to help, to give her any support he could. For a moment he felt her begin to draw on his strength, then, abruptly, she shut him out and, as though nothing had happened, said out loud, 'We need to land some-where safe and check these dataspikes.'

Taro looked around. 'Fenya's,' he said. He felt Nual nod and they flew off hubwards, towards the water-trader's homespace. 'Won't it be encrypted?'

'It's meant for me. My com and password will decode it, even a copy.' She slowed as they approached Fenya's.

Taro shook the water-trader's alarm and a few seconds later Federin's

185

wrinkled face peered out. His surprise at seeing Taro gave way to awe when he saw who was with him. He almost tripped over his robes getting the door open. 'Lady, it's an honour to see you again so soon,' he said.

Nual led Taro inside. 'Thank you. Would you bar the door again, please?'

Federin had nearly pulled the door off its hinges in his haste to let the Angel in. Taro gave him a hand shutting it. It looked like Fenya was out, which was good; he'd caused her enough grief.

Federin crossed his arms, dipped his head and asked, 'May I get you anything, lady? Water? Food?'

'No, thank you. If anything I owe you, and your partner, for all you have done for me, and for Taro.'

Federin gave Taro a look that said that he wasn't sure that honour was deserved, but he just said, 'Then I'll leave you alone,' and scuttled off into a back room.

Nual sank to the floor and arranged herself comfortably cross-legged. 'Dataspike, please. Any one will do.'

Taro squatted next to her and handed her a 'spike from the bag. As his fingers brushed hers he felt her tremble.

She flicked the screen of her com up and clicked the first dataspike holder into a slot on the side. While she worked Taro bound his fleck sheaves to his wrists. When he had finished he looked over at Nual.

Without looking up from the screen she said, 'Nice blackmail material but not what we want. Next, please.'

This one had a single red line on the holder. While Nual slotted it in, Taro searched the bag and spotted two others with the same mark.

He looked up at Nual's hiss of indrawn breath in time to see her raise her head and close her eyes.

'No,' she said distinctly. She shook her head slowly, eyes still closed, then opened them and looked down at her com again. Taro was glad her mental shields were back in place. From the look on her face whatever was happening in her head wasn't pretty. 'That is not possible,' she whispered.

Taro reached out to touch her, to comfort her, but she had already whirled to her feet. 'Last chance, Taro,' she murmured with a softness at odds with the twisted look on her face. 'This is your last chance to cut and run.'

As though he could let Scarrion get away with it! As though he could let Malia die unavenged! *As though he could leave Nual* ... 'No, I'm with you,' he said.

She nodded. 'Then let's go.'

'To perform the hit?'

'Oh no. This is one mission I would never take. We're going to see the Minister.'

CHAPTER TWENTY-SIX

Grace Street was further proof, as though Elarn needed it, that everything was for sale in Khesh City: temples, churches and shrines lined the Street, selling nearly every human religion Elarn had heard of, and several she had not. She almost expected to find an Ascensionist Chantry here, but the Sidhe religion had disappeared from the universe, even if the Sidhe themselves had not.

The Cathedral of Christos and the Almighty was one of the largest buildings on the Street, towering over its immediate neighbours. The frontage had high arches and a small spire.

She paid the pedicab driver and walked to the entrance porch, which was faced in stone bas-reliefs showing the suffering and sacrifice of the Manifest Son. A board outside announced that the cathedral was temporary closed, but the guard on the door had already spotted her and was on his way over. Once he'd satisfied himself she was indeed Medame Reen, he let her in.

Inside, the architects had worked wonders. The ceiling had to be a holo, but the vaulting looked perfect, the stained glass shone and the golden icons gazed down at her from their niches. A group of some thirty sombrely dressed men and women were milling about at the end of the chancel.

This was the first time she had been in a Salvatine church since her parents had died, and the strange mix of memory and novelty gave her a sense of dissociation. As she started down the aisle she barely resisted the urge to cross herself.

A man peeled off from the crowd of singers and came towards her. His expression was uncertain and it suddenly occurred to her what she must look like: still wearing last night's clothes, hair a mess, no make-up … and reeking of sex. She stopped.

He halted a few steps away. 'Medame Reen?' When she nodded the man frowned and continued, 'We were getting worried. You're quite late and we only have an hour before the cathedral is re-opened to the public.'

A huge, skeletally-thin Christos-figure hung over the altar. The statue's drooping head said that there was little hope, even for believers, and none at all for the damned.

Elarn forced herself to look away from the image. 'Of course. I'm sorry.'

'We can do introductions later. Shall we go straight into the *Requiem*?'

Elarn followed him up the nave to where the singers had arranged themselves in four neat rows in the choir stalls, leaving her alone in the middle. The glorious rose window at the end of the aisle showed scenes of martyrdom and redemption. She looked away.

The organ played the first few bars of the familiar music. The choir came in softly and Elarn closed her eyes, waiting for the music to carry her away. The moment passed. Her voice deserted her.

The singers faltered, then stopped. Elarn opened her eyes to see their conductor frowning at her, hand upraised. 'Shall we start again?' he said.

Elarn nodded dumbly.

This time she tensed, ready to jump in on her cue, and she managed to force out a note that was in tune and in time, but it sounded strained and unnatural. Her breath wouldn't come and, as she raised her voice, as the sound started to build, she felt something else rising within her.

The scream.

In surrendering herself to Vidoran she had removed one more barrier. It wanted to come out.

She stopped, biting down on the note.

The conductor looked at her, consternation on his face. Unable to return his gaze she muttered, 'I'm sorry. I can't do this, not now.' She fled down the aisle, tears making the candles swim and dip in her vision.

What little comfort had ever been offered by the church was no longer available to her. She was damned. She should never have come here.

Outside she hailed the first pedicab she saw, but when the driver turned to ask her destination she hesitated. Her hotel room was the closest she had to a safe space, but if Salik didn't get an answer from her com, he might go there to find her. If she saw him in the flesh, she would not be able to resist him. She would believe whatever he told her.

She needed to know the truth. And she needed to go somewhere Salik would not find her, for she didn't dare see him again until she knew she could trust him.

She told the driver to head for Talisman Street.

Taro stumbled out of Nual's arms into the noise and bustle of Chow Street. The sounds and scents of the 'Street of a Thousand Flavours' wafted up to greet him and he drew in a deep breath, inhaling the smells of frying meats, spices and burnt sugar. The early morning crowds scattered, casting curious, fearful glances at the Angel and the half-naked downsider. Taro swayed for a moment, gravity pulling at his battered body.

Nual raised her wrist. 'All right, you bastard,' she said into her com. 'You've got my attention.'

She lowered her arm and gave Taro a tired smile. 'He'll be here soon. Meantime, we should eat.'

She took his hand and led him across the Street to a stall with a brightly striped awning. The small queue at the stall moved aside as they approached. Nual ordered two steaming paper cups of noodle soup, then led him to a seat near the fence where they sat down side by side. Though it felt odd to be stuffing noodles into his mouth when the world was falling apart, Taro found he was ravenous.

He was halfway through his soup when she placed her barely touched cup down by the seat and stood.

The Minister was coming down the steps from the circle-car station. Though his face below the shadow of his hat wore its usual expression of faint, fatherly interest, he was actually hurrying, taking the steps two at a time. Taro found his haste freaky; downside legend had it that he never hurried for anything.

Taro stood too, but he didn't cross his arms or drop his gaze. He doubted the Minister would have noticed anyway; all his attention was on Nual, and hers on him. Something about the way they looked at each other told Taro that, as he'd suspected, their relationship went beyond master and minion. For a wild moment he wondered if they'd once been lovers.

They faced each other silently for half a dozen heartbeats. Then the Minister looked away from Nual and addressed Taro. 'I see you have thrown your lot in with her. I thought that might happen.'

'Aye, sirrah, I 'ave,' he said, trying to keep the shake out of his voice.

The Minister looked back at Nual. 'What surprises me more is that you chose to let him live.'

Nual spoke in a low, even tone. 'Aye. And I decided to trust him too. In fact, I trust him more than I trust you.'

The Minister raised a slender eyebrow. 'I'm hurt.'

'So hurt you felt the need to set your Angels on me.'

'You ignored a direct order. I had no choice.'

'The orders were intercepted. It took a while to recover them.'

'Intercepted?' The Minister gave Taro a cool look. Taro, to his surprise, found he wasn't afraid. He'd done his best to obey the Minister. He'd nearly died trying to protect the orders. He no longer felt any guilt at his failure; if anything, he felt angry. He'd let himself be used, and what had he received in return? He'd had no help, been given no reward. He said nothing.

The Minister cleared his throat. 'Is there anything you – either of you – feel I should know about recent events in the Undertow?'

Taro looked at Nual, and saw her mouth curl into a smile. 'No,' she said.

'You always did like your privacy,' the Minister said. 'I can't make you explain yourself, but I can order your death if you disobey me. Or should I tell my loyal Angels that you have not gone rogue after all?'

'If you mean,' said Nual slowly, 'will I perform the removal, then the answer is no, of course not. Elarn Reen is not a politician and ordering me to kill her is illegal.'

'Technically, that is entirely true,' the Minister agreed affably. 'But one must adapt to survive, and such desperate times sometimes call for a little rule-breaking. And asking you to kill her *did* finally get your attention.'

'Simply telling me she was on Vellern would have done that.'

The Minister looked sceptical. 'Are you telling me that you really had no idea she was here?'

Taro wondered who in the City's name Elarn Reen was, and what she'd done that was so bad the Minister wanted her dead.

Nual, sensing his confusion, turned to him. 'Elarn Reen was someone I trusted, long ago. She was listed as my legal guardian on the ID I had when I arrived in Khesh City, which is how he' – she nodded in the Minister's direction – 'knows about her. She lives on a world a long way from here and, given that she never wanted to see me again, I had assumed that was where she would stay.'

'As had I,' the Minister agreed. 'From what little you told me I hardly expected her to follow you here.' His voice grew hard. 'Incidentally, my dear, just how far did you say you trusted this young downsider?'

Nual laughed, as though she had been caught out but didn't care. She lowered her voice and whispered to Taro, 'He hates it when I answer questions before they are asked.'

Taro gawped, then stuttered, 'You mean he knows—?'

'—what she is?' interrupted the Minister. 'Of course I know she's Sidhe. But it was a condition of her remaining in my City that she never use her powers without my consent.'

Nual finally looked at the Minister. 'And the rules of the Concord state that only politicians can be removed. Desperate times, as you say.'

'Ah.' He turned to Taro and said, 'That's me told.'

Taro couldn't tell whether the Minister was amused or furious.

Nual sighed and shook her head. 'I have spent seven years pretending not to be what I am – but no more, not if my sisters are coming after me. And to answer your question, I meant what I said. I trust Taro completely.'

Taro felt a terrifying rush of pleasure – she *did* love him. He just hoped he could survive that love.

'And, sirrah,' she drawled the title mockingly, 'believe it or not, I had no idea Elarn was here until I read your order to kill her.'

The Minister nodded, ignoring her tone. 'I have no reason to doubt that. Nevertheless, she is here, and she has already invested considerable effort in trying to trace you. I have yet to establish precisely why, but I feel it is unlikely that she wants to renew your friendship.'

'You think the Sidhe sent her?'

'None of my scanners have picked up anything, so she's not a glamoured Sidhe, or anything as unsubtle as that. She's not even, as far as I can tell, under direct Sidhe influence. But we both know how devious those bitches can be, and I hardly think the woman would come to the Three Cities by choice. The most logical conclusion is that they are behind her decision to visit Vellern.'

'And what do you want me to do about it? You can hardly expect me to kill my friend simply because you tell me to.'

'If she is still your friend,' the Minister pointed out. 'No, I didn't really expect you to accept the removal; ordering you to kill her was a way of shaking you up, to see how you responded. I took your lack of response to mean that you had your own agenda, possibly even that you knew she was here and had been in contact with her. I declared you rogue on the assumption that whatever you were up to, you were no longer loyal to me. However, given that you have – *finally* – started talking to me, I will call my Angels off.'

'I would appreciate that.'

'And as for what to do about Elarn Reen, well—' He paused, and spread his hands, 'I give you full leave to perform whatever obscene magics you require to find out why she's really here. If she is a Sidhe agent, then at the very least you must convince her to leave my City – though I suspect if that is the case you might want to change your own plan and kill her. But I do need to know what she is really up to and who else is involved.'

Nual nodded. 'Fair enough. I will go to her and I will find out why she's here. But I will not kill her.'

'Even if she is a Sidhe agent?'

Nual paused. After a moment she said, 'Elarn is terrified of the Sidhe. If she is serving them willingly then she is no longer the woman I knew.'

'Which would make it easier. And if her presence here is just a co-incidence, then you can always just make her forget she ever met you, can't you?'

Taro felt Nual rein in her anger. All she said was, 'Where is she now?'

'She is currently en route from Grace Street to the offices of a certain Ando Meraint, infobroker. You'll find him about halfway down Talisman Street, above a big antiques emporium specialising in offworld fetish gear.'

'I'll find it.' She shrugged her gun off her shoulder.

The Minister frowned. 'What are you doing?'

'I am going as Elarn's friend, not as your assassin, so I won't be needing this.' She handed the gun to Taro. When he hesitated, she whispered, 'Don't worry. It's safe enough if you keep your fingers clear of the trigger-pad.'

Taro took the gun. It was lighter than he expected, almost as if this symbol of the Angels' power no longer held the weight it once had – but he was still careful to hold it by the strap.

Nual turned back to the Minister. 'I want you to re-code the gun so Taro can use it too.'

'Now why should I want to do that?'

'Because I am not likely to need it, given that you've as much as ordered me to use other methods. And because Taro has lost his family and his status, he's been jerked around by everyone – including you, and me, at first – and yet he still remains loyal to the City. He deserves to be given the means to fight back. And he deserves honesty.'

'Meaning?'

Nual turned back to Taro. 'Ask him anything you need to know. If he doesn't answer, ask me when I get back.' She looked sideways at the Minister. 'And you know, I think, just how biased my answers are likely to be.'

She was leaving him. Taro said, 'D'you have to go alone? I mean, can't I help?'

Nual smiled at him. 'You can help, by staying alive. And by making our *master* here as uncomfortable as possible with awkward questions while you wait for me.' She hesitated for a moment before leaning forwards and kissing him briefly on the mouth. The taste of her thrilled through him.

When he opened his eyes she was gone. He looked up and saw her, now just a dark streak against the orange sky.

CHAPTER TWENTY-SEVEN

When the door buzzer went, Meraint assumed Scarrion had come back for the results of his decryption job. The bastard would have to wait; the encryption on the file was complex and difficult, requiring carefully timed input from several subordinate algorithms, and he had just reached a crucial point. 'You're early!' he said without looking up from his work. 'I haven't finished yet.'

'I'm sorry?'

That wasn't the Screamer. He hastily collated the final two sub-files and checked the image inset at the top of his screen. Elarn Reen was staring up into the camera; she looked a mess: no make-up, tangled hair loose over her shoulders and dark circles showing under puffy eyes. But much as he might feel sorry for her, she was a complication he could not afford right now. 'Medame Reen, I'm sorry, I didn't know it was you. I don't suppose you could maybe come back in a couple of hours—'

'I'm afraid not. I did try calling you but I couldn't get through. I need your help.'

'I'm afraid this isn't a good time, medame.'

She blinked and he saw that she was close to tears. Meraint wondered what had happened to her since they'd last spoken.

'Unfortunately,' she said slowly, 'I have run out of people to turn to, so if you can't see me now, I'll just wait here until you can.'

He considered calling her bluff but he didn't like to think what would happen if she was still on his doorstep when the Screamer arrived.

'You'd better come in, but this will have to be quick; I really am on a deadline.'

A moment after he pressed the door release the decrypt routine pinged to indicate completion. Meraint, gratified at his success, started to read the words turning from gibberish to text on his screen.

Oh shit.

The Screamer had to be kidding.

Elarn paused on the landing outside the infobroker's office and took a deep breath. On the pedicab ride over she had found herself murmuring over and over, under her breath, 'Let him be true, let him be true.' More than anything, she wanted Meraint to tell her that Salik had nothing to hide, and if so, she would take that as a sign she could trust the Consul. She would call him from the infobroker's office and meet up with him and he would put his arms around her and tell her that everything was going to be all right.

Or, if he had lied, the infobroker might be able to tell her where she could get help to fulfil her mission. She would enlist whatever aid she needed, spend whatever credit it took to kill Lia, then return home and try to forget Salik.

Those were her options. Simple as that. She opened the door.

The infobroker, staring intently at something on the screen before him, did not look up as she entered.

She cleared her throat.

Ando Meraint pulled his gaze away from the screen. For a moment she glimpsed shock in his face, then the professional mask was back in place. 'Ah, Medame Reen. I must apologise for my rudeness, but—'

Elarn cut across him. 'You're obviously busy, so I won't keep you long, but I do need to know what you found.'

'What I found?' He sounded frightened, as though she were accusing him of something other than making a professional enquiry.

'Yes. I asked you to find out whether Salik Vidoran had any business interests outside Vellern.'

The infobroker refused to meet her eyes. 'Well, I— As I said at the time, getting access to information held outside the City is more complicated, takes longer—'

'You haven't done it yet.'

'No. I'm sorry ... I will, but as I said, I have other problems at the moment.'

'I will pay whatever it takes to make this a priority.'

'It's not a matter of money.'

He kept looking back at the screen, as if hoping that if he ignored her she might go away. But he was her last hope, and she wasn't going anywhere. Quietly she said, 'I have another request which, your present problems allowing, I would like you to also consider. If one were – *hypothetically* speaking – to want someone killed, someone ... someone hard to kill ... how would one go about it?'

'What?' He looked up at her, than back at the screen again, as though whatever was displayed there had somehow anticipated her question.

'I said, if I wanted someone killed—'

'Medame Reen, I think you should leave now,' Meraint said, his forehead shiny with sweat. 'I'm sorry, but I don't think I can help you any more.'

He was scared. Fine, so was she, and desperate. She needed to make him see just how desperate. She fumbled in the bag hanging at her shoulder. 'I don't want to make things more difficult for you when you have been so helpful—' *Where was the damn thing?* 'But I'm pretty sure you must know the kind of people I need to get in contact with.' There it was. 'And if money won't motivate you, perhaps the threat of violence will.' She pulled the gun from her bag and pointed it at him in what she hoped was a convincing manner.

He watched the tip of the weapon, which jittered despite her attempts to hold it steady, and said quietly, 'Why don't you put that thing away before someone gets hurt?' As he spoke he started to edge one hand under the desk.

'Don't move! I don't want to shoot you, but I will if you don't co-operate. Now, I have to arrange to have someone killed and it goes without saying that I'll need help to do it. I will pay whatever it takes.' Her hands wouldn't stay still. The gun felt like a venomous animal, a creature with its own mind that could turn on her in an instant.

He nodded slowly, his eyes still on the gun. 'It isn't about money any more. You are obviously an innocent caught up in matters you've no control over, which, believe it or not, is a position I can sympathise with. I can see that you're frightened, and frightened people do things they regret. I'll do what I can to help you. But please, put the gun down.'

At last he appeared to have grasped how desperate she was. She let the gun fall to her side, relieved that she hadn't needed to use it.

'Thank you.' He hesitated, then continued, 'Before we go any further, there's something you need to see.' He reached forward and swivelled his screen round to face her.

Elarn started to read the text displayed there. 'By order of the head of the Kheshi League of Concord, and in accordance with the will of the people ...' She looked at him. 'What is this? I don't understand.'

'It's orders for a removal.'

'Why are you showing this to me?'

'Keep reading.'

Her eyes scanned the file. The first time she saw her name she didn't make the connection. She read the line out loud. 'For the death of Elarn Reen, citizen of Khathryn.'

She staggered and almost collapsed 'That's *impossible*! I mean I'm just— I'm not even *from* the Confederacy! How can I be—? They can't do this, can they?'

'Not legally, no,' the infobroker told her. 'But, Medame Reen, if I were you, I would walk right out of here, take a pedicab to the transit hall and leave Vellern as quickly as you possibly can.'

Orders to kill her. Elarn's head swam. 'You're sure this is genuine? I mean, where did you get this? Surely these things aren't—'

There was a buzz from the desk and a window popped up in the corner of the screen. Elarn leapt back as Lia's image appeared – not Lia as she had known her on Khathryn, but as she was now, the woman in the clip Meraint had sent her.

Meraint grabbed the screen and swung it back round to face him. 'Oh shit,' he muttered, 'just when I thought my day couldn't get any worse.' He looked up at Elarn. 'Medame Reen, I have a back door. I recommend you use it.'

Elarn stared at the screen. Lia was here, now. Lia the Angel. Here to kill her.

'Medame Reen! You can't stay here! If you go into the kitchen alcove next to the door you came in by and open the cupboard door at the end, you'll find a staircase. The stairs loop round to come out at the side of the building, out of sight of the Street. I'll try to stall the Angel for a while, long enough for you to get clear. I'm sorry, but that's all I can do for you.'

Every instinct screamed *run!* – run, or be killed. She looked round at Meraint's escape route. Out the back door, into the sidestreets ... and then where? Lia would find her, if not now, then soon enough. She looked down at the gun in her hand. It wasn't run or be killed; it was *kill* or be killed. 'Thank you, but no, I won't run. Not any more.'

'She'll kill you, you know that, don't you?' Meraint sounded as frightened as she felt.

'Quite possibly.' Was Lia really here to kill her? Did Lia even know she was here? Maybe she was only responding to the infobroker's curiosity, trying to find out why he had been trawling for data on her; a slim hope, but something to hold on to. And if she was looking for Elarn, well, she might still have a moment, a fraction of a second to act before Nual's Sidhe magic stole her will. She looked back at Meraint. 'Listen, whatever you were doing, keep doing it.'

'What?'

'Just keep working.' She backed away from him. She needed to get the position just right. She would only get one chance.

'Yes, of course, I'll pretend I've been alone all morning when the Angel arrives. I'll say that I have no idea why she's here and obviously I won't mention you. If she asks I can claim I haven't seen you since yesterday. Or perhaps you would prefer I said I've never met you—'

She cut across his nervous babble. 'That won't work with her.' She looked round the room then adjusted her position, taking another step backwards and turning towards the door. 'What I need is for you to pretend I'm not here.'

'What?' Meraint's gaze flicked over her, to the door, then back. 'Wait! Medame Reen – Elarn – this is insane! You can't be thinking of ambushing an Angel! She's a trained killer—'

'I know exactly what she is.'

The buzzer sounded again and Meraint involuntarily looked at the screen.

'Don't look at her!' Elarn Reen found she was shouting. She forced herself to calm down. 'Let her in, but don't look at her, don't think of her. Think about ... think about your holidays, your family, your work. You have to try to forget I'm here. You have to *believe* you're alone.'

'But—'

'Do it! Please, just focus on something other than me, then let her in!' She raised the gun, sighting on the door. 'I am *not* leaving, and she *will* come in. The longer we try and stall her, the more difficult this will be.'

Meraint wiped his forehead with the back of his hand, composed his expression and bent over his screen.

Elarn stretched the gun out in front of her, arms locked. She found herself muttering under her breath, 'Divine father, who watches us all—'

Empty your mind, the priests always said, empty your mind when you pray.

'Blessings on thy name ...'

As a child she had questioned their instruction; how could an empty mind comprehend anything?

'Thy wishes true, thy servants willing ...'

But an empty mind cannot easily be sensed.

'In our lives and in our deaths ...'

The litany was silent now, the effortless, familiar cadences filling her head.

Protect those who serve you ...

The door opened towards her, so for a moment she could see nothing. Then Lia stepped into the room.

And forgive those who wrong you ...

She was taller than Elarn remembered, her dark hair worn in a plait coiled round her head. She wore panels of scarlet over skin-tight black: sexy, deadly, outrageous. Elarn saw her in profile; she was looking at Meraint sitting behind his desk with his head bowed. She had no idea Elarn was there.

Shoot now! This is what the Sidhe want. Kill her, and you will be free.

But she had never killed. She could not kill. Not even Lia, the abomination she had once loved, the destroyer of her comfortable life. She might wish she had never met Lia, but that was a long way from killing her.

Her finger froze on the trigger. She couldn't do it.

Meraint looked up and a fraction of a second later Lia's head whipped round. Without registering where the impulse came from, Elarn flung the gun away with so much force that it bounced off the infobroker's desk.

Running was the only option now: she had to get away— But Lia was between her and the door. There was no way out. She backed away until she came up against the wall. Her knees buckled and she reached out to a cabinet for support.

Lia released Elarn from her gaze and started to close the distance slowly, almost reluctantly. Elarn watched her booted feet approach across the infobroker's plush carpet. She didn't dare to raise her head for fear of falling into the Sidhe's eyes.

Lia stopped a couple of paces off and spoke, her voice cold. 'You should have shot me. You won't get another chance.'

Elarn, calmer now her fate was sealed, said quietly, 'You would never have let me.'

'Of course not, had I known you were there. I assumed, incorrectly – and foolishly – that I had arrived here before you. I only realised you were waiting in ambush when the gentleman whose office we find ourselves in wondered why you had failed to shoot me. Which is something I find myself wondering too.'

'Because I'm a fool,' whispered Elarn.

'No.' Lia's voice was as musical as Elarn remembered, though deeper, calmer, more melancholy. 'You did not shoot because you do not really want to kill me. You always were much better at fear than hate.'

'For all the good it's done me.' Her fate had been sealed from the moment her brother had returned with this fascinating refugee from a lost age.

'Why did you come here, Elarn?'

Elarn didn't consider lying. There was no point. 'They traced you to Vellern. They came to me and told me I had to come here to find you. What could I do?'

'Ah. So you had no choice.'

She straightened slightly, though she still kept her head down, avoiding Lia's eyes. 'I am not their creature, Lia. I am their victim.'

Lia murmured, 'You forget, they're my enemies too. And my name is Nual now.'

Elarn looked over at the gun lying next to the desk. This would be so much easier if she could feel hatred, or even anger, but all she felt was a distant sorrow at the unfairness of it all. 'Lia, Nual, whatever you choose to call yourself, whatever you pretend to be, they're still your sisters.'

Lia said quietly, as though to herself, 'If you understood what I have done, and what I have given up, you would know that is no longer true. I can never go back.'

Elarn didn't want to sympathise with her. She must not forget what this woman was. 'But they don't want you back. They want you dead.'

'Aye, no doubt they do.' Lia's voice was cold again, cold and tired. 'They want me dead and they dare not come to Vellern in person so they sent you to do their will.'

'But I didn't come here by choice! And I didn't kill you – I could have, you said so yourself. But I didn't.' Elarn raised her eyes to see Meraint watching the encounter with rapt attention.

Lia continued, 'And I will always remember that. But what now? You had your chance, but you didn't take it, so you have failed. What will you do?'

'I don't know,' Elarn said, trying not to let despair colour her voice. 'Leave, if you will let me. They will be watching for me, but maybe I'll get lucky.'

'And when they find you again? Aren't you scared of what they'll do to you?'

'Of course I'm scared,' she whispered, 'I'm terrified. But I can't kill you, and I can't spend the rest of my life hiding out on this crazy world of assassins and muggers.'

'You're right enough there. Hiding only postpones the inevitable.'

'But would you let me go, just like that? You know I'm— what's the term they use here? Marked? I'm marked for removal. And you're an Angel now. I thought you had come here to kill me.'

'Those are my orders, but I had no intention of killing you … not unless you were their creature.'

'Which I am not!'

'So you believe.' She stepped back, giving Elarn a clear path to the door. 'Go. Walk out of here and leave Vellern.'

'You're really going to let me leave, just like that?'

'I will not stop you. Go now.'

She should go … but she did not move; she *could not* move. Her body refused to obey her. 'No!' she screamed, as though force of will or hysteria could force movement from her rebellious muscles, 'stop it!'

'I'm not doing anything,' Lia said. 'Save for disarming you when I saw the gun I have not influenced you.'

'But I can't move,' Elarn said plaintively. Her limbs were frozen, locked. Her body thrummed painfully with the effort of trying to break free from the compulsion. *Move, damn you!*

Lia sighed. 'Forgive me for saying this, Elarn, but you are not the ideal choice for an assassin. They knew this. Did you really think they wouldn't build in safety measures? I assume they went to considerable effort to track you down and persuade you to come here, and even though you were strong enough not to pull the trigger when it came to it, I will bet they put in safeguards to make sure that you would not shirk your duty. Most will be subtle, choices you make that you could later rationalise as your own. But anything as blatant as an attempt to leave without completing your mission would simply remove your ability to act.'

'Oh God.' Elarn closed her eyes. Now that she was no longer trying to move she found herself relaxing and control returned to her quivering limbs. But her mind was in turmoil. 'So I can't know how far it goes, if anything I've done is *real*.'

'I would like to think,' said Lia quietly, 'that the woman who chose not to shoot me was the real Elarn Reen.'

She blinked her eyes open again; tears escaped down her cheeks. 'How ironic. I finally found the strength to disobey them in the one thing they wanted most – the one thing I *think* they wanted – but how can I know? I can't know *anything*: every action I've performed, every choice I've made … I can't know if any of it was me, or their implanted compulsions.' She began to laugh hysterically.

'Elarn, stop. I can know. I can try to find out the truth – if you let me.'

Elarn choked out, 'No!' What choice did she have? After a few moments, she whispered, 'Is there no other way?'

'This has to be your choice, Elarn. I am not going to coerce you.'

'Swear it,' Elarn cried, 'swear you're not forcing me, you won't force me, and all you'll do is look. Swear on the memory of what we once were to each other.'

Lia flinched, but said clearly, 'I swear on the love I had for you, and for Jarek, that I will not coerce you, I will only look, and that I will try to help you, if you let me.'

Elarn sighed. 'What do I have to do, to make this work?'

'Nothing, other than give your permission.'

She took a step forward. 'Well if it's that simple … You have my permission.'

Lia turned to look at the bemused infobroker, who had been following their exchange with mounting incomprehension. 'Be so kind as to watch over us,' she said to him.

He nodded agreement, and Elarn decided not to let herself wonder how much coercion or beguilement Lia might be employing with poor Ando Meraint.

Lia stepped up to her and Elarn finally met her eyes. *Christos, she had forgotten how beautiful the girl was.* Lia blinked, deliberately breaking contact, and offered her hands. Elarn hesitated for a moment, then placed her hands in Lia's. Her palms felt cold and hard, alien – as she was.

'What now?' Elarn whispered.

'Look at me.'

CHAPTER TWENTY-EIGHT

Taro kept staring at the sky long after Nual had disappeared over the rooftops. He had a terrible, growing conviction that he'd never see her again.

When he finally looked back, the Minister was watching him. It reminded him of the way Malia had looked at him when he did something well-meaning but dumb.

'So,' said the Minister finally, 'do you think I should recode Nual's gun for you?'

With Nual gone, Taro's earlier confidence was fading, but even so, he'd never think of the Minister in quite the same way again. 'It's what she asked you to do, sirrah,' he said politely.

'Hmm.' The Minister sat in the seat Nual had occupied. 'Yes, it was. And you think I should do something that is against the rules of the Concord just because one of my Angels asked me to?'

Taro eased himself down next to his master. 'Like you said yerself, some rules can be broken, if there's a good reason. And she ain't just one of yer Angels, is she, sirrah?'

'Quite true, quite true. Gun, please.'

Taro handed over Nual's gun. It looked simpler than Malia's; the black barrel was undecorated, the stock narrow and skeletal. Taro watched, fascinated, as the Minister ran his hands over the weapon until he said without looking up, 'This isn't a procedure generally carried out in public. Eat your food or something.'

Taro watched the crowds thronging the Street. Some people shot curious glances at the shirtless, mirror-cloaked downsider sitting next to the well-dressed topsider. They looked away fast enough when they spotted the gun.

'Finger!'

'Sorry, sirrah?' Taro looked round to see the Minister holding the gun out to him, butt-end first.

'Put a finger on the trigger-pad, whichever hand you'll be firing it with. Quickly, now.'

Taro didn't much like the idea of firing the gun at all, but this was what Nual wanted. He reached over and slipped a finger over the pad on the trigger, careful not to apply any pressure. The pad warmed beneath his fingertip.

'That should do it.' The Minister passed the gun back to him. 'I haven't erased her ID from the gun, just added yours. I recommend you give it back to her as soon as you see her again, as she's going to be far more effective with it than you are. But I have done what she asked.'

Taro put the gun on his lap, pulling the folds of the cloak round it. His relationship with the Minister had changed. Nual had practically ordered him to question the head of the League of Concord, and there was one thing Taro wanted to know more than anything. 'Sirrah?' he began cautiously.

The Minister inclined his head. 'Yes?'

'Why din't you call feud on Scarrion?'

'You don't give up, do you? All right, we may as well have this conversation while we wait for Nual to return. Politics: that was my initial reason. Scarrion was on the verge of going rogue, and by sending an agent on the edge as a "gesture of support" for Consul Vidoran's recent unwise political decisions, Yazil was saying, "Thanks, but yours is not the kind of help we need". For me to call feud on him would have been to return the insult. In the morass of intrigue that is the Concord, that was not a move to be made lightly. But I would have called feud, once I had confirmation that he had killed one of ours, if he were not so useful to me as a free agent. Scarrion knew his league had abandoned him, and he transferred his loyalty completely to his new master. He serves Salik Vidoran now, no one else, and he can go places his master cannot go and do things that a politician cannot do. But he's not exactly subtle. I had hoped that by watching him I would be able to get some idea of what the Consul is up to.'

'Vidoran? The politician in Confed Square? So this is all about him is it?'

'So I believe. I put you in Confederacy Square because you had been keeping company with Vidoran's Screamer. I wanted to know whether you were just a night's diversion, or if there was something more to your relationship; specifically, whether you were part of whatever Vidoran was up to. It was unlikely, of course, but I had to be sure. When I assigned you as a watcher I had not had confirmation of your line-mother's death. As it was, your understandable but ill-timed outburst during Vidoran's botched removal did at least convince me you were not the Screamer's ally. Unfortunately, it also ruined Nual's shot, thus invalidating my reasons for assigning her to perform the removal.'

Taro remembered the Angel from the Exquisite Corpse, the one probably still sleeping like a baby on a mazeway somewhere below them. 'Nual weren't meant to 'ave the next removal, was she?'

'Indeed not. I have a system that allows all my Angels a fair and equal share of the action, but I wanted Nual to be the one who pulled the trig-ger on Vidoran.' For a moment Taro thought he was going to stop there, but he gave a little sigh and went on, 'I suppose I had better explain why, or risk Nual's ire. This is rather complex, so pay attention.'

Taro wondered if the Minister thought everyone was stupid, or whether he just liked being rude, but he said nothing.

'In the past few weeks there have been two attempts to access Nual's records; this after years of silence. Both attempts were subtle, and both failed and were traced. The second was made a couple of days ago from the office of the infobroker where Nual has just now gone to meet Elarn Reen. It was made at Medame Reen's request. When Nual returns I hope she will be able to explain Elarn Reen's motivations for making that request.

'The first attempt was made just over a week earlier. I traced it to an unscrupulous sidestreet infobroker who turned up dead in an alley with a broken neck later that same day. Interestingly, that was not a search for "Lia Reen" – which was the name Nual had on her ID when she first came here – but for *anyone* with the surname of Reen and a Khathryn

ID who had arrived in Khesh City in the past seven years.

'Nual has her own topside agents monitoring all enquiries made about her. Being hunted by your entire race makes one justifiably paranoid. The first attempt was enough to drive her into hiding. I doubt she even knew of the second, as she hasn't spent more than a few minutes topside since then – until today, of course.'

The Minister paused and Taro asked, 'How does Consul Vidoran fit in with this?'

'Patience, boy, patience. Certain circumstantial evidence – particularly the nature of the sidestreet infobroker's untimely death – suggested a link between the psychopath that Yazil had rather ill-advisedly assigned to the Consul and that infobroker. Combined with earlier events, that was enough to convince me that Vidoran had to die, and Nual, whose loyalty I was no longer sure of, had to perform the hit.'

'You mean you rigged the Concord?' Taro had never bothered much with the ins and outs of how a politician came to be marked but he'd always assumed the system was, at some level, fair.

'Goodness no, I don't do that – at least, not as such,' the Minister protested. 'But the citizens of the Confederacy of Three aren't always aware of – or interested in – the big picture and sometimes I have to give them a bit of a nudge, just to ensure they make the right decision. It's generally just a matter of throwing money at the media and letting them do the job for me: tell people someone is bad enough times and they'll start to believe you.' He smiled benignly.

Taro decided to let that one go. This was the head of the Kheshi League of Concord he was talking to. Respect for life was obviously not top of his agenda. 'So what was this earlier stuff that Consul Vidoran did?'

'A few weeks ago Salik Vidoran made an unscheduled and highly uncharacteristic trip to the outer habitats of the Tri-Confed system. During his absence certain political misdealings of his were uncovered, but when attempts were made to contact him, he had disappeared. He turned up some days later claiming to have been stranded at the extreme edge of the system on a transport that had experienced technical difficulties. By the time he got back to Vellern his career was on the slide and my suspicions were alerted. I checked with the pilot of the transport, who swore blind she had never met him. Maybe she hadn't; maybe she just *thought* she hadn't. That kind of thing happens a lot with the Sidhe. And then Vidoran's Screamer tried to find out about the Sidhe who is now the Angel Nual. That was enough for me.'

'You put him on the hot-list just 'cause he might've left the system without tellin' anyone an' 'cause he might have been asking about Nual?' And he thought Nual was paranoid!

The Minister observed Taro from under the brim of his hat. 'No, I decided that his otherwise minor political mistake would cost him his life because I believe he has had direct dealings with the Sidhe. And I will not permit Sidhe influence in my City.'

'But I thought they never came here.'

'I wouldn't say that. They constructed everything on Vellern.'

'The Sidhe built Khesh City?' A day ago Taro had barely heard of the lost race; now he found he was living in one of their Cities.

'A faction within the Sidhe built Khesh and the other two Cities. That faction was made up of rebels who were opposed to the Sidhe Protectorate: hence the impressive array of scanners at immigration, all tuned to detect Sidhe minds and devices. The founders of the Confederacy were very keen to keep the other Sidhe out, and this remains true today. The Sidhe are as much my enemies as they are Nual's.'

Nual finds herself standing in the bedroom of the house she shared with Elarn for those few confused but happy months seven years ago.

The detail is perfect, provided she doesn't look too closely. The pale yellow-and-gold carpet is soft and warm beneath her bare feet. The walk-in wardrobe is there, the shelves with the statuettes of saints carved from translucent pink coral above the hardcopy antique books. And there is the bed of sea-oak beams with its coverlet of azure silk: the place where Elarn finally discovered what Nual was.

The Sidhe made this, creating a perfect illusion in Elarn's mind. It is a trap; Nual is not sure of its nature and purpose, but she knows she has fallen into it. She tries to withdraw her presence, to bring herself out, or at least to raise herself up from the depths of Elarn's unconsciousness.

The room wavers for a moment, solidifies again. She is still here, in Elarn's reconstructed memory.

The only choice is to go on. She walks round the bed, slowly.

A storm is in full force outside, but above the rain and wind she can hear another sound coming from the wardrobe. It sounds like someone crying. She tries to extend her mind out to sense the presence, but nothing happens. She is as limited as a human here.

She walks towards the wardrobe. As she does so she sees her own reflection in the burnished front.

She is seventeen again, waif-thin, with cropped hair, wearing the long umber robe she favoured when in the cliff-house. Naturally she would look like this here. After all, this is how Elarn remembers her.

The sobs are suddenly silenced, as though the person hiding in the wardrobe has sensed that someone is in the room.

Nual pulls open the door.

Elarn is crouched in the corner of the wardrobe, dressed in her white nightgown, hair a messy halo, face puffy with tears and white with terror.

She flinches at the figure looming over her, then recognition dawns in her eyes. 'Lia?'

Nual decides against asking Elarn to use her chosen name; this is Elarn's dream, after all, and she would be wise to obey the logic of the dream world. She nods.

Elarn regards her warily, the fear still in her eyes. Outside, the storm throws itself at the house with renewed force. 'How do I know it's really you? How do I know they haven't chosen to wear your face to trick me?' Her voice is rising into a hysterical scream, mirroring the howling wind. 'After all, you left me and now you're back—'

'I didn't leave you,' says Nual, her calm assertion cutting across Elarn's terror, 'I wanted to stay with you, to regain some of the unity I lost when I left my people. But in order to do that, I had to show my true self, and that was not something you could deal with, so you told me to leave. And I did. I was hurt, but I understand now why you did what you did. I forgive you. I hope you can forgive me for being what I am.'

'Lia, it's really you, isn't it? How did you get here? Wherever here is ... I'm not sure where I am, or how I came to be here. I mean, I think this is my room, but—'

If Elarn starts to question the illusion it may start to unravel, taking both women's sanity with it. 'Elarn.' Elarn looks at her, her eyes wild and unfocused. 'What are you hiding from?'

'You know what. *Them*. They're coming for me. And for you. And when they find me they'll bore their way into my soul and leave their seed in me, the *scream*— Oh God, I can't—'

Nual reaches in and takes Elarn's hand. Elarn lets her. 'Then perhaps we should not be here when they arrive.' Nual starts to help her up.

Elarn stares at Nual, then nods. 'Yes. Why didn't I think of that? There are still places to run ...' She levers herself up with Nual's help, then stumbles out into the room, frowning at the familiar but not-quite-perfect illusion.

Nual, wishing she could tell how much of what is happening now is Sidhe programming and how much is Elarn breaking free of that programming, follows her.

Standing outside the bedroom, they hear a door slam in the house below – the wind, perhaps. Or maybe not. Elarn freezes. Nual pulls at her, but the other woman does not move. Elarn's much-repressed maternal instinct had been stirred up when Nual – *Lia* – first came to her; she can use that.

'Please Elarn, you have to protect me from them,' she cries. 'They have come to take me back.'

Elarn shakes herself, looking at Nual as though seeing her for the first time. 'Yes, I have to help you. There's a way down, one they don't know about—' She starts to walk slowly, and around a corner they find a door which, as far as Nual remembers, should lead to one of the spare bedrooms. Elarn opens it to reveal a metal staircase spiralling down a rough-hewn tunnel. Crystals in the wall emit a pallid yellow-green light.

From her knowledge of the human psyche, Nual is far from sure that down is the right direction, but fear of their enemies' proximity is sending chill prickles down her spine. She is losing her objectivity, being drawn deeper into Elarn's nightmare.

There's a footfall from behind: someone is on the landing.

Nual hurries onto the stairs, Elarn following. Behind them, an incoherent shout – of victory? frustration? – echoes down the hall.

The stairs burn cold on Nual's bare feet, but the terror is real now as recollections of her own flight from her people flash through her mind. She must run, run, *run*!

The staircase ends abruptly: one moment they are in the green twilight, the next, on the beach below – except it is not the beach Nual remembers. There is no storm and no sea either, though the rising sun fires the wet sand before them into molten gold. For the first time she notices smell in the illusion, less like the tang of salt than the scent of fresh blood. And there is a reason the sand is whiter and harder than the sand below the cliff-house. It is not sand; it is finely ground bone.

In running away they have done exactly what the Sidhe wanted.

CHAPTER TWENTY-NINE

'Is that why you let Nual in? 'Cause she's one of these Sidhe rebels?'

The Minister laughed. 'Goodness, no. That rebellion ended a thousand years ago. Perhaps she would have been, if she had lived back then; she's not a normal Sidhe, if such a creature can be said to exist. That's why I let her stay here. The surviving Sidhe, hiding behind the complacent humans they secretly control, know what Vellern is and they steer clear. They'd never be stupid enough to send a Sidhe here. And then this child turns up, lighting up my monitors like a star. My first thought was to have her killed, but she was young, confused, and all but destitute. I let her live, watched her and arranged to meet her. After talking to her I decided to give her sanctuary here – under certain conditions – and here she has remained. You would think that after all the help I've given her she might try trusting me occasionally.' A small, tight smile crossed his face.

'Why don't she? Trust you, I mean.'

'She believes that I would betray her to the Sidhe if it were the only way to save the City.'

'Are things that bad? And—' He paused, but continued, 'would you?'

The Minister tilted his head to regard Taro. 'My, my, boy: you appear to have developed quite a backbone. Until recently you were terrified I'd kill you.'

'That was before I met Nual, an' before I knew you broke yer own rules,' he said boldly. Which didn't mean he wasn't still scared; he just wasn't going to let fear stop him from finding out what was going on.

'Ah. Touché. Nual chose well when she decided to trust you. What do you think, then: when all this is over, should I perhaps consider replacing Malia with her son?

Taro said nothing. Not so long ago, this would've been his dream come true, but so much had happened in the past few days: the world wasn't the place he'd thought it was, and his place in it wasn't what he'd imagined. Besides, the Minister hadn't answered his question yet.

'It's what you've always wanted, isn't it?' the Minister continued. 'I prefer to avoid Angel dynasties, and there are very few male Angels but, as you say, exceptions are some—'

The Minister stopped speaking, biting off his words mid-sentence.

For a moment Taro wondered if there was some threat approaching that he hadn't noticed. He tensed, ready to leap up and defend his master but the Street was quiet, people going about their business as usual.

Taro looked back at the Minister. He had stopped with one hand half-raised and a gappy look on his face. He looked like he'd just passed out, but forgotten to fall over. Though he didn't see his lips move, Taro heard him mutter, 'I think we may have underestimated our enemies.'

Nual turns to beg Elarn to go back, but the crystal-glazed rocks behind them are featureless and there is no sign of the staircase. Her companion is staring out towards where the sea should be, her face calm and expectant. Nual follows her gaze; now she can make out something on the horizon, a glint, like water held in check. At the edge of hearing is a faint rumble.

'Elarn!' she cries, 'this is wrong! We have to leave, now. I cannot help you; you must find the power within yourself to fight this. Elarn, it is still your mind. Reclaim it!'

She gives no sign of having heard. Instead, she opens her mouth and starts to sing:

> *When my true love comes to me,*
> *We will walk on the clear blue sea,*
> *Our skin will thrill to the ocean breeze,*
> *When my true love comes to me.*

See, my true love comes to me,
My soul and his will at last be free,
Our flesh is nothing, shed with ease,
Come my love, now come to me.

Nual recognises the words, a sentimental ditty they used to sing together.

Elarn stops singing and looks sideways, past Nual, down the beach. As her voice dies away the sound of rushing water grows to a roar.

Nual steps across to block her view and tries to reach for her, but suddenly Elarn is too far away. Elarn frowns at her and Nual's arms drop to her sides. A little petulantly, Elarn says, 'Please, don't be difficult. I have to do this.'

Nual knows now that she can do nothing that interferes directly with Elarn's mission, so she stays still. At least she can still speak. 'Do what?' she asks.

Elarn shifts so she can see down the beach. Nual looks too. There is someone coming towards them, walking like a sleepwalker along the base of the cliff.

Elarn sighs. 'You shouldn't have tried to help me. This was going to happen sooner or later, but you've seen this place, so it has to be now.'

Nual gives up trying to make out who the approaching figure is. She looks at Elarn. 'You have to fight this, Elarn. You are doing exactly what they want.' The noise of distant water is loud enough now that she has to shout; below the roar there is another sound: a high single note, mesmerising and perfect, sung in Elarn's voice. It chills and fascinates, and Nual has to resist the urge to stop talking so she can hear it more clearly.

Elarn looks sad but calm. 'I can't fight them. I never could. But if I do this one thing for them, they'll leave me in peace. I'm sorry you're here too, but it can't be helped. You'll have to stay now, even though this wasn't meant for you. This is who it was meant for all along. See? Here he comes.'

Nual turns to see a boy of about the same age she is in this dream. He wears a one-piece suit of unfamiliar design, and walks stiffly, eyes half closed. His is not a single face but a collection, all manner of men's features of all ages, from youth to old age. The features flicker and change from one to another as Nual watches. A distinguished gentleman seems half-familiar but then he is gone, morphed into a younger, leaner man she has never seen before. Then it shifts again, into a face she knows well.

The face of the Minister.

Meraint sat behind his desk, watching the two women on the far side of the room. They were holding hands loosely and their faces looked relaxed, as if in a trance, their eyes staring sightlessly at each other. If he hadn't known better, he might have thought he had fallen into one of the ancient stories and here were two Sidhe queens silently battling over the fate of humanity.

When he had awakened this morning Meraint had been looking forward to a quiet day with the family, maybe they'd even visit the Zoo ... He had still been under the illusion that he could make a life here.

Not any more. Once these two had finished doing – well, whatever it was they were doing – and the Angel was safely out of his office, he would go home to Bera, tell her how much he loved her – and then insist that they leave this place as soon as arrangements could be made. Damn making their fortunes. Khesh City was no place to bring up their children.

Just as soon as the Angel was gone.

While she was climbing the stairs up to his office he had activated the desk's defences so he could shoot her if she threatened his client – not kill her; he would never kill one of his City's agents, but he could stun the Angel if things turned nasty. But when she came through the door and looked him in the eye he knew he could never harm her. He had never met an Angel before; he had had no idea how magnificent they were. No wonder they were the mistresses of the Undertow, revered by all. And now he would stay here and watch over her, just as she had asked.

When the door buzzer went this time he felt only irritation. Did everyone in the City feel they had a right to visit him today?

Irritation turned to fear when he saw that he was finally getting the one visitor he had been most dreading ... and to think he'd almost forgotten the Screamer.

He couldn't let him in, not now, not with Elarn and the Angel standing entranced in the middle of his office.

Perhaps he should run, try to draw the Screamer away. He could use his back door, hide himself in the sidestreets. But what if the Screamer caught him? And the bastard knew where he lived. If he couldn't find Meraint here, he might go to the house where, even now, Bera and their daughters would be having lunch together. And he couldn't just abandon Elarn and the Angel. In their current state they would be defenceless. Scarrion had broken into his office once before, he could do it again.

Meraint checked his screen inset. The Screamer was holding his finger on the buzzer and staring up at the camera. He did not look happy. Meraint keyed the com. 'Hello. I have your file, I'll be down with it in a minute. Wait there, please.'

Scarrion narrowed his eyes and spoke into the open com. 'Every other time we've met I have been unable to persuade you to leave your desk. Now why would you suddenly want to come and meet me down on the Street, Sirrah Meraint? I think I'll come up, if it's all the same to you.'

Mouth dry and armpits damp, Meraint cut the com. Now that narrowed his options. As he stood up, the inset showing the camera feed went blank. The screen was full of static.

Elarn ignores Nual and steps forward to take the boy's hand.

He reaches out blindly to her, motions clumsy and slow, his face still shifting between a dozen different people. Nual recognises the head of one of the City's major maintenance corporations and, on the second pass, the High Speaker of the Assembly.

'You must come too,' says Elarn, and holds out her other hand to Nual. Without volition, Nual sees her hand reach for Elarn's.

They are doomed, and there is nothing they can do about it.

Singing, Elarn leads the pair of them towards the glistening wall of destruction hovering at the horizon. With every step the siren song beneath the water's rush grows louder, and Nual finds it increasingly hard to maintain concentration in the face of the beautiful scream of destruction.

Meraint felt horribly exposed when he stepped out from the protection of his desk, but his defences wouldn't be much help against the Screamer. All the assassin had to do was stand in the doorway and use his implant and he could take down all of them without even entering into the room. He bent down to pick up Elarn Reen's dart-gun; nothing more than a handbag weapon, but dangerous enough at close quarters. He slipped it into his pocket.

His best chance, perhaps his only chance, would be to enlist Nual's help. She was an Angel, used to dealing with such situations, so she should decide whether they ran, or stayed and faced Scarrion. It must be her call.

He looked over at the two women. Something had changed. Elarn Reen's expression was no longer serene; it looked slack, more like death than trance, and the Angel's face was twisted as though she were caught in a waking nightmare.

'Medame Reen? Lady Nual?' he called, 'can you hear me?'

There was no response. He stepped up to them and laid a hand gently on Elarn Reen's shoulder. The pulse that beat in her neck was rapid and uneven, and her posture was rigid and unnatural. 'Medame Reen,' he tried again, 'we have to leave now. Please, wake up.'

Overhead, the lights flickered.

At first Meraint thought he'd imagined it, but then it happened again. He felt a ripple of motion in the floor below him, as if the building were being shaken by the wind ... *But there is no wind in the City.* It was designed to be perfectly balanced, always controlled.

Without thinking, he pulled Elarn towards him, breaking the contact.

In eerie unison, both women gave a high, incoherent cry, like no sound Meraint had ever heard from human lips.

Then Nual flew backwards, as if she had been electrocuted, and collapsed on the floor by the desk.

Elarn fell against him and he managed to catch her before she crashed to the floor. She started howling like an injured animal, thrashing feebly against his restraining arm.

On the other side of the room, Nual lay still as death.

Meraint was so intent on calming the hysterical woman that it took him a couple of seconds to register what else was wrong. The room was shaking harder now. The walls swayed and the floor shifted and bucked beneath his feet. The door of the cabinet Elarn Reen had clung to earlier flew open, dumping a box of hardcopies onto the floor. The holo-pic of Meraint's girls toppled off the edge of the desk and smashed into glassy fragments.

Taro stared, confused. He'd never seen anyone do that. It was as though the Minister had turned into a statue.

Confusion started to give way to fear. Was the Minister dead? He *couldn't* be dead.

A weird silence fell over the Street and the air suddenly felt cold. Something well smoky was going on here.

The first shudder hit and Taro grabbed the edge of the seat. Panicked shouts erupted all around him and people started running in all directions, while others stood frozen in the middle of the Street, clutching each other. Those not screaming were staring upwards in horror.

Above him, the forcedome started to hiss, the sound building in intensity second by second into an uneven roar. The sky was rippling, colours shifting between sickly yellow and the red of dried blood.

Taro curled his fingers tighter around the seat and held on, his mind blank with terror, as the sky flickered and crackled over a world gone mad.

CHAPTER THIRTY

Meraint and Elarn Reen held onto each other while the room shook and the lights flickered. Cracks snaked across the walls and plaster rained down from the ceiling but, despite Meraint's constant terrified expectation, the building did not collapse.

The lights went out and though the quake continued, in the dark Meraint felt calmer, as though what he could not see could not harm him. He just wished Elarn Reen would loosen her grip a little, and maybe stop screeching quite so loudly in his ear.

After an indeterminate period of darkness, the emergency lights over the doors came on. The tremors started to subside at the same time.

Elarn Reen's howls faded to a faint whimper as the shaking died away, but still she clung to him, her fingers digging painfully into his arms.

'Medame Reen? Elarn? Can you hear me?' he tried again, desperate to rouse her.

'Is this the end of the world?' she muttered, her head hunched into his shoulder. 'I always thought it would end in fire. That's what the Salvatine texts say, you know ...'

'I have no idea, but we have to leave, now.'

She tilted her head to focus on him. 'Do I know you?'

'Yes, you do, and I'm trying to help you. You've had some sort of shock and I think there's something wrong with the City, but those crises are both going to have to wait. Right now we have to get out of this building. Do you understand?'

'Why does everything hurt so much? My head ... Can I lie down please? I think I need to lie down.'

Meraint heard a faint click, then a scrape and a bang. The door. Someone was trying to open the door. The lock must have gone offline in the quake but it sounded like the door itself was jammed, probably warped in the frame. Another grinding scrape, this time loud enough to attract Elarn's attention. The Screamer was certainly persistent.

Meraint swung Elarn Reen round to face him, grasped her shoulders and whispered, 'Listen! That is the sound of a man who is going to kill us both just as soon as he finishes breaking down the door.'

'What man? Why does he want to kill us?' She sounded like a hurt child asking why a treat was forbidden.

'It's complicated, so you'll just have to trust me. But right now we have to go.'

She nodded vaguely, her eyes wild, her cheeks soaked with tears. 'Yes. Go. We should go ...'

He started to steer her towards the alcove but then she spotted the Angel sprawled on the floor in front of the desk. 'Lia! Oh God!' she wailed, trying to break free from Meraint's grasp.

'There's nothing you can do for her.' Meraint had no idea if that was true, but he wasn't going to be distracted. 'We have to get out of here. Quickly, quietly. Come now.'

She let him lead her through the office, though she kept looking back at the Angel. He could hear her muttering under her breath, over and over, 'What have I done? What have I done?' From back inside the office the scraping at the door had given way to a strident banging as the Screamer battered his way in.

He pulled her into the alcove after him. She was at least compliant, if not entirely sane. He kept hold of her wrist in his left hand and used his right hand to open the cupboard door at the back of the alcove. Inside, cleaning equipment was stacked against what looked like a blank wall. He pulled the equipment out and gave the wall a sharp kick. The back of the cupboard swung away to reveal a narrow staircase disappearing into darkness. He turned back to his charge. She had stopped muttering, but there was a look of distracted fear on her face.

'It's all my fault,' she whispered, and looked away.

He leaned in to switch on the stairwell light. 'Possibly, but we can do blame later. Right now we're going to run down those steps and out into the sidestreets. After that I suggest hiding might be a good idea.'

'But Lia—'

'No time. We have to go,' he said firmly.

'No,' she sobbed, 'I can't leave her, not like this!' She tried to pull away from him but he held firmly onto her wrist.

It didn't sound as if Scarrion's efforts were having much effect on the office door, so perhaps he had a little time. '*City's sake!*' he swore. 'Look, you go ahead and I'll check out the Angel. I promise I'll try to get her out, assuming she's not— as long as she can walk. But you have to go!' He pulled her past him.

She nodded and stumbled into the stairwell. At the top of the stairs she turned, looked back at Meraint over her shoulder and said distinctly, 'The scream almost broke free of me. I must not let it break free. I have to destroy the vessel.'

Meraint met her eyes and for a moment glimpsed something irrevocably broken. Then she was gone, half-running, half-falling down the stairs.

He retraced his steps and peered out of the alcove. He could see only the middle third of the room, but through the still-settling plaster he could make out a figure in red and black crawling towards him, head down, hands snaking along the floor, pulling herself forward slowly, painfully.

'Lady! Nual?' he called, as quietly as he could, 'in here, quickly.'

At first he thought she hadn't heard him but then, head still down, she hissed, 'Leave. Now. Help Elarn. Don't look at me!' Despite himself he had started to walk towards her, was already reaching out to help—

From his left came a loud bang, followed by a splintering noise. He jumped back into the cover of the alcove.

A man's voice, unpleasantly familiar, said, 'Now what have we here?'

Meraint saw Nual start to raise her head.

A figure dressed in green and gold streaked into Meraint's field of view and barrelled into the Angel.

*

223

After several shit-scary minutes the shaking stopped and the terrible sound from above died away to a faint fizzing. Taro's vision was blurred, his fingers hurt and no matter how hard he breathed he felt a nasty tightness in his chest. But he was alive.

As soon as he was sure the world had really stopped moving he looked around. People were shouting for help or helping others; some sat, dazed, against buildings, and a few were lying suspiciously still on the Street. The stall where he and Nual had bought their noodles earlier had collapsed, but the actual buildings had stayed up, though most now had cracks running down their fronts. The sky buzzed like a broken light fitting, but at least it was orange again. Whatever had happened, the worst appeared to be over.

Taro looked across at the Minister. The shaking must've jolted him out of his trance; the head of the Kheshi League of Concord had fallen off the seat and was now lying on his side, still in a sitting position, hand still half-raised, eyes still open, staring blankly ahead. His hat lay in a puddle of noodle soup next to the seat.

Taro slid off the seat and crouched down next to the Minister, ignoring Nual's gun, which clattered to the ground as it fell from his lap. He'd seen death before, but nothing like this. He reached out to touch the Minister's neck. Cold as a vane at dawn. *Shit!* He really was dead. What the fuck would happen now?

The Minister blinked once, slowly.

Taro jumped, then caught himself and leaned over. 'Sirrah?' he croaked, 'you're alive?'

The Minister's hands twitched. He blinked again and started to push himself upright, moving like a meatbaby who'd been at the burnt mash, slow and clumsy, like he didn't fit his body. Taro reached out to help, pulling him round and leaning him up against the seat, easing his legs out so they stretched in front of him.

Taro waved a hand in front of his master's face. 'Sirrah?'

The Minister didn't seem to be able to see Taro; he stared into space like a blind man. When he finally spoke, his words were slow and slurred. 'Ah. Taro. The answer to your question is no.'

'My question, sirrah?'

'You asked if I am alive. The answer is no.' His speech was getting clearer but his face still had a gappy, vacant look. 'At least not in the way you think of as being alive.'

'Sirrah? I don't understand—'

'No, I wouldn't expect you to. I haven't been entirely honest with you, Taro. In fact, for the last thousand years I haven't been entirely honest with anyone except Nual.'

Taro's grasp of numbers might not go much beyond counting credits from punters, but even he knew that a thousand years was longer than *anyone* lived, even someone as important as the Minister.

'Taro? Are you still there?'

'Aye, sirrah, I'm here.' He reached out to cover the Minister's hand, which lay limp on his lap. The skin was cold and smooth and hard, like Nual's palm.

'Good. I'm blind now. Paralysed, too. And not just ... this body. My other avatars have shut down completely. I've lost surveillance across the City. Environmental control too. Fail-safes have cut in but it's taking all my current processing power just to maintain them.'

Taro had no idea what the Minister was talking about, but it sounded serious. 'Is there anythin' I can do?' he asked. He couldn't think of anything offhand.

'Oh yes, Taro. Now that I know what we're up against, there is something extremely important that you must do. But first there are a few things you need to know, about how the world works.'

'You mean,' Taro found himself saying a little wildly, 'the way you rig the Concord to kill who you want. Oh, that's prime with me. You know best.'

'Yes, we do. The three of us. My brothers and I. Better than you humans, but, unlike our bitch sisters, we don't presume to control you, just to watch. If you damn yourselves, so be it.'

'You've lost me, sirrah.'

'Yes. We need to focus, relate this to the current avatar. Become the *I* before you. Aye. Taro, the Minister – *I* – run rather more than the Kheshi League of Concord. I run the City. In fact, I *am* the City.'

Taro looked at the soup-stained cove sprawled on the ground in front of him. 'If you say so, sirrah,' he said in a calming tone of voice, patting the cold hand again. Obviously whatever had struck the Minister had left him well gappy.

'No, Taro,' the Minister said, 'it's not just what I say. It's the truth. I'll try to make it clear for you. Do you know what a puppet is?'

'We have shadow-shows in the Undertow, fer children. That what you mean?'

'Precisely so. Well, this body is a puppet, a puppet of the City, not just serving it, but acting out its wishes. My thoughts are the City's thoughts. The City's thoughts are mine. Do you understand?'

'Fuck me.' So Federin had been right all along. The City *was* alive.

'I will take that as a yes. The consciousness that inhabits this form also inhabits several other bodies, and controls the City's basic functions, but it has been damaged.'

'Damaged? How? Was that what caused the shakes?'

'Yes, it was – perhaps stunned might be a better word than damaged, for it is repairable. As for how it happened, that I do not yet know. All we can be certain of is that the weapon that caused the damage originates from the Sidhe. Humans would have no idea how to create such a device. This time, the attack was broken off. I have no idea why, for this weapon is capable of doing far worse, perhaps even killing us. It could certainly knock out our consciousness for long enough that control would be lost.'

Taro, his head reeling, asked, 'If yer the City, an' you've been the City fer a thousand years, then if you take a nap, that's a very bad thing, ain't it? World-endin' kind of bad?'

'Yes, it's bad, but not the end of everything, not if someone else takes over. I believe this weapon will be employed by Salik Vidoran, so that he can take my place.'

'You mean that's what the Consul's up to? He wants to use this Sidhe weapon to get control of the whole City? Fuck.' Put like that it sounded completely gappy – or it would have, a few minutes ago. Now, surrounded by the wreckage of buildings and dead and injured people, it made a kind of scary sense. 'Makes all the shit with the Concord and the Assembly look like pissin' off a mazeway,' he added gloomily.

'Quite.'

'But ... how?' he asked again. 'Vidoran can't just use this weapon an' take yer place, can he? I mean, he'd've done that already if he could, wouldn't he?'

'Correct. There is only one location from which control can be assumed. Those who built me into this City put an override mechanism there, to allow one still bound in the flesh to take over if I am incapacitated. There are defences, but the Sidhe will have told Vidoran how to deal with them – that is why he stole your line-mother's gun. Now the one weapon that can destroy me is active, he will take it to the only place where he can use it and live.'

'It's the Heart of the City, ain't it? That's where he'll go.'

'Exactly. And you, Taro, must kill him before he gets there.'

The initial blow knocked Nual onto her back. Meraint saw a flash of silver in the dim light and for a moment he thought she already had her spurs out. If so, the Screamer was in trouble. But when Scarrion straightened, Meraint saw he was kneeling over her, pinning her to the ground. He held a thin curved blade in his hand.

The Screamer leaned over her and whispered, 'So you're the infamous Nual. We meet at last.'

The Angel lay still, eyelids flickering, blades sheathed. Scarrion gave a dismissive snort. 'But what's wrong with you – been at the happy dust? Guess I'll never know. Makes things simpler, if less interesting.'

Almost casually, he slashed for her throat—

Meraint choked back a cry, then blinked, when he saw that the Angel was not quite as badly hurt as she had appeared to be. With a surprising show of strength she bucked the Screamer off her, and as he overbalanced, a look of dismayed surprise flashed across his normally emotionless face. He almost fell – Meraint saw the tip of his knife snag the carpet – but he recovered at once and sprang back into position.

The Angel already had her knees under her and was edging backwards on her forearms, ready to lever herself onto all fours.

Scarrion waited in a defensive crouch next to the Angel, rather than pressing home his attack. Meraint wondered why the damn Screamer was hesitating; then he heard a faint chuckle and realised the bastard was so confident that he was playing with her. He hoped the Screamer had underestimated the Angel, or that she was deliberately feinting.

227

And there was another reason he was being cautious, Meraint realised: with her hands flat on the floor she couldn't extend her spurs.

Sure enough, as soon as she was on all fours Scarrion sprang forward and kicked her in the face. She fell backwards against the desk.

It didn't look like she was feinting; it looked like she was having trouble staying conscious.

Scarrion settled next to her, leaning low with knife poised, shifting his weight from foot to foot, ready to attack or defend. 'Dear me, dear me,' he murmured gleefully, 'is this really the best you can do? I was hoping for a challenge for once. Perhaps I should just knock you out with my little song? Ah, but where would be the fun in that?'

The Screamer was focused on his adversary, and had no idea anyone else was in the office. Meraint had to do something; he couldn't let his enemy kill this Angel.

As if tired of waiting for Nual to make a move, Scarrion lunged. The Angel ducked his blade, just, but at least the attack got her moving again. She began to crawl away.

The Screamer started after her, but she kicked out backwards, catching him on the shin. He staggered back with a surprised yelp.

She used her brief advantage to pull herself upright on the edge of the desk. The Screamer must have broken her nose when he kicked her; blood spattered the lower half of her face and dripped onto the carpet.

They were both on their feet now, but while Scarrion stood relaxed and alert, Nual moved like a woman in a dream. Meraint was afraid that if she let go of the desk, she would fall, and he wasn't convinced she'd be able to get herself back up.

He had to help her. There were knives in the kitchenette unit in the alcove, but he'd have to open a cupboard, and that was bound to attract the Screamer's attention – and besides, what did he think *he* would be able to do with a kitchen knife against a Yazil assassin?

Then, finally, he remembered Elarn Reen's dart-gun.

The Screamer drove forward and Nual fell back, out of Meraint's sight. He winced at the sound of a chair crashing to the ground. It was impossible to tell who was winning, but the Angel didn't look like she would last long. He drew the little gun. If they would just come back this way, he'd even the odds.

He heard a blade swish through the air and a grunt from the Screamer. 'Too slow, switch-bitch,' he taunted her.

Meraint raised the gun.

Another crash, and a gasp of pain that sounded distinctly feminine.

'Now, really!' said Scarrion, his voice calm and mocking, 'you should have seen that coming! What *is* your problem?'

A couple of seconds later a hunched figure backed into view. In the bad light and dust it took a moment for Meraint to identify it as Nual; her head was down and she had one arm wrapped round her midriff. The other arm, the blade still only half extended, was stretched out in front of her to ward off the next blow.

Meraint's finger tightened on the trigger. *Come on you bastard. Walk into my trap.*

There was movement from the left.

Meraint fired—

—but Scarrion was already halfway across the room, Nual falling in front of him, when Meraint squeezed the trigger, and he knew he had missed even as he saw the tiny dart fly through the space the Screamer had occupied a fraction of a second before. The faint *ffssstt!* of compressed air as the gun fired was lost in the Screamer's incoherent war-cry.

The Screamer had looked sure to floor Nual when he ran into her, but in his haste to finish her off his ankle clipped the fallen chair and he stumbled. He fell into Nual, but she was too weak to take immediate advantage and they swung around each other.

She didn't let go; Meraint couldn't see if she was trying to keep her opponent off-balance, or if she was just trying to keep herself upright by holding onto him. It was getting increasingly hard to keep track of who was who as they spun through the ruined office. He could hear Scarrion's wild laughter and Nual's laboured breathing, but as they clung together their figures merged into one in the dim emergency lighting. They were already heading out of his view again.

The Angel wasn't going to last much longer. He had to act now.

He fired a second time.

At first he thought he had missed again. Then Nual stumbled and sagged in Scarrion's grasp.

He hadn't missed. He had shot the wrong person.

The Angel slid to the floor. Scarrion stared at her for a moment, confused. Then he straightened and looked around, taking in the rest of the room for the first time.

Meraint sighted on the Screamer, his finger tightening on the trigger—

—Scarrion spotted him a fraction of a second before he fired—

—and Meraint saw the shot go wide as the Screamer ducked and the dart flew over his shoulder.

Scarrion danced across the room towards him, weaving to throw off Meraint's aim. Without breaking stride he opened his mouth in a rapid, impossible movement. His jaws snapped shut, and Meraint felt the sonic wave hit him.

The gun slipped from his fingers and his knees buckled. Singing pain exploded from the roots of his teeth to fill his head. His bowels, already loosened by fear, emptied. Every blood vessel in his body felt like it was expanding, while his heartbeat slowed to a great unwieldy thump.

He clawed at the worktop with numb, tingling hands, then collapsed, his body now nothing but a useless lump of meat.

As the darkness started to close in on him, a detached part of his mind wondered whether it was against the Concord for a Screamer to use his implant on a civilian – as though the rules mattered any more.

Footsteps approached and he braced himself for the killing blow, but the Screamer ran past, heading for the open back door.

Well, Elarn Reen, he thought, *you're on your own now, just you and your madness.* Then the darkness met in the centre of his vision and he stopped thinking at all.

CHAPTER THIRTY-ONE

Taro steadied himself on the seat edge and bent down to pick up Nual's gun.

The Minister lay still. Taro wondered if he'd ever move again. He resisted the urge to close the glassy, staring eyes. After all, it wasn't like the Minister was really dead; apparently he'd never been alive.

Taro shivered. The air was freezing, colder than night in the Gardens, and it smelled wrong, as though something huge had died and started rotting beneath the City. Around him the uninjured coves and rollers had withdrawn into frightened huddles. A couple of baton-boys were trying to organise them and look over the casualties, but they had no more idea what was going on than the other topsiders.

Taro turned away from the empty shell that had once been the greatest power in the City and walked to the end of the Street. One of the pillars supporting the circle-car track had a large crack running up it, but the fence running beneath it was intact and it didn't look like there was much danger of the track falling.

He stopped in front of the fence. There was no hum of power now; it was dead and couldn't hurt him ... but he still needed to get through it. He pointed Nual's gun at it and slipped a finger onto the trigger-pad. When it warmed he pulled his finger back, firmly and gently, at the same time sweeping the gun in a slow arc before him. There was no sound, no light, just the faintest vibration from the gun, like the last shudder of a dying animal. For a moment he thought nothing had happened.

Then the fence in front of him parted as the links melted and fell to the ground.

He was used to coming onto the ledge through one of the gaps in the fence at the end of apparently dead-end alleys. Finding a way into the Undertow from a hole he'd made himself felt freaky, in some ways freakier than everything else he'd already lived through today.

He loped along the ledge until he got to the right area, then slowed and started to pace, stopping every now and again to look into the semi-darkness of the sidestreets for familiar alleyways that marked a place where nets hung from the rim of the City. It didn't help that he couldn't see properly. Tiny flakes of white stuff had started to drift through the air, messing with his vision. As he watched, one of them landed on the back of his hand and evaporated, leaving a cold damp patch on his skin. Taro stared at it for a moment, then shook his head. He had to stay focused.

When he thought he'd reached the right place he stopped and knelt down at the edge, feeling for marker pegs. Nothing. He moved along another couple of paces and tried again. There! A single bolt, just over the edge. He lay flat and felt over the lip until his hand brushed something. He recognised the rope by touch, the way in which four cords had been woven together; this was a route down he had used a lot. It came out near his old homespace.

He slung the gun over his shoulder, pushed the cloak back to free his hands and eased himself over the lip of the City and into the nets.

The gun and cloak made the climb harder but his body remembered the route, tuning in to the familiar pattern of the nets under his hands and feet … except something was wrong. Part of the net was missing. The shaking had been bad enough topside, where you couldn't fall off; here in the Undertow it must've been terrible. He pulled himself over to the intact part of the nets and carried on.

Taro had spent his whole life in the mazeways. Now, for the first time, he had to get below them to get a clear view across the Undertow. That's how he would take out Vidoran as he headed towards the Heart of the City. Taro found himself remembering his flights with Nual; it'd be easy enough for an Angel, but she was gone, perhaps even dead. The thought stung like a fleck to the heart, but he had to put her out of his mind. As he couldn't fly, he needed another way to get into position. Leaning over the edge of a mazeway was a well smoky option; even if he'd had a harness and tether, he wouldn't be able to use the gun while dangling upside down. He briefly considered Solo, but even if the alien was willing – and able – to carry him, the Exquisite Corpse was on the other side of the City.

What else? He *had* to find a way ...

'Water-traps!' he said out loud. They hung below the mazeways, and they were pretty sturdy, had to be, to take the weight of all that water. If he emptied out a big one, he could stand in it and get lowered down that way. And who had the biggest 'traps?

Water-traders.

He pulled up the hood of Nual's cloak and set off hubwards and sun-wise, towards Fenya's – surely she'd let him use one of hers, 'specially when he turned up with an Angel's gun and cloak.

The usual murmurous sounds of the Undertow had a panicked edge, and Taro soon came across more damage: torn nets, mazeways out of true or, where the ropes supporting them had snapped, missing com-pletely. The few people he met either didn't spot him under the cloak or, if they saw him at all, assumed he must be an Angel and quickly got out the way.

He was making a minor detour to avoid a missing mazeway when he caught movement out of the corner of his eye: a furtive shadow, gone almost at once. A few seconds later a whistle sounded from just behind him.

Odd time for a meatbaby hunt.

As he rounded the next corner he saw a section of mazeway about four metres long had fallen. The nets were gone too, though some sup-port ropes still hung from bolts just above head-height and the lower line of bolts that had once supported the mazeway were still intact. The only other route he knew was a long way out of his way and would take him deep into Limnel's territory. The missing stretch wasn't that long, and the ropes and bolts were still there. He'd have to chance it.

He stopped at the end of the mazeway and, careful not to look down, reached up to grasp the first support rope. He pressed his cheek to the vane and edged out with his left foot until his toes found the first bolt.

He raised his right arm and grabbed the support rope so he was hanging from it with both hands. Finally he slid his right leg along the vane and eased it in behind his left foot. With both feet splayed out he had a fairly secure, if less than comfortable, perch on the bolt. He let go of the rope with his left hand and slid it along the wall until he reached the next rope. He repeated the procedure until he was standing on the second bolt, hands twisted in the second hanging rope. The third rope was shorter, having snapped just below the bolt, so he'd have to be careful ...

He was straddled between the second and third sets of bolts when something hit him in the back, not hard, but enough to send the adrenalin surging through his already stressed-out system. He stopped, quivering. Another impact.

He turned his head to look back the way he'd come, scraping his chin along the vane, his neck creaking in protest.

A lag he didn't immediately recognise stood at the end of the broken vane he'd just left. He had a handful of bolts.

'Shit!' said the boy, taking a step back. Then louder, 'It's him!' He gave a short double whistle.

Hidden in the folds of Nual's cloak Taro had been nothing but a vague outline against the vane. By throwing the bolts the boy had made him turn his head and show himself. Shit and blood! If he'd just stayed still the lag might've given up and left him alone – he obviously didn't have a gun, just bolts.

As he watched, the boy turned and ran back along the mazeway. Taro saw him more clearly now: one of Limnel's general thugs and dog's-bodies, reporting to Resh. Just what he needed.

He eased his head back to face the way he was going and carried on.

By the time he'd got himself onto the third bolt and was reaching for the fourth his ribs were slick with sweat, despite the chill. Any second now he expected to see a gang member with a boltgun step onto the ledge ahead, but it stayed clear. From the sounds of the whistles, he guessed that most of the gang were still behind him.

He had just leapt from the final bolt, grateful to have a mazeway under his feet again, when he heard a familiar *shhwoop!* and ducked without thinking. Someone swore and Taro looked back to see the boy who'd found him and an older girl standing on the mazeway behind. The girl was just lowering her boltgun, looking pissed off. That's right, thought Taro with relief, you don't have the range.

But there was no reason to think other hunters weren't already on their way round to cut him off. Taro took a deep breath, spoke a prayer he knew the City wouldn't hear, and ran into the mazeways.

Elarn wasn't sure how she had managed to find her way back to the Street. As she stood in the mouth of the alley it took her a moment to register that the damage – people lying on the ground, a crashed pedicab, a spray of dirt and flowers from an upturned planter, cracks in the façades of some of the buildings – existed outside her own head.

Somehow, she had caused this. She remembered little after submitting to Nual's probe but she knew that the scream – the chaotic force hidden in her soul by the Sidhe – was responsible for the devastation around her. She had always thought Salvatine notions of possession little more than symbol and psychobabble ... the irony of discovering that it really could happen, and worse, that it had happened to her, an unbeliever, almost made her laugh. But a laugh could so easily turn into a scream—

Control, control, control. She must keep control. The scream was dormant inside her for now, though she had to keep gulping to make sure it stayed there. She needed to act quickly, before it rose up her throat again.

She frowned at the sky, trying to get her bearings. The orange of the forcedome was scabbed with irregular dark patches but the thin needle of the central spine was still distinct against it. She needed to head away from that.

As she stepped out onto the Street she almost walked into an elderly man holding a cloth to his bloody face. He looked at her, dazed but not hostile. 'I'm so sorry,' she said. He muttered that it was all right, but he obviously didn't know what she was apologising for. 'No, really,' she said, 'this is all my fault, you know: everything. But I know how to stop it getting worse.'

He stared at her for a moment, then hurried away. Perhaps he hadn't heard her. The infernal buzzing in her head made it hard to know whether she was really speaking out loud or just to herself.

The cold was bitter and each step jarred her vision. She found herself crying, tears leaking down her cheeks to drop onto the ground.

The end of the Street was still blocked by a fence. Fine, there were other ways. She turned around. Was that movement, someone coming towards her through the wreckage? She felt her lips part and forced them shut.

Out of the corner of her eye she saw something – steps? A way up: that was what she needed.

The steps were covered in debris and she had to pick her way through with care. The effort made the buzz rise to a roar and she could feel the scream rising with it. Lia must have let it out when she had tried to see what the Sidhe had put in her head. She had only been trying to help, but she was probably dead now. *And soon we will all be dead, unless I can destroy the scream before it escapes*, she thought sadly.

Control. Keep control. Just a little longer now and it will all be over.

The barrier at the top of the steps had collapsed into a pile of plastic and metal. As she heaved herself up onto it her cloak snagged on a jagged edge. She pulled and it tore, but held. In desperation she unclasped it and half-slid, half-fell down the other side. On the far side of the barrier she stopped to catch her breath and wait for her pulse to stop deafening her.

Snow had started to fall, possibly just in her head, but still she found herself smiling at this incongruous detail: snow at the end of the world. How peculiar.

The platform was divided by the circle-car track, but the bridge over the track was more or less intact. The far side was wider, with an air-taxi pad off to the side. There were a few people on the platforms, but most looked to be injured, or helping those who were. Elarn crossed the bridge to the far platform and found another fence at the edge. For a City that was meant to be dangerous, they did their best to make the environment safe, but there was a small gap, where the pylon nearest the air-taxi pad had buckled and torn the chainlink. That was where she needed to go.

'Medame, kindly keep away from the edge.'

At first she assumed the voice was in her head. At least her hallucinations were giving sensible advice now, even if she had no intention of following it. But this was a man's voice, vaguely familiar.

So, not a hallucination. She glanced over her shoulder to see Salik's bodyguard standing on the bridge between the platforms. What was he doing here? She didn't have time for this creepy psycho now. She reached for her bag, before remembering that both bag and gun were long gone. She said nothing, but he seemed to consider the fact that she was no longer walking towards the fence reply enough.

'That's right, medame. Come back here.' The Screamer continued to walk towards her. She didn't turn, but kept watching him over her shoulder. He looked as beaten up as the City, and wore the same wary look as the old man she had tried to speak to earlier. A killer like that regarding her with a caution amounting to fear was quite disconcerting. 'Sirrah Vidoran is very concerned for you, Medame Reen.'

'Oh.' Now why did the vile assassin have to mention Salik? Things were so much simpler if she avoided thinking about him.

'Why don't you come back over here and wait for him? He'll look after you, medame.'

Elarn found her head filling with images of Salik; of his elegant hands, of the way his mouth quirked when he smiled, of ... other parts. If only he had been the saviour she had wanted him to be, not the liar she now knew him to be.

Without another word she turned away and began to run towards the fence. The gap was bigger than it had first looked, and it wasn't far.

She was nearly there when something landed on her back and she slammed into the floor, winded, her nostrils suddenly filled with the smell of sweat and blood.

She shrieked and raged, but she was pinned fast.

A shadow entered her vision and a figure crouched next to her. Salik. Despite herself, she found hope entering her heart at the sight of him. 'Make him let me go! Salik, he's hurting me!'

He said, his eyes full of pity, 'Let her get up, Scarrion.'

The weight decreased and he held out a hand to help her. She got as far as sitting before giving up.

'Oh Elarn,' he said, 'you have suffered so much.'

'Yes, yes, and I deserve it all!' she cried. 'You have to leave me alone, let me break the vessel, so the scream can't use it.'

He crouched down beside her. 'What vessel?'

He was doubting her. The same fear that everyone else viewed her with was creeping into his eyes.

'Me, me,' she tried to explain. 'They made me a vessel for the song that kills. The scream, it's in me, trying to get out. I have to kill myself, or I'll find I'm singing it and then everyone will die.'

'I love you, Elarn.' He reached out to stroke her cheek.

Now, finally, he was telling her. She fell silent, looking into his eyes. She loved him too, of course. She was about to tell him when he interrupted her.

'That's why I can't let you do this.' He leaned forward, and for a moment she thought he was going to kiss her but instead he blew something into her face and sense flew away.

CHAPTER THIRTY-TWO

The hunters' whistles were all around him now.

Taro trailed one hand along the vane, using the other to fend off support ropes as he ducked under them. Running in the Undertow was a gappy idea at the best of times. At midday, with the sun blotted out by the City above, and with large chunks damaged or missing completely, it was downright suicidal.

But it sure-as-shit beat getting shot in the back.

This mazeway was long and straight, with a lot of exits – too many ambush points – but once he reached the end it was just a dogleg through another enclosed mazeway, a small netted gap to leap, and he'd be at Fenya's.

Light flared ahead as an old woman emerged from the opening to a homespace. She was moving slow and steady, looking back over her shoulder, talking to someone inside. He was going to run into her.

'Shift it, sister!' he yelped.

The woman looked up, alarmed. As she started to duck back into the homespace, Taro glimpsed another figure, carrying a boltgun, near the end of the mazeway.

Shit.

Turning coming up. Taro grabbed the corner of the vane and swung himself round, his feet scrabbling for purchase. His mental map adjusted itself. Short stretch of close-netted mazeway leading onto a large open area, a four-way junction like the one outside the Exquisite Corpse, only a bit smaller, and fully netted. Far side of that he needed to bear left, the long way round, but there wasn't much choice.

He broke out into the light. Something was wrong – *no mazeway!* – but he was a fraction of a second too late.

He started to fall.

He landed at once, but relief gave way to panic when the surface under him started to tip. He flailed for balance, but he was already leaning over too far to recover. He landed face-down on what felt like a stretch of mazeway.

When the stars stopped dancing in front of his eyes he raised his head.

He *was* on a mazeway – the very one he'd been expecting to take. Unfortunately, it was no longer attached to the rest of the Undertow. He reckoned it had been shaken loose from its vane and caught by the nets, then he'd landed on it and his weight had unbalanced it, starting its slide out of the nets. By landing face-down he'd stopped it moving. For now.

So, here he was, lying on a bit of mazeway in the nets. It could be worse.

The piercing whistle came from just behind him. Despite himself he glanced back over his shoulder, cursing as the nets started to swing. Resh was standing on the ledge Taro had just run off the end of, holding a vane-cutter. He looked down into the nets and grinned. A cutter was a close-combat weapon; he had no chance of reaching Taro with it from there. But he didn't appear bothered. 'Yer dead, yer ungrateful little shit,' he sneered. Two more gang members emerged behind him.

Taro ignored him and put his head down again, to take full advantage of the cloak. He had another edge they didn't know about – Nual's gun – but he needed to move it round to reach the trigger.

'Nice cloak. Girlfriend give it ya?'

He raised his head to see Limnel standing on the ledge in front of him. Taro looked away. 'Not now, Limnel.'

'Sorry?' said Limnel, his expression ready to tip over from humour to anger any moment. 'Din't quite catch that, neh?'

'Listen to me,' Taro said urgently, 'whatever was between us before, whatever business you got with me now, we gotta put that aside. There's more at stake here than our feud.'

'Like what?' Limnel drawled.

'Like all our lives. That 'quake, the shakin': the City's in the shit. We're all in the shit. Someone's tryin' to bring the City down an' I gotta stop them.'

'Yer sayin' this,' Limnel indicated the damage around them, 'is just the start of somethin' worse? That unless I let ya go, we're all gonna die? That right?'

Taro nodded. 'Aye. I have to—'

'Shut up! Even if we're in fer more shit – an' it looks to be pretty much over to me – d'yer really think one useless little waster is gonna be able to do anythin' about it? Taro the whore, saviour of the City? Now that I'd like t'see.' He started to laugh.

'You got no idea what's goin' on here!'

Limnel looked hard at Taro. 'An' y'do, neh? What about yer Angel friend? Why ain't she flyin' to the City's rescue? Why ain't she flyin' to yer rescue fer that matter?'

Taro called back defiantly, 'Who says she ain't?'

'Don't think so. Reckon she's abandoned ya, pretty boy. What a shame. But what'm I sayin'? I don't give a shit about 'er, about any of them crazy killers who do their murder fer the rollers.'

Taro suddenly saw how much Limnel envied the Agents of the Concord, and how much he hated the fact that his own small atrocities went unnoticed next to their actions.

Limnel carried on, 'But yer've caused me too much pers'nal grief. I 'ad the chance at real power; found meself some prime new friends, topside movers and shakers who need downside agents. But I haven't 'eard shit from 'em since ya crawled off last night. I'm thinkin' yer escape may've caused 'em to figure I'm too smoky fer 'em. So, whatever ya think, yer comin' back with me and yer'd better hope they still want ya, 'cause if not I can't think of no other use fer you 'cept as extra protein.'

While Limnel had been sounding off, Taro had shifted his shoulders and eased one hand behind his back. The angle made his shoulder joint pop and he didn't dare move too fast in case someone guessed he was up to something, but he'd managed to get the gun into more-or-less the right position, though the strap fell off his shoulder in the process.

More because he needed to keep Limnel talking than because he wanted to know, he asked, 'An' what if I do come back with you?'

Limnel laughed again. 'Once our Screamer friend's finished with ya, ya can go back t'workin' fer me. Assumin' ya still can. Depends on how much ya pissed 'im off, don't it?'

Taro clamped the gun to his body with his right arm. He needed to get his forefinger under the trigger-guard, then he'd have to lever himself up with his left arm and swing the gun round so it was pointing in the right direction – a tricky manoeuvre on a surface like this. Meanwhile, Limnel was waiting for his answer. He could lie, but he was done bending over for the likes of Limnel. He looked up at the gang-boss.

'So lemme see. You gave Scarrion the weapon that killed me linemother, you sold me to the Screamer an' yer too dumb to see that there might be somethin' bigger goin' on here than yer pathetic little gang. So I'm afraid I'm gonna decline yer kind offer, you slimy, treacherous, shit-sucking ratfuck.'

Limnel sighed. 'Thought ya might say somethin' like that.' He called over Taro's head, 'Cut the ropes.'

Taro almost had his finger under the trigger-guard. He tensed his left arm, ready to push himself up the moment the pad warmed, wincing at the twinge from his dislocated little finger.

Behind him, rope twanged and parted.

The vane started to slide out from under him. He threw himself forward.

His hand brushed rope and he closed his fingers on the knot between two strands just as the broken mazeway shot out from under him. The gun slipped and he grabbed for it, catching it by the strap as the nets bucked and sprang upwards. The mazeway slid free, but Taro, grasping the knot, held on grimly.

When the ropes stopped twitching and hung slack again, Taro found himself stretched along the nets, his feet braced on a single strand. On the plus side, the gun lying next to him was pointed in approximately the right direction now.

Above him Limnel swore and shouted, 'Bring the damn cutter over 'ere, arseholes.' Though Resh had cut all the ropes he could reach, the nets had been anchored on all four sides and he'd only managed to take out part of the side behind Taro, leaving the other three sides still attached.

But not for long.

Taro picked up the gun and crooked his leg to support it on his knee. He fumbled for the trigger. Just one shot, that was all he needed. Take out Limnel with an Angel's weapon and the others would run. Then he could climb to safety.

Limnel grinned down at Taro. 'Be with yer in a moment – unless ya wanna save us th'effort an' let go now?'

Taro, busy trying to keep the gun out of sight under the cloak while he got into position, ignored him. He'd lifted the gun too high: his hand wouldn't reach under the trigger-guard. He wriggled, lowered his leg a little.

'Nothin' t'say, Taro?'

He'd moved his leg, but now the problem was the strap. He'd have to let go of it to get a finger under the trigger-guard, and just hope the gun stayed put. Even if he did manage to balance it on his leg long enough to get his finger on the trigger he'd only get one shot. Better make it count.

'No matter. Ah, here we are,' Limnel said, satisfaction in his voice.

Taro looked up. Resh, now standing next to Limnel, ceremoniously handed his boss the vane-cutter. Limnel crouched down and thumbed the control and a tongue of blue flame sprang to life.

'Last chance, pretty boy.'

Taro released the strap and slid his finger under the trigger-guard, keeping his grip as the gun shifted, though his wrist complained at being twisted at such an unnatural angle.

Limnel raised the cutter in a mock salute, then swept it down and severed all the ropes in front of him.

As the cutter came down Taro's world shrank to the feel of the trigger-pad warming under his finger, the sound of parting rope, the sight of the strands twisting away. He felt the muscles in his arms tighten as he gripped the net with his left hand and fired the gun with his right hand.

No sound, no light. Taro thought the gun hadn't gone off ...

... then Resh, standing on the ledge behind Limnel, made a strangled sound and looked down as his head, upper chest and shoulder started to slide to the side. The rest of his body stayed where it was.

Limnel glanced back at Resh, then looked at himself. His face broke into a grin. Taro's shot had gone over his head.

Taro could feel his weight pulling down the nets still attached to the vanes on either side. Then the side-ropes snapped and the net went from diagonal to vertical instantly. Taro's feet slipped and a burst of agony ran from neck to dislocated finger as he felt something tear in his shoulder. He screamed, but clung tightly to the rope with his left hand; he wasn't falling, so this must be one of the few intact cables left. Nual's gun was gone, but things could've been worse.

Above Limnel's head, a thin line of blackness began to open: a break in the vane, an extension of the shot that had cut Resh in half. Limnel stopped laughing when the mazeway shifted under him. He tried to keep his balance, shuffling backwards, then his expression turned to panic. He opened his mouth, but before he could say anything, he was bowled over by Resh's torso. The grisly missile swept him off the maze-way and followed him down, narrowly missing Taro.

The gap yawned wider.

As well as hitting the mazeway directly in front of him, Taro's wildly random shot had partially sliced through the next vane along, where the ledge Resh and Limnel had recently occupied had been anchored. The now-empty mazeway ripped free of the rest of the Undertow with a noise like giant bones being smashed. As it fell, it tore a chunk out of the damaged vane next to it.

Taro thought that wouldn't have been a problem, if only the rope he was gripping with all his strength hadn't been attached to that vane.

He just had time to mutter, 'Oh, fer fuck's sake—'

Then he was falling too.

Elarn opened her eyes and, after a moment of disorientation, focused on her surroundings. She was sitting in a plush seat, her head cushioned on the headrest. She felt giddy and there was a strange roaring in her ears. Salik sat beside her. They were riding in an air-taxi. He was escorting her home from the successful concert, after a wonderful meal. She had had a little too much to drink—

No. That had been days ago. This was another journey. She wasn't sure where they were going, or why. She felt good, in a vague, dislocated way … but she also suspected that something was wrong, though she could not quite remember what.

Salik was leaning forward to talk to someone. She swung her head round – slowly, because she felt a little sick – to see who. It was a person with blond hair; his bodyguard, what was his name? Never mind. The bodyguard was sitting in a seat in front of them. Beyond him, a dramatic view commanded what was left of Elarn's attention: a dark mass above, rocky red earth below, and ahead, the eye-burning orange of the forcedome. But the view was blurred; there were dark smears over the windscreen in front of the bodyguard. There were disturbing memories associated with those red smears, something bad the bodyguard had done to the man who had been in the taxi before them, something that Salik thought she hadn't seen. Perhaps she hadn't. Perhaps she had just imagined it.

Salik leaned back and picked up a long black thing inlaid with a pattern of silver and red. Elarn squinted. What was that? It looked like some sort of stripped-down rifle, the elegant ghost of a gun. Salik handed the gun-thing over the seat to his bodyguard, holding it as though it might explode in his face. The bodyguard took it equally carefully and poked it out of the open window next to him. Salik was looking that way too, so there must be something interesting over there. She craned her neck carefully to look past Salik. No, nothing there but a black column running vertically through their field of view.

They stayed like that a while, but Elarn could feel herself falling forward, so she flopped back into the seat. Salik looked round at her briefly, then back out of the window again. He was saying something to the bodyguard, something about not being sure if they had hit it. Hit what? With what?

She had to trust that Salik would tell her. What other choice did she have?

CHAPTER THIRTY-THREE

Undertow lore had it that when you fell off the world you had three dozen heartbeats before you hit the ground, long enough to make peace with yourself and the City.

Taro wasn't counting. He was too busy screaming.

His hands clenched as the nets dropped away and he squeezed his eyes shut. As he tumbled through the air his guts twisted in counterpoint, while the wind shrieked in his ears and Nual's cloak whipped and twisted around him.

The scream ended: empty lungs. No point breathing in again. Too much effort.

Shouldn't he be dead by now? He started trying to count heartbeats, but that meant concentrating on something other than being terrified. It did occur to him that when he did come down among the rocks – which must be soon, surely – the end might be less painful if he were face-down. Shame he had no idea which way was up.

Impact!

Pain.

He'd landed on something. It wasn't the ground. He could tell it wasn't the ground because he wasn't dead and whatever it was, it was falling too, but slower. And it was hot, a soft covering over something hard. But it wasn't flat and it wasn't very big and he felt himself sliding off. He dug his fingers in. Flesh, he had landed on flesh. Something squealed.

He opened his eyes to see grey fur. He hadn't landed on some*thing*, he'd landed on some*one*. He released his grip slightly.

A soft, neutral voice said, 'Put your arms around my neck. Quickly, or we will both fall.'

Taro obeyed, ignoring the protests from his damaged shoulder to reach round and link his hands around its neck – not *its* neck, *her* neck. Her skin burned like fever, but perhaps that was normal for her. Beyond the alien's head he could see the ground, way too close and getting closer by the second. He could hear Solo's breathing, harsh and laboured. Beneath him, muscles bunched. He felt her wings shift and spread and rise and his panic eased off for a moment, as he couldn't slide off when her wings were raised. The muscles released and the wings dropped with a dull *whoommmph!* of displaced air. Taro tightened his grip round her neck as her back rounded. Ahead, the ground was still rushing up, but slower now, at a less scary angle. Taro laid his cheek against the heat of Solo's back, trying to make himself as small a burden as possible. Her musty smell, freaky but not unpleasant, filled his nostrils. The thinly-padded bones of her shoulders and ribcage rubbed against his face as her back muscles moved over them.

Solo spoke again; her voicebox sounded as flat and emotionless as ever, but the clipped sentences implied she was putting a lot of effort into keeping them in the air. 'Where is Nual?'

'Don't know.' *Please don't let her be dead,* he thought. But he didn't have time to deal with that possibility now; he was still getting used to not being dead himself.

'Last night Nual went to find you. Not seen her since. When the City shook I went to where you live. Looked for her there. I found you instead, falling. The City is damaged, Taro, badly damaged. Nual will know what to do.'

'I know, but she's ... I dunno where she is. But the Minister told me what's happening.' For the first time in several minutes he thought about why he'd come downside. He raised his head. Solo's flight was under control now but they were still losing height with every upstroke. He'd got his view across the Undertow, though from rather nearer the ground than he'd hoped. He scanned the horizon as best he could from the alien's back. Off to the left, near the Heart of the City, he spotted a dark shape circling downwards. 'Solo! You see that?'

Solo swung her head round to look. 'Yes. Air-taxi. Not allowed below the City.'

'I know, they shouldn't be here. I gotta—' He stopped. *I gotta shoot anyone who tries to fly under the City*. But he had to do it with Nual's gun, wherever that was.

'You have to what, Taro sanMalia?'

'I lost Nual's gun,' he said, despair in his voice. 'I was meant to stop those people. Shit! Can you— Can we get any closer?'

'Bad idea. The City has defences, maybe still active.'

The Minister had told him the automatic defences put in by the City builders could be disarmed at a distance by a shot from – what'd he called the Angel's guns? – an x-ray laser, that was it, if you hit the narrow band running round the spine near the base.

Except Taro had lost Nual's gun.

'Aye, I know about the defences. But the air-taxi is gonna be in range of them before we are.' The vehicle had veered inwards; it was only a few hundred metres from the spine now. If the defences were active they'd soon find out.

Nothing happened. So whoever was in the air-taxi had an Angel's gun and knew how to disarm the defences. Which meant it must be Scarrion and his master. 'We gotta stop them, Solo. Nual should be doin' this, but she ain't here. There's only me.'

'I will take you closer. It will be hard work, so no more talking.'

Solo's wing-beats changed pace, the strokes becoming longer and harder. Beneath Taro's chest, the alien's back flexed and heaved.

'Shit and blood!'

Elarn had never heard Salik swear. He sounded agitated, eager in a way she had not known before, not even when he had made love to her.

The bodyguard turned his head to speak to his master. 'I'm sorry, sirrah. The terrain won't allow a vehicle this size to land.'

'What about the autopilot? If we find an area where the rocks aren't too high can you set it to hover, low enough that we can climb down?'

'I will try, sirrah.'

Her head was beginning to clear, though the strange buzzing at the edge of her hearing remained. She had heard all of that conversation. Some of it had even made sense. She marshalled her energy to speak, but all that came out was a dry croak. She tried again. 'Wh— where are we?'

Salik's head swung round and for a moment his face was not that of the man she loved, but of a driven stranger. Then he smiled. 'Elarn. How do you feel?'

'Woozy. Not sure what happened.'

'I'm afraid I had to give you something to calm you down. You were hysterical. Things must seem very confusing right now, but everything's going to be fine.'

She hoped so, but she was no longer sure. She suspected that what she wanted to think of as perfect love might be near-perfect deception.

The bodyguard spoke again. 'This is the best I can do, sirrah.'

Salik turned away and looked back out of his window. With some effort Elarn managed to focus on their surroundings. They were hovering a couple of metres above a rugged rust-coloured landscape. Some of the more distant rocks were tall enough that they were at eye-level with their current position. Salik turned back to her. 'We're going to get out now,' he said gently. 'I'll help you.'

'Get out—?'

'We need to climb to the ground. Scarrion will go first and give you a hand down.'

The bodyguard opened the cab door and lowered himself down. The air-taxi rocked, before readjusting to the change in passenger weight. Elarn looked at Salik, hoping for further explanation. He just smiled reassuringly and covered her hands, lying inert in her lap, with one of his own. A double rap sounded from near her feet. She jumped.

'It's all right, Elarn. It's only Scarrion. Open your door now. There's a catch on the right. That's it, just pull it down.'

Elarn did as Salik had asked. Cold air swirled into the cab, making her head hurt even more and triggering a sudden flash of fear. Wherever they were, she was sure they shouldn't be there.

'You have to try to move now,' said Salik, gently but firmly.

She looked back at him. She wanted to ask him what was happening, but words were so slippery. Perhaps she should refuse to get out until he told her the full truth. It wasn't as though moving would be easy anyway in her current state. But there was something in his expression that said that one way or another, she would be getting out here. Below, the bodyguard – Scarrion, that was his name, of course – stood on a boulder, reaching up to her.

It took all her concentration to force her limbs to move, but once she had pulled free of the seat things got easier. She slid down into the assassin's arms, trying not to flinch at his touch. He reeked of blood. As soon as her feet touched the ground she stumbled free of his grasp, feeling strangely weightless. At first she thought it was whatever Salik had given her earlier, but then she realised she really was lighter. They were somewhere with lower-than-normal gravity.

When Scarrion turned back to help his master down, Elarn noticed the gun slung across the assassin's back, the same elegant black weapon he had pointed out of the window earlier. Now she was able to focus on it properly she saw that its sleek lines were marred by a small box-like contraption of wires and gauze, taped just in front of the position she would expect the trigger to be.

As soon as his feet touched the ground, Salik reached over and took Elarn's hand, as though he thought she might float away. Or run.

'There's a short walk now. Are you up to it?'

Elarn nodded, then realised that by agreeing that she *could* do it, she had agreed that she *would*. She had missed another chance to try to slow down Salik's relentless progress towards his mysterious goal. He had already pulled her round to face the dark column she had seen from the air-taxi earlier, and now she found herself walking alongside him, her body moving automatically. With every step their feet sent up clouds of ochre dust that stuck to her clothes and made her nose itch. They had to take frequent detours round large boulders and more than once she tripped on smaller rocks half hidden in the dust.

She knew where they were now: on the surface of Vellern, below the City. But there was nothing down here. Why had Salik brought her to this place?

As they neared the column she saw that it was not black after all, it just appeared so in contrast to the glow of the distant forcedome beyond. It was made of the same dark-grey material as the City above, save for a narrow red band running round it a few metres up. When they were thirty or forty metres from it Scarrion held up a hand. At the same time, he slid the gun off his shoulder. The ease with which he managed both manoeuvres simultaneously sent a flash of alarm through Elarn. Lost in the rhythm of their footsteps and the strangeness of their surroundings she had almost forgotten that she was travelling with a killer.

He addressed Salik. 'Sirrah, company. About fifty metres up and to the left of the spine.'

Elarn looked up. Flying towards them was what looked for all the world like a great black bird.

Three people? Taro was sure he had seen three figures climb down from the taxi and disappear among the rocks. Who was the third one?

Solo had managed to find her rhythm. Her breathing was steadier now, her wing beats longer and stronger. Taro shifted into a more comfortable position.

'*Skkrreeeee!*' Solo screeched and lurched to the side, sending Taro sliding across her back. He barely managed to keep his hold round her neck. His head was filled with an agonised screech, a noise both heard and felt.

The alien's wings were at the end of their down-stroke and though her left wing came up her right one stayed down. She lurched to the right. Taro slipped again; now he was hanging near-vertical.

Solo's wings started heaving and fluttering, not flying so much as trying to break their fall. Taro was tossed around like a doll; his already damaged shoulders felt like they were being wrenched out of their sockets. Below, he glimpsed the ground, coming up fast. He stubbed his bandaged finger on something small and hard at Solo's throat, which took his mind off his other problems for a moment.

With the ground so close that Taro could see individual rocks, Solo managed to get some sort of rhythm back into her flight, though she was still keening to herself. Taro pulled himself up onto her back. The muscles beneath him bucked and twitched.

Something near his right ear tore with a sound like wet cloth being ripped. Solo shrieked again and they dropped from the sky.

Taro let go. A second later his feet hit rock, then, before the pain of the impact could register, slipped off again. He flexed and rolled, landing sprawled and breathless with his head a few centimetres away from a torso-sized rock. Red dust puffed up around him.

More bruises to add to his collection, but nothing actually broken. He rolled over, blinked the dust out of his eyes and sat up. Solo had come down a few metres away on a flat-topped rock – at least, he assumed that pile of fur and skin was Solo. He pulled himself to his feet and went over to her, started to reach out, then drew back his hand and said, 'Are you all right?' Stupid question! One wing was all but shredded and though he didn't know what angle was right for her limbs, he was sure the leg nearest him shouldn't be bent like that.

Just as he had resigned himself to the fact that the alien was dead, she raised her head. Her golden eyes focused on him but he heard only a faint thrumming sigh, like the wind in a water-trap rope. He must've knocked off her voice-box when they fell.

'I know you can't speak, in fact, don't try to, but— Oh!' A gentle warmth filled his mind. Solo didn't need the voice-box to communicate after all. Her presence in his head was less insistent, more subtle than Nual's. Wordlessly she reassured him that she would survive and reminded him of the urgent need to carry on and not waste any more time.

'I understand.' He reached up to hug her. She pressed her cheek against his briefly before pulling back.

'Thank you,' he whispered, then turned and started to run towards the spine.

Smell returned first, the smell of blood and dust. The blood, Nual knew, was hers; unconscious healing processes would have already blocked the pain and slowed the flow from her wounds. The dust was from the quake. She was still in the infobroker's office. No other active minds were here, though she felt an unconscious presence behind her. The infobroker? Had to be, though she was too exhausted to probe further.

Scarrion must have left her for dead, which she probably would have been, had she been human. From the sting of toxins in her system, she assumed that Ando Meraint had shot her with a dart-gun loaded with lethal ammo, accidentally, no doubt. He would have been trying to help her, acting under the desperate and unsubtle compulsion she had laid on him before taking her foolish journey into poor Elarn's head.

She had been an idiot to think she could just slip into Elarn's mind. The Sidhe would have left nothing to chance. They knew that Elarn wasn't capable of murder, and that the love the two women had once shared was likely to lead Nual to help her, rather than killing her. And Nual had fallen into their trap, reverting to the frightened child who had run from them seven years ago. In some ways she had never grown up, for she had been too afraid to develop and explore her natural power for fear of giving herself away, or hurting those around her again. She would be dead now if someone – presumably Ando Meraint – had not intervened and broken the mental link.

She opened her eyes and sat up carefully, one hand across her abdomen. That huddled form in the alcove would be the luckless infobroker. She shuffled over to him and lifted his eyelids. The whites of his eyes were red with burst blood vessels. The Screamer must have used his implant on him. She briefly considered bringing him round, but she needed to conserve her energy and she doubted he would be able to tell her much.

She pulled open cupboards until she found a first-aid kit, and sprayed synth-skin over the worst of her wounds, covering clothes, flesh and, she noticed with a grimace, open guts. No time for niceties, she just needed to survive for long enough to get to the Heart of the City.

If she wasn't already too late.

CHAPTER THIRTY-FOUR

The spine towered over him, a solid column of unbroken grey. There had to be a way in somewhere. He worked his way round, keeping Nual's cloak pulled tight for camouflage, until he came on the door suddenly, caught out by the curve of the spine. Beside it he spotted the charred remains of some sort of instrument panel.

Taro ducked inside, alert for possible ambushes. A short passage stretched ahead. The walls and floor were the same featureless grey material as the City, though where the vanes of the Undertow often had a slight warmth to them, here the walls radiated cold.

The passage ended in a spiral staircase carved into the rock. A faint hum, felt in guts and jaw rather than heard, began to seep through him as he started down. After one twist of the stairs the light from outside faded, leaving him in darkness. He felt his way forward with toes and fingertips, pausing after each step, listening for any sign that he was not alone. After the open space of the planet's surface, the inside of the spine felt like a trap, but its very closeness made it a bad place for an ambush.

Taro wondered how much Vidoran and Scarrion knew about this place. The Sidhe would've told them all they knew, but from what the Minister said that wouldn't be much as they'd never got a spy this far. It was possible that no one had set foot here in more than a thousand years. Not that the Minister had said that. Taro guessed he'd told him only what he needed to know to get the job done. He'd hoped Taro would stop Vidoran before he got this far. Taro paused, one foot in mid-air;

he had to stop thinking of that man as the Minister. He – *it* – was just a tool, or an organ, like a hand or an eye.

And now Taro was heading into the City's heart.

As he reached the final twist of the staircase a dim red light oozed up from below. A topsider would be left blinking in the semi-darkness, but Taro's eyes were adapted to the Undertow; his night-vision allowed him to make out the view clearly.

The staircase opened out onto the strangest place he had ever seen. The Minister had explained what a cavern was, and Taro had thought he'd understood, but he hadn't been sure what the Minister had meant by 'honeycomb'. He'd seen something like this before, though: when Scarrion had first picked him up on Soft Street – it seemed like a lifetime ago now – he had ordered him to wash. He'd run Taro a bath – a prime waste of water – and had him scrub himself with a pale squishy thing riddled with holes. This, the Screamer had explained with amused patience, was called a sponge.

And now Taro had come out in the centre of a giant sponge carved into the rock of Vellern itself. Some of the gaps between the rock pillars were filled with shimmering curtains of red, the only light in the place. The way the light flickered reminded Taro of the forcedome. When Federin had spoken of the spirits of the dead feeding the City, this must be what he meant. The Minister's brief description hadn't mentioned the curtains of light, but Taro suspected it would be a bad idea to get too close. As he watched, one directly ahead flickered off. After half a dozen frantic heartbeats, a new one appeared in the distance, off to his right. Oh shit, they moved.

The air felt warm and thick and damp. Breathing took effort, and every breath stung his nose. The smell of decay, of wrongness, was stronger than ever. As he stepped down from the bottom step onto the bare earth, the pull on his legs increased. This was something the Minister *had* warned him about: the gravity here varied, not only in strength but in direction.

He needed to get to the centre of the maze. The only advice the Minister'd had time to give him was to spiral left and down. The Minister had also told him not to touch anything down here, but looking into the red-lit tunnels Taro decided that warning was unnecessary.

He checked the possible ways out from the open area around the steps. There were exits on every side, including several sloping down, some steeply enough to be called holes.

He glimpsed a flash of white light off to the left. That had to be Scarrion and Vidoran.

The light was a long way off; he was too far behind. He started to run, taking large uneven steps into the passage leading towards the intruders. Almost at once the passage started to slope down at a scary angle, but just as Taro's sense of balance was about to trip him up, the gravity shifted to match. Looked like down was the new up. The passage twisted back on itself, but he ignored the side turnings and whenever it forked he chose the left path. Soon after the third fork a curtain flickered out just as he passed it and freezing air whooshed across the passage, making him stumble.

He slowed down a bit and turned the next corner. At first he thought he'd reached a dead end, but as he drew closer he realised it was a T-junction, with paths going off at steep angles to the left and right. Left would be the default choice, but he could see the leftmost passage doglegged back to the right again a few steps along. He paused at the junction, trying to work out which path to take ...

He heard a crack like the sting of a stun-baton, felt a blast of heat on his back and threw himself forward with a yelp. When he looked behind him, he saw that he had only one choice now; a flame curtain had sprung up across the left passage, half a step behind the spot where he'd stopped to check his options.

Right, this way.

Elarn caught herself chewing the inside of her lip and forced herself to stop. This was hell. It had to be: the red-lit cavern, the heat, the vile, thick air. Salik, whom she had trusted, whom she loved, had brought her to hell.

He had spoken to the Screamer when they'd reached the spine, while Elarn stared up at the looming bulk of the City hanging over them and wondered how she could have been stupid enough to let herself be brought here. The Screamer had used the gun again, shooting out a near-invisible panel and triggering an opening to appear from what had looked like a blank wall. Then he'd slung it over his shoulder and drawn a nasty-looking curved knife from his boot. Elarn remembered that knife now. She remembered how Scarrion had slit the throat of the air-car driver. She flinched away. Salik turned to her and smiled what he must have hoped was a reassuring smile, but the drug-induced haze was already receding and Elarn saw how the smile did not reach his eyes, how it was as much an act as everything else he had ever said to her and done with her.

She had descended the spiral staircase between Salik and his bodyguard. At the bottom Salik took hold of her hand; the gesture that had once been reassuring was now threatening. He did not look at her or speak to her as they set off into the labyrinth, Scarrion picking out their path with the aid of a small flashlight.

And now she was in hell. The only light beyond the circle of torchlight came from the sudden snapping fires. Pits like gaping black mouths peppered the floor as they went down, ever down, and sudden drafts of cold or warm air whooshed from side-passages or holes in the ceiling. Yes, this was hell, a place of punishment and damnation. She felt herself slipping into the merciful oblivion of madness, accepting her fate, whatever it might be. After all, if this was hell, she was already damned. Soon they would reach the ultimate pit and the scream within her would be released.

Suddenly Scarrion, walking a couple of paces ahead, stopped. Salik, his whisper loud in the gloom, said, 'I heard that too. Go.'

The assassin nodded and slipped back past them.

Taro suspected this passage might not've been the best choice. There appeared to be more holes than floor, some no more than dips – though still enough to trip him up if he wasn't paying attention – while others were wide and deep enough that the only way past them was to edge along the wall. He thought momentarily about taking a side-passage, but then he'd get even more lost. Perhaps he should start leaving some sort of marker to show where he'd already been – but what? He had his flecks, but he wasn't going to throw away his only weapons. He might be able to use them to carve marks on the wall, but that would take time – and he remembered the Minister's advice about not touching anything.

He would just have to keep to the leftmost path, and hope.

It looked like things opened up a bit ahead, where rock pillars stood in a slightly larger cavern. There were still too many pits for comfort, but perhaps he might be able to get a clearer view from there, maybe even see the flashlight again if he was lucky. If not, he'd try going back to the junction to see if the curtain had gone, then try the other way.

Two steps into the cavern he stopped dead.

The rock pillars that supported the roof here were all sorts of shapes. In the weird-shit way of this place, the one ahead and to the left was thinner at the base and wider near the roof. Something stuck out from the base of the pillar, something shaped exactly like the toe of a boot.

He edged back into the passage and drew both flecks. A glance at the rock pillar showed that the boot-tip had gone, which probably meant Scarrion – it had to be Scarrion – had heard him. But he still had a couple of advantages.

Firstly, he could see far better than the Screamer; secondly, though the hem of Nual's cloak had been shredded when he fell, it was still good enough to hide behind. Ignoring the protest from his shoulder, he raised the left-hand side of the cloak like a shield in front of his face. Scarrion shouldn't be able to see him until he dropped the cloak and hit out with his right hand. Only thing was, though the cloak would hide him, it meant he couldn't see where he was going either.

He advanced slowly, ears straining to hear above the ever-present buzz from the fire curtains, eyes focused on the ground just ahead of his toes.

When he glimpsed the base of the rock pillar beneath the ragged hem of the cloak he tensed, breath frozen in his throat. The next half-step showed something black. Scarrion's foot. Before he could lose his nerve he dropped the cloak and stabbed for the Screamer's throat.

Scarrion was fast. Though he could only have seen the threat at the very last moment, his left hand flew up to deflect the blow. The fleck missed his neck and grazed his forehead. He slammed Taro's hand into the pillar and pain exploded in his wrist. Taro dropped the fleck and through a mist of agony heard the blade skitter away.

He staggered back, hugging his arm to his chest. Scarrion's face swam before him, feral and inhuman. Without the element of surprise, and with what felt like a broken wrist, Taro stood very little chance. But he was done running.

He crouched low, extended his remaining fleck in his left hand and met the assassin's eyes.

With the bodyguard gone Elarn felt some of her composure return. Most of the effects of the drug Salik had given her had faded, leaving her with shaking limbs and a splitting headache. The roaring not-quite-sound that hovered at the edge of her consciousness was nothing to do with the drug, it was the precursor of the scream, a sign that the barriers holding it back were badly damaged.

She knew what she was now: the Sidhe's tool, nothing more. And Salik was their agent.

She had been running to him, thinking he was her saviour, when all the time he was her enemy and she should have been running like hell in the other direction.

She stopped. Salik pulled on her arm, then, realising she was no longer following, frowned over his shoulder at her.

'I have to know something,' she said. Her voice was swallowed by the walls, drowned in the rush of on-coming destruction.

Salik turned to face her and said, 'What is it, Elarn?' He spoke as though to a child, or an idiot.

'Did you ever, at any point, care for me at all?'

Without waiting for an answer, Elarn brought her heel down hard on his foot. When he let go of her arm with a grunt of pain, she snatched the torch out of his hand and ran down the passage.

'You little fucker,' said Scarrion, more offended than angry. 'I'd say you're pretty much screwed now. Only question is, do I burst your organs with my song or gut you with my knife?'

Taro had already spotted the Screamer's third weapon: the slender muzzle of Malia's gun showed above his shoulder. Even the Screamer wouldn't be stupid enough to use a weapon like that in here.

'How about neither?' Taro snarled, slashing with his remaining fleck. His blade was shorter than the flesher's knife in Scarrion's hand

and both his hand and shoulder were damaged already. The blow went well wide.

'Oh,' said Scarrion, 'knives it is.' He darted forward, his blade flashing like a spurt of blood in the eerie light. The blood from his cut forehead must've thrown his aim. He missed too.

Scarrion saw Taro glance at the wound and his expression of cold amusement changed. Taro had hurt him. That wasn't allowed. It was against the natural order; he was a giver of pain, not a receiver. Before Taro could react to the change from arrogance to anger, Scarrion charged.

Taro staggered back and realised, not for the first time today, that he'd run out of ground. His right leg dropped, then hit rock. He toppled backwards. He flailed his arms, reeling back as he tried to adjust to the new direction of gravity, but he was already off-balance and by the time a fizz and a pop announced the arrival of a fire-curtain above him, he was half-rolling, half-falling down a hole.

She could hear Salik shouting behind her, but she kept running. She had to leap over holes and dodge pillars of rock and at one point she found her feet dragging as gravity doubled in a couple of steps. But she kept running, swerving down a side-passage as a curtain of red sprang into life across the corridor in front of her.

Only when her heart threatened to burst and she could no longer catch her breath did she stop. She heard no immediate sounds of pursuit, though she doubted she would hear much over the roaring in her head. She bent over to try to clear the stitch eating into her side, then set off more slowly.

Without his own light to see by, Salik would have to move slowly. Maybe she had lost him.

A faint skittering sounded ahead, ahead and above. She played the torch across the ceiling, her shaking hand making the beam waver. The torch revealed a patch of darkness, and a fraction of a second later something small dropped out of the hole. She took a tentative step towards the object, shining the torch onto it. It was a knife, a jagged blade made of a dull grey material. She picked it up by the rag-wrapped handle.

There was a shout from above, followed by a scatter of stones. She stepped back, dropping the knife into the pocket of her jacket.

A couple of seconds later a scrawny downsider youth tumbled out of the hole and landed in a crouch in front of her, so close she could have reached out and touched him. Her first instinct was to run, but he was blocking the passage. She shone the light in his face and he threw up his arms. In his bandaged left hand he held a knife like the one which had preceded him down the hole, though he wasn't making any threatening moves with it. Quite the contrary; he appeared as disorientated as she was. She lowered the light.

For several heartbeats, they just stared at each other. Finally he un-curled, stood upright and said, 'Now I don't mean to be rude but who the fuck are you and what the fuck you doin' down 'ere?'

'My name is Elarn Reen. And who the … Who are you?'

He grinned. 'I'm Taro sanMalia. Yer Elarn Reen? Nual went to find you. Where is she?'

'Nual? Yes, she did. I … I'm not sure what happened to her. I think she may be dead.'

From the expression that flickered across the boy's face, Elarn guessed he cared for Lia – for Nual. She wondered who he was – and why he wasn't more surprised to see her here. She might have assumed he was a hallucination, except the blade had felt real enough when she picked it up and she doubted her subconscious could fill in this level of detail, right down to the smell.

The downsider gulped and said, more suspiciously, 'And what're you doin' down here, Medame Reen?'

'I'm not sure,' she answered honestly, adding, 'Well, right now I'm running away from Consul Vidoran.'

He nodded, and pushed past her back up the passage. 'If yer runnin' away from him, then you won't mind if I kill him.'

She pressed herself into the wall to let him pass. 'Kill— I … No. I mean yes, kill him. But his bodyguard—'

'Is just up there' – he nodded back at the hole he had fallen through – 'so we'd best not be standin' here when that fire-curtain goes off again.' He began to stride up the passage.

There was something compelling about the youth's certainty. Elarn started after him. 'Listen, Taro. You obviously have some sort of un-finished business with Consul Vidoran, but I just want to get out of here, and preferably off Vellern altogether, though I'm not sure I can … Anyway, if you could tell me the best way out, I'll leave you to do … what you're here to do.'

'Sorry, medame, I'm lost meself.' The downsider's longer stride meant he was already pulling ahead of her. He didn't seem to need a flashlight to see where he was going either.

'You don't understand,' she said, a little plaintively. 'I can't go back to Salik. He tricked me. I think he means to kill me down here.'

Taro stopped and turned slowly. 'Yer sayin' he brought you down here to kill ya?'

'Yes! At least that's what I think. I don't know – all I know is that he's been deceiving me all along so he could get me into this place, and that he means me harm.'

'Oh shit!' Taro stared at her as though she was about to explode. 'Shit and blood!' He glanced at the knife in his hand, then back at her, and for a moment Elarn thought he was about to attack her. Then he grimaced and said, 'You know, yer so right, Medame Reen. It'd be a real smoky deal fer you to run into Salik Vidoran. Or Scarrion. Or anyone. Aye, leavin' the City would be a prime idea. Leavin' right fuckin' now.' He looked around him, his dirty face serious with fear. 'The tunnel forks ahead. You came that way; d'you remember which fork yer came down?'

'The right, I think.'

'C'mon.' He started to run and Elarn followed. They stopped at the fork; the tunnels looked identical and Elarn was no longer so sure where she had come from. Taro checked down both tunnels and said, 'I need t'go left to get to the throne room, so if you keep goin' right you should get back to the surface.'

'The throne room? What's that?'

'Not somewhere you wanna go, trust me. It's where Vidoran's headin'.'

'What about you?'

'Think of me as yer diversion. Now go!'

Elarn went.

CHAPTER THIRTY-FIVE

The Minister had been right – and wrong ... right that the Sidhe had given Salik Vidoran a weapon to disable the City, wrong that it was an object. It was a person.

Taro wondered if Elarn Reen had any idea what she was. Nual may've known, at the end, but Nual was probably dead. He was on his own now.

Perhaps he should've killed her back there, when he had the chance. But he wasn't sure he'd have been able to; not just for practical reasons – Scarrion had badly bruised, perhaps broken, his right wrist – but because she was a stranger and, as far as he could tell, innocent. Besides, killing her might be part of the Sidhe plan, given that it was what she reckoned Vidoran wanted to do to her.

So it was up to him to make sure Vidoran and the Screamer didn't get the chance. They mustn't find Elarn Reen again.

He paused for a moment, drew a deep breath and then shouted, as loud as he could, 'Come and get me, you fuckers!'

With the light, they'd be able to see her. Without it, she might fall down a hole or walk into a wall. Compromise then. Elarn played the torch beam along the passage ahead – it looked straight enough, with only a few holes – then turned it off again. She started to grope her way forward, one hand on the wall.

She froze at the shout. No, it was all right. That was the downsider, back behind her. He was leading them away.

Just when she had thought she was beyond hope, she had found an ally, someone who appeared to want her out of here as much as she wanted to leave. She wasn't going to consider the full implications of his urgency, or face the fear she had seen in his eyes when he had offered to sacrifice himself so she could escape.

She strained to see ahead, murmuring under her breath, 'Let the path go upwards soon, please let it go up soon.' If only she had the faith to pray. If only she could believe there was a chance her prayer might be heard.

The rough wall under her fingertips ended and she felt open space. Side-passage on the left. Taro had said something about bearing left, hadn't he? And this current passage wasn't going up. So, left here.

It was a mercifully straight passage but the next section looked tricky, with holes every few steps and eerily-still cold air that made her nose itch. She had no choice but to keep the torch on. She pointed it up for a moment. There were still gaps in the roof, so she wasn't on the top level yet.

A couple of steps down the passage, her feet failed to come down. Or rather, she floated slowly back to the ground, her stomach sending nauseous warnings to her head. Gravity playing tricks again. She bounced her next step and flew slowly through the air to come down several metres along, uncomfortably close to one of the holes. Another two bouncing steps and she landed hard as gravity returned to full strength. The sudden jolt sent her heart leaping into her mouth.

She needed to stay calm, take things slowly and carefully. The roar in her head was constant, but the scream was locked down for the moment. She had control. Things would be fine as long as Vidoran didn't find her. She could worry about how to get back up to the City later. Right now, she needed to use the diversion the downsider boy was providing to get to the surface.

Keeping the torch pointed at her feet, she edged along the passage. After a few dozen metres she risked a brief look ahead. The passage ended in a blank wall. She felt tears of frustration sting the corners of her eyes. Just when she had thought she was getting somewhere, she had run into a dead end.

Finally, the passage was sloping down.

Taro had settled into a rhythm. He took it slow and steady, ready for the frequent changes in gravity or other hazards. He kept glancing behind, shouting to attract attention every now and again, stopping to check every time he came to a junction to see if anyone was on his tail, but it looked like he was alone.

After spending so long trying to avoid the Screamer and his master, now that he needed to find them there was no sign of them.

It might not be a dead end at all. The only way to be sure would be to play the torch over it ... except if it was not a dead end, she risked giving away her position to anyone further down the passage. Keeping the torch focused on the ground directly in front of her, she advanced, slowly and carefully.

The holes in the floor were becoming smaller, less frequent. That was good. And it didn't look like a dead end any more. The angles of the walls just gave that illusion from a distance. Half a dozen steps from the end of the passage she turned the torch off and edged along the last few metres. This passage ended at another, wider one. A smaller passage doglegged away from the other side of the main passage.

She stepped into the wide passage and looked around. Three metres ahead, a heavyset figure with blond hair emerged from another side turning. He had his back to her but as she watched he cocked his head to one side and started to turn.

From somewhere ahead, she heard a distant shout, the downsider's distinctive high tones.

Without waiting to see how Scarrion would react Elarn dashed into the other side-passage and started to run.

Ahead, the red light brightened and Taro felt the ever-present hum grow more intense. Strange energies stirred the roots of his hair. The air had a faint taint, tasting rather than smelling of blood, or cold metal. He was getting close.

He rounded a corner and found himself facing a wall of red fire. The curtain of flame made his scalp itch and filled his nose with the scent of naked power as he squinted through. Beyond it he could make out a huge open space.

That had to be the throne room. All he had to do was get to it.

There must be more than one way in. He started to retrace his steps, but after a couple of dozen steps the hissing from behind him died. He stopped and turned slowly. The curtain of flame was gone. Beyond it, Taro glimpsed a dark shape in the centre of the open area.

He turned and started to run back down the passage.

The air cracked as the curtain sprang up again.

Taro threw himself to the side, barely avoiding plunging into the curtain of flame. He slammed into the wall, hitting the rock with a wordless cry.

Elarn ran blindly. She should turn the torch on, but that would mean stopping, and the assassin could be right behind her, could be about to reach out for her—

The floor disappeared.

Before she could scream she was tumbling. She tried to catch herself against the wall of the hole, to slow down, but her body wouldn't respond. It was as though she was already dead and was watching herself fall in helpless terror, unable to intervene.

The walls disappeared. She hit the floor.

Taro stared at the wall of flame. Beyond, the glow of the throne room tantalised him. There had to be a way through. The Minister would never've told him to head for the throne room as a last resort if there wasn't a way to get to it. He just needed to find it.

Watching for a few moments, he thought the ruddy glow that lit the room ahead wasn't constant. The only light down here came from the fire curtains, and they went on and off, so there would have to be openings into the room that didn't have flames blocking them. There was probably some pattern to the way they went on and off, if only he could work it out.

Standing by a curtain that'd just gone off might not be the best way to find a way in. Maybe there were some passages that didn't have curtains at all. Either way, he wasn't going to get anywhere by waiting here. He turned and started back up the corridor.

Elarn came to with a frantic gasp. Pain shot through her chest. She was lying face-down in darkness. She hesitated before taking another breath, but her body demanded air and she inhaled with a whimper. She couldn't let pain stop her. She had to get up, find the torch and keep moving.

She pulled in one outstretched arm, feeling the bruised and exhausted muscles quiver in protest. Now, get the other arm under her, sit up—

Something landed on her wrist, pinning it to the ground. Torchlight played over her face. Elarn squinted up, trying to pull her hand free.

'Let's calm down, shall we?' Salik had one foot on her wrist. He sounded anything but calm.

Elarn said nothing. Escape was no longer an option. She turned her head away from him, pressing her cheek into the rock floor. She felt him slip something over her wrist.

'Up you get,' said Salik, his voice brusque.

When she didn't move he hauled her into a sitting position. Stars whizzed through her vision and her chest felt like it was being crushed but she was too weak to resist. She let him manhandle her upright but when he stepped close to tighten the security restraints round her other wrist, she lashed out at him. He jumped back, then grabbed her hand and clicked it into the restraints.

'Looks like we're doing this the hard way,' muttered Salik. He tugged her upright with the cord attached to the restraints and started to pull her along behind him.

The first side-passage led away from the throne room. Taro retraced his steps to the junction. A quick check back showed the original fire curtain still in place, but as he turned away he caught a flash of white light. Someone with a torch was on the far side of the throne room. If it was Elarn, she was lost. If it was Vidoran or Scarrion, then there was a whole lot of space and fire between them. Either way, it was bad news for him.

He sprinted back up the passage he'd originally come down and took the next side-passage, which traced a long sweeping arc upwards. A line of holes just deep enough to trip him up ran along the edge.

Ahead, the red light grew again. A gap on the left-hand wall of the passage was filled by a curtain of light. Taro approached it cautiously. The light beyond was brighter and the direction felt right. This gap must lead into the throne room, though at a higher level than the first opening he'd found.

He leant back against the wall and settled down to catch his breath. He'd wait a couple of minutes to see if the curtain went off, and if it didn't, he'd move on.

Vidoran dragged Elarn round a corner. A curtain of fire filled the passage ahead. Elarn felt a small satisfaction at finding their progress blocked, but Salik appeared nonplussed. She expected him to turn round, but instead he walked up to the curtain, looked through it and then pushed her back against the rock wall. This close the fearsome energy made the roots of her teeth sing and raised goose-bumps on her flesh.

Salik turned off the torch, put it in his pocket and withdrew a dart-gun. In the red light of the flame wall he looked inhuman, the once-beautiful planes of his face transformed into the caricature of a seductive devil.

Cold panic seeped through her. He was going to kill her here, in this anonymous passage.

She closed her eyes. 'Do it. Do it now.'

Salik laughed.

She opened her eyes. His gaze flicked between her and the curtain beyond his right elbow.

'Do what, Elarn?' He sounded bored.

'Just ... kill me.'

He met her eyes, raising his eyebrows dismissively. 'Ever the drama queen, Elarn, ever the drama queen. What makes you think you're going to die?' She got the impression he was keeping up the pretence of interest in her because it entertained him.

Elarn hated him now, with the same mindless intensity she had loved him, for all the good that would do. He had a gun. She had cracked ribs, bound hands and no weapon—

Except that she did have a weapon. Her jacket pocket was deep; the downsider's knife might still be in it. She slid her hands over to the right and extended two fingers into the pocket. To distract him from her actions she spoke as casually as she could manage, keeping eye contact all the while. 'You can't trust them, you know.'

'Trust whom, Elarn?'

He still held the cord attached to her hand restraints; she had to be careful not to tug on it as that would alert him to what her hands were doing. 'You know who. The Sidhe.'

'Finally worked it out, hmm?'

'They can't be trusted. They trick people.' Yes, there it was, she could feel the rag-bound handle with one fingertip. But she'd never get the knife out while he was watching.

He hadn't noticed her furtive activity. 'They're not demons, you know. We've just made them into bogey-men to make ourselves feel better for trying to wipe them out. People forget that they always had humanity's best interests at heart.'

'So they told our ancestors. And even if that was true during the Protectorate, it isn't now. You're more of an idiot than I ever was if you can't see that,' she said bitterly. 'They *use* people, they *destroy* us.'

'Use, yes. Destroy? No, these days they need all the allies they can get. They'll give me what I want, and I'll give them what they want.'

'And what is it that you want?'

He had relaxed into the smug assurance of a born liar indulging in the truth now it no longer mattered. 'I want power. It's as simple as that. They want their renegade back, or dead, and from what Scarrion said, it looks like they already have that. And that is thanks in part to you – or rather, thanks to the "gift" they gave you.' Mockingly he sketched a bow in her direction.

That confirmed it, if she had had any remaining doubts. He knew, better than her, what the Sidhe had done to her.

The curtain popped out of existence.

Salik pulled her through the gap.

Now he had stopped moving, Taro's right wrist began to throb hard enough to distract him from his many other discomforts. Time to try

269

another way in. He sighed, stepped away from the wall—

And froze.

Through the curtain of flame he glimpsed something moving below him. Somebody was in the throne room. He pressed as close to the crackling energy as he dared, trying to make out details, but all he could see was a vague shape moving towards the centre of the room.

'Waiting for anything in particular?'

The domed chamber was massive, large enough for her entire house to fit in. Glowing red gaps opened into it at several levels, the flames flashing on and off in a not-quite-random pattern. The only object in the chamber was a statue of a kneeling figure, head bowed, arms by its sides. From the back of its neck a frozen multi-coloured fountain of wires, pipes and cables spread up and out to cover the ceiling, branching and expanding, disappearing off into the rock.

The air felt thick and heavy, a physical weight on the top of her head, like the moment before the first lightning discharge of a massive storm.

Salik dragged her towards the statue.

He stopped when they were a few metres from the figure. It was far larger than life and its surface was an oily blackness that looked almost alive to her dazed vision. Though the form was superficially human, an alien potency emanated from it.

Salik swung her round to face the statue, then let go of the tether holding her hands and raised the gun. He started to back towards the figure, the tip of the gun pointing unwaveringly at her head.

The figure's body and kneeling legs formed a human-sized seat. Salik started to climb into the lap. It was a stretch and he had to reach out to pull himself up on the arm. As he did so, the tip of the gun rose momentarily.

And in that instant, Elarn dived away. She heard him scramble off the statue, but she was already running round the far side.

'Come back here, you *bitch*!' he screamed.

Scarrion stood four or five metres away up the passage. The flaming light played on the blood running down his face but he was smiling, holding his knife casually.

Even if Taro hadn't already been hurt, even without the variable gravity, he doubted he could've hit Scarrion with a thrown fleck from here. And the Screamer had a far more effective range weapon.

From below, Taro heard a man's voice shouting, but all his attention was focused on Scarrion.

With a tiny nod as if to say, *This time we finish it*, the Screamer stepped away from the wall and opened his mouth.

Elarn paused on the far side of the statue and shoved her bound hands into her pocket.

Over the ever-present hiss of the flaming energy and the roar in her head she heard Salik's gun going off. She flinched and dodged away, still fumbling in her pocket. The tip of the downsider's blade tore her finger. *Other end, get hold of the other end, stupid!* she told herself.

She ran towards a gap in the wall, head down, zigzagging as best as she could, on the verge of falling with every step, sure every breath was going to be her last. She had to buy herself enough time to get hold of the knife.

Her hand brushed rag and her fingers closed on the hilt. She slowed and glanced back. Salik was no more than three metres behind.

She stopped, turned to face him and started to totter back towards him.

He raised the gun, a feral grin on his face. Elarn watched his finger squeeze the trigger.

She felt the sting of the dart and barely resisted the urge to raise a hand to her cheek. The chill spread with terrifying speed, but she made herself close the distance, though her limbs were sluggish and the final darkness was already rising up within her.

Two steps away, with the last of her strength, she pulled the knife from her pocket and launched herself at him.

Nothing happened.

Scarrion closed his mouth and shook his head, perplexed.

Taro had a brief thought: *The City allows no blasphemy in its Heart.*

Scarrion smiled, and started to run down the slope.

They met in front of the flame wall.

271

Taro screamed, 'I'll kill you!' and swiped out with his fleck. The Screamer laughed as he ducked; as Taro ran past he felt the sharp metal of the flesher's knife rake his ribs. The wound was shallow; either Scarrion was playing with him, or blood was getting in his eyes.

Taro grunted and swung back round to face the Screamer. Though he couldn't win, he had to fight.

He slashed again, though he didn't hold out much hope of actually wounding Scarrion.

He didn't – but the sight of Scarrion's upraised arm silhouetted against the flame wall gave him an idea: given he was gonna die anyway, he may as well take the bastard with him.

Taro backed off, angling himself to get into the best position. Scarrion must've thought he was giving up, as his smile broadened.

One step back. Two. Taro was where he needed to be now.

He threw away his fleck.

Scarrion lifted his arm to wipe his eyes, as if to check that he really had just seen his opponent disarm himself. The moment he let his guard down, Taro charged.

He slammed his hands palm-first into Scarrion's chest. The Screamer started to raise his knife, but either he was thrown by Taro's bizarre change of tactics or his depth of vision was screwed by the blood in his eyes; whatever the reason, he was too slow and the blow connected. Agony spiked in Taro's broken wrist and damaged finger but he didn't stop. Caught by surprise and his attacker's momentum, the Screamer had no choice: he staggered backwards.

One step. Two. Three.

Red light flared in Taro's eyes. He braced himself for the final agony and pushed with all his strength. Just as he did so, Scarrion worked out what Taro was up to – but it was already too late—

Power erupted around the Screamer as he hit the curtain and disintegrated.

Taro, expecting the same fate, had his eyes shut. He felt the sudden intense heat—

And fell into emptiness …

There was a jarring impact and Taro found himself lying on the floor of the throne room with a fine black dust raining down on him and the stench of burnt flesh all around him. As it hit his nostrils he gulped back overwhelming nausea.

But it wasn't over: on the far side of the room, two figures struggled together.

Taro picked himself up and started to run towards the throne.

She had finally surprised him. She saw it in his eyes as he raised a hand to fend her off, and saw the surprise grow into terror as her desperate backhand slash got past his guard and tore up into his neck.

Something hot covered her face and hands: blood, more of it than she had ever seen before. *Salik's blood.* His body heat splashed over the coldness that gripped her. Then they were falling, he backwards, she on top of him. He was screaming but finally she had her silence, the silence of the breath drawn before the final note is sung. She was beyond fear now, already in the arms of darkness.

By the time they hit the floor, her heart had stopped.

From the corner of his eye he saw Elarn and Vidoran fall, but he was focused on only one thing.

A few steps from the throne a note sounded in his head. The pure, perfect tone filled his mind. Suddenly it rose into a scream, climbing beyond hearing, an unheard sound tearing at the fabric of the world.

He fell to the ground, hands over his ears, eyes screwed shut.

As quickly as it'd begun, the scream ended.

Every light went out. Every sound died.

In the ringing silence, alone in the darkness, Taro raised himself onto all fours and started to crawl towards the throne.

The earth began to shake.

His fingers touched a chill, smooth surface. He had made it to his goal. He pulled himself up onto the seat and pressed himself back into it.

Cold needles found his neck. Instantly the growing tremors, the feel of the cold hard throne, the crushing darkness were all gone.

And so was his body. A wave of nothingness picked him up and carried him away.

The world returned in a mad, crazy rush, like sex, like chemicals, like being born. He had a body again.

Except it wasn't his.

CHAPTER THIRTY-SIX

In the Assembly Hall politicians cower under their benches while the High Speaker lies sprawled on his dais. A lone fragment of consciousness tries to slip back into the Speaker's inert body, but it's like trying to flex a deadened limb.

I am filled with echoes of other amputated islands of consciousness: one slumped at the head of a table in a boardroom on Silk Street; another on the floor by a bed in an Opera Street penthouse; a third lying in a pool of noodle soup by a bench at the end of Chow Street. All beyond reach now.

How can I be all those people?

Through half-blind eyes I see hundreds of others who are not part of me:

... below an ancient tree in the Gardens two strangers fuck like beasts, bodies sliding over each other, desperate that their end should be in ecstasy, not terror ...

... outside a Memento Street hotel whose gilt and marble facings are cracked and skewed, a man is trying to pull the body of a child from under a fallen pillar, his cries for help ignored by the few people still standing ...

... on Chance Street a riot has evolved, a confused rush of desperate humanity looting and screaming purposelessly ...

... on Grace Street isolated groups of people pray together, while others stand transfixed, turning eyes wide with fear to the disintegrating heavens ...

… Amnesia Street, the haunt of those already halfway out of reality back when reality was still a viable option, is empty now, save for the occasional prone figure, dead or paralysed …

How can I be in all these places?

Who am I?

What am I?

I look beyond sight for the answer.

Above the Streets the skin that covers me is breaking down. Soon the bubble of warmth that has endured a millennium against the thin air will disperse to the winds. Soon I will lose myself to the void.

The deep engines of decay and rebirth have fallen silent: the great breaths that take in foul air and excrete oxygen have faltered, the water that trickles down through filters and back up has dried up, the ingestion of used matter, the molecule-by-molecule conversions that create nourishment or structure from waste – all have stopped now.

My thousand-year heartbeat is slowing to nothing …

I am dying.

I do not know who I am, but I know that I am dying.

But I cannot die. I am eternal.

This must not happen. I must take control.

First, the skin that encloses me, and the million minds I watch and protect: I must draw energy from the planet's core to feed the processes of transformation deep underground. Slowly, slowly, the swirl of energy starts to coalesce, to strengthen. I start to rebuild the forcedome—

But something else is wrong. While I am concentrating my efforts on my skin, I realise my very body is tipping off-balance, and if my unimaginable mass comes crashing down— I have to catch myself, stabilise myself, and centre myself, reach down to access the great devices that offset gravity. I must juggle the forces that bind the universe and harness them to my service …

But while I work on gravity, my control on the forcedome is slipping. The pressure of the gases trying to escape is ripping holes in the damaged fabric of my skin.

So many processes, so much to think about: too much. I cannot do this alone.

<You are not alone.>

I cannot control all this—

<No, but together, we can.>

The other presence slips in gently, supporting, augmenting his efforts, taking control of the forcedome, healing the wounds in his skin. He concentrates on the gravitational trickery that keeps the City afloat. It is stable, just. The other presence is here too, underpinning his own efforts, buoying him up in the vortex.

Soon he – *they* – start to deal with the myriad other problems. Deep down, the recycling systems start up again: water flows, power surges and the chill air starts to warm.

Together they are strong.

<This is not the real you.>

Now, for the first time, he wonders who he was before he was the City.

<You are human. Your name is Taro.>

Human, like the tiny beings cowering and running about and dying: small, pathetic, insignificant, and yet strangely compelling beings. Could he really be one of them?

<You – we – are not meant to live like this. We still have flesh.>

He addresses the unknown presence that is supporting and comforting him. *<But the City still needs us. We are the City now, we are in control. In charge.>*

<No – even together we can barely manage to keep the City alive. Basic processes that should require no conscious thought are taking all our combined effort. Once the City is stable we must return control.>

<Return control? Who to?>

<Look.>

He looks, though he has no eyes. In a dark limbo, protected by the same presence sharing control of the City with him, a small pearl of life is curled in on itself. As he watches the pearl grows, strengthens.

He feels an invasion at the edges of his consciousness: the original mind, feeling its way back? No! This City is theirs now!

He starts to resist.

The voice is soft and sad. *<You must let him take back what is his, Taro.>*

<What if I don't?>

<Then he will fight us when he recovers, and he will win. He will destroy us.>

<Only if you help him! He's still weak. I can feel you giving as much power to him as you are to the City's functions. If you let him fade away we can stay here, ruling together, always!>

<Do not let the power blind you. You will no longer be you.>

<But I will be with you.>

<A part of you will always be with me. Let go, Taro.>

She is right. He starts to comply, reluctantly allowing the growing consciousness that Nual has nurtured begin to take the reins of power from him.

He can no longer see the whole world, no longer sense the thousand complex processes that keep the City alive. He is shrinking, becoming reduced to a mere human boy. He starts to panic; if he is no longer the City he will no longer be anyone.

But she is still here, the presence that supported him and sheltered the City: his goddess, his love.

Suddenly he has a body again, a tiny, confining thing, damaged and insignificant. His soul is filled with the dull ache of pain and loss. He begins to collapse in on himself, fading, fading to nothing—

He is embraced, and knows it is her.

Taro opened his eyes. He was lying at the base of the throne. Nual's arms were wrapped around him as she cradled him in her lap.

With a supreme effort he looked up and focused. Her face was pale as bone beneath the dust and dried blood. Through the link they still shared he felt the other, more serious, physical injuries she was repressing.

Speaking was too much effort so he just thought at her, *<You look terrible.>*

Nual smiled and, safe in the shared knowledge that they had done what had to be done and could finally let go, they slipped together into a place beyond thought.

CHAPTER THIRTY-SEVEN

The glass dome of the transit hall had taken more than its fair share of damage during what the media, with a typical mixture of irony and understatement, were calling 'the Cityquakes', but it was already well on the way to being mended. After all, it was the first thing the rollers saw when they arrived.

Taro looked up at the scaffolding over the main doors as he walked into the transit hall. There was barely a building that hadn't been affected by the City's recent near-destruction, but given the amount of money Khesh City attracted, the only place where the scars might never be healed was the Undertow. The entrance into the transit hall was one of many once-forbidden thresholds he'd crossed in the week since he and Nual had woken together in the Heart of the City. There was no place in the City he couldn't go now – but he had already seen the whole City, with senses that were not his own.

The Minister stood a little way off from the main flow of the crowd, talking to Nual. They turned as Taro approached and he allowed himself to meet Nual's eyes. She held his gaze just long enough for a brief surge of warmth to flash through him. Perhaps love – ordinary, human love – was like this. In some ways the deeper union they'd shared, an experience beyond that of even the most intense human lovers, was as far away from him now as his days as whore and victim. But it'd changed him in ways he'd yet to come to terms with.

If Taro hadn't known better he would've said the Minister was embarrassed by their wordless exchange.

'There you are. Goodbyes all said?'

Taro nodded. It had been a hard decision to make, and the thought of the vast unknown universe beyond the forcedome filled him with apprehension, but he couldn't stay in Khesh City now, not when Nual was leaving. And not when he'd experienced what it was like to *be* the City. Even life as an Angel seemed nothing more than an indulgence of the City's ongoing fascination with the squabbles of the self-absorbed humans it sheltered. He'd accepted the offer of Angel implants, though: hidden blades and the ability to fly might come in handy, and he had an idea that once he got out into the big wide world he was going to need every advantage he could get.

It occurred to him that the Minister expected more than a nod in reply and though he no longer felt any obligation to show respect he said, 'Not that many people to say goodbye to. The survivors're busy rebuildin' and lickin' their wounds, though Solo's almost healed. By the way, he says the topside bakery where he gets his bread insists on not chargin' him any more.'

'Oh, she's male already? Must have been the stress. Yes, I try to be fair, which includes rewarding those who deserve it. Not knowing much about the alien's lifestyle, that seemed the least I could do. I was just telling Nual that the infobroker – his name is Ando Meraint; I don't think either of you were formally introduced to him, and he's mercifully oblivious of the significance of what he did – came out of hospital to discover a mysterious increase in his credit balance. The man had the good sense to use it to relocate his family off Vellern.' He looked around at the bustle of rollers coming and going. 'The resiliency of the human mind never fails to amaze me. That and its capacity for self-deception.'

Nual said softly, 'And of course, we Sidhe would never deceive ourselves, only others.'

The Minister *hurrumphed*. '*We* Sidhe? I hardly think of myself as Sidhe, whatever race the body I originally had might have been.' He looked at Nual and raised an eyebrow. 'Ah, I see, you're baiting me. Old habits die hard. You know, I think I'm going to miss you. Sometimes the games can get a little wearing, all that pretending to be human. Nice to drop the mask occasionally.'

'Having spent so long thinking of you as my reluctant protector, I can't yet say whether I will miss you or not.' Nual spoke lightly, though Taro sensed the undercurrent of gratitude and affection in her words. Despite their inability to completely trust each other, these two minds were closer in nature than Taro liked to consider.

'Touched, I'm sure.' The Minister sounded almost emotional as he said, 'I will tell you again that I think you are very unwise to even consider taking your late guardian's ashes back to Khathryn. You realise they'll be watching out for you?'

Nual shrugged. 'I know, but I have to do this. It is the least I can do for her.'

'A shame you weren't so fastidious about Vidoran's remains,' said the Minister, which struck Taro as a deeply insensitive remark – no doubt why he'd said it.

Nual chose not to take offence. 'You still disapprove of me leaving Vidoran's body in the throne room?'

'Yes, though it's not as though I can do anything about it. I can hardly send someone in there to clean up after you. Tell me, was he already dead when you regained consciousness?' The Minister directed the question at Taro but Taro signalled wordlessly to Nual that he had no intention of answering it. He had come to in the throne room to see Nual bending over the Consul's prone form. He knew what she'd been doing – reaming his dying mind for every piece of information he'd gained from his contact with the Sidhe – but he'd never mentioned it, and neither had she.

Nual said coldly, 'I gave him his wish, to be at the centre of power.'

The Minister barked a laugh. 'Quite. The man's arrogance still astounds me. To think a mere human could ever consider taking on all this.' He gestured around him, then looked at Nual. 'Or even an untrained Sidhe female.'

He turned to Taro and said conversationally, 'You do know that the woman you love is an inhuman monster who may well destroy you?'

Taro let his hand brush Nual's, a momentary touch. 'Aye. I know.'

The Minister shook his head. 'So then, you're on your own now. Both of you. Goodbye— And, I suppose, good luck.'

'And to you,' said Nual.

'Goodbye … sirrah.' Taro used the honorific with only slight irony.

As the Minister walked off, Taro heard him mutter, 'Gods of our ancestors, what have I let loose on the universe?'

ACKNOWLEDGEMENTS

Being the first, this one took a long time gestating and had many hands to help it into the world. Though he might not recognise where I've ended up, it all started with Christopher Patrick. Since then many critiquers have helped me get where I wanted to go: Mike Lewis, Liz Holliday, Jim Anderson, Frances Beardsley and Milford Class of '04. I've also had much useful feedback from first readers Dave Weddell, Kari Sperring and Emma O'Connell and proofreader Lucya Szachowski. 'Zero5um' provided soundtracks and visualisations. James Cooke gave last-minute advice on weaponry. Jo Fletcher of Gollancz has guided me gently and expertly towards the finished article. My thanks to you all.